*The Scientific Marvel Fiction
of the French H.-G. Wells*

# THE DOCTORED MAN
## And Other Stories

*The Scientific Marvel Fiction
of the French H.-G. Wells*

# THE DOCTORED MAN
# And Other Stories

by
**Maurice Renard**

translated, annotated and introduced by
**Brian Stableford**

A Black Coat Press Book

ISBN 978-1-935558-18-7. First Printing. May 2010. Published
by Black Coat Press, an imprint of Hollywood Comics.com,
LLC, P.O. Box 17270, Encino, CA 91416. All rights reserved.
Except for review purposes, no part of this book may be reproduced or transmitted in any form or by any means, elec-
tronic or mechanical, including photocopying, recording, or by
any information storage and retrieval system, without permission in writing from the publisher. The stories and characters
depicted in this novel are entirely fictional. Printed in the
United States of America.

# Table of Contents

## Introduction

This is the fourth volume of a set of five, which includes most of the "scientific marvel fiction" of Maurice Renard, and some related works. It includes translations of four stories from the collection *Monsieur d'Outremort et autres histoires singulières* (Louis Michaud, 1913), the novella "L'Homme truqué," first published in *Je Sais Tout* in March 1921, and a miscellany of later articles and short stories taken from various sources.

The first volume of the series, *Doctor Lerne*, includes translations of the novella "Les Vacances de Monsieur Dupont," first published in *Fantômes et Fantoches* [Phantoms and Marionettes] (Plon, 1905), the novel *Le Docteur Lerne, sous-dieu* (Mercure de France, 1908) and the essay "Du Roman merveilleux-scientifique et de son action sur l'intelligence du progrès," first published in the sixth issue of *Le Spectateur* in October 1909.

The second volume, *A Man Among the Microbes and Other Stories*, includes translations of the novel *Un Homme chez les microbes*, the first version of which was written in 1907-08, although no version was actually published until Crès released one in 1928, and the entire contents of the collection *Le Voyage Immobile suivi d'autres histoires singulières* (Mercure de France, 1909).

The third volume, *The Blue Peril*, comprises a translation of the novel *Le Péril bleu* (Louis Michaud, 1911).

The fifth volume, *The Master of Light*, comprises a translation of the novel *Le Maître de la lumière*, which first appeared as a *feuilleton* serial in *L'Intransigeant* between March 8 and May 2, 1933.

The introduction to the first of the five volumes includes a general overview of Renard's life and career in relation to his scientific marvel fiction, which I shall not reiterate here, confining the remainder of this introduction to the specific works featured in this volume. Some further discussion of the themes developed in some of the stories—especially that of the title story—will be undertaken in an afterword, in order not to spoil the reader's enjoyment of the stories by giving away too much in advance.

"Monsieur d'Outremort, un gentilhomme physicien," here translated as "Monsieur d'Outremort, Gentleman Physicist," echoes Renard's fascination with the works of Edgar Allan Poe in a much less earnest fashion than "Le Rendez-vous" (tr. in volume two of the series as "The Rendezvous"), to the point of sarcastic caricature; its representation of Renard's own political opinions and affection for automobiles is equally parodic. He had always been a humorist and his comedy had always had a black edge, but the affected bitterness of this story might have an element of double bluff about it, representing a significant step in the course of his own disillusionment with his prospects as a writer of scientific marvel fiction.

"La Cantatrice," here translated as "The Cantatrice," is not strictly relevant to the series' theme, but is included here because it completes an eccentric thematic triptych with two stories included in volume two, there translated as "Death and the Seashell" and "Parthenope; or, The Unforeseen Port of Call."

"L'Homme au corps subtil," here translated as "The Man with the Rarefied Body," is a sequel to "La Singulière destinée de Bouvancourt" (tr. in volume two as "The Singular Fate of Bouvancourt"), featuring an earlier exploit of the ingenious experimenter with invisible radiations.

An earlier English version of "Le Brouillard du 26 Octobre," here translated as "The Fog of October 26," was featured in the April 1941 issue of the American pulp science fiction magazine *Thrilling Wonder Stories*, as "Five After Five." That version is, however, severely abridged—including the omission of the last few pages of the story—and altered to such an extent that it barely qualifies as a translation; it might be more accurately described as a synoptic paraphrase. The story carries forward the fascination with remote prehistory and evolutionary theory exemplified in "Les Vacances de Monsieur Dupont" (tr. as "Monsieur Dupont's Vacation") and laid some imaginative groundwork for the central premise extrapolated in *Le Maître de la lumière* (tr. in volume five as *The Master of Light*).

These four stories in *Monsieur d'Outremort et autres histoires singulières* included the last three items of scientific marvel fiction that Renard published before the outbreak of the Great War, although he might have done some work then on one, two, or even three of the longer works to which he returned his attention afterwards.

"L'Homme truqué," here translated as "The Doctored Man," was the first new item of scientific marvel fiction that Renard published after the Great War, although the version published in *Je sais tout* was probably not the work that he envisaged writing when he advertized the title in the 1920 reprint of *Le Péril bleu* (tr. as *The Blue Peril*) as "*a paraître*" [forthcoming], where he described it as a "*roman*" [novel]. It seems probable that the work was still incomplete when he placed that advertisement, and that he intended at that time to develop it as a full-length novel, but that he subsequently decided to modify the project and redevelop the incomplete text as a novella, perhaps as a result of his increasing despair regarding the imminent future of scientific marvel fiction in general and his own endeavors of that sort in particular. Although it remains an interesting story, it does give the impression of leaving off at the point at which it was just becoming more interesting, effectively aborting what might have been a visionary text in the same radical vein as *Le Péril bleu* in favor of a calculatedly-limited story of a type that would eventually come to be known as "technothrillers."

"L'Homme qui voulait être invisible," here translated as "The Man Who Wanted to be Invisible," first appeared in *Oeuvres Libres* 19 (January 1923), thus becoming one of the very few stories Renard published in an upmarket literary periodical. He had little opportunity to do so; *Oeuvres Libres* published speculative fiction by Pierre Mille, J.-H. Rosny Aîné and, most prolifically, André Couvreur before its editors apparently decided, in the late 1920s, that such material was either too outré or too disreputable to be entertained there any longer, but it was the last reputable literary periodical to do so regularly, although many of those specializing in popular fiction had no such qualms.

Although it is not, strictly speaking, a scientific marvel story, "L'Homme qui voulait être invisible" constitutes an important response to one of the most famous works in that genre. It was reprinted in *Invitation à la peur*, a collection issued by Crès in 1926, where it was given a section of its own, headed "Intermède critique" [Critical Interlude], placed between "Quatre contes au stylographe" [Four Fountain-Pen Tales] and "Quatre contes à la plume d'oie" [Four Goose-Quill Tales], the former group being contemporary stories with a horrific element and the latter historical fantasies with a horrific element.

The article "Depuis Sinbad," here translated as "Since Sinbad," was written at the request of Jean Ray, who interviewed Renard at his home in the Rue de Tournon in 1923; it was published in the same issue of *L'Ami des livres* (June 15, 1923) as the interview and an overview of Renard's work by Ray. It updates and revises the manifesto for the "roman merveilleux-scientifique" (tr. in volume one as "Scientific Marvel Fiction and its Effect on the Consciousness of Progress") that Renard had published in *Le Spectateur* in 1909, and gives clear expression to Renard's disillusionment with the genre's prospects—a disillusionment not unconnected with his explicit rejection in the essay of the earlier label, the example of which I have obviously not followed in compiling this collection.

The second story from *Invitation à la peur* included here, "La Grenouille," translated as "The Frog," reflects the manner in which Renard was to make use of the raw materials of scientific marvel fiction from then on, as fuel for *contes cruels*

10

and whimsical vignettes. This one retains a complexity that his later ventures of a similar kind lack, but it is nevertheless strictly limited in its use of marvelous material.

The second article included, "Le Roman d'hypothèse," translated as "Hypothetical Fiction," first appeared in the December 15, 1928 issue of *A.B.C.*, and represents yet another attempt to find a more useful label for the kind of fiction to which Renard had just been enabled to return, albeit briefly, by the belated publication of *Un Homme chez les microbes* (tr. as *A Man Among the Microbes*).

"La Découverte," translated as "The Discovery," and "La Verité sur Faust," translated as "The Truth About Faust," are both taken from the collection *Le Carnaval du mystère* (Crès, 1929), the contents of which provided a fine illustration of Renard's craftsman-like development of ultra-short fiction. The former is the only story in the collection that can qualify, even marginally, as scientific marvel fiction, but the latter is an interesting, if rather oblique, revision of the modern legend of the man who was reputed to have sold his soul for scientific insight, and it provides yet another interesting illustration of Renard's own disillusionment.

"Eux," here translated as "Them," and originally published in *La Revue des Vivants* 8 (August 1934), was Renard's last revisitation of a theme he had touched on several times before, perhaps reflecting his regret at not having been able to develop it more elaborately in "L'Homme truqué."

The three remaining stories all appeared in the newspaper *Le Matin*, as elements in a series of ultra-short stories entitled "Les Mille et un matins"—a title that had been used before but undoubtedly seemed particularly apposite to the paper's editor. All of them appeared in 1939, the year of Renard's death. I do not know the specific date of "Le Requin," here translated as "The Shark," but it probably appeared somewhere between "Quand les poules avaient des dents" ("When Hens Had Teeth"), which appeared in the February 11 issue, and "Sur la planète Mars" ("On the Planet Mars"), which appeared in the August 5 issue. The last-named was

Renard's last contribution to the scientific marvel genre, but—in spite of its blithe triviality—not quite his least.

The translations from *Monsieur d'Outremort et autres histoires singulières* were made from the Louis Michaud edition published in 1913 (although it bears no date). The translations of "L'Homme truqué," "Depuis Sinbad," "Le Roman d'hypothèse" and "Le Requin" were made from the versions in *Maurice Renard: Romans et Contes Fantastiques* published by Robert Laffont in 1990. The translations from *Invitation à la peur* were made from the Crès edition of 1926. The translations from *Le Carnaval du mystère* were made from the Crès edition of 1929. The translations of "Eux," "Quand les poules avaient dents" and "Sur la planète Mars" were made from the Gramma collection *Les Vacances de Monsieur Dupont* (1994).

Brian Stableford

# MONSIEUR D'OUTREMORT, GENTLEMAN PHYSICIST

*To Léo Larguier*[1]

*Extract from the Memoirs of Monsieur de La Commandière, dated July 15, 1911*

This morning newspapers did not refrain from commenting at length on an astonishing drama that took place yesterday, and whose protagonist I knew quite well—a certain Marquis Savinien d'Outremort. He was my fellow student at the Ecole Polytechnique, where I met him for the first time. We soon formed ties of friendship, impelled by our common nobility—which did not reside in our titles and surnames, as so often happens, but in our beliefs, manners and breeding.

I believe, moreover, that I was Monsieur d'Outremort's only friend. The sepulchral name that he bears was the first thing that led our comrades to distance themselves; his personality, moreover, did not provoke advances. He was handsome, to be sure, but singularly so, in a simultaneously cruel and archangelic fashion. His bearing was always that of a wrathful seraphim—in a word, that of Azrael, the Angel of Death. He was to retain until his declining years the same adolescent face and judgmental expression that he offered to our 20-year-old eyes; at 60, he still seemed to be what he had been then: a splenetic and silent young man.

---

[1] Léo Larguier (1878-1950) was a prolific poet and novelist who contributed the same periodicals as Renard in the years preceding the Great War and was one of the younger writers in regular attendance at his salon.

It is doubtless to the severity of his external appearance that one must attribute the unusual deference mingled with dread that he soon inspired in each of us, for which I can find no better comparison than the respect with which one customarily surrounds those who are the instigators of formidable events.

However, as I was not long delayed in learning from his own lips, he had never perpetrated anything out of the ordinary, any more than any of his ancestors. Their name, he added, did not derive from some ancient fantastic adventure, and had obtained its present consonance by a simple process of etymological corruption, the *n* in Outremo*n*t having mutated into an *r* by virtue of being mispronounced by the inhabitants of the marquisate.[2]

This confidence was unable to weaken Monsieur d'Outremort's prestige to the slightest degree in my eyes, and as I experienced no less veneration in his regard once I knew about the nullity of his accomplishments to date, I fell into the habit of regarding him as a man predestined, for whom Dame Fortune was reserving her most dazzling favors—Bonaparte at Brienne, if you wish.

In spite of my presentiments, Monsieur d'Outremort has lived in obscurity; and I doubt, at present, that he will know glory—for that word is inappropriate to describe the ephemeral, frightful and bizarre kind of reputation that he has recently acquired, the cause of which, after all, might well be that of his imminent demise.

The most curious and objectionable thing is that he is being held up simply as an illustration of the present century. You shall see why.

On leaving the Ecole, when my inclination led me to the Inspection des Finances, Monsieur d'Outremort, whose private income was by no means paltry, undertook private research projects in the domain of physics. Directed especially

---

[2] Outremont signifies "beyond the mountain" whereas Outremort signifies "beyond death."

toward electricity, they gave rise to remarkable discoveries. In truth, it appears to be to Monsieur d'Outremort that we owe the principles of "telemechanics." I am not very well-versed in that subject, but someone has undertaken to instruct me. By "telemechanics" it is necessary to understand the government of machines at a distance, without wires and by the sole inter-mediation of so-called "Hertzian waves," which operate in space.

If the experts can be believed, that was something which might have led the inventor to great renown, if only he had followed his invention through and manifested it in reality rather than in formulas. Why did my friend leave it to other engineers to put his work into practice? Telemechanical torpedoes, which can be operated from several kilometers away, are in current usage today, I am told. Was it not Monsieur d'Outremort who laid the groundwork for them? And why did he not even point out the other practical utilizations of his theory which are easily imaginable and numerous, even to a layman?

Monsieur d'Outremort has always been capricious. As the extreme descendant of a lineage that emerges from Me-dieval darkness, ten centuries of nobility press down upon him the crushing weight of their heredity. Ten centuries of nobili-ty—which is to say, let us admit, 1000 years of increasingly refined existence; 1000 years of turmoil, preoccupation and ardent ambition; a millennium of luxury, passion and debau-chery. Each generation of d'Outremorts was a step the family took toward what a few call "the perfection of being," and many others "degeneracy." For you cannot peruse the se-quence of their unions and find a single one of those fine pro-letarian misalliances which so propitiously renew the blood of an ancient house from time to time, nor a single bastard issued from a rustic mistress or a plebeian lover: nothing but nobles emerged from nobles. That is a great calamity for a lineage. The La Commandières have been well-protected from such hazards, where the Outremorts have failed.

That is why the Marquis Savinien, my comrade, inherited from his ancestors the sort of excessive and sensitive soul in which genius is sometimes tainted with delusion in disturbing ambivalence. With him, the loftiest genealogical tree in the Vosges terminated in a precious and morbid branch: an élite ornament or monstrous bough. The interest he provoked remained ambiguous; one hesitated between admiring its rarity and deploring its anomaly. In consequence, no family in France possesses a sense of status to such a high degree. And it must be said that the sentiment in question was maintained in him by a state of affairs that was scarcely banal and which is scarcely to be found anywhere else. No matter how far back one went in his archives, one never ceased to find traces of an eternal discord between the lords of that name and their vassals. The history of the fief was a violent series of revolts and repressions, rebellions and punishments—an interminable drama in which not the least tragic act was staged in 1793, involving the ambassador François-Joseph d'Outremort and his sister, a canoness: Savinien's great-great grandfather and great-aunt.

Too proud to emigrate, like their son and nephew Théophane, the two old people, having not quit the paternal château, busied themselves, one with his administrative duties and the other with her charities, in the midst of the atrocities of the provincial Revolution. And the Terror was terrible—more terrible than anywhere else in the Republic—in its effects on the welfare of the d'Outremorts. After many riots, Jacques Bonhomme had passed his Master of Arts; the peasants were pitiless. They were led by a furious patriot named Houlon, who played the same role as Carrier in Nantes.[3] On his decree, the local *sans-culottes* and *tricoteuses* seized the ambassador and the canoness. A thousand derisions were reserved for them, at the climax of which they were hanged from the lantern of a shop overlooking the village square, at the foot of the

---

[3] Jean-Baptiste Carrier (1756-1794), the instigator of notorious atrocities in that city before he was guillotined himself.

manor. A faithful servant cut them down during the night, and placed them in the family vault in the château. The Consulate saw that good man restore the property to Marquis Théophane on his return from Coblentz—where he might perhaps have met Ludovic de La Commandière, who is to the author of these lines what Théophane is to Savinien d'Outremort.

The latter, even as an adolescent, could not relate all that without bitterness. His voice trembled with anger at the story of the execution of the ambassador and the canoness. His time was more taken up with reverie than it should have been, and within his reverie the losses of his family and the hostility of the rabble to the successive chatelains of Outremort were too preponderant. Even so, this obsession remained secondary for quite a long time, and the love of science held sway over such cares in Monsieur d'Outremort's thoughts until the day that his father, Marquis Fulbert, expired.

Marquis Fulbert! He had never been anything but a master of hounds, utterly and completely—but he was that to the maximum. I can easily evoke the memory of his awkward appearance: that of a robust, unpolished, grumbling country squire, always gaitered in leather and mud, always reeking of gunpowder, fur and feathers. Nothing amused him but hunting. He devoted all the time to it that he did not spent ruminating on his disgust for democratic government and his regret for the monarchy. His gamekeepers, chosen like pugilists, were very hard on poachers; they had orders to be so, under threat of dismissal. Their master diverted to poachers his aristocratic fury against the triumphant mob. One evening, when he was 50 years old, the Master of hounds was found stone dead in a corner of the woods, his torso riddled with buckshot.

I took part in his funeral ceremony. We laid him to rest not far from the ambassador and the canoness, in the midst of a quantity of ancestors, in the crypt rounded out beneath the manor's chapel.

Savinien took this new blow of fate badly. He did everything possible to avenge the memory of the murdered man. For want of proof, however, the assassins escaped, and my friend turned to hypochondria. From that day forward, he shut himself up at Outremort, and was never seen to go out again. He ceased all active participation in the scientific movement; at least, if he continued to work, it was in secret, given that the Academies received no further communication of his endeavors. Some claimed that he had given up; others accused him not of idleness but of mutism, saying that he was only depriving his fatherland of the results of his experiments in order to cheat the government.

He had married—in 1884 or thereabouts, if my memory serves me right—his cousin d'Aspreval, who died in childbirth the following year. Their son, Comte Cyril, died three years ago. The last time I made the journey to Outremort was to pay my last respects—for it is worthy of note, and passably ominous, that my relationship with the Marquis was now only marked out by funerals. That was in 1908; Monsieur d'Outremort no longer left his château any more than the Pope left the Vatican; but, being alarmed by his eccentricities, I had lost any interest in meeting him. He appeared to me then in the full perfection of his gloom and strangeness. His Raphaelesque mask might have served as a model for some wax figure representing Rancor. What am I saying? Did he not seem to be the wax figure itself?

He attributed his recent misfortune to the insatiable rascality of the country-folk, and I reckon that he was right. The late Comte Cyril, an adventurous sportsman, drove automobiles at high speed. A number of dogs and chickens run over, and several serfs brushed a little too closely, had served to win a bad reputation for the crimson vehicle, known to our manufacturers as a double phaeton, in which he burned up the Republic's tar macadam. One night, when he was returning to the château, a metal wire stretched across the gateway had caught him under the chin. The wire had broken, thanks to some capricious Providence, which did not extend its protection of the wounded man beyond that rupture. Indeed, complications set in as a result of the injury. Favored by the impoverished constitution of the gentleman, which a marriage within the family had further reduced, they annihilated the escutcheon's last hope. Many quarters come to that poor terminus, to that sorry omega. Savinien alone remained—and, by a striking coincidence, the crypt had room for only one more tomb.

Monsieur d'Outremort retained me beside his own sarcophagus when the rest of the funeral party had gone back up. Whether I liked it or not, I had to listen to his recriminations. He got increasingly excited as his monologue progressed. The scene rapidly became theatrical.

We were in the depths of a vast subterranean tower, damp and glacial. The wall was checkered with sepulchers, and the funerary flagstones rang hollow beneath Savinien's footsteps. He strode back and forth. An air-vent—a grille fitted above our heads into the pavement of the chapel's choir—poured a grey twilight into the place, scarcely the half-light of a cellar; the smoke from the incense-burner ended up dissipating in an undulating stream like a long and living spider's web; its ecclesiastical aroma accorded admirably with the cavernous and mortal odor of the *in pace*. The Marquis' complaints sounded muffled, the air of the tomb being a milieu of silence, dully resonating with the names of the dead that he harangued one by one. I saw him circling the rotunda in the imperfect darkness, pointing to the epitaphs in the order of decease, summoning the knights, the noblemen, the Constables, the squires and the commandants, the chamberlains, the Ladies of the Bedchamber, the Marshals, the ambassador, the canoness, the Master of hounds and Comte Cyril as witnesses to his misfortune, and swearing to their spirits on his eternal salvation that they would be revenged.

I, meanwhile, thought I saw them all: the surrounding dead, lying in their suits of armor or uniforms, courtly dress or mantles of the Holy Spirit. At that apparition, I felt nausea overwhelming me, the damp transpiercing me more deeply, and chilling me with a new iciness. I attempted to calm the Marquis down as quickly as possible. His exuberance faded away, and a stupor took hold of him. We finally quit the crypt—and I slipped away that same evening, retaining the most painful impression of Monsieur d'Outremort.

The episode in the tomb that I had just witnessed was renewed many times in solitude. I knew, in fact, that Monsieur d'Outremort divided his existence between the crypt and the workshop. His heart full of resentment and his soul full of science, it was said that he passed from one to the other, mediating here, working here, without anyone figuring out the object of his ecstasies or the goal of his studies. He passed from one to the other as from an invincible regret to a joyless hope, and the ancestral manor in which his family would become extinct with him had never been so dismal.

And yet, it had always been a sad dwelling. The Outremorts of the 11th century had built on a mount at the center of their tenure. Imagine, at the heart of a somber forest, a colossal somber rock whose summit is carved into a fortress, and you have the Château d'Outremort at the top of its pedestal. That bluff ending in architecture, that basalt crowned with an abundance of pointed turrets, made one think of cyclopean stalagmites. Shadowed, feudal and gigantic, elegiac and romantic, with something of the fabulous about it—Rhenish, for want of a better word—it was reminiscent of something imagined by Gustave Doré as a location in the most heart-rending of Perrault's tales; or, better still, of the original of one of those frightful sketches that Victor Hugo traced in ink, coffee and charcoal according to his redoubtable fantasy, and which he called Heppeneff or Corbus.[4]

---

[4] The reference to Heppeneff remains obscure, but Corbus is a castle featured in the section of *La Légende des siècles* entitled "Eviradnus," which offers an account of heroic knight errantry. Hugo was an inveterate sketch-artist, whose innovative work anticipates numerous later schools of painting; he used such endeavors as a method of imaginative stimulus and as a means of showing off. He often finished off sketches he did for an audience by sprinkling them with coffee to provide a sort of sepia finish. The images available for viewing on the

If the exterior of that Vosgian burg seems geological, the interior is monastic. Galleries sustained by arches connect up vaulted chambers and courtyards like cloisters. No décor is more appropriate to the pensive walking of a solitary individual charged with knowledge and melancholy—an Edgar Poe décor haunted by a Hoffmann creation: Château Usher.

Monsieur d'Outremort invited me there frequently during our youth, while Marquis Fulbert was there, hunting. I did not like it there, and I felt a sudden relief whenever I left, as if I had escaped some great misfortune. The proximity of that defunct crowd spread an atmosphere of torment and disquiet throughout the edifice. In my eyes, the crypt extended itself throughout the citadel; its mustiness, reminiscent of churches and catacombs, rose up, for my nostrils, to the attics. I declined more than one invitation to hunt deer in the Outremort forest without any other reason, and I always avoided sleeping in the dwelling, which had no bed in which someone had not died.

Thus I remember the burg. Thus I remember the astonishing burgrave who brought into the 20th century the anachronistic existence of the noble alchemist, Roman and modern, Romantic and laborious—as if legendary.

I made allusion above to the village situated beneath the château: Bourseuil.[5] Presently the administrative center of the canton, it was once a very humble hamlet overshadowed by the enormous proximity of Outremort. It has not ceased growing since the end of the 17th century, to the annoyance of the chatelains, who could not see all the rancor of the region concentrated within its walls without irritation. They could not do anything about it. Bourseuil prospered. Its leading citizens

---

internet include one of a Rhine valley castle, which might well be the one that Renard had in mind when concocting his description of Outremort.

[5] Like Outremort, Bourseuil is significant, roughly translatable as "the threshold of the Stock Exchange."

struggled against a suzerainty that was baptized as tyranny. In that ultra-republican town, the bloodthirsty Houlon established his headquarters and put the district guillotine to work, after the hanging of the ambassador and the canoness.

Having related all this, I leave it to the reader to imagine Monsieur d'Outremort's state of mind when he learned recently that a statue of Houlon was to be erected in the Bourseuil's town square. It would be visible from the château. A public subscription was opened.

From that moment, it appears that Monsieur d'Outremort—whom I have not seen again—went so far as to surpass his own self-perfection, that superlative of his personality about which I have already said a few words. He absorbed himself in work and contemplation. Nevertheless, his domestics observed that now, of the crypt and the workshop, it was the latter that attracted him more. He augmented it with an immense garage, in which two post-chaises and a tilbury kept close company with huntsman Fulbert's shooting-brake and Comte Cyril's red automobile. At all hours, the noise of hammering and filing were audible there. It was Monsieur le Marquis playing the locksmith and the blacksmith, to erode his pain and pound his heart. What he was making was unimportant, in truth; he was tiring himself out in order to tire himself out, without any other aim—he, the scientist, the father of telemechanics!

Then it became evident that Monsieur d'Outremort had succeeded in killing his excessively dolorous soul, for he appeared to become joyful, and laughter was heard by night, in the garage, amid the rasping and the ringing. His people loved him for his magnificent indulgence. They feared a fatal outcome occasioned by the inauguration of the statue, which was to take place on July 14, the national holiday.

From his window, Monsieur d'Outremort doubtless saw the stone demagogue perched on his pedestal, in his carmagnole, coiffed with a bonnet that one imagined to be red in spite of its white color, if I might venture to write such a silly sentence. Houlon was depicted in an attitude of bravado. His eyes stared brazenly up at the château. He was the very personification of the conquering lout.

Watching the festivities, Monsieur d'Outremort scrutinized the simulacrum with the aid of binoculars, and smiled. This is certified by his manservant Nazaire, a very devoted old fellow who swears that his master was never more cheerful than on July 11, 12, 13 and 14, 1911. He concluded that Marquis Savinien was putting on a brave face against ill-fortune, and that insanity is sometimes a blessing. Fortified by that opinion, and Monsieur d'Outremort having instructed him and the other valets to go and mingle with the people in order to report back to him what the rabble was saying, Nazaire went down to Bourseuil at about 1 p.m., the ceremony being fixed for 2 p.m. The entire household staff accompanied him.

The village was furiously overpopulated. The reported statistic alleges that 5000 people crowded into the commune of 900 souls. This is clear evidence of the importance attached in the region to that libertarian demonstration, and provides as measure of the ardent "citizenship" that still animates the former tenants of the marquisate. In spite of the torrid heat, the entire society packed the square around the statue, which was covered by an almost-immaculate linen sheet. A makeshift podium emerged from the crowd like a pontoon from a turbulent pond. Four oriflammes hung from four flagpoles; colored flags decorated the windows garnished with spectators; Venetian lanterns were already interlacing their garlands for the evening ball—and the animation continued all along the main street, at the end of which the looming Château d'Outremort provided a taciturn image of the Bastille whose storming was being commemorated.

From the utmost depths of his retrenchment, Monsieur d'Outremort clearly heard the *Marseillaise* that opened the solemnities. Houlon, unveiled, appeared to universal applause. A deputé of the extreme left took the floor. His speech was not so much socialist as Jacobin. A native of Bourseuil, he was familiar with the kind of bombast that it was necessary to proclaim to move his fellow citizens. The populist made facile and pitiless allusions to Outremort. Listening devotedly, the audience contained its jubilation, several bumpkins squinting at the castle with expressions of evil delight. They saw someone at the latticed-window of a corner turret, which did not cause them any anxiety at all; they were unable to tell, at that distance, who the curious person was.

Nazaire, however, could not be mistaken on that score. While his peers were busy drinking in an inn, he had scrupulously obeyed the instructions he had received, and kept his ears pricked in the direction of the podium. As soon as he noticed Monsieur d'Outremort's presence at the turret window, he knew that it portended nothing good, and he set off on the return journey. Weaving through the crowd in the main street, addressing frowning glances to the château, he suddenly perceived something that caused him to go pale: the drawbridge had been lowered, the portcullis raised and the doors opened wide.

Nazaire accelerated his pace, gripped by an indefinable anxiety. Meanwhile, Monsieur d'Outremort had not left his post, and that was reassuring. Indeed, he did not seem to be interested in the distant spectacle of the rustic celebration, since, from closer range, he seemed to be manipulating something... yes, that was reassuring.

Even so, as soon as he had disengaged himself from the crowd, the honest manservant began to run. He came to a sudden stop, and uttered a piercing scream that was heard as far away as the square, thanks to the attentive silence engendered by the speech.

Five thousand heads turned toward Outremort.

They saw no reason to be afraid. Everything offered the most placid appearance. An automobile, having emerged from the château, was coming along the inclined ledge whose triple-zigzag slope led to the drawbridge between Outremort and the entrance to Bourseuil. Four travelers were grouped in it. A stream of dust extended behind it.

Was there anything there to justify the slightest cry of alarm? No, thought the majority. Yes, thought the Bourseuilians, when they recognized, by its red color, the double phaeton whose speed had driven them to revolt three years before. It was necessary to see the employment of that machine, which they had condemned, as a challenge on Monsieur d'Outremort's part. That spoiled their pleasure. They refused, however, to admit that the arrogant vehicle would come to them on a day like this. At the bottom of the hill it would turn, follow the departmental highway, and disappear, along with the four lackeys charged with making this miserable protest.

Senator Collin-Barnard, the president, got up in order to redirect attention to the statue with a tirade-but all eyes were following the descent of that insulting automobile—and the stone Houlon seemed to be following it too. It arrived at the bottom of the rocky decline. At that moment, the Sun illuminated its sides with an unusual reflected gleam.

Monsieur d'Outremort, still unrecognized, watched from the height of his turret.

The car did not turn on to the highway as everyone had presumed; it took the narrow road that transformed into the main street. It would arrive, therefore, in Bourseuil, and speedily! Perhaps it was the Marquis himself, with partisans, who was coming to sneer at the proletariat? Who were the impertinent *aristos* bringing the machine down?

A dusty whirlwind approached. The four travelers were hidden from the sight of the crowd. They were astonished by the muteness of its progress; previously, the motor had rattled. They had been astonished by the rapidity of its progress previously...but...

Ha! Everything became abruptly clear in their minds.
*The automobile was charging the crowd!*

There was a convulsive movement in the main street, a prompt consolidation of the assembly to either side, forming two ranks. In the blink of an eye, an open pathway opened up through the mass of compressed humanity. For whatever reason, it yielded passage to the seigneurial procession, as in times of old when resounding carriages had jolted along the

25

King's highway. *Look out! Look out! Stand aside! Get out of the way!*

The automobile plunged into the vacant space. A meteor! And not a single blast of the horn! Not a single warning shout from the driver! Not a single gesture from the four individuals masked with goggles and swathed in capes, who were maintaining a frightful tranquility!

The bolide brushed the mob to the right, then swerved toward the mob to the left, then swung back to the right, and so on—and atrocious clamors accompanied each of the car's sinuosities, while people fell down in sheaves to either side...because it was *mowing them down* with large scythes disposed at shin-level, as in the military chariots of Antiquity.

Like a momentary lightning-bolt, launched at top speed, it ran in this manner through the ditch of flesh, lurching from one bank to the other and leaving horrible butchery in its wake.

Blood ran in the gutters like water in a rainstorm.

In this manner, it reached the crammed square, and there, rather than following the alleyway they made for it in a straight line, it turned sharply and plowed straight into the midst of the audience.

Now, such was the speed that it had built up, and its power, that it followed a considerable further trajectory before coming to a halt. Its gait imitated the yawing motion of a boat bobbing on a stormy wave. It rose up only to plunge down again, pitching and rolling. Soft impacts battered the hood. The tires caused bloody splashes to spring forth. It advanced amid howls of pain.

The terrifying reaper of a field of humankind, it cut an abominable swathe through the mass. The killing surpassed all the carnages that those who were there could remember.

To top everything else, though, no crazier massacre had ever been carried out by murderers so cold. An impassive driver directed the hecatomb. By a subtle refinement, his costume was that of Comte Cyril d'Outremort, whose passage from life to death the peasants had contrived. The detail was recognized; the terror increased. Everyone fled.

Every man for himself! The rout scattered the crowd in all directions.

A large number of gawkers had, however, piled into a side-street opening into the square, which was a dead end, and the danger cornered them there. There was an indescribable agglomeration at that spot of bewildered creatures, who were trampling one another down, climbing on top of one another and stifling one another.

The automobile headed toward them.

An ailing monster covered with innumerable stains, a final effort precipitated it into the heart of the panic-stricken mass. The car cut right through the crowd, crushing its victims with its quivering bumper as it smashed into the wall.

The beast was dead! The four executioners lay among the debris. Immediately, ferocious laborers drunk with hatred ran to finish them off.

One of them, a mechanic by trade, saw the motor beneath a heap of twisted metal, and was astonished to be unable to make out the quadruple silhouette of the cylinders; a large dynamo replaced their familiar block—but the avenger had better things to do than hang around examining an electrical system. His acolytes were already grabbing hold of the criminal chauffeur. The latter was seized, and the goggles masking his bandit's face were torn away...by the man who was the first to let go of him....

For it was Death, in person, who had piloted the reaper-car.

I can tell you this: it was a frightful jeering skeleton, half-denuded of its greenish shreds of flesh...

Three other skeletons, divested of their dust-covers, appeared at the same time. One was clad in Marquis Fulbert's button-up hunting-jacket, the second in a silken coat and knee-breeches, with a sheathed sword, the third in a dress with petticoats, held up by a blue sash...

They all agreed, then, that Comte Cyril, having come from *beyond the grave*, had guided the revenge of the huntsman, the ambassador and the canoness. All eyes turned as one to look at the macabre château from which the dead had escaped. The majority were haggard eyes fixed in a permanent stare. Many expected visions of Jehoshaphat...

But the château did not flinch, and someone therein calmly closed a turret-window.

# THE CANTATRICE

*To Louis Cochet*[6]

Old Hauval—who is still the director of the Opéra-Dramatique—smoothed his flowing beard with a gnarled hand and said: "This is what happened!"

In 189-, in the month of March, there was a performance of *Siegfried* at Monte Carlo. An extraordinary interpretation made that revival the great lyrical event of the season. I had decided to see it, and I left Paris with a group of artistes, critics and dilettantes who were racing, without knowing it, to the most troubling auditory experience that living men might undergo. I shall spare you the vicissitudes of the journey, for our journey was nothing but vicissitudes: pauses, delays, and a forced two-hour halt in Marseilles caused by a railway accident, which I employed as best I could in visiting the city. Suffice it to say that I went, reached Monaco, and arrived at the performance.

It commenced in splendor and continued without a hitch. The program was a list of celebrities. The finest singers in the world were realizing the Wagnerian drama. Caruso played Siegfried, and we were in the depths of the delight into which his power and timbre had plunged us when the bird sang.[7]

---

[6] Louis Cochet is quite a common name, and there were several notable people of that name when the story was written; the one most likely to be the intended dedicatee is the architect Philip-Louis Cochet.

[7] Enrico Caruso (1873-1921) was world famous by the time this story was published, but in the 1890s, when it is set, he was still singing in provincial Italian theaters; he did not make

You will recall that there is in *Siegfried* a singing bird—which is to say, a woman, in the wings, who lends the bird the prestige of words and melody. Thus, an invisible woman suddenly began to sing—and then it seemed to us that all the other singers had merely been mewling, roaring or braying since the curtain went up. The sonorous sounds of the impeccable orchestra immediately became screechy and annoying, so magical was that voice. Its purity was only equaled by its strength. It combined all the virtues that sounds can acquire, and did so in a manner so incomparable, unprecedented and superhuman, that everyone wondered, at first, whether a human throat was really emitting that prodigious song, or whether it might be some strange independent voice with a life of its own...

But on listening to it, no, no: that tender soprano revealed a feminine soul, the ardent heart of a young woman who was breathing it out in a charmingly natural fashion, as a flower yields its perfume...

On listening to it, one divined as its source a vermilion mouth and palpitating white breasts...

One shivered, on listening to it, as if gazing at the freshness of an excessively beautiful virgin...

Who, then, was singing in that fashion? My memory recalled, one by one, the voices of the world's most famous singers. I knew them all. I thought for a moment that one of them had taken us by surprise by accepting that minor role—but no prima donna could have rivaled, in voice or skill, the fairy who was singing the bird in the wings.

She fell silent. There was a sensational rustle in the audience. The program was consulted. It bore only one name that was obscure, which every eye sought out: *Borelli.*

The public awaited with bizarre impatience the bird's next entrance in the scene and the moment when the unknown

---

it to La Scala until 1900 and his recording career did not begin until 1902.

woman would begin to sing again. For my part, I was subject to a tyrannical desire to hear her voice…

It finally sprang forth, and streamed over us like a subtle and bewitching wave, in which one could have wished to bathe forever…

When La Borelli stopped singing for the second and last time that evening, the crowd must have suffered a chagrin akin to pain, for a great dolorous sigh was heard to swell, from the stalls to the highest boxes. Then the applause burst forth, so impetuous that the orchestra stopped playing. The standing spectators clapped their hands, demanding that the diva appear and take a bow. It was in vain, however, that Caruso extended an inviting arm toward the wings; Mademoiselle—or Madame—Borelli refused, presumably unwilling to exhibit her pretty face in the stage-lights without make-up.

I took advantage of the mundane tumult to slip away to the wings in order to discover the phenomenon. Gunsbourg, the director, intercepted me. He was radiant.

"What a revelation, eh, my dear chap!"

"But who is she? Borelli, Borelli…a pseudonym? It's miraculous, the voice of a maiden with the experience of a seasoned artiste! Amazing! What authority! What warmth! What…"

"What a revelation, eh!"

Gunsbourg could not get over it. As for me, I had but one idea: to engage La Borelli at the Opéra-Dramatique—and I admit that frankly. But Gunsbourg shook his head mockingly. "That, you know, is something else!"

I assumed that he had contracted with the singer for a long series of performances. He corrected my misapprehension, but swore nevertheless—still in a bantering tone—that Madame Borelli would never appear on the stage of my theater.

"Is it that she doesn't know how to act?" I asked. "Bah! She'll learn. It's a mere detail. Her diction already leaves nothing to be desired. Introduce me to her, my dear chap—quickly. I'll take responsibility for the rest."

"Hold on! She's already leaving! There she is at the end of the corridor with her husband. Well, are you coming?"

A couple had just emerged into the corridor through a side-door and, having turned their backs toward us, were drawing away. I glimpsed them for a few seconds before they reached the far corner: he, an imposing stature enveloped in dark clothing; she, a meager imprecise form propped up on two crutches that made her shoulders rise and fall rhythmically and dug into her armpits at every tottering step.

The unparalleled cantatrice was a cripple!

I felt a cruel disappointment, whose violence astonished me when I recovered from my stupor.

The Borellis were on their way out. Gunsbourg was waiting.

"What does it matter!" I eventually exclaimed, in the ardor of my enthusiasm. "There's no lameness that can hold her back! After they've heard her sing, every composer will want her as an interpreter. They'll write roles to suit her, episodic, motionless or hidden—roles of admirable originality! Roles for voices, not for characters! What do I know? Then again, we have the resource of concerts—in that respect, the field is wide open. In any case, my dear chap, it's *essential* that she be heard. Think of it! Centuries might pass before such a vocal prodigy is reproduced—if it ever is reproduced! I'm astonished that your company-member isn't famous in spite of her infirmity. Where the Devil did you unearth that nightingale?"

"I saw her for the first time a week ago. She arrived in my office one evening, escorted by her husband, or at least by an individual who claimed to be her husband. He's a rather disquieting character, shady in appearance and manner. Both of them, decked out in unspeakable rags, seemed to be very poor. Their bearing, however, respired the health of vagabonds accustomed to the open air. I thought they'd come from Italy, perhaps as beggars…but in sum, no one knows where they come from. Monsieur Borelli argued the conditions of the engagement with revolting rudeness. He has his hooks into his companion, that's obvious. She has that constrained physiognomy of Lakmés or Mignons,[8] and surely wouldn't sing unless someone were forcing her to do it. Poor girl! Did you notice the melancholy quality of her voice?"

No, I hadn't noticed that. Besides, my project was preoccupying my mind.

"Give me their address," I said, brusquely. "I must take that woman to Paris."

The Bohemians' household occupied two small rooms in a fourth-rate hotel called *Villa des Mouettes*,[9] overlooking the sea. It happened that I was staying nearby. I went there the next day, early in the morning.

Without the least protocol, a boy led me to their apartment. "They're on the first floor," he told me, "because of the lady's incapacity. There's no lift here, and no rooms on the ground floor." As the blast of a trumpet shook the whole the building, he added: "He's the one playing the hunting-horn. He's already been told three times to shut up."

We arrived in front of a door that the interior fanfare— savage and scandalous, but not without a certain crude beauty—was causing to vibrate.

My guide knocked. Silence fell abruptly. I perceived a muffled dialogue, the sound of something moving away, being dragged across the carpet, the closing of a door, then the opening of a window…the click-click of a key…

Finally, Borelli appeared.

Face to face, we recoiled. For my part, it was surprise, at the sight of that astonishingly chubby, suntanned, curly-haired gallows-bird—a sort of dangerous Hercules, half-dressed in

---

[8] *Lakmé* (1883) and *Mignon* (1866) are both light operas. The former has words by Edmond Gondinet and Philippe Gille and music by Léo Delibes; it is based on a work by Pierre Loti and set in India; the latter has words by Michel Carré and Jules Barbier, inspired by Goethe (Mignon is a character in *Wilhelm Meister*) and music by Ambroise Thomas.

[9] "Seagulls Villa."

33

trousers and a loose jacket, and who...in truth, I don't know how to express it...

I had a vague sensation of having met that man somewhere before—and recently, damn it!—but *in circumstances such that I should never have seen him again.* Do you see? The fact of seeing him again seemed—obscurely—impossible. It was a vague impression—so vague that a moment's reasoning immediately attributed it to the remembrance of some dream.

Borelli's suspicion was not so quick to dissipate. Anxiety widened his eyes, and I didn't understand the reason for it— for, far from explaining my reminiscence, my host's attitude seemed to contradict it. I had a muted consciousness of that relationship.

I bowed. Borelli's face lit up.

"Damn!" he said, blowing into his abnormal cheeks. "You frightened me, with your big white beard! *Perbacco, signore*—you should warn people, when you resemble someone else so closely!"[10]

I offered him my card. He burst into loud laugher, from which I inferred that he could not read. That is why I told him my name and my position. Then he invited me to sit down.

I explained the purpose of my visit, neglecting to mention crutches and lameness, while surreptitiously taking inventory of the lodgings. Borelli, impelled by false modesty, had hidden his hunting-horn. I was only able to discover miserable impersonal furniture: two chairs; an iron-framed bed; a chest of drawers; a cheapjack clock flanked by two large spiny seashells on the mantelpiece; lithographs and coat-pegs on the walls; and the most wretched trunk imaginable—moldy and falling apart—in a corner, like debris washed on shore after a shipwreck.

---

[10] The Italian exclamation "*Perbacco!*" is an approximate equivalent of the English "Wow!"

Confronted by that indigence, pity gradually softened my attitude. My offers reflected that. They were…what they needed to be.

Borelli listened to them without saying a word. He gazed through the open window at the sea, with piercing eyes. The toes of his bare, sun-bronzed feet played with their sandals. In the opening of his jacket, the brown torso of a Neapolitan athlete could be seen swelling with the rhythm of life. Oh, what a handsome fellow! But where had I seen him before?

Furrowing his brows and clenching his fists, he muttered: "Just my luck!" And he began laughing sarcastically. "I knew I'd be offered loads of gold and silver," he went on. "Just my luck! *I can't, perbacco!* We *can't* accept. We can't go to Paris, you see, Monsieur Director. I'm obliged to refuse. Oh, existence on land isn't easy! I even wonder if we'll succeed in living here…you know, don't you, that Madame Borelli is a cripple?"

"I don't care about that. No one will care about it. She sings, and one is all ears. She sings, and one no longer has eyes…"

"Isn't that so? Isn't it? You've never heard singing like that, eh? Can you believe that she has such treasures in her throat? Oh, tell me, anyway—do you think I could make a lot of money with her? What would you say to concerts in the dark? Darkness and music—they go together. No one ever saw her…then again, it would economize on lighting. What do you think? Tell me, Monsieur Director? I'm thinking about a tour along the coat: Nice, Marseilles…"

Profoundly sickened by the manners of this boor, who spoke of his wife and a great artiste as a curious object, I nevertheless replied: "But why don't you want to try Paris? I guarantee…"

The enormous lout cut me off, curtly. "Basta! Basta! I said the coast; it will be the coast! We only do seaside resorts. It's for health reasons, Madame's whim, family secrets—anything you want, but *that's—the—way—it—is!* The coast or nothing."

He had the same effect on me as a rare wild beast. My opinion was further reinforced when Borelli, having distinguished the splashing sound of ablutions in the next room—which, moreover, must have splashed the surroundings copiously—ran to the connecting door, opened it by a crack, and cursed the author of the splashing in singularly barbarous terms. He was terrible in his fury and vehemence.

There was no response, but Madame Borelli—at least, I assume that it was her—continued taking her bath in a more subdued fashion.

The other, mollified, returned to me. "I regret it, damn it! I regret it, *perbacco!*—for the wages, as is reasonable…and also…you seem like a nice old fellow. We'd be fixed up…"

He looked me up and down with disdainful benevolence.

"I'm at your disposal," I replied, politely.

The bumpkin misunderstood the conventional meaning of the formula. "Really?" he said. "Really and truly?" Drawing closer, he looked me in the eye without restraint. "Really, truly and honestly?"

The sad lot of the singer moved me to such pity that I made a sign of acquiescence with my eyes and head.

With that, Borelli said to me in a low voice: "Well then listen: you can do me a big favor."

"Go on."

"If you…" He stared at me severely, then, satisfied with my attitude, resumed in a confidential mode, perhaps a trifle hesitantly: "If you see a man hereabouts *who resembles you like your mirror image*, tell me right away."

I pretended to accept the mission. "A man with a long white beard? Very old?"

"Rather!" said Borelli, with a bitterly ironic smile.

"How is he dressed?"

He seemed perplexed. "Dressed? In faith…not very fashionably, doubtless. Baroque, probably. Ah! There's this: try to get a look at his forehead. His forehead ought to bear the mark of a…an overly heavy hat, worn for a long time. Just now, when you appeared, that's how I knew you weren't him…but it's the beard, most of all, that you'll pick out."

"What if he's shaved?"

My interlocutor smiled again, this time without bitterness. The thought of my mysterious double stripped of his beard seemed to fill him with delight. "Have no fear, Monsieur Director. There are beards one does not shave off. And thanks, you know—he is, so to speak, a creditor…who's tracking me…"

He looked at the sea, thoughtfully.

In order to prolong the conversation and, if possible, get more deeply into the confidence of the enigmatic churl, I ventured: "I can see that you love the sea."

He emerged from his reverie, and his reddened cheeks puffed out. "Me? The sea?" he gasped. "Ugh…why ask me that? No, I don't love the sea. It stinks, doesn't it? You can smell the tide. Don't you think that you can smell the fish even from here? No? That's not what you were trying to insinuate? No? I can!" He raised his voice abruptly, in a menacing fashion: "I can! It smells of fish here!"

His keen eyes sparkled, fixed on mine. I thought I ought to withdraw without further ado, and took my leave of the irritable nomad, asking him to convey to Madame Borelli the assurance of my utter admiration and the regret I bore for not having been able to offer my homage to her.

"She's getting dressed," Borelli countered.

I was not yet outside when the fanfare thundered more loudly than before.

The Hercules with the pygean[11] cheeks had closed his window—but I perceived, at the next one, the desperate face of a woman who was gazing at the sea and weeping.

---

[11] This Greek-derived adjective does not appear in the English dictionary any more than the French one, but it signifies "buttock-shaped."

I saw the Borellis again that same evening, at the theater and in the wings. A veritable multitude was crowding the auditorium to heard *Siegfried*'s bird sing. Our Parisian party had remained in Monte Carlo in its entirety, contrary to the plans we had made to return to Paris the day after the performance. The previous night's audience had returned in full, replete with melomaniac fervor. For lack of a smaller folding-seat, Gunsbourg had offered me a stool behind one of the scenery-supports. It was the best way of getting close to Madame Borelli. I watched out for her.

They arrived. The most lamentable of all the memories I have is that of the invalid advancing jerkily on her crutches in the midst of other actors magnificent in their carriage and radiant with pride. The unfortunate woman was clad in poverty-stricken Sunday clothes. I shall long remember her shapeless and colorless bonnet, undoubtedly the victim of many a downpour, diabolically positioned, but on a superb chignon whose fawn-colored tresses were tightly wound, compressing their fabulous opulence. And her bodice! The poor woman! How many times had she laundered that smock to get it into that urine-colored state? And her skirt! Her pitiful skirt, with its faded hues, superannuated petticoats, "decorated" with garlands and worn braid—her sinister skirt, knotted at the base like a sack, upon the secret monstrosity of her legs!

She moved heavily, positioning the sack, then the crutches, then the sack...

I couldn't tell you whether she was pretty; one only saw her sadness. She looked as if she had been born on the Day of the Dead.

Monsieur Borelli held her close. I perceived a vague similarity between them, like a family resemblance, a certain wild, russet, suntanned quality that linked them confusedly together. Brother and sister? Cousins? Or simply compatriots?

On seeing me, the man stopped short. He resumed walking immediately, his expression reassured and his cheeks puffed out.

"It's a bit strong! I can't get used to your beard!" he said to me, as he shook my hand. Then, very quickly, he whispered in my ear: "No news? The old man? Good." He straightened up again. "This is my wife, Monsieur Director."

I tried to get the cantatrice to talk. She murmured a few *yesses* and a few discouraging *noes*...besides, the performance was under way; we didn't have the right to talk. The music reigned.

Siegfried's horn resounded. Borelli gripped my shoulder and whispered; "Isn't that beautiful? Isn't that trumpet beautiful? That's what I call a nice piece, easy to remember..."

Suddenly, the voice of the bird emerged from the lips of the invalid, so close to me that my throat resonated with it. It was as if the atmosphere were saturated with a maddening sonorous aroma. Seized by vertigo, intoxication, gratitude, I became unsteady on my feet. Scene-shifters, chorus girls, bit-part players and even singers—the entire personnel of the theater—formed a circle around the cripple. There was something in her voice other than genius and sweetness; there was an inexplicable power of attraction. And in the half-light of the place, magnified, transfigured by the love of her art, the golden-haired cripple acquired an irresistible beauty...

She finished. The continuing opera was a tiresome racket. I emerged from an opium dream. La Borelli was no longer anything more than a sad and badly-dressed creature, who could not be cheered up by my praises. The ovations left her indifferent. Her escort led her away hurriedly—"to avoid indiscretions at the exit," he said. I wanted to go with them; he refused, will an ill grace.

An hour later, unable to calm the agitation that the emotion, though brief, had left within me, I was wandering along the edge of the sea, some distance away from the houses. The silhouette of a man standing on a rock was suddenly outlined in the darkness.

The new Moon illuminated the marine landscape faintly. I thought I recognized Borelli. Divided between dread and curiosity, I advanced furtively through the boulders on the shore, continually losing sight of him only to discover him closer at hand, as motionless as his pedestal. It was definitely him, like a statue.

Where had I met him before?

Remembering the scares that the unexpected sight of me gave him, I paused some distance away and announced myself joyfully. He shivered nonetheless upon his rock, like a cypress in a gust of wind.

Borelli seemed to be lost in contemplation before the nocturnal sea. A large cloak draped him in Romanticism. Diffuse objects were heaped at his feet.

"You can't tell me that you don't love Amphitrite!" I exclaimed, in a bantering tone. "To come at this hour to admire her..."

"So what?" he grunted. "Is it any of your business? Yes, I love the sea, but not so much as solitude, you know!"

I was astonished to hear him speaking so loudly, in a voice that overwhelmed the sound of the waves, when I was so close to him. I felt his anger. He said to me, point-blank: "Why don't you dare to interrogate me about what's on the ground beside me?"

"But I hadn't even given it a thought..." I replied, disconcerted.

Borelli shrugged his shoulders. I observed that his eyes were uniquely occupied with the sea. He studied its moving expanse unrelentingly. It was quiet and pallid in the moonlight. A dolphin was playing in the waves; its contortions and the flips of its tail were visible from time to time in fugitive gleams. The lighthouses, all in a line, gesticulated variously with their infinite arms of light.

"You haven't given it a thought?" he mocked. "Go on! You're scared. I hate intruders—you know that very well. Leave me in peace, my dear Monsieur!"

I was only an old man, devoid of vigor...

"Listen, Borelli—I'm going, that's understood. It's far from my intention to be disagreeable to you, my lad. But don't say that I'm scared. I'm not scared. What are those things at your feet?"

"Go away!" bellowed the colossus. "Peace! Peace! Peace! If not..."

I beat the retreat at a steady pace, mastering a furious desire to run away as fast as my legs could carry me.

As I went back into Monte Carlo, I wondered if it might be wise to take advantage of the absence of the redoubtable cicisbeo to attempt to have a conversation with Madame Borelli. The lateness of the hour held me back. Both the adventurers' windows were dark; the invalid's slumber seemed to be a delight that should only be broken in exchange for another. I passed on.

The adventure seemed supremely exciting to me; a voice captivated me; a woman excited my charity; a man intrigued my suspicion. I allowed my traveling companions to leave without me.

In the early afternoon, Borelli had himself announced. I received him in my room. It was a social visit, or so he claimed. No allusion was made to the previous night's incident. After a few superfluous remarks, though, he asked me straight out to lend him 25 louis.

Very annoyed, I procrastinated, changing the subject; I offered him my compliments with regard to the affluence that the singer was attracting to the theater and the principality. Thanks to her, the accommodation was fully booked for a fortnight and the hotels were overflowing.

On that, the husband-impresario told me that he was going to demand a serious pay-increase from Gunsbourg, or his wife would not sing again. I assume that he was on the point of reiterating his request for 500 francs, but an unexpected occurrence interrupted him.

His face changed. With his ear cocked, he gestured to me to be silent. Before I had heard whatever it was, the fanatic hurled himself on to the balcony.

All the passers-by and strollers were heading in the same direction at a hurried pace, with a hypnotic and taciturn gait that was alarming at first glance. In the distance, in the direction of the *Villa des Mouettes*, an extraordinary voice launched forth in disorganized song—and it was toward that voice that all those people were marching like sleep-walkers.

My visitor lost his temper. "I've forbidden her, though…"

What happened next was immediate. Four bounds had taken him to the foot of the staircase, as he too hastened toward the magnetic singer.

Was it the effect of the indomitable curiosity that linked me to their destiny? Was it by virtue of the melodious magnetism? At any rate, the fact is that I bounded after him.

From every direction, people were running toward the barbed call of the voice. What she was singing resembled nothing familiar. It sprang forth, twisting and overflowing in delightful cries. It was the entirety of springtime, singing the entirety of love. Men, subjugated, were heading toward the infernal canticle as little birds head toward the eyes of a serpent. There were some women trying to hold some of them back, and others who were following them toward the voice. Arms extended, eyes crazed, their feverish legs were working mechanically. A host of fanatical automata was pressing at the doorway of the *Villa des Mouettes* and beneath the singer's open window. Borelli threw himself into it with a forceful leap, waving his arms and legs, progressing with great thrusts of the hips and shoulders into the bosom of that living wave, with the gestures and a swimmer and an amphibious flexibility. The ecstatic members of the crowd allowed themselves to be brutalized. They were listening, with their mouths open and their nostrils flared, as if their mouths and nostrils were listening, drinking and breathing in the voice, obedient to its despotic tones: *Closer! Closer! Forwards!* That was what was being ordered without being spoken.

Like everyone else, I was held voluptuously captive by the toils of the melody, and I immersed myself involuntarily in the human heap in order to get closer, at any price, my ear-drums fascinated, my soul numbed...

It was resonating in the depths of a gulf, into which all those amorous individuals withed to precipitate themselves.

The charm lasted until the intervention of the plump manager. His outburst reached us as a fearful summons, proffered in an idiom that was impossible to comprehend...

Then, crushed by a silence more silent than any other, we looked at one another as if emerging from an adorable and shameful dementia. Everyone resumed his interrupted journey, head empty, nerves jangling, full of astonishment and confusion. Many had glided as far as the threshold of the room; they slipped away, blushing. A few were weeping. Life recommenced; the noises of it set all their teeth on edge.


That kind of scandal only had fortunate consequences for my friend Gunsbourg. Madame Borelli sang the bird as she had the night before, in the presence of an elite audience which crammed the corridors and blocked the exits, a noisy and profuse crush; but Wagner's music on her lips was not sufficiently imperious a spell to draw the legion of her admirers into the wings.

I was placed in the orchestra stalls.

On raising my eyes, I perceived in the balcony, directly above my head, an old gentleman whose long white beard made me shiver. The opera-glasses revealed the image that mirrors habitually relay back to me, with the difference that, of the two of us, it was me that was the reflection. I was the faded, soft and discolored replica of that august old man; the copy of which he was the original. With the complexion of an old sea-dog,[12] a Roman nose, two turquoise flames beneath

---

[12] The term I have construed metaphorically in substituting the English "sea-dog" is *loup de mer* [sea wolf], which is applied more literally to several different fish and marine mammals, nowadays most commonly to the sea bass. It is conceivable that Renard might have a comparison of that genre in mind.

shadowy eyebrows, and his forehead barred by a reddish line like those left by heavy helmets, he looked like the venerable admiral of a squadron of yore, a commander grown old in naval glory, a doge of Venice, mistress of the sea, immortal or resurrected. A frock-coat constrained the amplitude of his torso. Many a lady was peering at that combined patriarchal and military majesty through her opera-glasses. Royal names were running from mouth to mouth in his respect.

There was no doubt about it: this was Signor Borelli's enemy—perhaps even his ancestor and the ancestor of the singer; for, it must be admitted, the family resemblance I had already noted assimilated all three of their faces.

That of the old man took on an expression of tragic grandeur when the bird began to sing. Its ancient solemn rectitude shifted nervously, as if to deplore...

Bravos. Encores, Hurrahs. Disorder.

I tried to find him again. He had disappeared.

Ought I to warn the interested party? I hesitated over that until the final act and concluded by opting in favor of the old man, against the persecutor of my protégée. Borelli's adversary could only be a friend of the oppressed woman, an ally for me; it was, therefore, her and not the Italian who had to be informed as soon as possible.

In the hope that the plump man would devote himself once again to the shadowy task in which I had disturbed him on the strand on the previous night, and which, no doubt, would prevent him from leaving the shore, I went to the *Mouettes*.

The drowsy concierge mumbled that neither Monsieur nor Madame Borelli had come back from the theater—to which he swore—and that, moreover, they never came back before 3 or 4 a.m., *which he had already told me a little while ago*, and that he did not understand why I had woken him up twice in succession to ask him the same thing.

The news of this double absence confused my ideas and upset my plan. Moreover, *the old man had been there*. I resolved to bring the matter into the light, and set off resolutely for the rocks where Borelli had snapped at me. Having had second thoughts, though, I turned back; I climbed to the top of the cliff that bordered that part of the shore, from whose heights I would be able to look down on the setting and the action.

My heart was beating rapidly. I felt strange.

The nebulous night was not as favorable to watchers as the one before, and the moon was still on the point of rising. The sea—the ancient sea, the Latin sea—lulling its eternal insomnia, was reciting its pagan legends and the poem of its mythology in the darkness. Flecks of foam whitened it here and there. Clouds being sparse, the clarity of the sky showed me the fugitive gleams of the nautical play of a dolphin in the far distance. But then the thunderous clamor of a horn went up—a horn sounding Siegfried's fanfare!

I stopped.

Beneath my post, there was a statue standing on a pedestal: Borelli, who was sounding the trumpet-call on an instrument so small that it could not be seen; Borelli *alone*; a sculptural Borelli.

Ah! I thought, suddenly. God, how stupid I am! I didn't realize it until now. He doesn't resemble any *actual* citizen! It's the Tritons he resembles, with his bloated cheeks! The Tritons of painters and sculptors! The two decorative Tritons of the water-pavilion at the Palais de Longchamp, in Marseilles, at which I was looking only the other day! All well and good! That's why it seemed impossible to encounter him, since he wasn't in the land of dreams!"

The fanfare having concluded, Borelli called out to someone—but he was still alone. I was looking at him from behind. He was standing between the sea and me, on the rock, in his overcoat. His calls multiplied, and became more precipitate, to the point at which he seemed to be hurling invective at the waves. He really was calling out, but to whom? Darkness. No one.

He crouched down, and leapt down from the rock. He was no longer visible…

Oh! Yes: at the very edge, on the fringe of the waves.

And the horn began to sound again—no longer Siegfried's leitmotiv but long howls reminiscent of what hunting jargon terms a *compulsory summons*. And then again, another bitter discourse shouted in the solitude, into the Mediterranean darkness: the liquid desert where a single dolphin was frolicking. And then the insistent trumpet call again, imperative, roaring....

Nothing more.

The Moon was veiled with cloud.

Borelli was dragging something out of the sea—something that resisted him. Like a fisherman hauling in his net—the simulacrum of a fisherman hauling in his net, of which absolutely nothing could be seen. Ah! The thing had yielded, had broken; having fallen backwards, he blasphemed. I heard foreign words, imprecations...

He was struggling on the spot. Suddenly, I saw that he was naked. In the same instant, he slid sinuously into the water, swimming with the rapidity of a seal, with great thrusts of his shoulders and hips, just as he had surged through the middle of the crowd...

Fascination, equal to a passion, made me tremble. The most fantastic thing of all, however, had not yet occurred.

While the Hercules was swimming out into the open sea, becoming blurred in the depths of the darkness—heading almost directly for the dolphin, which could no longer be made out—I heard a kind of whinnying sound, *out at sea*. Several others followed, mingling together; gigantic, paradoxical whinnying sounds, with an unusual resonance; a choir of stallions imitating the barking concert of seals; horses crossed with walruses; ambiguous striders of the shadows and the sea...

At that moment, another of Borelli's calls reached me, above the din.

An infinitely distant voice answered him...

I just had time to throw myself flat on the ground and stick my fingers I my ears. I had just felt myself marching

46

forward, toward the edge of the cliff. One more step, and I would have been dead. For that faraway voice, from the remotest distance, as the hallucinatory voice of Madame Borelli, frenzied now, and triumphant, who was singing her springtime song like a hymn of deliverance!

Slowly, I relaxed the vice-like grip of my fists upon my ears; by that means I established that the human voice and the whinnyings had vanished.

The Moon emerged from a mass of cloud.

In the sea, a moving dot was heading straight for the shore; another dot, gleaming was following it a few fathoms behind: two men. The first came ashore. That was Borelli again. Dripping and painting, he headed for Monte Carlo. The second stood up at the same spot, and immediately launched himself on the heels of the fugitive. That one was an old man, and he was a giant—the old man whose feeble miniature I was. His long white beard floated in the wind of the pursuit. A golden crown helmeted him with spikes and fire. Although devoid of clothes, he would have been reminiscent of Charlemagne had he not been more sovereign than any emperor. At the end of one superb and menacing arm he was brandishing a sort of fork, like a lance and like a scepter.

The pursuit disappeared into the unknown.

I remained alone with the immensity.

After an hour of waiting in the moonlight, I decided to leave the theater of that equivocal drama. Before doing anything else, however, I went down a path to the place that Borelli had haunted for two nights in a row, to my knowledge—and every night, in my belief.

I found his felt hat there and his Romantic cloak. Next to them, on a parcel of old clothes, easily recognizable as Madame Borelli's, were two crutches forming a cross. There was also a large spiny seashell on the cloak: a conch.

By virtue of searching for the place where I had glimpsed the nocturnal wanderer trying to haul in the thing whose rupture had made him fall over, I ended up discovering a stake solidly planted in the sand, on the tide-line. It still retained a fine and resilient steel cord, which plunged into the sea. I pulled out about two hundred meters—all of it. It ended in a large collar, or rather a girdle—a leather girdle with a padlock, which had been cut a little while before.

As for Borelli, his body was blocking the path half way to Monte Carlo. He was lying face down, facing Monaco. Death, aided by the moonlight, was whitening his colossal back to the point of giving it a green tinge. Three parallel wounds, equidistant and in the same line, offered evidence of a single thrust of an avenging trident.

# THE MAN WITH THE RAREFIED BODY

*To René Martin-Guelliot*[13]

*From the hand of Dr. Sambreuil of Pontargis*

The delay that Bouvancourt imposed upon me expires today, March 14, 1912. It is therefore permissible for me to relate the history of the prodigious event of which he served as the thaumaturge. It is a story as fine as a legend. One sees therein, so to speak, an electric spark relighting Aladdin's lamp.

The friend that we are still mourning had this adventure at Pontargis, a few months after his installation there, some years before his tragic death. It is well-known that the physicist had retired there to work in a more leisurely manner and that it was in the Picard sub-prefecture that he carried out his most remarkable investigations of X-rays.

One night in the winter of 1901-02—without being equipped with either an overcoat or a hat, oddly enough—Bouvancourt was walking the pavements of Pontargis with a firm and sonorous step, with the expression of a fellow who feels extremely contented with himself.

He had kept watch from his window for the moment when the streets would be deserted, and then he had gone out for the first time in seven days—for, throughout the week, his passion for research had kept him cloistered in his laboratory,

---

[13] René Martin-Guelliot (1879-1962) was the editor of *Le Spectateur*, one of the periodicals to which Renard contributed before the outbreak of the Great War, and the one in which he published his manifesto for "*le roman merveilleux-scintifique*" [scientific marvel fiction].

preoccupied with an imminent discovery. For seven days and seven nights—a fateful interval—he had pursued the Truth like a goddess accustomed to being hunted and skilled in evasion. She had surrendered to him at 9 p.m. Immediately, her conqueror, quivering with pride, had recovered the consciousness of his muscles and his nerves; a furious desire had taken hold of him to walk energetically, and thoughtlessly, in the open air...

In spite of the authority of his desire, however, Bouvancourt had kept watch from his window for the moment when the streets would be deserted. Then he had woken his housekeeper, Mariette, and asked her to open the door for him; and, after having convinced her of the necessity of waiting behind the door for his return, in order to undo the latch when she heard his voice—only then did he go out for the first time in seven days. And Mariette never contrived to understand why her master had gone out without a hat and an overcoat, nor why he had woken her up in order to have the door opened as he left and when he came back, in response to the sound of his voice, when he could so easily have undone the latch himself, or made use of the doorbell and a key.

Mariette was also worried about the "Morand gang"—an association of evildoers which was terrorizing the canton. The domestic, without giving any thought to the perils of a late and solitary walk, reckoned that only a boorish egotist would leave a poor woman all alone by night in a small house in the Boulevard Poincaré while the Morand gang was ravaging the Pontargisians—but Mariette knew that Bouvancourt did not like criticism, so she did not make her sentiments manifest.

The professor, therefore, was striding through the sinister desert of the pitch-black town. Everything that could be distinguished within that provincial darkness was depressingly ugly. The avenues and esplanades rivaled one another in shame with their cul-de-sacs and side-streets. The rare gaslights, with their dimly-illuminating, paltry yellow flames, gave the impression of soiling the darkness; the cold rendered you wretched; the very silence seemed lamentable, because it was nothing but the mutism of 35,000 citizens.

Bouvancourt did not give a hoot for any of that. Neither the place nor the season had any purchase on his cheerfulness. Head held high, his step resounding, he marched victoriously; a permanent smile lit up his face, sometimes being amplified into laughter. He felt as if he were Archimedes wandering through the streets of Syracuse shouting to the people: "I've found it!" He marched triumphantly, as if beneath the bright Sicilian Sun, in a city full of Palaces.

It was thus, with his eyes elsewhere and his mind absent, that Bouvancourt ventured into the Saint-Charles district, where someone suddenly loomed up in front of him.

Bouvancourt was brutally snatched out of his dream. He experienced a sensation of having been transported by magic to the place he perceived: a dark crossroads where four muddy streets lined by blind walls intersected. Isolated and distant, a lantern shed a little crepuscular light, limning the gallows-bird silhouette that had just surged forth.

Let me open a parenthesis at this point. The following scene lasted about a quarter of a minute. The narrator cannot reproduce it as briskly, for fear of insufficiency. He will therefore function, if you wish, in the manner of a cinematograph that is turned slowly in order that the film might be analyzed and the event decomposed.

Bouvancourt stopped dead in front of the human obstacle. His soul was the theater of a remarkably instantaneous change of viewpoint. Before the apache's lips had moved, he had recalled all the crimes of the Morand gang. God knows that he had only scanned the story with a distracted eye, given that science was, for him, the only reality—but the fact is that, at that moment, he remembered the slightest details of every crime. Even the names of the victims came back to him as naturally as radiographic terms, and his mind's eye fixed itself upon a frightful series of cadavers worthy of some foreign wax museum: old women with their throats cut, broken-hearted girls, charred rentiers, mutilated cashiers, all of whose

51

biographical details he knew! Between the widow Canut, her blue features grimacing, and little Angèle Braquard, exposing the gaping wounds slashed in her thin neck, was the sexagenarian Adolphe Piat, bloated and burned to a crisp....

The cut-throat's filthy, reeking breath got up Bouvancourt's nose as he said: "Can you tell me what time it is, boss?"

At the same time, the physicist heard the muffled sound of footsteps approaching him from behind. Everything within him told him to back up against the nearest wall. He was not allowed to do it. Something passed before his eyes, moving downwards—something dark, which he identified immediately: it was the joined hands of his posterior enemy, which intended to perpetrate upon his person the ritual *coup du Père François*.

Bouvancourt, whose knowledge was not confined to physics, anticipated his destiny in a second, and saw himself strangled, held by that devil of an invisible animal, while the other went through his pockets in comfort.

The living lasso closed violently upon the professor's Adam's apple, and he uttered a strangled exclamation, half cry and half cough—rather incongruous, in sum, and, in any case, quite unjustified, for he had felt almost nothing, and reason alone had caused the abrupt recoil he had just effected. The offensive hands had vanished; Bouvancourt's ears told him that the assailant behind him was in the process of falling heavily and that, although his curse was brief, it could not have been any more forceful.

"To you, Julot!" said the *Père François*, in a muffled roar, less bellicose than fearful.

*It's true! It's true!* thought the scientist. *It had slipped my mind!*

And Julot saw Bouvancourt's smile return.

For two seconds, but no more, the aggression was suspended. The *Père François* got to his feet painfully and Julot wondered whether he had really seen what had just happened—whether he had really seen *his accomplice's joined hands disappear through the intended victim's neck, cutting through it, and yet leaving it exactly as before, atop that robust upright body, beneath that smiling head.*

Julot hesitated. But...bah! That decapitation, those cutting arms, were an effect of the poor lighting, an artifact of glimmers and shadows. He pronounced a silent obscenity, which served him as a war-cry, and bent over, intending to attack Bouvancourt like a ram and butt him in the stomach.

This was done at the risk of hurling the physicist backwards on to the *Père François*, who had completed his painful readjustment and was meditating singular hypotheses while watching the action—but the poor fellow was not yet done with pratfalls and amazement. Scarcely had he understood Julot's plan than he received his charge in the pit of his stomach, not without having seen his comrade *passing clean though his phenomenal adversary and emerging from his back like a clown leaping through a paper hoop!*

Bouvancourt burst out laughing and turned round. His two aggressors, tangled up, were writhing as each strove to be the first to get to his feet. It was Julot who succeeded. He ran off. The other followed hot on his heels, clutching his abdomen with his left hand while he made signs of the cross with his right. Both of them, however, were blaspheming madly.

"I must be daft!" murmured Bouvancourt. "I'd completely forgotten...hare-brained. To go out at night because of it, without a hat because of it, without an overcoat because of it, and not to remember it! Truly, I must be more exhausted than I thought. Let's go to bed, then. But first, where am I?"

His course had taken him to the edge of town. One of the walls was that of the cemetery—a circumstance that explained the superstitious terror of the *Père François*.

The nocturnal stroller headed for his lodgings, with a considerably less swaggering gait. He went back in—but I am not sufficiently well-informed to offer the most meager description of what he did then. I only know in broad terms, and I would prefer to report that second-hand explanation as I received it from his own lips—at the end of the story.

At any rate, the following morning, at about 8 a.m., while I was passing by, I rang the doorbell of the physicist's apartment on the first floor of 25 Boulevard Poincaré. As usual, I went in without standing on ceremony.

Bouvancourt seemed put out by my visit—and I hasten to say that, on that day, I saw no evidence of the nocturnal attack. I found him in his bedroom. He must have got up earlier, unless he hadn't gone to bed at all, the bed having been made, or having not been unmade. Disquiet was written all over his face. Standing in front of the clock, my friend was studying it with an anxiety that could not have been feigned. Something—an unaccustomed untidiness...slovenliness, even—had overtaken his entire person.

I offered him my hand.

"No, not today," he said, excusing himself with a snigger. "I shan't shake your hand, Sambreuil. Gout, you know. I've got very sensitive fingers. You can't imagine how painful it is. Then again, old chap, your visit is inconvenient this morning. Forgive me, but could you possibly come back this afternoon? You don't have any urgent communication to make? No? Well, see you soon, then? You have no idea...until then, my friend, and all my most humble excuses...*au revoir...*"

Being received in that manner threw me into a dark and fearful astonishment. I had observed that Bouvancourt had carefully stood to one side, with his back to the light, as if he were contagious. Normally, he escorted me to the top of the stairs; this time, I left him in his bedroom, alone with the clock. He kicked the door shut behind me.

I was filled with alarm and grief.

At 4 p.m., as soon as my medical consultation had concluded, I hastened to the Boulevard Poincaré.

Everything had resumed its normal appearance. Bouvancourt was waiting for me, in order to take a walk along the canal—the canal that was to prove deadly to him! I still recall that he was wearing his hazelnut-brown overcoat and his chestnut-brown felt hat. The professor's handshake crushed my finger-bones, but that grip could not have made me happier.

We started out. I expected a clarification…I solicited one by making allusions…but my friend remained coy. There was, moreover, no gaiety in his manner. I suspected that he had suffered a disappointment. I presumed that his current project had hit a snag, and did not insist any further.

A week later, Madame Sambreuil and I were eating lunch when Bouvancourt burst into the dining-room. His distress astonished us.

I gave him two glasses of ratafia, one after another, which revived him. After a certain number of sighs and exclamations—such as "Oh, my God!...Oh God, is it possible! Me! Me! My dear doctor…! Oh, Madame, if you only knew!" and so on—the excellent fellow dissolved in tears and began to tell us what you have already read, just as you have read it.

A few hours earlier—it was, I think, 9 a.m.—Bouvancourt had begun his day's work in a rather bad temper, because an employee of the railway, carrying a crate of laboratory equipment, had bumped into him awkwardly, bruising his shoulder. Even so, he had immediately set about unpacking the precious glassware contained in the crate and arranging them on his laboratory shelves.

The job was approaching completion when an exceptionally handsome youth came in without having himself announced, closed and locked the room's three doors, put the keys in his pocket, and came forward.

Bouvancourt was kneeling beside the crate, in the straw, and looked up at him in amazement.

"Monsieur," said the unknown, "May I introduce myself, at least!" His voice was soft, musical, amiable and polite. "I'm Morand…you know…of the Morand gang."

Bouvancourt leapt to his feet, not merely troubled at being at the rogue's mercy, but also astounded to see the features of a student of good family and to recognize in that gracious bandit, relieved of his disguise, the porter that had bumped into him a little while ago.

"Have no fear!" said the intruder, with an exquisite laugh, so feminine and so child-like that my friend scented subterfuge and trickery. "Have no fear! I don't mean to do you any harm!"

"What? Are you really Morand? Are you the man who had the teller at the Crédit Foncier knocked unconscious? Are you the author of the sextuple murder in Vautremont?" Are you the crook…"

His tone acid and his face stern, the Antinous replied: "Yes, Monsieur Bouvancourt, that's me. *I have no reason to hide it from my future accomplice.* For it's also me who's responsible for the theft of 500,000 francs from the Comptoir d'Escompte de Pontargis."

"Eh? What are you saying? I didn't know…when did that robbery…"

"That robbery *will be* committed tomorrow night, my dear Monsieur Bouvancourt. And it's *you* who'll help me carry it out."

"Me!"

"You'll help me," the youth continued, with an expression of vice and cruelty. "You'll help me, I tell you. As true as my name's Morand. Sit down, and let's have a little chat."

The master of the house sat down at his guest's bidding. Dominated by the gaze of a tiger, he thought of the youth of imperial brutes—Nero, Caracalla, Tiberius—and accepted that this was the terrible gang-leader.

The latter continued: "Two of my employees have given me an incredible report. A strange humiliation was inflicted on them on Tuesday, at about midnight, near the cemetery. The arms of the first, suddenly becoming yataghans, went through a certain stroller without doing him the slightest damage. As for the second, he passed through the supernatural individual, for whom that perception was sufficient to make him to break out in diabolical laughter.

"This late stroller, Monsieur could not be anyone else but the magician Bouvancourt. I know the Pontargeois directory; it includes but one sorcerer's name—yours. And, as the date of my baccalaureate in science is not very distant, I understood that, by the intervention of radiography, you had discovered a means of making yourself traversable, as ungraspable as a man of gas...or liquid..."

"It's not that, exactly," remarked Bouvancourt, with a thin smile. "The comparison..."

"Is of no importance!" declared the perverse Adonis. "The interest, for me lies not in the cause, but in the effect. The cause, however....X-rays, isn't it?"

"Yes," Bouvancourt admitted, carried away by his favorite hobby-horse. "Oh, nothing's simpler, in principle. The problem was this: to endow sold bodies—opaque or transparent—with the qualities of penetration that dark light enjoys. To put it another way, to treat these solids in such a way that they could traverse other, untreated solids, and, in consequence, could be traversed by them—which amounts to the same thing.

"To do that, it was necessary to succeed in impregnating them, if I might put it thus, with dark light, in order that they would be profoundly modified, at the level of their most arcane molecules, thus acquiring the property of the invasive fluid—which is to say, the property of traversing masses without disturbing them...without disturbing them, for example in the fashion of a swimmer moving through water or as we move through the atmosphere, but passing though by a sort of *immediate osmosis*, like two regiments intersecting, man by man, without being subject to dilatation. That came back to varying the porosity of matter, which is never dense enough not to be imaginable as a troop of atoms.

"Well, the other day—Tuesday—I was charged with this...fluid...as a condenser is charged with electricity. To be strictly accurate, though, the...fluid...is not merely dark light, for it's necessary that the treated body should also penetrate substances that X-rays cannot pass through, or only pass through with difficulty. So…"

"Good, good," said Morand. "It's almost exactly as I supposed. In brief, if we change the terminology, you have the power to render a fully-dressed man ungraspable. By means of the same operation, a man might laugh at bullets and daggers; and, as he can pass through all closed doors—including bank doors and prison doors—it's mere child's play for him to plunge his arm into some unbreakable strong-box, as meekly as an X-ray beam!"

"Oh!" exclaimed Bouvancourt, finally realizing the object of the visit. "But…ah! But…that's….yes…except that…"

"Except that it doesn't last forever, no? That's what you were about to say? I know that. To assure myself of it, I bumped into you a little while ago, as a station porter."

"I've recognized you. In fact, though, what did it matter to you whether I was tangible or not?"

"This," replied the brigand. "That if you had not yet returned to your normal state this morning, I would have varied this dialogue, and if you had retained the gift of rarefaction forever, I would never have come back."

"Why?"

"Because it's essential to my plan that you aren't invulnerable, Master, in view of the fact that I need to keep you under my thumb and in my sight—otherwise you could decamp through the very doors whose keys I've put in my pocket, and laugh at this little implement here."

So saying, the redoubtable baccalaureate-holder pointed a revolver at the scientist—a melodramatic attitude too hackneyed to have the slightest effect on the reader, but always new—strangely enough—for the person thus threatened.

Bouvancourt reflected. His head was buzzing like a hive in which a swarm of ideas was whirling. For a few minutes, he had been wondering whether the ambiguous Morand might be a 30-year-old woman rather than a young man of 18. He expressed himself with such aplomb! He spoke with so much assurance and testified to the fact that he was well used to speaking. And then again, what grace and beauty! Simultaneously, though, Bouvancourt recalled the crimes committed by this male or female wild animal. The victims of the Morand gang rose up again in his horror, uttering cries of agony…

And all of that was drowned by the great confused perplexity in which the physicist's will recoiled before the evil act that he was on the point of committing. In that regard, a thousand conceptions were so impetuously entangled in the hive of his brain that he could no longer see clearly within himself.

The creature that held him in check raised his weapon again. The gesture was imprinted with professional ease and effeminate delicacy—Cartouche and Mademoiselle de Maupin rolled into one. After a brief pause, Morand continued: "I therefore know, Monsieur Bouvancourt, that the ungraspability only lasts for a short time. That's annoying, for it would otherwise by synonymous with impunity. No more possible arrests, escaping as simple as saying hello, and, finally, the blade of the guillotine…" Morand paused, and finished with a sardonic smile. "One would never be…culpable.[14] So much the worse! But tell me—how many days does the property of rarefaction last?"

"Sixteen hours and 12 minutes," replied Bouvancourt, trembling at the thought of the request he was anticipating.

"No more than that! But after all, it's more than I'll need today to carry out the raid on the Comptoir d'Escompte. By midnight the trick will have been played."

Bouvancourt shuddered. "But…but there's always a guard on watch in the vault, and…"

"Let's get started right away," instructed Morand.

Bouvancourt uttered an exclamation of revolt: "And what if I don't want to?"

---

[14] The literal significance of the French *coupable*, of which "culpable" is the nearest English equivalent, is "strikeable"— the pun does not translate.

"I can force you to do it. I could force you to do it any time I like. For the present, this will suffice…"

The revolver touched the venerable physicist's forehead. Bouvancourt closed his eyes…

When he opened them again, a different intention was reflected therein.

Morand, who was waiting for the change of heart, put his instrument of persuasion back in his pocket.

"All right!" said Bouvancourt, in a tone that was perhaps resigned, but more likely resolute. "Fifteen minutes—I need 15 minutes to accomplish your metamorphosis." He added, lightly: "Naturally, you want your *entire* body to become ungraspable."

"Of course—that goes without saying. From head to foot."

"From head to foot—very well. I asked you the question because it was my duty. When you go to a photographer, he has to ask you…"

"Full length. My dear Master, I want to be intangible in full length. You can't think otherwise—what good would it do me to have the ability to introduce myself into a strong-room if my heels, for example, had to remain outside and would hold me back? Come on, my associate!"

"Good, good…it's your business. Indeed. Come this way."

Bouvancourt headed toward a door—curtain. Before moving that mysterious threshold aside, he stopped and said: "Will you swear to me that you are Morand?"

The demand gave the murderer a sense of the ascendancy that his fashionable infamy exercised and how right he had been to reveal his identity. Pride warmed his temples. "And how!" was his vainglorious response.

"Come in, then," said Bouvancourt, decisively.

He introduced the other into a cul-de-sac closet. The walls and the ceiling, the linoleum covering the floor and the internal face of the door-curtain—in sum, all the surfaces of the room—were gleaming with silver paint. The window had been daubed with an analogous coating, as translucent as frosted glass. One might have believed that one was inside a silver cube. In the middle, something resembling a coiled spring was set up—which was not a spring, since it was rigid. The apparatus was about two meters high. Its extended spiral consisted of a metal tube wound around thirty times to form a cylindrical cage. Two flexible wires, silvered and twisted, emerged from either end of the tube; the one from the top met up with the one from the bottom and their two threads, twisted into one, terminated in a plug. The power-point was located in the wall next to the entrance.

And that was all there was in the silver chamber.

"There's the apparatus," said Bouvancourt.

He tapped the spiral, which rang like a bell; it was like a knell tolling in some other world.

Morand questioned the physicist about the silver tint, He did not like it. The white metal displayed a funeral pomp that affected him.

"You have to place yourself inside it," said the operator, tipping back the upper part of the coil. "You mustn't be surprised when it becomes luminous. I was there for a quarter of an hour."

Moran asked again for an explanation of the paint.

"It's a solution immune to the light that I've called *Y-light*," replied the scientist. "It's a protective layer."

"You mean that the objects that it's shielding are no longer traversable by objects saturated with Y-light?"

"No. I mean that the objects painted with the *antilux* gum—with that silvering—escape the action of Y-light, so that, the rays being reflected by the gum, they don't become rarefied. Those objects stay as they are, instead of acquiring the gift of absolute permeability. Thanks to the *antilux* that you see here, the effect of my radiation is confined to the interior of this closet, and the panes of that window aren't rendered traversable—which would be inconvenient, if you think about it. The cold, rain and wind would come in as if the panes weren't there!"

"Oh? Yes, that's true. But in that case, when you're ungraspable, you can feel the wind blowing through you?"

"Of course. Come on, quickly—let's get on with it…"

"And knife-thrusts, pistol bullets, dogs' teeth—one feels those too?"

"Inevitably; sensitivity….but let's make haste. My housekeeper wasn't there to let you in, and I'd prefer it if you left before she comes back."

"And the walls that one goes through?" Morand persisted, ignoring Bouvancourt's solicitations. "And the embankment in which one might have to hide? Oh! And what about the lack of air? You can't breathe inside an embankment, can you? So you have to get through it double quick. Hmm…"

"Eh? What's that?" said Bouvancourt. "Come on, is this for today or tomorrow?"

He was supporting the heavy spiral cage with rigid arms.

"Oh! But…it's just…" The trickster was obviously perplexed; Bouvancourt put the apparatus back and said to him brusquely: "After all, you're right not to hurry. Our contract seems to me to be imperfect. I understand that you'll kill me if I refuse to obey; I also presume that capturing you here, as in a mouse-trap, would doubtless lead to my execution by your…subordinates. But what will you give me in return for my services, for my submission? What will you give me from the Comptoir d'Escompte's 500,000 francs?"

"Hang on!" grumbled the thief. "Ten thousand—is that enough?"

Bouvancourt held out his hand.

"Trust rules, damn it!" Morand retorted. "We'll talk again. You have my word. To work!"

"It's just…"

"To work, I tell you." Morand took up a standing position within the spiral.

"Ah! I've just thought—give me back my keys," said the physicist.

"Why? What's the hurry? I'll give them to you in a little while."

"Oh no! In a little while, if you keep them, they'll be transformed and permeable, like you, and then I won't be able to get hold of them for 16 hours and 12 minutes...oh!" He interrupted himself to exclaim, in a curiously abrupt and excited fashion: "How stupid! I've forgotten the most important thing. You see, I've got to protect myself against the Y-light, otherwise..."

He opened a cupboard in which several silvered garments were hanging He chose one and parted to put it on. It was a large hooded cape that came down over his head, concealing him entirely, as if permanently. A penitent, a figure from some expiatory procession or auto-da-fe, replaced the professor. The hood was fitted with goggles, whose glass disks were silvered like the window-panes; Bouvancourt's eyes could see without being seen behind these skull-like orbits whose inanimate tint stared into space. Only the hands remained bare; gloves silvered them. The robe was too long; silvery folds piled up on the silver floor. This apparition of repentance and luxury stood as still as a statue, like an allegory of inestimable value and a representation of the *De profundis*.

While donning this costume, the physicist joked continuously about the forbidding appearance that he would present once costumed. His loquacity never let up, but acquired a muffled, subterranean and quasi-sepulchral tone beneath the fabric.

"Quickly," he said. "The keys!" His statuesque hand passed through a gap between two turns of the spiral.

"There they are," said Morand, who had gone slightly pale. "Whether you have them now or later is of no importance." He tried to laugh, and added: "On the contrary, it proves that you're not going to electrocute me—because then you'd have taken them back afterwards..."

"Exactly!" Bouvancourt said, approvingly. "I can see that we understand one another. Don't worry—I give you my word of honor that I'll rarefy you, nothing more."

He tucked up the penitential frock, the color of the absolute, and slid the keys into his old jacket. Morand shook the slender tower that imprisoned him, afraid that it might suddenly become riveted to the floor. The machine shifted and swayed, emitting the music of some celestial campanile...

"You mustn't touch anything during the irradiation," the penitent recommended. "The solenoid would freeze you grievously. Stand up straight, in the very center. Are you ready? A quarter of an hour!"

He picked up the flexible wire that was dangling and placed the plug in the power-point.

Immediately, one might have thought that the sunlight had been amplified; the spiral lit up with a dazzling glare that was to broad daylight what broad daylight is to moonlight. It became a magical light, continuously rising and swirling. A serpent of white fire ringed Morand with its splendid coils. That light gave a velvety appearance to the contours of the incandescent tubulature; its drill ran from the bottom to the top with a fiery rapidity. Thus, the machine appeared to be rotating in a frantic ascent.

Morand shut his eyes. He was resplendent. So young and so handsome, so wicked, so pale and so radiant, he was the living portrait of Lucifer, a split second before the fall.

There was no crackle of sparks. The miracle was accomplished with humble simplicity. The igneous snake wound around indefatigably in the quiet bosom of its motionless ascent. Cold made itself felt, radiating all around.

Morand, his eyelids partly open and blinking, was the first to speak. "It's certainly not warm in here! But I don't feel anything else...does it have to happen like this? Can't the rarefaction be done gradually?"

"No," replied the voice from beyond the Earth. "After a quarter of an hour, when the saturation point is reached, you'll enter that state abruptly. Impalpability has no degrees."

"But I don't understand..." objected the superirradiated individual, imparting all his juvenile innocence to his tone.

The penitent lifted his arm in a priestly pose: "It would be better if you remained silent."

The other obeyed.

Bouvancourt took out his watch; holding his two hands tightly together, he shielded it from the radiation. "Twelve minutes more...11...10..."

The refrigerating hearth continued to lower the temperature. The physicist knew that leaves of frost were beginning to coat the windows. The patient was shivering. Bouvancourt went to lean on the wall to the left, almost directly behind him; his teeth were chattering like castanets beneath the hood, and shivers were galvanizing him, making his joined hands shake. In a laborious tone, with trembling jaws, he declared that it was much warmer inside the serpentine spiral—which was a lie.

"Eight...Seven...Six..."

The silence, broken from afar by the sound of motor cars and trams, was insistently re-established. Then the persistent little concert of the familiar sounds of the house became deafening; a sewing-machine started up on the ground floor; the clinking of bottles emerged from the cellar's ventilation shaft; there were intermittent footsteps on the floor above...

An in the meantime, in the glowing polar closet, whose walls seemed to be melting, the marvel followed its course, and the serpent of light continued to perform its incantatory swirl around the charming criminal.

"Three...Two...One..."

Suddenly, without anything more being heard, the reprobate sank into the floor, a thousand times faster than Méphisto at the Opéra. In the time it takes to fall, he had disappeared. There was no hole or trapdoor, and yet there was no longer anyone in the middle of the spiral, which persevered in vain.

The penitent, sprawled in a corner, felt a tightness in his chest. All the murmurs of intimacy fell silent, save for the footsteps on the second floor, which came and went as before.

Bouvancourt dragged himself along the wall and cut off the current. The spiral was extinguished. One might have supposed that night had fallen. A clock chimed ten, however, and daylight whitened the frost-caked windows.

The scientist took off his macabre domino and reappeared in the solitude. Was it really him? Was it even a man? Given the mechanical movements, the chalk-white hands and the plaster mask, who would have maintained that it was? But he was streaming with cold sweat, so he *was* a man. He said "Justice is done!" and began to weep, so he *was* Bouvancourt.

He wept in the silver chamber, and then, not wanting to remain alone with his secret, he ran to my house.

When he had finished his story, my wife and I looked at one another without understanding, and we listened to him groaning, desperately: "I've killed someone! Me—I've killed! Voluntarily! I've killed a child---perhaps a woman—deliberately! I'm a murderer! Oh. Sambreuil, it's horrible, isn't it?"

"Er...it's just that...I don't quite understand what happened..."

Bouvancourt fixed me with a hard and almost mistrustful state. "I had a higher expectation of your knowledge and intelligence."

"Ahem!" I resumed. "I can certainly see that Morand fell through the floor—but why? Since you, a few days earlier...oh! I get it. You deceived him! The operation wasn't the one..."

"Shut up! I haven't deceived anyone. I've rarefied him, as agreed. Except that I've rarefied him in both senses of the term. You see, Sambreuil, for myself, on Tuesday, I was very careful not to treat myself entirely. During my irradiation, I wore boots coated with *antilux*. Thus, my feet remained as they had been since my birth—which is to say, incapable of passing through other solids, and of being traversed by them.

"Remember that, once saturated with Y-light, it was no longer possible for me to lean against a tree—I would have passed through it! If I had attempted to put my coat and hat on, both of them would have fallen through my anatomy exactly as they would through a body of smoke! Do you think that I would even have been able to grasp them with my fingers? Of course not! My rarefied hands were incapable of getting hold of anything whatsoever, of acting upon anything whatsoever. That's why I asked my housekeeper to open the door for me and wait for me to come back when I went out. I had no way to turn a doorknob or ring a bell! I was only good for walking or kicking…I had no more material leverage except pedestrian.

"You'll understand that I could only go out decently in such a state by night. And when I came back…if you only knew! Impossible to lie down, no matter how much I wanted to! For—it was frightful—my body would have gone through the bed, the floor and everything, until my benevolent feet finally retained it. But how, then, in that posture, could I have disengaged myself, without any leverage, without even being able to touch anything, however ineffectively! Oh, a strange night—spent standing up, in idleness, transparent to impacts, diaphanous to touch, and thus an authentic phantom! I was falling over with fatigue, but I couldn't sit down!

"According to my calculations—which were defective— the rarefaction should have lasted for ten hours. Imagine my anguish during the six supplementary hours that its possession inflicted on me. It was at that moment that you came to see me, Sambreuil. I couldn't shake your hand. I was unable to dress myself or to shave. Water went through me! But it is only fair to add that nothing had the power to make me dirty, since I was intangible, dust no longer accumulating anywhere but on my shoes. Oh, my shoes! Oh, my feet! What treasures they were, on that occasion! Because, damn it, ungraspable doesn't mean weightless! Gravity still acted on the mass of my physique, attracting it mercilessly…"

"In that case," I said, fearfully, "Morand…"

Bouvancourt drank his third glass of ratafia. "Morand…oh, Madame, when I think of it…Morand, at his request and by means of my treatment, had been prepared in his totality. Morand no longer had two very solid limbs at the base of his body, two objects of good firm flesh. In the matter of contact, he had nothing but dematerialized feet—things without leverage. His entire body became suddenly traversable, and capable of traversing, after the fashion of a body steeped in X-rays—or, rather, Y-light. So, as gravity…"

"So? So?"

"So he lost his footing, falling toward the center of the Earth, plunging directly into the heat of the dense gulf. First he went through the floor, then the sewing-machine, whose operator fainted at the sight of that indistinct prodigy, then, without even snuffing it out, the candle lit by a cooper who was washing the bottles in my cellar. After that, he went through the geological strata…without being able to catch hold of anything, as disarmed as his surroundings, an etherized man falling through a solid milieu, like an ordinary man falling through the atmosphere…"

"What became of him in the end?" asked my wife, urgently.

"If there's an interior fire, his account is settled!" Bouvancourt declared. "If not, I don't doubt that he's been asphyxiated as a result of his plunge, in the course of that burial by immersion…there's no air to breathe down there!"

"In that case," I put in, "will his cadaver be at the very center of the Earth?"

"I don't think so. I'm quite sure that it isn't there at the present moment. Wherever it is, it's only passing through. It's necessary to take account of the acquired momentum, you see. Morand fell toward the center of the Earth, almost in free fall, with a uniformly accelerating velocity; he will therefore have reached the same speed as an unlucky person falling to Earth from a height of 6371 kilometers. A momentum of that sort only dies down gradually, and the poor devil, passing the center of gravity, will have continued his trajectory in a straight line, beyond the center toward the antipodes. But then his acquired velocity would have been countered by the force of gravity, and his momentum wouldn't have been sufficient for him to reach the opposite surface of the globe. When he came within a few leagues of that surface, Morand, whose velocity was progressively slowing, undoubtedly began to fall back toward the center of the Earth, which he would have overshot again to return in the direction of Pontargis...that might last quite a long time![15] In order to get a better understanding, imagine that someone threw you into a diametric well, a chimney gong all the way through the planet...

"After hundreds of comings and goings, progressively reduced, Morand's cadaver would finally come to rest at the center of the Earth, if 16 hours and 12 minutes were sufficient for the affair to reach its conclusion. But 16 hours and 12 minutes won't be sufficient, and, having suddenly become tangible again—brutally immobilized during one of his frightful falls, then bogged down, penetrated, invaded, crushed cell by cell, transformed into a sudden amalgam of rock, clay and flesh—the wretch will remain eternally blended into the profound paste!"

My wife, who has an imagination, was not reluctant to give proof of it. "Wait a minute!" she cried. "Provided that there's a sea at the antipodes, Morand might drown!"

Bouvancourt sketched a mournful moue with the corner of his mouth. "Madame, he'll be dead before then, asphyxiated. Anyway, we're quibbling idly, given that the existence of the interior fire is proven. There is not a shadow of a doubt regarding Morand's incineration—for I can fabricate a human specter, but not a human salamander. I've conquered the resistance of solids, liquids and gases, but not their other de-

---

[15] This was not the first time this kind of oscillation had been envisaged, although it is unlikely that Renard had read Clément Fézandie's "Through the Earth" when it was serialized in the American periodical *St. Nicholas Magazine* in 1898. Fézandie's story features a temporary hole penetrating the Earth from periphery to periphery rather than an alternative state of matter.

fenses—not their asphyxiating envelopment. I've vanquished the water that moistens, not the water that drowns, nor the fire that burns! It's a frightful death!"

"It's an execution!" I rectified. "Thank God! Thank Bouvancourt, for having broken up the Morand gang!"

"My invention will do no other service than that. In the final analysis, you see, it would do more harm than good. The wretched thing shall disappear! I'll burn my notes and calculations this evening, and I'll destroy the spiral. Nothing must remain…Morand won't talk…and I ask you, my dear friends, on your honor, not to tell this story until ten years have gone by."

We had to do leave it at that. I agreed, reluctantly, to the ten year delay, without understanding why the invention would then be impossible to recover. If my reader happens to be a Berthelot—or, if female, a Curie—perhaps he will perceive what I cannot. But perhaps he will also criticize me sternly for having made a promise that deprived science of a considerable enrichment. I made it because there are certain critical moments at which one cannot refuse certain supplicants. The overexcitement of the placid and wise Bouvancourt frightened me. He did not omit to tell us about the mortal terror to which he had been subject during his dialogue with the handsome and softly-spoken villain, the alternatives of justice and pity that animated him, the tortures he endured between his duty and his emotions, his disgust at the indispensable tragicomedy, or how he feared at every moment that the demi-scientist with a smattering of physics might happen upon the truth.

"His reasoning was so naïve!" Bouvancourt remarked. "And so dangerous! Mistaken and immoral! Fifty times over I thought all was lost! Fortunately, he was fascinated by the final cause, hypnotized by his goal. What a crime! To put one's hand into a strong-box, through the door, and empty it! But how would he have been able to grip the gold and silver? And even if he had been able to grab those piles of louis and écus, how would they have been able to pass through the wall of the safe, being no more rarefied than the wall? Never! Never! As for the feet, that really was the ABC of deduction...oh, Sambreuil, the shame!—the shame of abusing that poor fool! And the torture of lying to the child that I had caught in the trap of my falsity! Oh, no, I wasn't born to be an executioner!"

I put my hand on his shoulder, looked him in the eyes and aid, gravely: "Don't you think you're reasoning falsely in your turn? You've purged the Earth of a monster; you stand alongside Hercules, Theseus and the One who precipitated Lucifer into the eternal flames, as you have done with the new Satan. Bouvancourt, it seems to me that you ought to feel a great divine satisfaction..."

"Yes," sighed the physicist, "I'm *racked* by satisfaction..."

And as I insisted on the fabulous character of the event, he demonstrated to me that it was an illusion.

"To imagine," he said, "that we might plunge into the Earth is as natural as thinking: *perhaps creatures exist that are incapable of passing through the air and traveling through gases*. The proposition isn't antiscientific—far from it. Solids have always been seen resting atop one another, and for centuries humanity has been resting on the surface of the world. Does it follow that I can deny the possibility of the contrary? Not at all! Until a man had thrown a cork into a river, all corks might have believed that water was as impermeable to them as the earth is to humans. Now, what that man did to the cork, I have done to Morand."

Having murmured that name, Bouvancourt lost the thread of what he was saying. He abandoned himself to the pursuit of a preoccupation from which I refrained from distracting him, for he gradually recovered the expression of wisdom, strength and forbearance that I should like to see in the features of the All-Powerful, if ever we should come face to face.

# THE FOG OF OCTOBER 26

*To J.-H. Rosny Aîné*[16]

> At this dark shadow I gazed wonderingly for many minutes.
> Its character stupefied me with astonishment.
> I looked upward. The tree was a palm.
> EDGAR ALLAN POE
> *A Tale of the Ragged Mountains*

The late director of the Museum, the botanist Chantelaine, has left some curious memoirs. If they are still unpublished, it is because too many revealing portraits are to be found there of contemporary figures; it is necessary to wait for those individuals to belong to History before publication is appropriate—that is what custom demands. We have extracted from the manuscript these exceptional descriptive pages, in which the author does not deal with men of the present day.

---

[16] J.-H. Rosny Aîné was the pseudonym employed in 1913 by Joseph-Henri Boëx, who had signed his earliest works "J.-H. Rosny" but had then allowed his younger brother, Séraphin-Justin, to share that pseudonym, with the result that they eventually began to distinguish themselves as "Aîné" and "Jeune." The elder Rosny, the foremost writer of scientific romance in France, had a particular interest in prehistory; in addition to prehistoric romances, he wrote several romances of exploration in which exotic survivals from the remote past are discovered, including an account of "La Contrée prodigieuse des cavernes" [The Amazing Cave Country] (1896), which proves to be inhabited by intelligent giant bats. The works of Rosny Aîné are available in translation from Black Coat Press.

"Put your coat on," Fleury-Moor said to me. "It's getting cold now, and I want to show you my state-of-the-art mushroom-farms."

"Is it far?"

"No, indeed. A few steps. It's up there." The geologist pointed to the top of the hill. "Do you see that hump, Chanteraine? It ought to be famous. More than a fraction of Notre-Dame-de-Reims came out of it. The whole ridge is perforated by subterranean tunnels, which are abandoned quarries. I use them to grow my cryptogams; they open on the far side of the hill. You can bring your rifle—the hunting rights belong to me. Come on!"

"It's already getting late—past 3 p.m."

"We'll be back well before nightfall. Let's get on with it!"

I brought my 12-caliber and my game bag. To be frank, the excursion was not at all unwelcome—save for its mycological aim—to an old landscape-lover and indefatigable sunset-watcher like me.

The date was October 26, 1907.

The path sloped gently upwards through the stripped vines and asparagus-fields that were running wild following the harvest. Peasants were pruning the high foliage and piling it up for burning. The gleam of fires was visible in every direction, and smoke ascending into the calm air. We went up unhurriedly toward a copper and rust-colored wood. I frequently looked back over my shoulder at the gorge and the plain that it revealed. There was a bend in the path at the edge of the wood, and along its border, set out before us, the rounded valley: a spacious semicircle, becoming funnel-shaped on the far side, which already offered an image of the foggy month that was about to begin. In spite of the cold and harsh weather, the dull sky and the mist whose precocious veil blurred the marshy depths, its mantle of yellow foliage dressed it with a kind of sunshine. No breeze stirred the branches. From time to time, a tree would shed its leaves in the forest with the dismal sound of a light shower. It was the sound of the invincible gathering, the precursor of winter. One could sense the countryside becoming torpid from moment to moment as the autumn ripened.

We called a halt before going into a sandy cutting, beneath a vault of thinned-out acacias. It was then that I mentioned the fog for the first time, observing that a malarial miasma was now misting all the low-lying ground like a mold whose grey plush was visibly thickening. A flat cloud laid siege to Cormonville, invisible spinners were weaving arachnid threads from one end of the gorge to the other, stagnant and ever-more-opaque, while long stationary vaporous steaks were multiplying on the indefinite plain without any visible cause. We would not be starting back until they had covered the whole area with down, all the way to the horizon where darkness would soon be falling.

"Let's hurry," said Fleury-Moor. "It's so easy to catch cold!"

I followed him into the narrow path.

Shortly thereafter, it seemed to me that the surroundings became blurred. I passed my hand over my eyes, thinking that they were becoming confused, but the grayness persisted. It was the mist; it had enveloped us in its muslin.

"Aren't you afraid of being caught in the fog?" I asked.

We were now moving between walls of fawn-colored sand stratified with floury earth. My colleague had taken a fistful of that earth and presented it to me, having crumbled it, I could see nothing there but an infinity of calcareous particles, the minuscule debris of shells, including those of ammonites and gastropods, some of which had survived intact thanks to their microscopic size.

"There! That's what I was telling you, this morning!"

I remembered perfectly well what he had told me that morning, and I immediately recalled the moment when the 35 horse-power machine in which we were traveling had emerged from the Ardenne forest. It was as if the Sun had suddenly risen for a second time. The Champagne plain had extended before us as far as the eye could see, white, chalky, broadly undulated by harmonious waves that seemed to be in motion, almost marine by virtue of being immense and seemingly meandering. The widely-scattered villages were reminiscent of rocky islets. The clumps of fir-trees, occasionally shaped into rectangles as if by a set-square, imitated strange geometric coral reefs. There was a highway in the distance so straight that one might have taken it for a jetty.

"We're going at 75 kph," said Fleury-Moor.

I would have preferred it had he said "We're traveling at 40 knots," so strongly was I experiencing the lovely nostalgia for the sea that is contained within the human heart, and so urgently was the territory reminding me of seaside regrets and naval illusions.

"Of course!" cried Fleury-Moor, when I confessed that. "Champagne resembles an ocean as a daughter resembles her father. The configuration of the region reveals its Neptunian origin, and the fact that the prehistoric sea once modeled it in its own image, with the broad strokes of waves and surges. Look, way down there are the hills that emerged first, in the Eocene epoch, when the waves were retreating from century to century—that's where the hills of the Vesle and the Aisne finish, and it's also where we're heading. Well, you see nothing there but the hillocks of sediments and alluvia, sandbanks and calcareous deposits that were once submarine, which are overflowing with shells.

That was what I remembered. "That's all very well, my dear chap," I replied. "But what about the fog? Aren't you afraid of getting lost in it, if it thickens?"

"There's no danger! I know these crannies by heart, you see. I could go to my beds with my eyes closed. Besides, fogs are never dense hereabouts. If you want, though, we can soon get ahead of it if we hurry."

Soon, in fact, as we came out of the corridor, the path sloped abruptly upwards, and the atmosphere became free of any confusion. I took advantage of that to glance around, and I observed—not without astonishment, given Fleury-Moor's assurance—that the whole of Cormonville was now invisible. The valley was full to half its depth with nebulous spirals; they extended into the remotest distance and submerged the vast intensity.

"Hey! Do you maintain that that fog isn't dense?"

"No, it isn't. If we were within it, you'd share my opinion. But we're looking at it from above, so it seems very thick."

A rabbit broke cover. I killed it. The shot rang out without echoing.

We were reaching the summit: a grassland strewn with outcrops of stone and scattered juniper bushes. The place seemed so desolate to me that I experienced a certain shame at passing through it without being in mourning or suicidal. The solitude, the silence and the immobility aggravated one another. The contours were already blurring with the effect of the rising mist. The location, vague with mystery and melancholy, was like the memory of a landscape; I took pleasure in imagining that we were haunting a pastel drawing that was in the process of being erased.

Fleury was still moving on. Our boots were trampling sharp-bladed grass. We were crossing the ridge.

"Damn!" exclaimed my guide. "It's absurd, all the same!"

From there, one would have thought that Champagne was no more than a vast snow-covered steppe: a Siberian surface, shining beneath a laborious sun, utterly flat. What was quite poignant was the abandonment that phenomenon seemed to have visited upon us. I had the impression that a universal fleecy deluge had only spared the two of us, upon that hill— and the spell would have been prolonged had it not been for the voices of woodcutters and the whistling of birds that resonated fantastically beneath the impenetrable layer.

Fleury informed me that the valleys usually formed delightfully-wooded half-moons at intervals. Even so, exceedingly boggy marshes soaked their floors, the last vestiges of the Paludean era that had followed the Lacustrian period, which had been substituted for the Marine epoch. Pointing at the concavity of the scallop that had just appeared in front of us, he said: "My mushroom-farms are down there."

He took a path whose track followed the curve of the crest at a lower level. A stand of fir-trees extended to our left, on a bank that rose up vertically. To the right, the downward slope—covered in brambles, sweet-briars and clematis, whose withered flowers were like a host of dead spiders—extended into the mist.

The setting Sun, which shone through momentarily, was now no more than a pale disk with vaporous make-up, so lunar that it would have fooled Pierrot.[17] The distant plains gradually vanished. Slanting ridges of stone, like monstrous strands of gossamer, meandered around the bushes—and the bulk of the mist furtively extended its assault on the slope.

I scarcely had time to notice five or six of the openings of quarries that cut dark holes directly into the slope at intervals. Suddenly, the sun was extinguished, like a Japanese lampshade when its candle goes out. A pallid night surrounded us. We passed clumps of hazel-trees, diffuse masses that appeared and disappeared again. The livid darkness was icy, and as a frost formed, the light diminished further.

Contrary to my advice, my mushroom-farmer pressed on doggedly toward his mushroom-farms. He advanced unhurriedly. I saw him less and less clearly, like a scarcely-perceptible shadow—as if his shadow had separated from him and started walking on its own. To find his way, he entrusted himself to the guidance of the path. We could no longer see anything other than that trace—or, to put it better, anything other than a circle of ground of which we were the center.

---

[17] Renard's wordplay refers to *Pierrot Lunaire: Rondels Bergamesques* (1884) by Albert Giraud; he probably wrote the story before the 1912 première of Arnold Schoenberg's musical accompaniment to a selection of the poems in the cycle, which is nowadays better known.

I marched through the fog as a creature with an aureole might march through the darkness, only being able to see by virtue of his nimbus—but, by God, it was uncomfortable! A dusty and moldy odor insinuated itself into the depths of my torso; my teeth were chattering; my eyelids and beard were soaked; innumerable droplets were forming on my clothes. I seemed to have become a human sponge soaked with melted snow: a human sorbet. And it was no good telling myself that all of that was, after all, no more than the customary illusions of fog; a disagreeable sensation reminded me that I, too, had once been a child who cried in the dark.

From then on, I wondered whether what was happening was really a sequence of imagined events, let out by my sub-conscious mind—but I don't know what might be worthy of dread, if not the intensity of an unhealthy ambiance, arctic and treacherous, in which the worst thing of all would be to get lost and fall ill at the same time.

Nevertheless, the mist closed in, indefatigably. It was an atmospheric malady. It had upholstered the void. It muffled the sound of our footsteps. It was so heavy that one might have suffocated in it, and so damp that in my place, a fish might not have choked any more. The air had become posi-tively aquatic.

I tried to translate my anxiety into humor. "Shall we have to swim, my dear chap, as in the time immemorial when the ocean weighed upon these hills?"

I had spoken as if through a gag. Fleury-Moor did not hear, or pretended not to have heard—but the padded footfalls of taciturn phantom in front of me slowed down. Until then, I had been able to keep track of the flattened ground, the color of ash, on which my boots, shiny with dew, were treading— but I could no longer see it.

Fleury-Moor stopped. I looked down at my feet; they had disappeared. Within the surrounding fog, a second fog was rapidly rising. It was up to our knees. Its icy temperature was eating into the flesh of our calves.

Fleury-Moor leaned toward me. "I'd prefer to wait for this to pass," he said, in the most natural tone in the world. "I believe we might go astray. It won't last long. Very interesting, you know—extremely rare!"

His tranquil words reached me as if through a broken megaphone. They were swirling like puffs of pipe smoke, of which the fog immediately took possession.

"I'm wondering what will happen to us," I said, effortfully. "My legs are suffering terribly...and it's rising..."

"What do you expect to happen to us?" jeered the murky specter.

I grabbed Fleury-Moor's arm, which offered no resistance, and we watched as we were enshrouded. We became shadow-torsos, then shadow-heads, and then nothing, before our own eyes. And while we were watching our bodies get bogged down in the invisible, those bodies were subjected to the abominable ordeal of being gradually plunged into an oppressive and icy fluid, more frightful than death. I could no longer see my fingers touching my eyelashes. Blinded by an atmospheric phenomenon, I was able to say that my every nerve was on edge.

Ah! A sudden certainty! The certainly that I might tremble in good conscience! My intuitions of a short while before had not been mistaken. *Something strange had occurred.* Professorial knowledge and animal instinct were agreed on that within me; both were now hoping for a marvel and dreading a cataclysm.

The geologist put his mouth close to my ear. He raised his voice placidly, in the manner of people who are speaking to one another through an obstacle. "What surprises me, you see, is that a fog as humid as this doesn't resolve itself into rain—what am I saying? Into snow! Into hailstones! And what's even more astonishing is that even with this dire cold, the water that's soaking us isn't freezing!"

I sucked my disgusting moustache then, and observed that the water of the fog, which was so very cold, was *salty*.

"Oh, Fleury, how horrid! One might think they were the tears of a cadaver!"

"Why yes! You're right. It's like sea-water." And he added: "That's why the fog can't condense."

"Tell me, then—have you ever heard mention of such an adventure? You and I might, perhaps, be the first to experience it. Don't move away, whatever you do!"

"No, I won't budge. We'll make a report. Definition: an absolute but whitish darkness, a dull whiteness...oh! Hang on—it seems to me that it's getting brighter..."

"Yes, it's beginning to brighten up..."

Our surroundings became luminous. The impalpable padding that sealed us in lightened with a suggestion of dawn. A feeble glow spread through it, hesitantly—but transparency did not come back in a hurry.

First, I saw Fleury-Moor's silhouette reappear, which gradually materialized in its entirety instead of reappearing bit by bit, as it had vanished. My excellent colleague was astonished. "Oh! What the Devil! Where...what...come on, come on...I'm quite certain that we stopped on the path..."

"So what?" I asked.

"So what's that red sand doing at my feet?"

"We've strayed..."

"Strayed where? Where? Red sand, here! Since when?"

"Perhaps it's the result of the salty fog...a combination of its chemistry with that of the soil. See how the appearance of the soil is still uncertain, floating..."

Fleury bent down and inspected the red sand.

"The wind's getting up now," I remarked.

He stood up, urgently. "What's that you said?"

"I said: the wind's getting up now. Can't you hear it in the fir-trees?"

"And can't you see that the fog is motionless, and that, in consequence, there isn't any wind? That there can't be any?"

"Just listen. There must be! Listen!"

"But that noise...that wind sound...it's to the right!"

"So?"

"So there aren't any fir-trees to the right."

"There aren't…but since we can hear the sound of the wind in the trees…"

"It's not the sound of the wind."

"What is it? What is it?"

"Don't lose your nerve. We'll soon find out. This accursed fog is dissipating."

The luminosity increased with a sort of weary fluctuation. At the same time, the cold relented. The circle of visibility increased. Vague things appeared there: pebbles, tufts of grass. The geologist, having considered these grasses, exclaimed: "Come and see!"

But then a strident clamor rang out in the impenetrable depths—a raucous and ferocious trumpet-call, reminiscent of menageries, circuses and zoological gardens…

We watched one another grow pale, with dilated eyes in which an impossible conjecture was legible.

In a low voice, with a wild expression, Fleury insisted nevertheless: "You're a botanist—look at these grasses!"

I did so. That was why I beat their air with my arms, to extricate myself from the element that was making us sticky. Possessed by the instinct of self-preservation, that rarely-salutary dementia, I was no longer anything but a creature of panic and flight. I hurled myself forward.

Fleury held me back. "Calm down! And stay here, for God's sake! I don't know exactly where we are…the ravine must be nearby, close at hand. You'll fall into it…" He paused, then offered imperious advice: "Then again, remember what you are, damn it! Think about your status. We ought to be thankful for what's happened to us. No one is better qualified for such meteorological phenomena! And tell yourself that all of it will finish up as a memoir for one of the sections of the Institute!"

That speech restored my self-possession. "Agreed," I said, ashamedly. "But you must admit that it's rather disconcerting to encounter *tropical grasses* in the middle of Champagne, and to hear…"

81

"Listen!" he said, extending his arm in the probably direction of the ravine. "That's what you call the wind!"

"It's getting louder…it isn't the wind."

"I told you it wasn't."

"The sound of a river…or a torrent…a huge river…"

"Look out! There's something new, Chanteraine!"

The tremulous daylight was still increasing, sketching out shapes in the surroundings—one of which, not far away, assumed the form of a moving column that was about to climb the slope. Behind it, others were beginning to display their slenderness. I make no claim, however, that the fog was disaggregating in the slightest degree. In truth, it was not. Let that be understood. Things were not emerging around us as if they were slowly released by the mist, but they seemed to be sketched out in grey, as if sculpted in the same fickle substance. They seemed to be constituted by the fog. More than that: even the sound of something flowing seemed to be nothing but a sonorous property of the fog, and the warmth that was now overtaking us seemed to be emerging from it, along with a resinous odor.

"Ah! Chanteraine! The tree! There!"

"Mercy!"

The top of the column emerged from the unknown. It was a bouquet of leaves. A palm tree was looming up before us! We could discern it in the false daylight and the gleaming haze that continually deformed it, making it undulate like a reptile. Further away, an entire groves of palms became manifest, stirred by the same waves, dancing like the reflection of a river-bank.

Everything that we could see was moving in a serpentine fashion in the iridescence. Furthermore, the vision was continually passing through alternate phases of light and darkness. And it did not take me long to realize that sight was not the only one of our senses to be affected in that way. The balsamic perfume was reinforced in one wave after another; the sound of the water involved a progression of loud phases followed by soft ones, and the heat increased in gusts, following a fantastic rhythm that could be described as general, for all these assertive and weakening phases coincided perfectly, whether they were olfactory, auditory or visual.

They were attenuated, however, as the environment gained in lucidity. It became more precise within the fog, like a projection on a screen when one brings it into focus, as its brightness flickers. Photography provides the best comparison: that of an image "coming out" on the sensitive plate in a revelatory bath that is agitated. From one moment to the next, that phantasmagoric location became more fixed, more positive, more profound.

The circle—or, rather, the cylinder—seemed to have a radius of about 20 meters when Fleury-Moor concluded: "It's a mirage, like those in the desert—except that it's a peculiar mirage that *surrounds us*, and instead of giving us the illusion of perceiving some unreal lake or oasis in the distance, gives us the illusion of *being* somewhere, in Africa or elsewhere."

"Yes," I added, "what's peculiar about it is, indeed, that it surrounds us—but also that it's produced at a considerable distance from the place reflected, and, above all, that it affects the senses of hearing and smell as well as that of sight!"

"Right. It's a mirage that we can see, hear and breathe, which is very far away from us. It's an optical, acoustic and osmological sympathy in space—at least in one sense—between the place where we really are and the place that is being projected on the fog around us. I know that red sand very well...let's see: it's Egypt, isn't it? No?"

"No," I repeated, astonished to the point of excitement. "Further south. I think...I think those are equatorial plants...but...there are cochineal figs...a baobab...and yet..."

"What?"

"My God, Fleury! That...that fan-palm, like a peacock's tail, over there, appearing in the fog...do you recognize it?"

"Oh! It's not possible. A dicot...a dicotyledon from the Cape...or Madagascar..."

"Yes: *Flabellaria lamanonis*. From the Cape, Madagascar, or the *Tertiary epoch!*"

"The Tertiary epoch? What are you saying?"

"Open your eyes! Look at those arborescent ferns near the aloes…"

"They're osmunds. Flowering ferns…from Ceylon…"

"No they're not! That species is *extinct!*"

"Are you sure? Ah! Yes. Look, look! That palm-tree! A parasol-palm. And what's that? Laurier-roses, with camphor-trees…myrtles…a birch!"

"Vine-stocks! An oak! Walnut trees!"

"Angiosperms! We're in the middle of the Neozoic Period!"

As soon as he had spoken, the murmur of the river became so loud that we turned round. On that side, there was nothing to be seen but the fog, and the red sand sloped gently down to disappear into it. Behind the misty curtain, the rumbling eased off. A foamy wave had just sprung forth and died back gracefully, like fizzing lace. A second wave succeeded it with the roar of a cataract. The sand became moist; the moss crackled; spray flew up.

"The sea!" I stammered. "The sea that existed here millions of years ago!"

Two black rocks sketched out their shapes on the edge of the surf.

"So it's not only a mirage in space!" declared Fleury-Moor, transported by enthusiasm. "It's also a mirage in time!"

"It's *only* a mirage in time," I retorted. "The space where we think we are really is the space where we are. We're subject to the illusion of having moved in duration; we haven't moved in extent. Look again."

The illustration of the fog was further enhanced. Rather low now, it still weighed on things like a nebulous ceiling, but in the other dimensions the landscape was marvelously clear-cut. We could see it well enough to recognize the approximate conformation of the hill of Cormonville, with its overhanging ridge here, and its ravine there, its curvature espoused by the antediluvian beach. There was no more doubt about it: some anachronistic freak of nature was permitting us to contemplate the Marne in its prehistoric aspect. Those oaks and those maples were the first European oaks and the first French maples, and that vine—O poignant charm!—was the first vine in Champagne!

It was, I think, at that moment that a horrible screech rent the cloud above our heads. We raised our eyes, without catching a glimpse of anything but the escape of a majestic flying shadow. I could not understand why the screech had upset me to the point of knowing, as I heard it, that I would never forget it.

Fleury-Moor's expression was distraught. We were trembling. It was in vain that we heard again, in the depths of the fog, the trumpet-call that had troubled us before. We could not be any paler. The horror of the cry put all others in the shade. The already familiar trumpet-call, however, was repeated several times in quick succession, from different points in the vastness, and Fleury-Moor, cocking an ear, interrogated me with his gaze. "Proboscidean, isn't it?" he said.

"Assuredly. *Elephas meridionalis* or *primogenius*."

"Damn! Is the mirage also susceptible to touch?"

He crouched down and touched a few sprigs of esparto-grass." "Hmm!" he muttered.

"What?"

"Feel it for yourself."

The result of my experiment was that I slid two cartridges into my rifle—at which sight Fleury-Moor said: "It's crazy! Are we dreaming? There's something insane about what you just did! We're dreaming; this fog is narcotic—or it's pestilential, and this is the product of delirium."

"People don't dream in pairs, and men like you and me aren't hallucinated in the same fashion simultaneously. No, no, Fleury; since no conjurer is capable of playing such a fakir's trick on us, this really is a mirage of a new order, *a mirage integral in time*. We can see, we can hear, we can smell, we can taste and we can touch a scene from the past, as one sometimes admires in the desert, with one's eyes alone, a scene that is taking place out of range."

The heat of a Turkish bath overwhelmed us. Our damp clothes exhaled abundant vapors. I took off my coat.

There was the sea, too, and the sky: a silver-plate sea beneath an indigo sky. The Sun, huge and pink, was climbing in a halo of mist. It was, therefore, *morning*, and yet...

I consulted my miniature pocket-compass. "Look at the sun, Fleury, how strangely placed it is..."

My companion could not help smiling. "You're forgetting," he said, "that since its birth, the Earth has not ceased to revolve relative to the ecliptic."

"That's true."

Fleury-Moor took out his watch and continued: "*Actually*, it's 4:20 p.m. Let's make a note of that. *Artificially*, however—which is to say, according to the Sun in the mirage—it's about 10 a.m. And...it's spring."

I confessed that so many anomalies robbed me of the greater part of my means, and I complimented the geologist on his resilience. He told me that he was only annoyed that he had not brought a notebook, or a pencil, or his fine binoculars.

We chatted, but without distracting one another from the immense magical apparition in which the infancy of the Earth was displayed. The fog-free zone grew around us. The first things to appear were now concise, material and immutable. However, the more distant view was still subject to a vibratory palpitation analogous to that presented during heat-waves. That caused us to think about animate presences. I expected that there would be movement in the distance, and I sought to assure myself that, if the occasion arose, the rocks at the edge of the sea would be able to provide us with a refuge. While doing that, I perceived a large dorsal fin garnished with spines out to sea. It had just emerged, and it plunged beneath the surface again.

The tyrannical sound of the sea swallowed us up. Its odor, combined with the resinous perfume, fortified our blood. We soon realized where the reek of gum and turpentine was coming from. The mixed grove of palms and occidental trees extended along the red beach on the same level, but further

86

inland the embankment still existed—pardon me, *already* existed—steeper and a little further away, and planted with pines. Its wall of marl clay, in which the entrance to a cavern yawned, was visible through a gap in the palm-grove.

As one might well imagine, the vegetation intrigued me more than anything else. Its dimensions were extravagant. Some plants, which were not fully-developed, bore voluminous and robust corollas, bright violet in color, with golden yellow pistils. Other unknown trees of the magnolia family displayed admirable bicolored leaves, more beautiful than flowers. At the bottom of the trunks, there was an exuberant and ferocious mêlée from some fantastic hothouse, an inextricable tangle in which aloes extended and curled their thorny tentacles like octopodes; where swollen opuntia cacti brandished hairy tufts and spiny manes; where stout pale-furred caterpillars, placed end-to-end, fattened themselves on ridiculous or redoubtable plants.

It was nothing but a lethargic riot of green and twisted limbs, a heap of lissome nudities and brunette fleeces beneath tree- ferns curling back their enormous hairy crosiers. The excess of life and the prohibition of life burst forth in the prosperity of pods, the rubicund turgidity of mucilage, the claws and horns of all those paralytic monsters, toothed and barbed into the resemblance of Jurassic dragons, some of which formed tips like Carib knives. It swarmed without moving, a stupendous winter garden in which mimosas, euphorbias and myrtles rubbed shoulders with vanished species—Dryophyllum, Doliostrobus, Callistris and Lepidodendron—and alders, aspens, oaks and chestnuts!

Pyramids projected from the half-light of the underwood, vague and bathed in blue, half-fern and half-larch, trees and plants at the same time. Baroque candelabras, singularly *art nouveau* in spite of being natural and prehistoric, deployed their espalier branches in the same vertical plane. Each one of them, speckled with buds, rose up like hat-stands, supporting monstrous, wrinkled, over-ripe pears which hung down heavily and gargantuan.

Sweat ran down our cheeks. The air became troubled; a hint of black was mingled with the indigo heavens. I made the observation that the atmosphere would not become any clearer, and was really that of a torrid and moist era. The moon, at the end of its course, traced a thin spectral crescent. In spite of the diurnal and radiant hour, a large round star tinted the zenith. We could see both of them at the same time. Oh, we had no need to exchange our impressions. A compassion of a great and inexpressible sort stirred in our hearts, and I thought that we were about to weep at the sight of that star: *that second satellite of our planet, irredeemably lost; the ancient tiny moon of our beloved Earth!*

We could not tear our eyes away from the zenith.

When we finally lowered them, the prodigy was complete. The last wisps of fog were melting in the distance like an exhalation of breath. The sea, rippled by wavelets, extended eastwards, and a rounded hillock emerged from the water as we had seen it emerge from the mist in a previous glimpse. It formed an inlet flanked by two lateral near-islands. We were on one of these promontories; the other extended in front of us. It was a reddish tongue of land, enlivened by a few lentisks and sequoias, which grew more densely the closer they approached the continent, with the result that the depths of the little gulf were already lined with the verdure that extended all the way to our position and then became sparser as it extended toward the tip of our own cape. In the middle of the horseshoe, the crest of the hill showed above the woods, bare, bad and red against the violet azure of the sky.

And it was from there that four elephants emerged, one by one, so colossal that in order to estimate the distance separating us from them—more than eight hundred meters as the crow flies—I had to recall the true proportions of the locality. At any rate, with common accord, we sought the shelter of the rocks before even being aware that we were moving.

"We must observe!" said the geologist.

"Then let's observe."

The titanic animals go past in Indian file, sharply silhouetted side-on. They stand out sharply. Their tusks are hard to make out. Fleury-Moor, who is short-sighted, claims that each individual has four of them. I hold out for two, curved. He maintains that they're furry; I maintain that they aren't. In brief, unable to decide between *Elephas meridionalis, antiquus* and *primogenius*, we can't arrive at a conclusion as to which period of the Neozoic era the mirage has transported us. It's not the Eocene, much less the Pliocene; the sea and the vegetation indicate that—but is it the Oligocene or the Miocene?

By chance, another incident resolves the difference of opinion.

The mammoth in the lead pauses momentarily. It opens its prodigious ears very wide, as if its skull were about to fly away, releases a loud clarion call, and gallops away over the ridge. Its comrades execute the same "left turn!" They make off. The earth trembles dully. And from the north, here comes some kind of black mountain advancing through the wood, surpassing the height of the tallest conifers. And behold!—it's a mastodon tapir, a pachyderm with a short trunk and low-set tusks, coming through the grandiose forest as a modern tapir might stride through a meadow.

"A dinotherium!" I whispered.

"Yes, a *Miocene* dinotherium!"

Fleury-Moor had pronounced *Miocene* with an indefinable emphasis. I looked at him; I knew that he was experiencing a boundless pride and thus being able, in the blink of an eye, to determine among the myriads of centuries a particular point in eternity.

Personally, I found the dinotherium amazing. A kind of terrestrial whale, it was not at the head of an entourage. It seemed out of place, built for a much more spacious Creation, or even for the colossal ocean. One divined that it was not at home on land, but that it had nowhere else to go.

We had the good fortune to be able to examine it at leisure. It raised its stump of a trunk toward the mammoths' retreat, hesitated, turned round, and headed for the extremity of the promontory that bounded the north like a devastation. There, it stretched itself out laboriously and started scraping the ground.

That had been going on for a few seconds when we noticed a flock of large birds—or, at least, large flying animals—over the sea. They were approaching the coast, brushing the surface of the water and sometimes even settling on it, with wings aloft, to catch fish in the manner of petrels. We counted them; there were 12, flying with remarkable elegance. Suddenly, all uttering in unison the supernatural screech that had the gift of terrifying us so completely, they fell like fletched javelins upon the dinotherium.

The latter straightened up. The great birds surrounded it with a discordant whirlwind. The screaming horde spiraled around it, persistent and malevolent. Then, one after another, its assailants settled on its mountainous back, where their company formed a sort of wriggling hydra. The animal shook itself. A quadruped palace, Notre-Dame-de-Fouvières turned upside-down, it turned tail and fled in a deafening tempest. It bellowed. Its protest resembled the vehemence of a steamboat, and its tormentors, which had taken to the air again, covered its retreat with howls. We followed it with our eyes for a long time.

Fleury-Moor shielded his eyes against the dazzling sunlight, and said: "I'd give five years of my life for a set of opera-glasses. Impossible to see! Oh, if I'd known. Think of all that I could have brought with me, Chanteraine! And all I have is my watch! What were those flying creatures? Oh, to know! What vile creatures! How horribly they sing!"

"My God yes! But I don't know…pterodactyls?"

"No…and yet…oh, no, no…the winged lizard no longer existed in this epoch; I'd bet my head on that." He wiped his glistening forehead and went on: "Oh, the vile beasts! That horrid cry! I can't recall any sensation more odious…since a certain occasion in my childhood…"

"What was that?"

"Oh, nothing. I mean the first time I ever saw a monkey. That parody…well, to hear that bird cry…"

"You're right," I told him, struck by the justice of the comparison. "But we'd better lower our voices. We don't know what might be hidden in there."

The dark blue shadow of the covert protected its mysterious hostility. The foliage quivered, animated by invisible small birds. Swarms of convulsive flies were hovering in the half-light. The jungle was waking up at every instant, sensitive to furtive passages. Wakes were curving the stalks, suddenly stopping with terrible abruptness, leaving me to imagine that some invisible monster had caught sight of us.

"We have to go around that rock," I said, "and interpose it between ourselves and the land. The ocean seems to me to be more inoffensive."

"If you think so!" said Fleury-Moor, while we were carrying out the maneuver. He added: "But I'm expecting the mirage to vanish at any moment. You'll keep observing, won't you?"

"Until then," I remarked, "we'll be rather uncomfortably situated." The sea was, in fact, lapping at the base of the monolith.

"Let's stay all the same," Fleury-Moor said, with one foot in the water and the other lifted up. The essential thing is not to make too many movements, which might reveal our existence. Besides, it's inherently dangerous to change position when one's in a mirage—which is to say, in a false terrain that masks the pitfalls of the veritable terrain. Don't forget that, Chanteraine, and whatever happens, try to avoid running away. The place we *see* is only superimposed on the place where we *are*. You might encounter a solid and exceedingly present tree-trunk in the apparent emptiness of that antediluvian clearing. That, I think, is the only danger threatening us, because…" He slapped himself on the forehead. "Yes, of course! However total a mirage may be, it's never anything but a decoy! Echoes, reflections, chimeras! Touching it is an illusion! In consequence, my dear chap—God, how naïve we are!—the image of elephants that died hundreds of thousands of years ago can't do us the slightest harm! It's trapped in its own epoch just as much as we are in ours!"

His confidence infected me. "That's excellent, my dear chap. Say, should I assume the creatures of yesteryear that we can see can't see us, because the mirage isn't reciprocal? African mirages are never reciprocal!"

"Of course!" the geologist confirmed. "One can quite easily have a direct impression of the past—every night, the firmament, with its more or less distant stars, shows us as many pasts as the stars it contains—but one can't have a sensation of the future. Thus, when we stood up and cried out just now, the dinotherium would not have seen anything or heard anything!"

"That's right! That's right!" I affirmed, laughing in relief.

On that note, we abandoned the screen of the rock, having recovered all our casual swagger. The imprints of our shoes stigmatized the moist sand: our American shoes; the prehistoric sand...

Fleury-Moor had folded his arms across his chest. He stood there watching the waves for a little while, and finally said: "You can't imagine the emotion I feel in facing that, which is the adolescent sea—the sea of the early ages of the world, so close to the primordial era when the Earth had only the one sea! All life came out of it! There's nothing that breathes and feels that did not come from the maternal ocean, which seems to breathe and feel itself like a multitude of fluid lungs. This is the original sea, in something very close to its original state. This is the admirable womb of all living beings, which the filial Frenchman calls by the same name as his mother.[18] This is the sea, mother of men, which already has the taste of tears, an appetite for blood and a sobbing voice.

---

[18] The French *mer* [sea] and *mère* [mother] are phonetically similar. The next phrase (*Voici la mer mère des hommes...*) inevitably loses some of its elegance in translation.

We have had the ineffable pleasure of glimpsing her in her youth!

"In the moment that has been reborn for us, she has just completed her Great Work. She has released onto continents, still very narrow, all the creatures that are due to emerge from her fecundity. The era of saurians has already been over for a long time. They have undergone metamorphosis. The bird and the mammal have surged forth from the reptile. The colossal dragons will never return. And now, someone else will soon arrive. Even now, in the obscure depths of a simian race, humankind is germinating, and Virgil is on the march in the brain of a chimpanzee…"

There was a moment of reverie, full of the sound of the sea.

"When it comes to journeys in prehistory," I hazarded, "I'd rather have gone further back, as far as the Secondary era, which preceded this one. The dinosaurs would make a fine spectacle, Fleury-Moor! The most bizarre, perhaps, in the entire extent and duration of the Earth!"

"Bah!" retorted Fleury-Moor. "All your diplodocuses, megatheria and other iguanodons…that was a pelagic population. They nearly always lived in the water, you know, not as the books and the museums represent them to us. Don't complain; isn't the dinotherium you've seen a belated survivor of the giant fauna?"

"It's not a saurian," I said, regretfully.

"As for me," he said, not neglecting to scan the sea, the palm grove, the beach and the pine forest with his eyes, "if I could choose, I'd rather not have gone back so far in the course of the ages, stopping in that season of geology when humanity finally broke through within the brute. Oh, to contemplate the first humans! The Adams and Eves of the indisputable evolutionary Genesis!"

"Excuse me!" I said, by way of contradiction. "By virtue of the theory of transformism itself—as you advanced it a moment ago—an ancestor of humankind existed in every period. In this Neozoic epoch, I grant you, our ancestors were no more human than those of the Stone Age, but they must certainly have constituted very special individuals!"[19]

Fleury-Moor shook his head. "I think," he said, "that they were apes like all the rest, imperceptibly craftier, more talkative and less inclined to go on all fours. They lived in groups, having sensed that union makes for strength...but they lived far away, very far away from here..."

"In Oceania, no? I'm aware of the intransigence of your theories."

"Yes, in Oceania, which is, in my view—and that of many others, Monsieur—the cradle of humankind, since Pliocene anthropomorphic fossils have not been found anywhere else."

"Chance..." I ventured—but he cut me off.

"In Java, on the other hand," he continued, "and in the Pliocene, in the terrain corresponding to periods immediately posterior to this one, you'll recall, Chanteraine, Eugène Dubois' *Pithecanthropus!*"[20]

---

[19] "Transformism" is the specific thesis that species are transformed by evolution into new species; in the Darwinian evolutionary theory that had become commonplace by the time Renard was writing, only a few species were imagined to be thus transformed, the great majority becoming extinct under the pressure of natural selection, but in the Lamarckian schema that had preceded Darwin's—which had recently been revitalized to some extent in France by Henri Bergson's *L'Evolution créatrice* (1907)—all species are considered to be in transition, ceaselessly in the process of becoming something else as a result of some innate progressive impulse. As the central speculative thesis of this story will eventually make clear, Renard still harbored Lamarckian sympathies.

[20] The term *Pithecanthropus* had been coined by Ernst Haeckel to refer to the hypothetical missing link that he believed, as an evolutionist, must connect humans to their apelike ancestors. When Renard wrote this story the only known example of an intermediate between such near-human paleon-

"Hmm!" Was that really an *ape-man*, Fleury-Moor? One can reconstruct it as one wishes on the insufficient evidence of a couple of molars, the upper part of a skull and femur!"

"I'm astonished to hear you talk like that. Mantell, Cuvier, the iguanodon..."[21]

"And what a femur!" I continued. "What an extraordinary thigh! Knotted with osseous protuberances that no one has ever explained, except by the ingenious hypothesis of rheumatism! Ha ha! Rheumatism, Fleury-Moor! The rheumatic ape-man! Ha ha! The primitive human of the glacial caverns still passes muster, but the ape-man of the tropical Pliocene? Ha ha! Let me laugh!"

"It's no joking matter," the geologist grumbled. "And the Java bones *are* the bones of *Pithecanthropus*. In any case, why shouldn't the hypertrophies of the femur bone be mechanical lesions, consequences of an accident? Reconnected fractures? It's been suggested—you know that as well as I do. Anyway, enough—what do you expect? It's annoying."

---

tological specimens as Neanderthal man (discovered in 1857) and the great apes was Dubois' "Java man," discovered in 1891 and initially classified as *Pithecanthropus erectus*. This lent some credence to the theory of an Oceanian origin for humankind, before Raymond Dart's discovery of the first Australopithecine skull in Africa in 1924—after which evidence for an African origin piled up prolifically and irresistibly.

[21] Georges Cuvier (1769-1832) was the inventor of a system of analytical deduction that allowed paleontologists to infer whole skeletons from limited samples of bones, by analogy with other species. His anticipations often proved correct when better skeletons were subsequently discovered, as in the case of the Iguanodon, but Chanteraine was not the only skeptic who wondered whether dubious analogies might sometimes lead to incorrect reconstructions. Gideon Mantell (1790-1852) was an English paleontologist whose works helped to popularize the science, including Cuvier's method.

He looked toward the land, and I looked out to sea. "There are the birds again," I declared. "They're fishing in the distance. One might suppose that their plumage is white, but perhaps it's an effect of the distance and the light. They're like formidable seagulls."

"I'd really like know what they are!" snapped Fleury-Moor. "But we'll have to give up on that. Let's not waste precious time, and at least try to recognize what we have at hand. There are monstrous pears over there that intrigue me. Let's try to go as far as the wood."

He took a few steps then, his feet testing the ground and his arm groping, as if he were deprived of the use of his sight. That was because he feared the obstacles hidden in the invisible contemporary landscape. "Hey!" he said. Having stopped and straightened up, turning toward me with a hesitant and wonderstruck expression, he whispered behind the screen of his hand. "The cavern! Look!"

Mutely, I signaled to him that he had to come back. I suddenly experienced an unparalleled despair, in thinking that we might be alone in a world in which humans did not exist. Phosphorescent gleams had just become perceptible in the darkness of the cavern. They were tiny glimmers, arranged in pairs, red-green and green-red—incontestably recognizable as eyes.

"I'm going in there!" Fleury-Moor decided.

"No!" I ran toward him.

"Given that the mirage will dissipate," he reasoned, "Wouldn't you be eternally regretful at having missed the opportunity? Let's take advantage of it, my dear chap! Let's take advantage of the practicable mirage!"

"Don't you see that those eyes are *looking at us*?"

"Eh? You're crazy! They're looking into the future?"

But I held firm, for I was governed at that moment by an internal master more powerful than common sense. He had to yield to my strength, and ended up by contenting himself with an examination at a distance.

The eyes gleamed, like pairs of somber stars, and sometimes blinked, beneath frighteningly unknown eyelids. My imagination forged behind them a family of terrible bears as large as rhinoceroses…

"Don't you notice anything?" I asked, abruptly.

"Pardon?"

"You can't see it? The ray of sunlight?"

"What ray?"

"The one that penetrates the cavern—that patch of oblique light…"

"So what?"

"Well, the two eyes that seem to be closest to the opening…aren't they *above* that bright patch?"

"Yes, that's true."

"So, if they really were the eyes on an animal standing on the ground, we'd be able to see that animal in the ray of sunlight…"

"Bravo! According to the evidence, those eyes must belong to some animal that's suspended from the vault, unless it's hovering in mid-air."

In the depths of the lair, which hollowed it out indefinitely, the pairs of flamboyant eyes were increasing in number.

We were out in the open, and I was careful not to interrupt my surveillance of the neighborhood, in spite of the absurdity of any such occupation. The palm grove, divided into two by the red sand clearing, plunged its undergrowth into shadow to the right and left of the cavern. I couldn't retain a gasp of amazement: that shadow was also punctuated by the bronzed gleam of eyes! There were two at the base of every pantagruelesque pear. There were hundreds of them. And that Argus forest was spying on us with all of its fascinating eyes.

The idea that the pear trees weren't vegetables crossed my mind like a hairy spider.

Fleury-Moor, however, gave his own opinion. "Your pears," he said, "are simply bats. They're giant vampires hanging head-down in their customary posture, holding on to the branches of those candelabras and the ceiling of the cavern. But they must be diurnal—because, you see, I'll wager that your so-called seagulls are also vampires. Those that surround us are probably taking a siesta."

"You mean they're waking up!"

I would have preferred not to have to correct him. Bat colonies disgust me to the point of nausea, and I leave it to the imagination to judge the impression made on me by that city of vampires, endowed with a supplementary monstrosity by virtue of their gigantism.

I looked at the cavern, the palm grove and the suspended pear-shaped bats. Fleury-Moor looked at the sea and the bats flying in the distance. We stood like that for a minute, without anything moving.

By incredible and contradictory trick of the mind, that passivity, which prolonged the anguish of expectation, moved me to action—me, the most timid person in the world! Impulsively, I picked up a handful of pebbles.

"Should I?" I proposed, aiming at the dark cave mouth.

Fleury-Moor approved with an evasive gesture.

My first pebble missed the target, striking the wall and falling back on to a heap of fish-bones near the opening. The second one flew straight into the depths of the retreat.

Immediately, a frightful concert went up in the bowels of the hill, which made the hair stand up on our heads. The cavern filled with demonic howling, as if it were a tunnel to Hell. Its darkness was constellated by ardent coals—and we finally saw something move in the heart of the darkness, becoming paler with each step as it advanced toward the light beneath the incandescent gleams.

*A man!* I thought.

"A monkey," murmured Fleury-Moor.

It was both, and it was neither: a frightfully thin upright biped with a wretched little rounded skull, a snub nose, a preeminent jaw, furry cabbage-ears and hair over its entire body. There was no doubt that we had before us a pithecanthropus, the ancestor of humankind. A pithecanthropus like the one reconstituted from the Javan bones by Eugène Dubois. The

*Pithecanthropus erectus* of the Pliocene, here in the Miocene, in Europe, in Champagne! Alive! And which, by some abominable singularity, was the ally of the vampires, sharing their habitat!

"Bah!" I said, for my own satisfaction. "He must employ them as slaves, or hunting-dogs—or, rather, fishing-dogs!"

The ape-man stopped on the threshold of the cyclopean burrow. He opened his close-set eyes, which had been half-closed...

The most amazing thing you could ever see appeared in the broad daylight—and you'd never guess what it was! Listen: this savage among savages, who might have been expected to be entirely nude, was draped in an ample cloak of supple leather, chestnut-brown and shiny, the folds of which fell symmetrically along the body, down to the heels.

"A cloak!" said the dismayed geologist.

Civilized, already! An ape that could clothe itself! But the diabolical garment prevented us from examining the monster's external anatomy.

The pithecanthropus furrowed its eyebrows in a simian manner, then turned its head in human fashion. The tumult inside the grotto died away.

"It's looking at us I tell you!"

"One would think so, all the same!" Fleury-Moor conceded "But if it's looking at us, can it also hear us? Come on! It's impossible." He wore an indefinable smile. He shouted at the human beast: "Hey! Grandpa!" And he burst out laughing, presumably in order to cheer me up.

I didn't want to cheer up; I had no license to do so.

Our ancestor extended an immoderately long arm, lifting up its leather toga. Its mouth opened, becoming a maw equipped with fangs. A yapping voice—a complicated barking—escaped therefrom, making its hungry throat vibrate like those of Italian singers. It was something like: "*Hallooee, tooee, tooee! Hirra-ah! Ratoh! Ratoh!*" I remember *Ratoh!*

quite well—which, after all, could be written as "râteau"[22] without any impropriety. And believe me, that was a genuine curiosity: that French word, that gardening term, evocative of mallets and bowling-greens, of Versailles and the Trianon, on the scarcely-rimmed lips of an Adamic gorilla.

Now, in the Miocene era, *Ratoh!* obviously meant "Come here, lads!" or even "All together!" In response to that call—or, rather, that order—a band of anthropoids erupted out of the cavern. Each side of the palm-grove disgorged a troop of our ancestors into the open space, and the crest of the hill was garnished with a cordon of sentries that emerged from the pine-wood. The ammoniac odor of a monkey-house gripped our nostrils. Vile howls filled the silence. A hostile and bestial population besieged us, formed into a circle. All of them, like the leader, were clad in capes in various shades of brown, whose flaps they agitated furiously.

I tried to get back to the rocks on the edge of the sea. A flutter of wings above the waves brought a hurrying flock of those huge kingfishers, or huge bats. We were now about to find out what we were dealing with: albatrosses or vampires, they were racing to the rescue, and…

"Flying men!" exclaimed Fleury-Moor.

Word of honor, they were flying men! And the brown cloak, the uniform cape of the primates that surround us—what was that? You will already have guessed: vast reptilian wings. The pears, the birds, the bats and the pithecanthropus were but one single creature: our paternal Adam, who had reigned over the Earth as he reigned in the sky.

We were surrounded by ancestors, therefore, coming from every direction. Their flight rounded out a dome of beating wings. They had put us under a bell, and that quivering cupola obscured the daylight. There was no longer any escape.

---

[22] *Râteau* means "rake;" I have refrained from translating the cry as *Raik!* because Chantelaine specifically says that the word sounds French, and some of the associations it evokes in his mind are specifically French.

Instinct stuck us back-to-back. Thus prepared, two in one—Janus of the double face—we cancelled out the deplorable inferiority of our rear. I clutched my rifle in nervous and spasmodic hands...

"You can see perfectly well that the mirage is reciprocal," I said, "since we can see them and they can see us!"

I felt him shrug his shoulders. "Natural phantoms!" he explained. "Natural phantoms. Do you get it? An exquisite illusion! Let's try to retain as much as we can. Ah! So man finally ended up losing them—his wings! By virtue of no longer making use of them! Evolution has punished his idleness, as with penguins. Ah! Let's try to retain all that we can."

"Yes, that's understood. You keep going back to the same thing."

The pithecanthropes—let us rather say, since they had wings, the pteropithecanthropes—were content for the moment to keep us under observation. We were the focal point of every gaze, which did not fail to intimidate me. Moreover, the incessant tumult, the riot of clamors and the beating of membranous wings brought on a dizziness of the eyes and eardrums. I stiffened myself as best I could against a weakness of purely physical origin. All my will-power was employed in fighting my eyelids, which wanted to close. I waited avidly for the prodigy to end.

Fleury-Moor, for his part, was thinking aloud within the mirage. In order to commit what he had observed more securely to memory, the incomparable scientist was taking verbal notes. I heard him recording them continually:

"Face Negroid. Prognathous. No civilization. No fire. Rudiments of language. The leader is the strongest, not the oldest. As among animals, equality of males and females. No weapons. The wings...oh, unparalleled...connect their arms and legs. Ha ha! The protuberances of Java! I hold the key to that enigma. In that respect, here are intermediary creatures, situated between the bat and the flying squirrel, but they're neither insectivores nor rodents, icthyophages...yes, fish-eaters. In sum, they proceed principally from pterodactyls, and the entire terrestrial fauna is definitely descended from saurians. That's your opinion, isn't it, Chanteraine?"

"Everything's spinning!" I replied. "I'm getting seasick! Everything's spinning! What can we do? I just want to do something, no matter what…"

My counterpart muttered his disdain: "Stupid…a representation devoid of danger…unworthy of his status…living pictures…gallery…family portraits…"

Finally, he resumed cursing his lack of equipment.

"At least make use of your chronometer!" I told him. "Look at it! What time is it?"

"5:05 p.m."

"Put it away!" I cried. "It's exciting them! It's shiny! Put your watch away! They'll do you harm…put it away…"

Something dark and heavy fell upon us. I moved sideways. A furry claw had struck the hand that held the gilded watch…

On the ground, covering the vanished body of Fleury-Moor, a pithecanthrope was struggling, with its wings furled, as abject as a Callot devil.[23] Agitated by somersaults, the brute offered me the nape of its neck, hollowed out beneath the occiput…

I put my rifle to my shoulder, and fired.

This time, the shot produced a thunderous noise. Thick smoke surrounded me, unexpectedly blowing out the immemorial Sun. It was followed by silence and cold.

The smoke was no longer there.

It could not be there, since the fog had reappeared. The detonation of my powder had shaken its heaviness and caused the astonishing retrospection that had played within it to vanish. We had come back to the 20th century.

Immediately, as a sequel to the same dislocation, the fog turned to drizzle. A tenuous and frigid rain sprinkled me…

---

[23] Jacques Callot (1592-1635) was an artist celebrated for his grotesque and fantastic designs.

The twilight of the twilight had arrived. In a gloom in which the night and the fog combined their negations, I perceived Fleury-Moor's feet at my own. He was lying full-length, face to the ground.

He recovered consciousness, groaning. "It's killed me!" he whined. "It's killed me!" And to tell the truth, it was as if he were lamenting thus from the other side of Death.

His hands were those of a man who has perished. I rubbed them, to no avail. He looked around, his features expressionless, bewildered by terror. He had the eyes that one must have behind one's eyelids when one is asleep.

I showed him the outline of a fir-tree in the gloom. That familiar sight calmed him down. He told me that the visibility was good enough for us to go back, and that he wanted to do so as quickly as possible.

Rapidly, I improvised a cross of branches, and I planted it in the ground in a particular fashion. Fleury urged me to get a move on.

Twenty meters away, we found the path. Another cross; more impatience from Fleury.

Further on, some stone-cutters from Nauroy-les-Cormonville, replied to my questions. They had not seen anything except the fog, nor heard anything, except the rifle-shot.

"The bizarrerie was localized in a narrowly restricted space," I said, when we had left them. "That's very fortunate. Otherwise, how many villages would have been submerged?"

I wanted to laugh—the attempt was vain. Fleury-Moor went down the hill as fast as his legs could carry him, making inexplicable detours and sudden halts, troubled by bats tracing their black lightning-streaks, disturbed by the green fog of an asparagus field that we could have crossed to take a short cut. The vaporous foliage of a willow frightened him like a thickening of the fog. An owl that flew away, as silent as a shadow, made him duck his head.

I followed him as best I could. We arrived at the château.

It had been agreed that we would keep the secret of the adventure that had happened to us. That was quite easy. That evening, my colleague felt weak. His hands were still corpse-like and his physiognomy was no longer able to translate the variations of his mind. He was put to bed. I watched over him, in company with his wife. All night, I had the feeling that Fleury-Moor, the celebrated geologist, was done with being a genius, and that he would henceforth be no more than a place where great things had happened.

In the morning, fortunately, his fever declined. The doctor prescribed rest, silence and sleep. Before commencing the treatment, Fleury asked to talk to me in private.

He wanted me to return to the location of the mirage, to determine the situation of the cavern. "We must find it, no matter what the cost. It must contain fossils of inestimable value." He congratulated me warmly for have planted markers, and implored me to be quick, for fear that the wind or some vagabond might carry them off.

I left with a party of laborers armed with digging-tools.

The two crosses had not been disturbed. The orientation of the first pointed to the second, and the orientation of the second pointed to the cavern. My retina conserved a picture of the distances, and counted about 30 meters between the place where Fleury-Moor had fallen and the entrance to the cave. At present, though, the legacy of the ages had brought the embankment some 20 meters closer, with the result that it would have been necessary for us to dig a tunnel of that length if a most opportune quarry had not been set two meters to the left and in the desired direction. I measured 20 meters along its side wall. The laborers attacked it from the right, and encountered clay almost immediately.

At about 3 p.m., I stopped the work. There was no cavern. I imagine that it had collapsed, in the course of various geological vicissitudes. By digging carefully in the glutinous marl, however, we discovered conglomerates of red earth mingled with bones.

I isolated fragments of skeletons analogous to that of the Javan pithecanthropus where they lay. The arm-bones and leg-bones all presented the famous excrescences of the Malayan femur, which were neither mechanical lesions nor stigmata of arthritis, but simply natural apophyses to which the tendons of the membranous wings had been attached. These fragments, fitted together, formed an almost-complete composite skeleton, which interested parties can see at the Museum under the reputedly-fantastic label *Pteropithecanthropus erectus*. It is also known as *Anthropopterix*, or, more commonly, "the winged man of Cormonville."

In accordance with my anticipations, the dig did not bring to light any pottery, however coarse, nor any flint tools, however crude. There were no elephant tibias, ready-made sledgehammers, nor any narwhal-horns that had served as pikes. So, it was greatly to my surprise that I exhumed an occipital portion of skull pierced by a round hole, which seemed to be evidence of the use of trepanning by the anthropoids of the Neozoic era. I was not unaware that Quaternary man, the master of fire and fabricator of axes, had practiced this precocious surgery, but Tertiary man! A mere baboon, less than the faun of legend!

I meditated upon this skull-fragment more gravely than Hamlet upon the entire skull of Yorick. That enigmatic void, that little circle of nothingness, obsessed me. I had the idea of measuring it. It had the same diameter as the bullets of my 12-caliber!

I was just getting used to the explanation that a simple numerical relationship had caused to explode within my uncertainty, when a laborer brought me something that he had disinterred: a right hand, intimately cemented to the lump of clay that molded its slender, white and fragile fingers. Its fist was clenched on something that I was determined to extricate.

For millions of years that right hand had been buried under a mountain. What it held, however, was a *fossilized chronometer*.

I had never seen such a disconcerting relic. Crumbs of glass, iridescent by virtue of the accumulation of several antiquities, speckled the ruins of the casing. The hinges of the watch were welded shut. I opened it with a knife, like an oyster. Nothing remained of the steel works but red granules of rusty powder—but the impenetrable gold had resisted the ravages of time. The name of the vendor was still legible on the dull inner surface of the case:

SAMUEL GOLDSCHMIDT
*19 Avenue de l'Opéra, Paris.*

And the hands, covered with a mineral crust, had been standing at five past five for an eternity of sorts.

I shall not try to describe the disorder of my thoughts.

Thirty minutes later, armed with the watch and the occiput, I disobeyed the doctor's orders and went into Fleury-Moor's sick-room. He was sitting on his bed with his arms folded.

His welcome disappointed me. The report that I gave to him scarcely interested him at all, and when he had handled the two rarities distractedly, he said, in a loud voice and a resolute tone: "Chanteraine!"

"What?"

"You mustn't say that about men."

"What, my friend?"

"That the men of long ago had wings…"

"Eh?"

"It would be too sad for them, you see. You mustn't tell them. I've been thinking a lot since you left… You see, Chanteraine, our need to streak through the sky, our immortal desire to fly, is no more than a hope, an impulse of the race in the direction of the best and most beautiful. It's nothing but an ill-defined regret…regret for lost wings…regret for a paradise lost! Is that what the Old Testament tries to symbolize by the expulsion of Adam and Eve? Perhaps. Probably. Oh, believe me—all the myths of the ancients have a basis in prehistoric reality. Each of their heroes, in his turn, represents the human species. Is not Prometheus the conquest of fire? Is not the loss of flight also the fall of Icarus? An elementary tradition, muffled but tenacious, transmits the rancor or the gratitude of the flesh within itself. When we desire to acquire wings, we are mourning, without knowing it, for the wings we have lost, just as, when we experience nostalgia for the sea, what moves us so greatly, without our knowing it, is the affection of the exile for his henceforth-forbidden fatherland. No, no, we mustn't inform men that they're fallen angels. It would be too sad!"

"What!" I fulminated, indignant and also consternated. "You'd have the courage to remain silent? But our discovery doesn't belong to us! It belongs to all the people of the world! And I can't help wondering what's *sad* about what we have to tell them: Long ago, men flew, but their souls crawled! Admit that we've gained by the exchange!"

"You mustn't tell them."

"And what about truth!" I cried. "The truth! Isn't it necessary to tell that, in spite of everything, no matter what? Isn't it necessary to sacrifice everything to it? The truth, Fleury! Isn't that the goal of our intellectual flight? Isn't it the truth that fits wings to our souls and enables them to rise higher than a hexapteran seraphim?"

"You mustn't tell, all the same," Fleury-Moor insisted.

Rightfully, only half of the honor of that indivisible discovery belonged to each of us. One of us could not dispose of his part without the consent of the other. I therefore resigned myself—and that's why so many days went by before the pteropithecanthrope made his entrance at the Museum. It owes that mercy to the invention of aeroplanes. On the day after the first decisive experiment, Fleury-Moor released me from my secrecy.[24]

---

[24] The first "decisive experiment" in heavier-than-air flight to take place in France is generally agreed to have been carried out by Alberto Santos-Dumont on October 23, 1906, a year before the date of Chanteraine and Fleury-Moor's supposed adventure. It is possible, however, that Fleury-Moor was unimpressed by the feat of flying 60 meters at a height of less than three meters, and found it difficult take such machines seriously until Louis Blériot flew across the English Channel

"Now that these orthopedic machines exist, which are to wings what a crutch is to an amputated leg," he said, "it seems to me that we may speak, since God is welcoming Adam back to paradise and Dedalus is climbing into the sky again."

We have spoken. Who believes us? No one. Why?

Because, on the one hand, the skeleton in the Museum is a skeleton, like the one in Java, and nothing more. The pithecanthrope's wings resembled those of a bat less than the membranes of a flying squirrel; they only possessed a muscular armature, which has disappeared.

On the other hand, we, the living, dare not recount the tribulation that testifies in favor of our thesis. Only posterity shall know about the mirage that assailed us in the fog of October 26 and gave us the unforgettable vision of the time when men could fly.

---

on July 25, 1909; that might well have been the event that provoked his change of mind.

# THE DOCTORED MAN

*To Léon Michaud*[25]

The body was found by gendarmes Mochon and Juliaz of the Belvoux brigade. They were returning from a patrol at daybreak and were riding along the departmental highway, coming from Salamont, when they noticed the ominous circumstance in the Thiots woods about six kilometers from Belvoux.

The dawn was grey. The rain, which had been falling for several days, had not ceased since the previous evening. A keen wind was stirring the water of the puddles and tormenting the illuminated foliage. Caught on a clump of thistles, a handkerchief was fluttering. The black and white form of a human body was extended by the roadside, visible at a distance, with other objects on the ground nearby.

The gendarmes, experienced in warfare and in their profession, knew at once that the man was dead. They got down some distance away and attached their horses to a telegraph pole. The two companions approached the cadaver, taking care to walk on the grass in order not to blur any tracks.

"Why, it's Doctor Bare!" said Juliaz.

The other looked on in silence.

"That's true—you're new," Juliaz went on. "Well, he's a physician from Belvoux."

---

[25] Léon Michaud is not an uncommon name, but this dedicatee does not seem to be one of the various writers who have used it as a by-line. Louis Michaud was the publisher of Renard's *Le Péril bleu* and *Monsieur d'Outremort* before the war, although the company did not survive the conflict; it is possible that Léon was Louis Michaud's son.

They were confronted with the body of a man in the prime of life, a tall fellow of 30 or 35, lying on his back, facing the sky, with a bullet-hole in his forehead. He was bareheaded and had no overcoat, but he wore large sporting gloves. His clothing having been unbuttoned, the contents of his turned-out pockets—watch; wallet, cigarette-case, lighter, instrument-case, fountain-pen, etc.—lay scattered on the ground.

Mochon picked up a revolver lying near the corpse. It was fully-loaded, with a cartridge in the chamber, and the inside of the barrel was shiny. The weapon, therefore, had not been fired.

"A crime," said Mochon. "But the motive wasn't theft. That silver, these banknotes..."

"We can't be sure. He must have had a notebook, a diary, this doctor, and there's none to be seen. There might have been many things on him that we don't know about..."

"What I meant," Mochon explained, "is that if it was theft, it isn't an ordinary theft. Did he have any enemies?"

"Not to my knowledge. He's been demobilized since January and since then has been quietly practicing in and around Belvoux. He's reputed to be a good doctor. I don't know him in any other capacity, you understand. He's been dead for several hours. What was he doing here last night?"

"Take note of his shoes," said Mochon. "They're almost free of mud."

"And there's no indication of a struggle. His clothes aren't torn, not even scuffed..."

Juliaz examined the road. As sticky as they could have wished, it retained the night's imprints with remarkable clarity. The doctor' footprints were located. There were three of them, no more and no less; three footprints arranged at right angles across the road, which came from nowhere and stopped abruptly. Then there was the imprint of a heavy body, the impact of whose fall had impressed the image of a thick fur in the muddy ground; a few hairs remained, stuck to the mold.

It was easy to conclude that Doctor Bare had been shot by a rifle after getting down from a vehicle, doubtless by an aggressor hidden in the woods, and that he had been dressed in a goatskin coat at the time; his murderer had dragged him aside to search and rob him at his ease.

Juliaz knew that the doctor possessed a small, rather speedy automobile, which he drive himself with considerable skill and which he used for his excursions into rural areas. The gendarme had often seen him pass by, at the wheel of his little sports car, sometimes executing rapid maneuvers in reverse or making skidding U-turns with bold skill.

The little car had left tracks on the road. Juliaz followed them, always staying off the roadway. The rear tire-marks covered the front ones. One of them was ribbed, the other studded. The car had gone past twice, in opposite directions, the studded tire first being on one side of the road, then the other. But in which direction had the car been going on each pass? This way, toward Belvoux, or that way, toward Salamont? How could its coming and going be determined? That being unrevealed by the tracks, one might assume that the Doctor had departed from Belvoux, but only further inquiries could confirm that.

Juliaz, who did not stay there long, informed himself of the above while he limited himself to inspecting the vicinity of the crime without any particular objective. On the road, about thirty meters from the cadaver in the direction of Salamont, he discovered evidence of a circular skid, facilitated by the slippery ground, which marked the terminal point of the nocturnal excursion. The two sets of tracks ended there, in a knot.

The doctor, therefore, had indeed been coming from Belvoux, and some mysterious cause had suddenly impelled him to retrace his steps by making an unceremonious U-turn in the dark. What, then, had his headlights lit up in front of him? What danger had suddenly emerged from the darkness?

The gendarme, going back toward Belvoux himself, inspected the tracks scrupulously—which, in reality, was an exceedingly difficult task. He observed lurches in one of them, which seemed to be evidence of high speed, then a skid-mark revealing a brutal application of the brake, and the stopping of the vehicle, indicated by a sort of heel-mark, which had hollowed out its ruts exactly opposite the three footprints, level with the cadaver—and he wondered what reason had obliged the automobilist to stop his car in mid-flight and leap out of it in order, it appeared, to run for the woods.

This initial research had taken time, though. The day had broadened. A peasant's cart came in sight. On the gendarmes' orders, it came to a halt in the middle of the road. It was necessary to take advantage of the terrain's helpfulness and close the road to all vehicles until the ground had, so to speak, completed its testimony.

"You see that he's definitely been robbed," said Juliaz. "Someone has taken his fur coat, his headgear and his automobile."

Indeed, the sports car had got under way again after the murder, heading toward Belvoux. Julian conscientiously took charge of that track while Mochon went back toward Salamont, on the chance that he might discover some clue to the mystery of why the victim of the ambush had turned round. They were perhaps five hundred meters apart when they hailed one another with expansive gestures. Mochon, being the younger, rejoined his comrade. The latter showed him new tracks, deep and widely-spaced, proving that a powerful automobile with a large wheelbase had swung across the road before it too had resumed the road to Belvoux.

"It's possible," said Juliaz, "that it was simply to turn round..."

"No, I don't think so," Mochon replied, "for I called you to observe exactly the same thing over there."

"Yes?"

"And mine was a different car," Mochon went on. "Your tires, here, show a kind of trellis pattern; mine, back there were differently made. Hold on! There they are—mine—also passing in front of us..."

"They're certainly not the same," Juliaz agreed. "Furthermore, mine don't go any further; they stop here, where we are. If I'm not mistaken, then...."

"There were two large automobiles, then, which blocked the road, 500 meters apart."

They looked at one another, satisfied by their success.

For some reason that they would surely discover later, Doctor Bare had been traveling through the pitch-black night on the road from Belvoux to Salamont. As he passed through the Thiots woods, the light of his headlamps had suddenly showed him the obstacle of a large automobile with all its lights out, set across the road in such a manner that he could only get past by swerving to the left or the right. That sight had certainly frightened him, and he must have suspected danger; the haste with which he had turned round was evidence of that.

By means of one of those U-turns that were his specialty, he had been able to reverse his direction within a second and head for Belvoux at top speed, thinking that the large automobile would only be able to give chase after a pause, and counting on the speed of his sports car to maintain its distance. Scarcely had he launched himself forward, though, than he perceived another obstacle in front of him, in the form of a second automobile. *He was trapped.* A hostile ruse had triumphed. While one automobile waited at a predetermined spot, the other had followed him, silently and obscurely, and had been transformed into a barricade in its turn, at an agreed spot.

The doctor had seen that he was blocked in. His sports car could no longer be of any assistance to him. He had stopped as quickly as possible, and tried to hurl himself into the woods—a decision foreseen by his adversaries, since one of them, posted in a thicket, had shot him down before he had taken four steps.

This hypothesis fitted the facts and it was the only one that no evidence contradicted. Whether the assassins had lured the unfortunate into an ambush, or whether they had laid their trap on his usual route, the tragedy had eventually unfolded. The subsequent investigation would doubtless clarify the mystery, exposing the reasons for the murder and the motives for the theft, and they would find out why such a scheme had been deployed against a humble provincial doctor. That was no longer the gendarmes' concern; they had done their duty.

Juliaz took notes for his written report. The remains of the unfortunate doctor were loaded on to the cart, requisitioned for that purpose, and the two horsemen, astride their mounts, escorted it as far as Belvoux. Let us note, however, that at the Trivieu crossroads, they discovered a divergence in the tracks of the three automobiles fleeing the crime-scene. One of the two large cars had headed for Trivieu, while the other, accompanied by the stolen sports car, had continued along the road to Belvoux. They followed the latter tracks as far as the town boundary, where the hard surface no longer permitted anything to be distinguished.

Doctor Bare lived in the High Street. It was 8 a.m. when Juliaz rang the bell, knowing that there would be no painful scenes to fear, the dead man having been a bachelor who lived alone with a single manservant. The latter came to open the door, looking pale and distressed. He had got up an hour before and had been roaming the house since then, having discovered his master's absence and the fact that the safe, cupboards, filing-cabinets and desk had been rifled, and not knowing what to do.

The lieutenant of the gendarmerie interrogated him almost immediately. And this, more or less, is what he obtained: "The doctor was working in his study yesterday evening, as usual; I saw his light under the door when I went to bed. I wasn't yet asleep, and Saint-Fortunat had just chimed 9 p.m., when I heard the telephone ring. A few minutes later, the doctor came upstairs and said to me through my bedroom door 'Auguste! Are you asleep?'

" 'No, Doctor.'

" 'Someone's just telephoned me from Salamont. The postmistress has had a stroke. They say she's dying. I'm going over there. I don't need you. I'll be back before midnight.' And he added: 'It really must be the postmistress, for them to phone me at this hour.' With that, he left. I saw the light of his headlamps in the courtyard—my window overlooks the yard—and I heard the car go out into the Rue de la Botasse, then the doctor closing the gate behind him…and that's all that happened yesterday evening.

"During the night, the noise of the automobile returning woke me up. I went to the window to ask whether the doctor needed me. I saw him just as he got out. He had his back to me. He replied: 'No—go to sleep,' as he put out the head-lamps. I was still half-asleep. He didn't turn round. It wasn't him, you say? What can I say in reply? I saw his goatskin coat and his fur helmet; the goatskin's collar was turned up…I went back to bed. And that's all that happened during the night.

"No, Monsieur, I didn't hear anything else, nothing extraordinary. No breaking, no prizing—but the thief had taken the keys from the doctor's pockets. All the cupboards and all the drawers were opened with keys. The strong-box too—but there, it was necessary to be truly clever, with respect to the combination…

"All the papers, Monsieur, yes, they took all the papers, but not a single item of jewelry, not a single clock, not even the silver cutlery. Nothing but papers! There was surely enough to fill two or here suitcases…

"In the safe? Yes, papers, neatly filed, in blue cardboard covers—I've seen them several times; the doctor had complete confidence in me…"

The interrogation had taken place in the doctor's study, and the police officer contemplated the empty, wide-open cupboards, the goatskin coat and the fur helmet thrown on a chair. He raised his head.

"Is the car there?" he asked the lad.

"Yes, Monsieur, and nothing's broken."

"What do you think, Juliaz? The large auto waited for the thief, didn't it? And now it's far away! What a plot!" Then he seized the telephone that was set on the desk among magnifying-glasses, forceps and other medical equipment. "Hello!" he said "Hello!" While tapping the call-signaler, he murmured: "I want to clear up yesterday evening's telephone call. *Hello! Hello!* No one's answering. It's no longer working. What's the meaning of that? Juliaz, go to the Post Office. At the same time, send this telegram to the court in Bourg."

Juliaz left at the double.

The receptionist referred him to the telephonist. She swore that number 18—that of Doctor Bare—had not emitted any call signal. As for the communication of 9 p.m. the previous evening, she thought that he was joking. Moreover, her supervisor confirmed that no one had telephoned Doctor Bare after the offices had been closed. No one ever telephoned after 7 p.m.

Juliaz recounted the drama. The functionary then placed a call to the receptionist at Salamont and offered the gendarme the second earpiece. The receptionist at Salamont was in perfect health, and could not explain what she called, in her ignorance, a "practical joke."

"Even so, someone telephoned number 18 yesterday evening," Juliaz insisted, to the supervisor. The brave man's tone made his interlocutor go slightly pale.

The latter, seeing himself implicated in a criminal affair, imagined that his job was at stake. Self-justification became his only objective. "Come on," he said, putting his hat on. "It can't have happened like that."

As soon as they arrived in the doctor's study, where the formalities were taking their course, the telephonist, adopting the telephonic apparatus as his point of departure, set out to follow the conducting wire, just as Mochon and Juliaz had followed the tracks of the automobiles. That operation took them outside, behind the house and out of the courtyard.

The aerial wire went along the Rue de la Botasse, upon which only courtyards and gardens opened. A certain distance away, it had been cut level with an isolator. The long part was dangling in the gutter; that was what remained connected to the doctor's apparatus. The telephonist picked it up, examined the end closely, and smiled triumphantly. A few centimeters from the end, the copper wire, freshly exposed, bore a little round scratch.

"The point of a screw!" said the telephonist to those surrounding him. "The screw of a terminal! Look, Messieurs! This wire has been in contact with a portable apparatus. It's from here that some unknown person sent the call to Doctor Bare. It's from here that the false news departed. My service had nothing to do with it, Messieurs! Nothing at all!"

"That explains everything," said Mochon.

"Everything as to *how*, but nothing as to *why*!" replied his lieutenant.

The full descent of the law took place that afternoon. The disorder of the dwelling had been carefully preserved from any modification. The doctor's body, transported to the Hospice, was lying in a little room. A medical examiner accompanied the magistrates. He carried out an autopsy, which provided no instructive result. The bullet, fired at long range, had passed right through the skull and been lost. Permission for burial was granted immediately,

The prosecutor, meanwhile, had undertaken to examine the house, and searched in vain for the motive for the murder. All that could be deduced from the doctor's death and the theft of his papers was that Bare had been in possession of an important secret, and that someone had wanted to prevent any possibility of his making use of it or divulging it. As for the nature of the secret, that was anyone's guess.

There are dead men who talk; the writings that they leave behind them preserve their ideas and lend them a voice from beyond the grave. The prosecutor wanted the furniture searched to the last crack. The marble tops of sideboards were lifted, he undersides of drawers inspected by the light of electric lamps; they riffled through all the books in the bookcase; the clothes in the wardrobe were subjected to an implacable search. Nothing was found. Not a single stub of paper blacked with ink, not a word of any writing whatsoever. That investigation, as they now had proof, had been carried out by the murderers in advance of the magistrates.

The latter withdrew. It was decided, however, for the convenience of the investigation, that the sports car would be put under seal, along with the goatskin and the fur helmet of which one of the malefactors had made use in order to borrow Doctor Bare's appearance.

As the vestment and the headgear were being removed, the clerk observed that the goatskin, by virtue of the special fate reserved for it, had escaped his investigations. He then had the idea of plunging his hand into one of the interior pockets.

Quite calmly, without suspecting the value of his find, he drew out a few sheets of white paper, folded in four. They were covered in fine, compact handwriting. The other pockets were empty.

Acquaintance with this manuscript demonstrated peremptorily that the assassins would not have left it behind if they had known that it was contained in the goatskin. In a hurry to put on his disguise, one of them had doubtless removed it from the doctor's body before the corpse had been searched. Thus, the goatskin had been taken out of consideration by virtue of the role it that had to play, in the same way that it had almost escaped the perspicacity of the law, by virtue of the role that it had already played—which is a rather curious trait of psychology that might provide a philosopher with food for thought.

The stupidity of the criminals was forgivable, however—if one might put it that way—for it was now known that the principal objective of their theft was the contents of the safe and, secondarily, the desk. The documents distributed in the other items of furniture, and perhaps on their victim's own person were, in the thieves' view, of little interest, because they believed them to be enigmatic in isolation. How could they have suspected that the goatskin, a cape for occasional use, contained such important revelations? It was necessary, in order to explain it, to indulge in conjectures, and assume that Doctor Bare had just added the final words to that summary account when he telephone rang in the silence of his office. He had been summoned urgently to Salamont. The life of a sick woman depended on his haste. He did not think that he ought to waste several minutes opening his safe, and thought it more prudent to take the document with him, resolving to put it in a safe place as soon as he returned.

It is this document that we publish hereafter. It tells a story to which the doctor's death is merely a bloody epilogue. Alas, what you are about to read is only a very imprecise relation of the observations made by the physician from Belvoux. It is merely an intimate history in which he recounts information that could not be placed in his technical memoir, which was stolen by the redoubtable burglars on the very eve of being sent to the Academy of Sciences. It is true that—according to the doctor—the technical memoir was itself very incomplete, but its loss is no less deplorable, if one considers all the light that might have been cast into depths of the unknown of which the manuscript from the goatskin one gives a faint glimpse.

Without further ado, we offer the reader these memoirs, which, mingling the precision of a report with the sincerity of a confession, retrace the vicissitudes of a tragic and marvelous adventure.

## I. Death on the Field of Honor

I believe, in all sincerity, that there are few men as calm and as unimpressionable as me. I think that love alone has been able to hasten the beating of my heart. And yet, every time the old doorbell rings in the corridor, I can't retain a slight start. My nerves themselves remember the apparition and the circumstances that accompanied it; insensible to explanations, they cannot lose that stupid habit so easily. And it's the persistence of such a phenomenon that gives me retrospective proof of my fear, for, at the time, I thought I was only able to experience surprise without disquiet, a sort of embarrassment in which a sense of impossibility, the suspicion of a practical joke and—very faintly—a suspicion of the trustworthiness of my senses, were in contention.

It must be the case, however, that fear struck me unaware, since, every time it rings, that bell makes me quiver imperceptibly, in the same way that a child raises an elbow and blinks when a hand that has previously beaten him moves. Furthermore, why should I make use of that word "apparition," which is false, if I didn't have some absurd individual within me, who has remained under the influence of astonishment and persists in his unreason?

I suppose that my nerves would be more tranquil if the day and the evening had not required them to work in a funereal mode and put me in a state of mind exceptionally favorable to certain weaknesses.

On the day in question, the town of Belvoux had celebrated the memory of its children killed on the field of honor, and Madame Lebris, an old friend of my late mother, a partially paralyzed old lady, had begged me, together with Maître Puysandieu, the notary, to help her move around. According to the order of the ceremonies, we had to take her from the church to the monument in the mall, and from the mall to the cemetery; then we would meet for an intimate dinner in the worthy woman's home.

Under the influence of an obsession that no longer left her, Madame Lebris made that dinner into one last ceremony dedicated to the memory of her son.

"He loved you very much!" she told us, in an emotional voice, in reaching out to us across the table. And we talked about nothing but him, until the moment of separation.

Madame Lebris is my neighbor. To go from her house to mine one only has to cross the High Street. I went home profoundly sad and sat down, as I do every evening, to work at the desk on which I am writing at present.

It was impossible for me to work. Usually, I have too much work to do to burden myself with respect the disappearance of the people who were my friends and whom the war had devoured, but a few hours of concentrated idleness had brought me much closer to their austere company. I was surrounded by cherished phantoms, and the thought of Jean Lebris was haunting me.

I saw him again, thin and pale, a trifle bowed down. I believed, in fact, that he had "love me very much," in spite of the ten years that made me his elder. His delicate health put him under the dependency of my solicitude. He was a talented young man, an artist, who would doubtless have been a painter. He was irreproachable, save for being unsociable, home-loving, and pushing timidity to the extent of a generalized phobia. His affection was all the more precious to me. He had written to me often, in the army. Then, one day in June 1918, a letter from his mother had come to notify me of the disaster: missing in action near Dormans during the German advance...and two months later, coming via the Swiss, the final confirmation:

*Died in the Saxon field-hospital at Thiérache (Aisne)...*

I put down my useless fountain-pen and put my head on my hands, over my open books. Those who have lost loved ones know the sacred game that consists in bringing them back to life in front of you, by concentrating all the forces of memory and imagination to create shades that resemble them. This was what I did, on that April evening.

It was then that the old doorbell rang, and I was suddenly standing up, repossessed by a down-to-earth sentiment and placed under the orders of my scientific nature again. At least, I thought so. I thought that existence—my existence as a physician—had abruptly taken hold of me again, and that my evocations of the world beyond the grave were far away. Some client had come in search of me—probably a client from the Saint-Fortunat quarter, since it was the bell connected to the back gate, in the Rue de la Botasse, that was ringing.

I opened the door at the end of the corridor. I stopped on the threshold. The darkness was impenetrable.

"Who's there?" I called across the courtyard.

The silence was heavy.

"Who's there?" I repeated, intrigued.

No one replied from outside, but the bell tinkled softly behind me. Was it the sick person who was ringing in person? Was he unable to speak?

The light in the corridor projected a corridor of light into the courtyard. Rapidly, I went to the gate to the street; the bolts clicked one by one, and the gate creaked on its hinges.

If anyone should read this story some day, that person will already know what was behind that gate, for I am not a novelist skilled at managing his effects but a straightforward man who reports what he sees as he sees it.

For a moment, I was dumbfounded. The apparition stood still, scarcely visible. I was looking at the frightfully pale face of Jean Lebris. His thinness was not of this world; his features seemed fixed in an eternal gravity, and his eyelids appeared to be closed in the final sleep. He was facing me, and he was neither lying down nor leaning against a wall, but standing upright—but I distinguished his body as a shadow within a shadow.

My seizure, as measured by the chronometer, only lasted for a tenth of a second. The phantom whispered: "Is that you, Doctor?"

A stout form, which I had not yet discerned, emerged from the shadows beside him. "Good evening, old chap!" said that form, in a low and joyful voice. "It's me, Noiret. I've brought you Jean Lebris! As surprises go, what do you think of that one?"

"Jean!" I exclaimed, taking the young man's hands. "My dear Jean!"

He smiled blissfully, and we embraced, although I am not much given to effusiveness.

"No noise!" said Jean. "No one must suspect, this evening…Mother mustn't know. You'll tell her tomorrow, won't you, taking precautions…?

Noiret—a friend of ours who lives in Lyon—explained: "I've left my car with the chauffeur at the corner of the Mall. We came by night so that Jean wouldn't be recognized."

"Come in," I said, joyfully.

"No, no—it's not worth the trouble, for me," Noiret insisted. "I'm going back. I've got 92 kilometers to cover."

"I don't know how to thank you..." Jean said to him. He began coughing.

"We have to go inside, Jean! Come on!" While I was speaking, though, I looked at Noiret, performing a mime as expressive as the half-light allowed, touching my eyes pointing at Jean's—which were still closed—and making interrogative movements with my head.

"*Au revoir*, Jean—see you soon!" said Noiret. "Look after yourself...*au revoir* Bare, old chap!" Then, murmuring close to my ear, he let slip the terrible word: "Blind!"

I saw him disappear with a desolate gesture. Meanwhile, utterly confused, with joy and sadness disputing over my thoughts, I took Jean Lebris' arm.

"We've come like thieves," he said, apologetically. "I didn't want to raise my voice to answer you, when you said 'Who's there?' I assume that no one can see or hear us. It's just that, if Mama found out about it all of a sudden...apparently, she believes me to be dead?"

"There are two steps to go up, Jean—be careful. There. To the left now. Here we are in my study. Sit down, and drink a little quinine. You can sleep in the guest-room, and tomorrow, as soon as it's light, I'll go to your mother's house. I'm so happy, Jean!"

"So am I!" he said, radiant with happiness, passing his hand over his forehead.

I examined him in the light. His appearance filled me with anxiety, and I understood how I had been able to hesitate for a little while, in the half-light, before recognizing him as the true and living Jean Lebris. His dry skin, tautly extended over his prominent cheekbones, was colored by the effect of emotion with an excessive brightness. In five years, the illness that I had combated before had run its course freely.

But Jean began to speak, with that slight quivering of the throat which great contentment produces.

"I arrived in Lyon yesterday evening, at my regiment's barracks. I was immediately demobilized. I had someone take me to Noiret's. He told me that you were in Belvoux, that you'd come back in January. Then we planned this nocturnal return. I didn't want to send you a telegram or telephone you, because of Mama. A careless indiscretion might have broken her! Finally, I wanted so desperately to avoid noise, questions, and stories in the newspapers..."

"We'll arrange everything for the best. Don't make yourself anxious, my dear Jean. Be tranquil."

"It was at Strasbourg, you know, that I made contact again...what an adventure! Oh, what an adventure. Just imagine: I'd been abducted—that's the right word—abducted from the German field-hospital! I could no longer see clearly. They took advantage of it. I don't know where I was taken. I was looked after very well. They were doctors, weren't they? People who wanted to experiment with some kind of ophthalmological treatment...except that they didn't keep me informed about anything, and I never went out! It was only that boy—a discontented servant—who told me about our victory, the armistice, the occupation...

"We left one evening, him and me. We were in a railway wagon for hours on end, and he left me on the Kehl Bridge. 'You're on your own,' he said. 'You're in Strasbourg. It's full of French soldiers.' I made myself known...it's curious, isn't it?"

"Curious," I said, "to be sure." But I wasn't thinking about what I was saying. Jean had just opened his eyes and I had been taken completely by surprise. Oh, those eyes! Imagine an antique statue brought to life; imagine a beautiful marble head raising its heavy eyelids upon the uniform orbs of its pupil-less eyes.

"What treatment have you been given?" I asked.

"For my eyes?" He suddenly closed them again. "Oh, bandages, I suppose. I can't tell. No one told me anything. I had the impression that my case had a captivating particularity, and that they were keeping me there to study me...but here I am, cured, and I no longer have any interest for Science."

"Cured, my dear Jean?"

"What I mean is that I don't need to be looked after any longer."

There was a hint of agitation submerged in his words. Before the conversation took a different direction, treating subjects that Jean brought up, there was a brief, rather unexpected silence between us.

We chatted long into the night. We still had a thousand things to tell one another. When I decided to go to bed, we had made no further mention of the blind eyes, nor of what had happened between his disappearance and his return to Belvoux.

Personally, I went to sleep without any difficulty. I don't know how to describe the bizarre and complex state in which I found myself. I was, if you will pardon the expression, a sort of human question mark. And most of all, I thought, with bewilderment, about those statuesque eyes, of which no example had offered itself to my eyes since life had begun to parade its faces of suffering and strangeness before me.

## II. The Revelatory Gesture

Early the next day, I went into the blind man's room. He was coughing in a heart-rending manner; nevertheless, I made no allusion to the state of his health.

I helped him to get dressed—which was easy, because, in spite of his blindness, Jean wasn't awkward. Youth works miracles and, in addition, the poor boy had already grown used to his disability.

I asked him whether he had lost his sight as soon as he was wounded. He told me that he had, and that he had been blind for six months.

"Here are some dark glasses," I said. "I think that you'd do well to put them on right away. It's for the sake of your Mama. Women are so impressionable. I'll go to her house as soon as the hour permits, and I'll come back to fetch you. But...she'll ask me questions, Jean, and I want to be able to tell her everything, in a few words. You see, my dear chap, I don't know how to approach it. Let's be precise. What happened to you? What has been done to you?"

"Exactly what I told you last night."

"Nothing more complete, then? No details? Come on, Jean!"

"No, nothing more." And he continued, in an irritated tone: "I'm desperate for rest and isolation. I want everyone to leave me alone, not worry about me, and not speak to me! I know, damn it! People will regard me as a sort of Lazarus emerged from the tomb. Oh, let me be left in peace, for God's sake!"

I always go straight to the heart of a matter. "Will you let me examine your eyes?" I asked.

"Here we go!" cried Jean, impatiently. "You too! For four days, since I set foot in France, I've had dealings with no one but investigating magistrates! If you knew how the military doctors have already questioned me!"

"Yes, that's true? What did they conclude?"

"Do they know? They think that they're provisional apparatus with which someone has equipped me, something preliminary, preparatory, and that I was rescued before the final operation. Go on, look! Look, if it'll give you any pleasure! But promise me that there won't be any more questions. I'm so tired!"

He opened his eyelids upon his Hermetic eyes, and I brought them fully into the light.

"But what about your eyes—*your own eyes?*" I asked, passionately.

"Destroyed. Enucleated. They were burned by gas from a shell."

"Would you like to take out these...these items for a moment?"

"But I can't! They're fixed in place! You're all the same, you doctors..."

"Fixed? And that doesn't inconvenience you?"

"Not only doesn't it inconvenience me, but I'm certainly much more comfortable since this apparatus has been set in place."

"What! What use are they to you?"

"None, if you like—but they fill a void that I found painful, quite agreeably. Look—the comparison is crude, but they give me a vague impression of well-adjusted molds. And I absolutely forbid anyone to touch them."

"Your obstinacy will do you a bad turn, Jean. That's an unhealthy idea, let me tell you. A foreign body resident in the orbit! Come on, that's not possible. You must feel some inflammation..."

Through my magnifying-glass, however, the eyelids seemed extraordinarily healthy and clean; their blinking kept the crystalline and motionless surface of each item of apparatus moist. The latter was white, tinted with blue. To the naked eye, it seemed perfectly uniform, but the magnification of my lens showed me that it was ribbed by vertical lines. In sum, it resembled a ball of capillary thread, coated with a layer of colorless enamel over which the eyelids slid. The "mold hypothesis" was sustainable, the two balls being unable to have any other function than to maintain the form of the orbital cavities, until some unknown definitive devices   presumably prosthetic instruments, artificial eyes of some new kind—could be inserted therein. But the fact that they were irremovable was what surprised me...and even frightened me.

I paused thoughtfully.

"All right!" I said. "So be it! And these Germans didn't inform you of their intentions. That would have been the least they could do!"

"I don't believe they were Germans. Those people were speaking an unknown language, and I swear to you—make no mistake—that I had no idea where I was."

My amazement was undiminished. "We'll resume this conversation later," I said. "For the moment, I can see Césarine, your old housekeeper, opening the shutters. Madame Lebris is awake…"

"No, we won't resume this conversation. You're a good friend, my dear Bare, but I beg you to let me experience the joy of being here, in my little town, close to Mama and to you, in all its plenitude. No going back! No stories! I'm here, alive; let that suffice. And as for you, the scientist, the researcher, well…." He started laughing, and groped to find my shoulder. "Well, leave me in peace! Go now, my dear friend, and come back soon. And thank you, with all my heart."

That same day, shortly before noon, having done my morning rounds, I was striding back and forth in my study. Jean had been welcomed back into his mother's house with the embraces you can imagine, but the thought of his incredible adventure was aggravating my ignorance.

I like things to be clear. All darkness irritates me. Bulls aim for the red; it's at the bull's-eye that I charge. To set me a puzzle is to place a bowl of soup in front of a starving man. When I feel the truth escaping me, I'm no longer alive.

It's all very well to say "No stories", and "Calm down." Jean Lebris had a right to rest; agreed! But that sequestration, those experimental operations, did all that not merit investigation? Were the French authorities mounting that investigation? It was necessary to clarify the conditions in which Jean Lebris had disappeared from the Saxon field-hospital, to establish responsibility, to exact sanctions, to discover who it was that had cared for him, after their fashion, and to verify whether the young soldier might, if better treated, have retained the use of his eyes. Finally, I confess, my medical curiosity was violently excited, and I would have given a great deal to know the mysterious objective that Jean's abductors had had in mind.

128

I knew from experience about administrative indifference, bureaucracy, piles of paper. They had only to let it lie; soon, there would no longer be any question of doing anything; the guilty parties would remain unpunished and the enigma would remain unsolved. Was it right to sacrifice justice and truth to the inertia—to the cowardice, almost—of a sullen young man? Oh, that misanthropic character, that skittish timidity, that morbid self-effacement—how could they be overcome? How could I triumph over my friend Jean?"

Someone had just opened his bedroom window, and I saw him through the gap in my curtains, groping his way around the familiar furniture. His mother was there, but she soon left him alone.

Jean was holding his brushes, and a palette. Alas! He put them down, sadly.

What would become of him? The Lebris were not rich; that little house constituted the bulk of their wealth. They only occupied the first floor; the ground floor, converted into a shop, was rented to a milliner, and the second floor had been vacant for several months. What future awaited them, in these expensive times, now that she was old and tormented by rheumatism, and he was blind!

But wasn't the future, for him, after a brief delay, the sanitarium?

The slow chime of noon began. My lunch, served, went cold. I was retained there by some confused anomaly…some indefinable contradiction between Jean Lebris' gestures and the fact that he was blind.

I followed his careful comings and goings with my eyes. His hands slid along the mantelpiece, feeling surfaces, making sure of contours. One of them suddenly moved toward his waistcoat pocket, and the gesture that he made was so natural, so normal, that, for the moment, I didn't have any sensation of an incredible phenomenon…

When the last vibration of the church bell died away over the town, though, I was still frozen in the same attitude…

At the last stroke of noon, Jean Lebris, the blind man, had checked his watch and set it right.

## III. The Adorable Fanny

What did it mean?

*Jean is lying,* I thought. *He can see. What! Without eyes? With those inanimate things? Go on! It's mad! I must be mistaken. I saw it wrongly. He took out his watch and he set it right be touching the hands, after raising the glass—nothing's easier; everyone knows where 12 o'clock is on the face of his watch, relative to the circle. But no, though—I was watching attentively... it requires confirmation. Lying? Why? If he really has been provided with visual apparatus, if he carries precious marvels beneath his eyelids for replacing sight, would he be so egotistical, so malevolently stupid, as to hide them?*

To this question an internal voice replied: *Yes.* And it was not without irony that I measured how much less pure and less perfect Jean Lebris appeared to me *now that he was no longer dead.* His return to the world of the living had stripped him of a halo, and I felt incapable of rendering to the living the reverence I had devoted to his memory. Small as his faults were, I recognized them—but the dead are gods.

*On the other hand,* I continued, silently, *there are pretences that the gaze of a physician can surely see through. Feigning blindness isn't easy, and I shan't be deceived by it. It's true that at present, all I have is a vague doubt... but I shall put the matter to the proof!*

Scarcely had I come to this decision than a beam of sunlight came directly into my study. Jean, at the back of his room, had turned toward me. His window was still open. I opened mine noiselessly, and I put a little pocket mirror into the path of the sunbeam. Reflected by the mirror, a tremulous circle played upon the shaded façade, then the wall at the back of the room; it superimposed itself like a mask of light on Jean Lebris' face...

The man did not flinch, nor did his eyes blink.

So? What was I to think?

I was perplexed. The wisest thing was to keep silent until there was something new. In any case, whatever it might be, Jean's secret did not affect his military honor in any way. From the beginning of the war until the end, he had conducted himself valiantly. Having fallen before the eyes of his commanders, in the course of an ordered retreat, he was now among the ranks of the presently demobilized. The peace was about to be signed; he was free—and thank God, I knew enough to be sure that, if his personal exile had been prolonged, it could only have been under duress.

I was obliged to be patient for a fortnight before finding the opportunity that revealed the truth.

The truth! It surpassed everything that my imagination had been able to foresee! Its revelation should have excited me, transported me with enthusiasm and left me confounded, as if I were some humble physician of the Middle Ages to whom the invention of the radiograph or the telegraph had been revealed by anticipation. I certainly can't say that my mind was resistant to dizziness. When I realized the immensity of the discovery, a shiver ran through m entire being…but a man is made as his heart dictates; mine was then palpitating with a nascent love, and nothing could any longer impassion me that was not the adorable Fanny.

Fanny…!

My hand trembles when I write her name. I did not believe that any creature as seductive existed on Earth, and at first I thought that I alone was subject to the attraction of her charms, by virtue of the secret mechanism of affinity. I had lived to the age of 35 without believing in the kind of love of which poets sing. I had passed among the women of my era with my mouth taut and my eye hard, without more than one of them having attracted me, and that one only had to appear to make me her avid and quivering servant. A little later, with as much pride as jealousy, I realized that Fanny had the same effect on everyone else that she had on me, and that her youth exercised a universal empire…

Fanny! Fanny!

It was like a presentiment.

About two weeks after Jean's return, Madame Lebris, justly anxious about her son's health, had asked me to examine him with my stethoscope. We were in the blind man's room. Dusk was falling. I could hear someone walking back and forth above our heads, and the sliding of heavy objects dragged across the floorboards…

"Well?" asked Madame Lebris, when he examination was finished.

"Well," I replied, dissimulating my private opinion, "it's not very serious, but I think mountain air would do him good."

"Never!" cried Jean. "Leave Belvoux! Oh, no! Spring's beginning, and the air here isn't bad. In the autumn, if you insist, we might go to the coast—to Nice or Cannes, for example…"

*In the autumn*, I thought. *Where will you be, my poor Jean, in the autumn?*

"Until then," he continued, "with all due respect, Doctor, we shan't budge, and we'll save up."

What psychologist or diviner could have explained why I was distracted—why, in spite of my grief, in spite of the pathological disaster of which the auscultation had just informed me, the sounds of house-moving hammering the ceiling were echoing in the depths of my being and claiming the better part of my attention?

"Oh, as for saving up…" Madame Lebris took up the thread. "Now that the second floor is let…"

"Time flies, Mama, and 1800 francs isn't very much."

"Ah!" I said. "You've let it?"

"Yes!" exulted the old lady. "We owe it to Maître Puysandieu. He's found us charming tenants—ladies from Lyon…"

"From Arras," Jean corrected. "But they were refugees in Lyon during the war. All their possessions have been destroyed. They were looking for a more rural residence. Puysandieu put advertisements for the apartment in the Lyon newspapers. 1800 francs fully furnished was very reasonable. The ladies came to visit this morning, and stayed. But I can hear from down here that they're modifying the décor. People have their own tastes and ideas!"

"Madame Fontan has gone back to Lyon," said Madame Lebris. "She won't be back until tomorrow, with the trunks. It's Mademoiselle Grive who's rearranging things up there.

"Mademoiselle Grive?" I asked.

"The niece," said Jean. "And Madame Fontan's the aunt. Mademoiselle Grive is the young woman who commands, Madame Fontan the brave woman who obeys. Would you like to meet the child, Bare? Nothing easier—she's dining with us. Mama will invite you, won't you, Mama?"

"Gladly!" said Madame Lebris, manifestly dreading that the leg of mutton might be too modest or the capon too slender.

I found some excuse in order to refuse and left, faithful to the mission that I had given myself—which is to say, without taking any more risks than I had on the preceding days, to find out all I could about the inconceivable blindness of Jean Lebris.

Mademoiselle Grive was coming down the stairs from the second floor in a rush of muslin. I flattened myself against the wall of the landing, gripped by a delightful disturbance, and made an awkward and mechanical bow—and when I found myself back home, it seemed to me that it was by enchantment, and that a magic wand had transported me instantaneously from Madame Lebris' landing to my study...

Fanny, I am nothing but a miserable coward. I have exerted all my strength to efface your charming image from my memory, but in vain; you have marked me with your red hot seal, and I have felt that sweet wound ever since the evening I first saw you, my beloved—since that night I passed in a fever of astonishment and boundless joy, repeating aloud that I was in love, in love, in love! Oh, the exquisite and frightful memory! Fanny! Blonde Fanny, who came down toward me, light and supple, amid the clouds of your hair and your petticoats, as Diana glided toward Endymion…

I love you still, alas!


I saw her again the following day, when I went to see Jean to take him for a walk—for Madame Lebris, being disabled, was unable to serve as her son's guide, and Césarine had other things to do—with the result that I had volunteered to devote one hour a day to Jean Lebris. When my patients did not leave me time and Maître Puysandieu could not take my place, my friend Jean risked going out alone, on a woodland path very familiar to him, whose hedge he felt with the tip of his cane. The woods, in fact, extended behind the Lebris house—and it appeared that it was the neighboring boscage that had decided Mademoiselle Grive to establish herself there for the summer.

I don't know what household matter was responsible for her presence in her landlady's apartment when I arrived there.

Madame Lebris introduced me.

On the previous evening I had scarcely had time to get a look at the young woman. I was still unfamiliar with the beauty of her face and body, the gracefulness of her movements, the velvet gaze of her pearl-grey eyes and the perfume of roses with which she was redolent. Her voice was musical…

I must have gone pale and trembled. I searched within myself for the man I no longer was. I wanted both to run away and never to leave her…

"I've come," I stammered, "for Jean's walk…"

Jean had just gone out. It was late. Thinking that I had broken my promise, he had resigned himself to going without me. Césarine, having taken him to the edge of the wood, came back upstairs.

"You'll soon catch him up," said Madame Lebris. "He'll be so glad!"

"Oh, Madame, why didn't you say anything to me?" said Mademoiselle Grive, reproachfully. "I would have accompanied your son..."

That was said in a tone full of humanity, so simple and so touching that the poor mother had tears in her eyes. And it was said in that tender voice, which seemed to lend to the slightest banal statement the passionate softness of the most tender promise.

I slipped away, my breast in a state of upheaval, intoxicated by happiness. Beautified Nature surrounded me with promises. I had never seen anything as lovely as that path of hectic grass, bordered by verdant embankments. The sun, shining through the young shoots, appeared to be holding a festival in my honor. The florets were only growing, and the little birds were only singing, in order to congratulate me. Spring only reigned because of my love. "I'm happy!" I whispered. "Thank you, daisies; thank you, bullfinches; thank you, thank you, Sun, sky, butterflies...so polite, bravo!" And I bore my heart like a monstrance!

That late afternoon was, however, more summery than spring-like, to tell the truth. A premature heat was cooking the ground, and a monstrous cloud-bank was massed in the southwest, like an enormous mountain of glistening snow.

I went on. Suddenly, as I emerged from my reverie, it occurred to me that Jean Lebris must have been walking with singular rapidity. Or had he gone in another direction? The path forked behind me; was it possible that the blind man had gone the wrong way? No. The path branched to the left, and I knew that Jean was careful to draw his cane along the hedge to the right. That, at least, was what he had told me. All things considered, though, was it necessary to believe him? The incident of the watch obsessed me.

I stopped. Nothing was audible but the rustling of the undergrowth in the stormy calm of the locality and, further away, the muffled murmur of the town. I refrained from calling out; on the contrary, my stratagem was silence. Jean thought he was alone in the midst of the thickets; to creep up on him, spy on him, that was the plan—to wait for him, if necessary, back there at the fork, without making a sound, perhaps even without showing myself…

But I seemed to perceive, in front of me, the hoarse sound of a coughing fit…

I went forward carefully.

The Sun was going down. Beneath the vault of foliage, darkness was gradually falling. A tortoise could have followed me.

Finally, I caught sight of Jean Lebris.

He was sitting on a fallen tree beside the path, which now snaked horizontally through the woods, and he had his back to me.

Slowly, selecting patches of moss in order to place my footfalls thereon, I reached the shelter of a thick bush. There, although I was still behind the walker, I was able to convince myself that he was *examining* something he was holding in his hands. What was it? My position and the increasing gloom prevented me from identifying it. The thing, however, was making a metallic clicking sound as it was handled.

The horizon rumbled. The abusive heat created one of those inhospitable ambiences that astonish and alarm the human body, as if the air were beginning to become unbreathable. I took out my handkerchief to mop my brow; my pocket-knife, slipping out, fell on to a stone.

In response to the noise, Jean Lebris sprang to his feet and turned to face me. "Who's there?" he said, in a cutting voice.

My stupefaction was indescribable. *He was looking at me through the opaque mass of the bush*, and his staring eyes—his large enigmatic eyes—*were shining with a faint gleam!*

I don't know what distressed me more: seeing those two glimmers in that face; being stared at by them in spite of the obstacle that separated me from Jean Lebris; or realizing that the man who was looking at me, and whose friend I was, *did not recognize me!*

"Who are you?" he went on, in a menacing tone. "What do you want? Answer me, or I'll shoot!"

The object he had just been holding was now revealed to me: it was a revolver. He aimed it at me with incontestable precision. Twenty meters, at most, separated us.

Quite deliberately, and not without seriousness, I said: "Doctor Bare! Don't be afraid, Jean."

He made a gesture of annoyance, almost of rage, and put his weapon back in his pocket.

I went closer to him. "My dear Jean," I said to him, affectionately, "you can't remain alone in the company of your secret. You need help. You're afraid of something, and if I can judge from the emotion you've just experienced—which you betrayed involuntarily—and from the radical means you don't hesitate to deploy against intruders, that danger is serious. Don't you think that an ally might be valuable? Do you think that you'll be able, without support, to hide from everyone the...particularity...of which you are...the host? Do you think you'll be able to defend yourself, with your own resources, against the curious and...your enemies? For it was an enemy, wasn't it, that you suspected of being behind that bush?"

After a moment of somber meditation, Jean raised his naked phosphorescent eyes toward me. "My dear Bare," he said, "I give you my word: the only reason for my silence is that I do not want, at any price, to be treated as a phenomenon: as a display-case specimen, a monster that physicians and scientists might pass from one to another..."

"It's not the physician but the friend who is talking to you."

"Give me your word, in your turn..."

"All this shall remain between the two of us, Jean, if that's your wish. It seems to me however, that Science..."

"Leave Science where it is. I know that I don't have much longer to live. Don't protest—the auscultation told you so. Well, I want to end my days, God willing, in tranquility."

"All right. I give you my word of honor that I'll keep your secret."

"When I'm no longer here, you can do as you wish. Until then, let it be understood: you won't tell a living soul about my adventure?"

"That's a promise, Jean."

He closed his eyelids momentarily, to collect himself. The seemed slightly pink, by virtue of their translucency.

## IV. Jean Lebris' Adventure

"The last vision that I perceived," said Jean Lebris. "Yes, Bare, I said 'vision'—you'll understand in due course—the last time I saw the spectacle of things as you see them, solid and colored, was in a marshy field north of Dormans.

"My company was retreating under shell-fire. Behind us, the fields rose up, and the exceedingly close horizon cut across the sky like a wall. In front of us, large trees limited the meadow, forming a patchy wood that extended indefinitely to the right and the left. I assume that a river must have been flowing there.

"We were running, surrounded by whistling sounds and detonations. The big trees were exploding into splinters, their foliage agitated by the wind of projectiles. The shells, falling densely, were making volcanoes spring up everywhere; the brutalized air was jostling us. It was a veritable inferno, in which we heard a mewling in the air, like a legion of invisible enraged cats, scorched and seething—for at such moments, everything seems to be alive.

"Comrades were falling down. Driven by the ancient and obsolete instinct that has survived the invention of heavy artillery, we were hurrying toward the wood. I never got there. Everything leads me to believe that there as a shell-burst behind me. I didn't see anything or feel anything. It was instantaneous oblivion—and I can't tell you how long I remained like that, lying in the long grass.

"I recovered consciousness with the sensation of an extremely painful aching. Immobility appeared to me to be the acme of happiness, and I remained in a state of weakness and torpor for a long time, from the depths of which I heard the cannonade rumbling. Then the sentiment of peril was born in the bosom of my slumber; nature, more and more imperious, enjoined me to shake off the numbness. Perhaps I was gravely wounded; perhaps my blood was running from a wound I could not feel...

"It was pitch dark, No Moon, not a single star. With a superhuman effort, I was able to find my fluid-lighter in my tunic pocket, but before I could make use of it, a terrifying idea crossed my mind: *the cannon are thundering; I can hear the trajectories of the shells overhead; I must, therefore, be in the middle of a battle—and yet, no glimmer of light is illuminating the darkness, one on side or the other.*

"With a flick of my thumb, I turned the flint-wheel of the lighter. No flame. I pinched the wick feverishly. A burn told me that I was blind.

"My eyes were causing me pain, it's true, but my entire body was aching so badly that nothing, until then, had indicated the most badly injured parts of my flesh. I felt myself, like a man in fear of having lost himself. I stood up. I took two steps; my hands recognized one another, finger by finger. I passed them over my face, and felt nothing frightful; my singed moustache, my burned eyelashes...a prickling sensation over my entire face. As for the rest: an unimaginable headache, and that fatigue, tearing at my muscles in every corner of my being.

"But was it really dark? It might be...the grass was covered in dew. It must be morning. The sharp odor of deflagrations hung over the meadow. Groans were audible. I called out to my comrades, by name. No one replied. Then, a breeze having risen, the rusting of the wood allowed me to get my bearings. Free France was that way...

"Suddenly, a dull and continuous drumming noise, about which I could not be mistaken, came from the west. I listened. It was the noise of artillery on the road, a rumble that extended from north to south. The enemy was still advancing! I tried to drag myself toward the wood, on all fours. The task was beyond my strength; even if the meadow hadn't been pock-marked by shell-holes and strewn with cadavers, I wouldn't have reached it. Having emptied my water-bottle without slaking my thirst, I lay down, with my face in the grass, and resigned myself to my fate.

"I remember coming to in a huddle, howling, after having made out some noise or other that had extracted me from stupidity. Indeed, voices were raised; men chatting to one another some distance away. One of them came. They were Germans. I was put on a stretcher and felt myself being carried away. I was placed, along with the stretcher, in an automobile; I lost consciousness again. After some lapse of time, I found myself lying in a bed, with my head swathed in bandages. The cannonade was more distant.

"The pharmaceutical odors, the surrounding murmurs and the noises from outside...

"*A field-hospital*, I thought. Although I had found the strength to cry out in the meadow, I was now too weak to say a word. Occasional questions were asked of me in German to which I could not reply, even though their simplicity permitted me to understand them. I shall not describe for you, one by one, my first impressions of being a blind man and a prisoner. You only need to know the sum, which was this:

"According to my suppositions, I must have reached the field-hospital as night fell. I had been placed, so far as I could tell, in a tent containing a large number of wounded men. From the exterior silence, and from the respiration of those who were asleep, I soon concluded that it was night. A cock chimed the hours. I lost consciousness again. At midnight, I was woken up by whispering. The words *Franzose, Augen* and *Dreitausend Marken* struck my ears. There were two people in conversation. One of them did nothing but acquiesce, repeating *So! So!* at the end of every statement. 'French' and 'eyes' was what I seemed to be understanding—but how did the sum of '3000 marks' arise from that?

" '*Da ist der Kamerad!*' said one of the two voices.

"And, with a frightful accent, someone said to me in French: 'Ow are you, old jap? Ve is goink to take you to nice place. *Also, also*, vill be many kvestion…can't spick at all? *Ach! Sehr gut! Och, Ludwig!'*

"Contentment made the man snigger. In a trice, I was bound and gagged. I was carried away from the bed on a litter. The automobile that received me on this occasion was so quiet this time that only its movement made me aware of its nature and rapidity. I had the impression that the journey lasted several hours. After that, I was embarked in a railway wagon that seemed to me to roll on forever. I've only retained the vaguest memory of all that. Lassitude overwhelmed my body, and indifference numbed my mind. The blast of the shell must have shaken me violently, but it's quite possible that they administered some narcotic substance—for I've forgotten to tell you that the most attentive care was lavished upon me during the journey; expert hands renewed my bandages, I was made to drink drugs with all desirable gentleness and a thousand precautions were taken in my regard. But no one addressed a single word to me, and no one in the wagons spoke at all. A continuous presence watched over me, silent but helpful.

"Where were they taking me? What was the destination of that interminable journey? I can certify, at present, that it was a house lost in a forest—but in what region of central Europe? I don't know, and I doubt that I shall ever know.

"Suddenly, it seemed that I woke up. Understand me: I had the illusion of waking up, after having dreamed the nightmare of the meadow, the shell, the field-hospital and the journey. I was in a small bed. A great calm had succeeded the rolling of the train. Someone was holding my head, and I felt a warmth moving over my eyes. *It's some powerful light*, I said to myself, *whose beam is being moved across one eye and the other. I'm being examined.* People gathered around me were engaged in animated discussion. I found out later that that was their habitual way of talking, and that their impenetrable language—guttural, singsong and accentuated—combined the ardor of debate with a liberal dispensation of exclamations.

Without seeing them, one imagined them gesticulating and grimacing. But that language had a barbarian crudity that puzzled me. Some Balkan dialect? Perhaps. Today, in spite of all the romanticism of the hypothesis, I believe that it was an artificial language, like Volapük[26] or Esperanto. I covered my eyes with my hands.

" 'What do you want?' I asked. 'What are you doing to me? Who are you? Tell me where I am.'

"Two affectionate hands were placed on mine, and the voice of a young man—a reassuring, compassionate, warmly inflected voice—said in impeccable French: 'Don't worry, Monsieur Lebris. This house is a house of science. Consider it, so far as you are concerned, as an ophthalmological clinic. I'm your physician, and—this is not said out of vanity, but to reassure you—I have a certain reputation in these parts.'

" 'But once again, Major, where am I?'

" 'I'm not in the military,' said the stranger, with a smile that I *heard*. 'Call me...call me Doctor Prosope.'[27]

" 'Are you Greek? Turkish? Austrian? Bulgarian?' I asked, with an intuitive anxiety.

---

[26] Volapük [world-speak] was invented by a German Roman Catholic priest, Johann Martin Schleyer, in 1879, after he received a message from God instructing him to invent a universal language; the third conference of Volapük speakers was held in Paris in 1889 but its fashionability declined rapidly thereafter, overtaken even in its own field by Esperanto, and the legacy of Babel continued to hold sway.

[27] Prosope is derived from a Greek term signifying "face." As a chosen pseudonym, it is obviously intended to be meaningful, but it may be worth noting that the names of the story's other major characters also have meaningful resonances; Lebris means "the wreck," Grive "thrush;" Bare is not a French word, but Renard would probably have been familiar with its English meaning.

" 'Science has no fatherland, Monsieur Lebris. What does it matter? Great gods, calm down! I don't know what you're imagining…'

"His strong hand squeezed mine. He added, solemnly: 'In the name of my collaborators here present, I swear to you that, in regard to you, medically speaking, we have only fraternal and helpful intentions. Everything that we can do to help you, to ameliorate your condition, will be done.'

"But I remembered the brutal fashion in which I had been taken out of the field-hospital and, in spite of all the protestations, the clandestine character of the adventure made me shiver. 'Why did your…agents choose me out of all the wounded men back there?'

" 'Your case is one of those in which we're interested.'

" 'My case…it doesn't seem remarkable to me…'

" 'We shall see. Hope, Monsieur Lebris. And let's be friends.'

"My dear Bare, there are tones of voice that are hardly ever deceptive. In truth, did these men not do everything possible to save my sight? And having not been able to conserve it for me, was it not in all the sincerity of an aberration that they judged it…? But let's not get ahead of ourselves.

"I lived in that unknown part of the world for three weeks, treated and cared for admirably. I had a well-aired room. My needs were attended to by furtive and mute servants. Doctor 'Prosope' spent long periods conversing with me, and it was a joy to listen to him, for he saw things from a lofty viewpoint, and he knew such a lot, such a lot…. I had no news of the war, though; the doctor claimed to be uninterested in it, regarding it as a distant event—distant in every respect. And when I asked him to write to my mother to soothe her anxieties, he simply said that it was impossible, for the moment. I have summoned up all my memories, and I don't recall that he ever lied to me…but isn't it the same thing to remain silent, not to reveal certain thoughts? Anyway, what do I know? Who is that man, after all? He had such need of my trust, my acceptance…

"One day, after carrying out his morning tasks, he said to me: 'My poor Lebris, I'm not satisfied. They're not coming along as I'd like, those eyes.'

"I must tell you, Bare, that I expected to remain blind for the rest of my life, and that that announcement had no great impact on me.

" 'The best thing,' Prosope went on, 'would be to relieve you of them. They can only do you harm, in affecting their surroundings. Besides, I wouldn't want to give you false hope, but it seems to me that, one that's done, we can, to some extent, temper your infirmity.'

" 'What are you saying? Once my eyes have gone, it would take a devilishly clever man…'

" 'That depends on what we find behind your eyes. Do you understand? It all depends on the state of the optic nerves. Anyway, we'll talk about it again, Lebris. For the moment, I advise you to have them taken out. The enucleation is necessary, my friend. I insist. We'll operate tomorrow morning, shall we?'

"I consented with a good grace. For some time, my useless eyes had become heavy and excruciating. They seemed to me to have swollen, and that pain had sometimes made me desire what he had just proposed. In the meantime, I repeat, Prosope had inspired trust in me. And the house was so peaceful! Never a scream, never a suspicious noise. During my hours of idleness and nostalgia, when I dreamed of the beautiful France that my eyes would never see again—save for some miracle in which I could scarcely believe—and even when I listened to the sounds of my prison in order to try to divine what was going on there, I could only make out the rumors of work and leisure. Often, machines were operated; the hum of a workshop reached me through the walls—but everything was placid, inoffensive, restful…

"The next day, I no longer had eyes. As I came out of the anesthesia, giving way to an instinctive sadness, Prosope told me with a strange enthusiasm that the operation had been accomplished in the best conditions, and that everything favored the experiment that he had mentioned to me. 'The optic nerves are intact! Let's heal them. Lebris, you were born under a lucky star! You'll be associated with some sensational re-search!'

"He told me that he had no idea whether the experiment in question would be successful. I think he was only hoping for an indicative result, but he had to encourage me. In any case, although I overwhelmed him with questions, I didn't obtain any clarification from him regarding the basis of the enterprise—and you can imagine how many conjectures were crowding my skull! I paused successively at the idea of a graft, then the idea of an optical invention; I sometimes saw myself provided with the eyes of some animal, sometimes in possession of artificial pupils, the works of some optician of genius. But, in whatever fashion, *I saw myself seeing!* Had not Prosope certified the integrity of the optic nerve?

"You will probably think me very credulous, my friend—but if you only knew everything that the little word 'see' implies, for a blind man! Besides isn't that which has been effected even more extraordinary and magnificently pro-digious than artificial sight would be? If you wish, some other day, I'll describe—at least to the extent that I was able to take account of them and remember them—all the preparations to which I was subjected: the various cares, measurements, orbit-al molds and, finally, the presentations of two perfectly smooth objects that were neatly fitted into their lodgments.

"They were taken away almost immediately. Their trial placement had taken place in the presence of several people, who did not hesitate to talk abundantly in their strange gibbe-rish—and that day, it wasn't Prosope who interrogated me with regard to my impressions, but an old man whose shrill voice seemed to emerge from a bird-caller. In French? Natu-rally, but without purity and with all the intonations of the mysterious *Volapük*. I told him that I hadn't experienced any painful sensation by virtue of having the two balls that had just been put into me, and I understood that my reply filled him with satisfaction.

"A few days later, I was put to sleep for the second time. The first time, my nauseous awakening had been accompanied by phenomena with which you're doubtless familiar: dazzling, fulgurance and other tricks determined by the reaction of the optic nerves, since that's their fashion of feeling pain and since their separation had just been effected with my eyes out of use. So, that second time, when the ether vapors began to dissipate and luminosities appeared to me in the form of streaks and blurs, I simply thought that a similar cause was giving rise to analogous effects.

"Gradually, though, as I emerged from the artificial oblivion, my own materiality reappeared to my senses. I felt myself lying down, with my eyes closed, beneath a thick bandage. And yet...

"*No, no!* I said to myself. *I'm not awake! I must, on the contrary, be plunged into the utmost depths of the operational sleep! I'm the victim of a phantasmagoria, and* this...this *can only be the result of the displacement of a pain...of a pain that the anesthesia is preventing me from feeling. It's the nervous repercussion of a surgical action: an injection, or a section, translated into a hallucination! Of course. Aren't my eyes shut? Don't I have a bandage over them?*

"Wrong. I was indisputably awake, conscious, lucid—and in front of me, upright and luminous, I could see a frightful and fantastic creature."

## V. The Marvel

"Imagine," Jean Lebris continued, "a human form constituted by a tangle of a quantity of threads of varying thickness—a sort of incandescent network, shining with violet fire, and reproducing, in its interlacements and aerial ramifications, the flimsy and anatomical appearance of one of our peers. One might have thought it a man constructed like the roots of a luminous tree, a branched man, whose brain made a mass of downy light in my darkness, and whose luminescent spinal cord stretched out like an active Geissler tube.[28]

"The specter moved. To me, it was as if its lines were traced in phosphorus on a blackboard. I noticed a sort of violet nebulosity between them—some of them were as thin as hairs—which, filling the empty spaces, completed the contours of the structure and outlined the mass of an individual.

" 'What am I seeing?' I cried, in horror.

"Then, in the lower part of the face, the phosphorescent threads began to expand and contract; those of the throat were similarly activated, while the brightness of the brain intensified on the left side of the front—and all these filaments glowed with a changing and concentrated light, like embers when one blows on them. The specter leaned over me and spoke.

" 'You can *see?* You can *see?* Lebris, is it really true?'

" 'Yes,' I said, recognizing the voice of Doctor Prosope. I see an unimaginable spectacle, through my eyelids and the layers of the bandage.'

" 'You're sure? Tell me—tell me what you can see…'

"I told him—and I had the supplementary surprise of seeing the thread-man execute a few sliding dance-steps as he spun around. Others might have fallen to their knees to thank the Lord; Prosope, content with Fate, danced the tango.

" 'Please, explain…' I implored.

" 'Soon. Wait a moment. We need to know…'

"I saw the bizarre aspect of Prosope suddenly diminishing and pivoting—the door clicked—changing appearance by an effect of perspective. I heard his footsteps going down the stairs—and I realized that he was moving away through an infinity of vaporous planes and more-or-less discernible

---

[28] A device invented by Heinrich Geissler in 1857, consisting of a glass tube containing a rarefied gas with an electrode at either end, which glowed when supplied with a current. It was the ultimate ancestor of numerous other experimental and practical devices, including modern neon lighting.

frames, which comprised for me a fogbound world, translucent here, transparent there, geometrically transected by vertical lines, partitioned by diaphanous walls and strewn with innumerable haloes.

"At that moment, at the very beginning of my prodigious transformation, the mixture in question was, from my viewpoint, only a very pale chaos, scarcely sensible; and behind those vague traces, colored in variable mauves, the ink-black darkness—the terrible night of blindness—subsisted. It was then that I looked at my own body, and was only able to perceive myself as a sort of monster similar to the one that had just gone away...

"Four forms—four frameworks, four human luminous ramifications—now hastened to my bedside. One of them was hunchbacked. Another was bent and wizened. I distinguished, on the torsos, the almost-imperceptible silhouettes of watches and chains, and other little round shadows, which might, it seemed to me, have been buttons and coins...

"Prosope was recognizable by his height and his vast encephalum. My bandage was removed and I opened my eyelids without any alteration in my sensations. As you can imagine, the idea of radiography came to mind; however, I reminded myself that with radiographic eyes, I would have seen the *skeletons* of people, not their *nervous systems*...

"Prosope, left alone with me, gave me the explanation for which I was waiting. 'Lebris,' he said, 'you asked me just now, with an astonishment tainted with fear, *what you were seeing*. Forgive me if, in order to explain it, I need to remind you of some principles that you already know—but I want everything to be clear.

" 'You know, Lebris, that the eye is connected to the brain by the optic nerve, which transmits to the brain the luminous impressions that the eye has received. You also know that the optic nerve cannot send the brain anything *but* luminous impressions, and no others. Pinch it, and the result is not pain but a sensation of brightness. Let us take note, in passing, of that luminous sensation of a contact, which is nothing other, all things considered than a *vision of touch*.

" 'Any excitation of the optic nerve is, therefore, translated for an individual into luminous manifestations, whether there is an eye at the end of the nerve or not. Consider a man in possession of his eyes. In him, the optic nerve communicates to the brain the indications furnished by the retina. That man has the sensation of images, colors, shadows and brightness; in brief, he perceives all that the eye registers by courtesy of its admirable complexity. Eliminate the eye and excite the nerve directly. No more images, alas, but merely confused luminosities, scarcely expressive, which reveal next to nothing of the external world and only inform the subject of some vague incident.

" 'But what if, instead of the eye, I were to install another organ, and put that organ in communication with the optic nerve? If, for example, I were to replace your eye with an auditory apparatus—or, which comes to the same thing, connect your ear to the optic nerve instead of leaving it connected to the auditory nerve—what would happen? This: your ear would continue to register sounds, but you would perceive those sounds in a luminous form, since that is the only language that the optic nerve is able to speak and transmit. *You would see sounds.* You would no longer hear them; you would have a visual perception of the sonorous world.

" 'Since we have five senses, we can imagine a series of five individuals in various conditions with respect to sight. One, being normal, sees all that is normally visible. Of the others—the four who have undergone operations—the first sees sounds, the second sees odors, the third sees tastes and the fourth, more difficult to imagine because our organs of touch are diffuse, sees contacts.

" 'Now, Lebris, a number of experiments convinced us that these physiological fantasies can be surgically realized, especially with respect to hearing, taste, odor and sight, the last-named sense being taken as the experimental base. Artificially, *everything is visible*, provided that the optic nerve is connected to the relevant organ. Everything: perfumes, pieces of music, varieties of succulence! You might tell me that such a demonstration is merely of speculative interest, almost comical, and that, all things considered, being able to hear with the eye is as unimportant as being able to walk on one's hands—and you'd be right, Lebris. But wait, though.

" 'You're not unaware that the five human senses cannot claim to offer a total perception of matter in its various states. Five senses! Perhaps there would need to be a hundred, perhaps a thousand, to obtain cognizance of everything that exists! Nature is enveloped by a large number of veils. Until now, humans have only been able to lift five of them—those which our cave-dwelling ancestors had already lifted. What do the other veils hide? They hide certain qualities of matter for which we have no perceptive organ, the existence of which reason alone leads us to presume, and the character of which we cannot suspect, because our senses will never perceive them—even indirectly, by echoes or reflections. They also hide certain other qualities for which we likewise do not possess an appropriate sense, but which reveal themselves to us sometimes, in exceptional circumstances, by some visible, odorous or noisy effects—escapes, or escapades, as it were, which bring these things into the domain of sight, odor or hearing...

" 'Certainly, Lebris, it's a fine thing for humans to lift the five veils that we have seized with our trembling hands a little further every day. It's a fine thing for the telephone to augment the acuity of our eardrum so mightily. It's a fine thing for the microscope and the telescope to give us, by turns the eyes of Lilliputians and Giants, and for our gaze to pierce walls by means of the light of X-rays. It's a fine thing, most of all, for the scientific mind to have made up for the inferiority of the senses, and even the absence of sensory organs, by means of intuition and calculation. But think: the man who could endow humankind with a *sixth sense*; the man who could adapt a new organ to the optic nerve, sensitive to vibrations hitherto unperceived, hitherto *imperceptible*, to any other nerve...how would he be rated?

" 'Listen: among the mysterious elements that are to humans what light is to the blind, but which nevertheless reveal their existence occasionally and furtively, in an indirect manner, there is one, Lebris, that is no longer unknowable *for you*. Of that element, which we occasionally distinguish, thanks to exceptional luminous, sonic, tactile, and even olfactory and gustatory manifestations; of that element, which our engineers utilize today without knowing exactly what it is, or how it acts; of that redoubtable, occult, universal element, you alone in all the world, Lebris, can receive a direct impression. I have replaced your eyes with an apparatus that grasps it as the ears grasp sound, as the eye grasps visible light. Personally, I only divine the presence of that element in the sound of thunder and the spark, in the sight of lightning and the odor of ozone, the vibration of a plated bottle, the spectacle of rotating machines and glowing bulbs. *Wherever it may be, you can see ELECTRICITY.*

" 'I have replaced each of your eyes with a much-improved sort of electroscope. They perceive the electrical aspect of the world, and no other—and your optic nerve, naturally, translates that aspect of the world in the form of luminosity.

" 'Note this: instead of putting the electroscope in place of an eye, one could equally well substitute it, let us say, for an ear. One could connect it to the auditory nerve rather than the optic nerve; and then the patient would *hear* the electromagnetic phenomena instead of *seeing* them. To understand why the optical nerve is preferable to all the others, it is sufficient to think for a moment; it is sufficient to remember that sight is our principal sense, and that electricity is much more closely analogous to light than to sound, odor or taste. That's why we asked our friends at the front to send us blind casualties for our experiments. You are only the first, Lebris! The first man who has lifted Nature's sixth veil!'

151

"Doctor Prosope fell silent after pronouncing that emphatic sentence in a proud tone. His victory was carrying him away; I could see his nervous system sparkling with luminescence. For myself, I remained confused. In the first place, it displeased me to play the passive role of a laboratory subject. I was ashamed of it; the man had reduced me to the status of a guinea-pig. If he had made use of a human being instead of an animal it was only because he needed his patient to be able to part his impressions to him. Then, as I've told you, after having accepted my blindness, I had hoped to recover my sight, and the deception left me sad and resentful. I had nothing of the explorer in me, and now I found myself suddenly deprived of my old familiar surroundings and thrown, alone—alone of all humankind—into the heart of unexplored physiological regions! Me, a phenomenon! Jean Lebris, a creature to be exhibited! Oh…!

" 'Don't you have anything to say?' Prosope resumed.

" 'I'd rather have been able to *see*,' I told him, ill-humoredly. "To *see again*, as before. Since you're capable of inventing extraordinary eyes, it would be child's play for you to fabricate ordinary ones, to replicate Nature, to render to the blind the faculty that they so cruelly lack.'

" 'That's a narrow and egotistical view of things—a paltry conception. Can you compare the curing of a disability—a repair—to the extension of human competence? We're not bone-setters, we're pioneers of a greater humanity! Furthermore, Lebris, it's necessary to know that these items of electroscopic apparatus with which you are equipped are, in a fundamental sense, nothing other than eyes. Yes—just now, a mentioned the analogy between light and electricity. The expression is insufficient; light and electricity are identical. What we call 'light' is merely that electricity whose oscillations are rapid enough to influence the retina. That which we call 'electricity' is merely light whose oscillations are too slow for our eye to be able to capture them. We have already produced electric currents of 50 billion oscillations a second; when we succeed in rendering these oscillations 10,000 times more frequent, the luminous waves themselves will be reproduced. Your electroscopes are, in the final analysis, merely *sloweddown eyes.*[29]

" 'You will now understand exactly why we have chosen the optic nerve rather than any other for our experiments One day, perhaps our successors will succeed in creating a complete eye: an eye that is capable of obtaining impressions from the slowest and the most rapid vibrations; an eye that will see both the infra-red rays and the ultra-violet rays, heat as well as electricity; an eye that will finally provide an integral vision of the world. Then there will no longer be any need to distinguish between visible and invisible light; there will no longer be anything but LIGHT. What beauty! If I were to tell you, Lebris, that thanks to you, the first step on that dazzling path has been taken; if I were to add that present-day Science tends to consider electricity as being *matter itself,* the fundamental principle of *everything,* would you not be proud of your mission?"

" 'You ought to have warned me,' I complained. 'I'm a prisoner of war; you've treated me like a slave. Besides, I can hardly see anything.'

" 'Your sight will gradually improve. Be patient. Give me a description, though…I'll take notes.'

" 'It's useless,' I said, firmly. 'I can't see anything.'

" 'What! What do you take me for, Lebris?'

" 'I can't see anything,' I repeated. 'You're mistaken, my dear chap. You've grossly abused my misfortune and my situation. I consider you and your accomplices to be scoundrels.

---

[29] This is, unfortunately, incorrect; electricity is not a form of electromagnetic radiation, being composed of electrons and not of photons. Renard's knowledge of physics seems to have been somewhat behind the times—perhaps forgivably, given that he had just spent more than four years fighting in the Great War. Prosope's subsequent elaboration of the notion is confused by the mistake. For further comments on the scientific foundations of the story, see the afterword to this volume.

One does not treat a free man, a French citizen, in this way. Wasted effort! You shall know nothing. Ah, these gentlemen carry our experiments on their fellows! Well, know this: I shall say no more than the poor dog that you would have lashed to a board and doctored with thrusts of the scalpel. I can't see anything, I tell you!'

" 'But Lebris, you're insane! My friend! Come on! We've involved you in our noble work, and...'

" 'Enough! Enough hypocrisy! Leave me my electroscopic eyes or remove them, but I demand that you have me taken immediately to a camp for French prisoners. Everything that is happening here is a violation of human rights!'

" 'No, no,' said the doctor, with irritating calmness. 'You won't leave us that way. You'll never leave...'

" 'I beg your pardon?'

" 'We need you. I hoped that you would be intelligent enough to put the love of Science above everything else. I hoped that the joy of no longer being blind, in the proper sense of the term, and the intoxication of new spectacles, would compensate you for the annoyance of a sedentary existence...'

" 'I shall never tell you what I see!' I proclaimed.

" 'Yes you will—in time.'

" 'You can torture me...'

" 'Oh, nonsense, Lebris! What do you take me for? We shall always treat you with the respect due to your remarkable ability...'

" 'But after all, you will surely have other subjects than me, in the same condition!'

" 'Quite probably. We shall never have enough of them. Come on, Lebris, don't get hysterical! Know that you're dead to the entire world. Your mother knows—or soon will—that her son has given his life for his country. There must have been a mix-up at the field-hospital; a nurse has misread a label. You, who cherish tranquility, will be quite happy with us.'

"I trembled with anger. 'Filthy Boche! Filthy Boche! You shan't know anything!'

"The other began to laugh, which gave his nervous system a macabre dancing appearance. 'But I'm not a Boche!' he protested. 'Ah, that's interesting! Let's make a note of that.'

"What was 'interesting' is that the electroscopes did not prevent me from weeping."

## VI. The Doctored Man's Escape

While Jean Lebris was telling me about his prodigious adventure, the darkness had become intense, and, the electrical tension being maintained, the narrator's eyes formed two cold clear-cut patches of brightness in the fluid shadows.

"Your mother will be getting worried," I told him. "Let's go. Does the gloom weaken your vision?"

"Not at all! Day and night are no longer, for me, anything but an almost inexpressible alteration in shade. Are you coming?"

He was the one who guided me, for, with my eyes designed for visible light, I could not see anything at all.

"Then you were putting on an act for me, my dear Jean, when you groped…"

"Oh! Yes and no. In certain atmospheric conditions, I'm far from being as perspicacious as I am this evening. Dry weather is, for me, gloomy weather, and fog is singularly favorable to my perception. I confess, though, that I've sometimes dissimulated…" He hesitated, but then said, not without confusion: "Let's leave it at that. I'll pick up the thread of my story. While we're walking, if you don't mind."

If I didn't mind!

"I stopped at that fit of angry resentment. To stem my tears, I rotated my fists furiously in my accursed eyes, and pressed down on them without any precaution to such an extent that Prosope warned me about my imprudence. By rubbing myself like that I risked compromising his work. The operation was too recent…

"He was right. My unconsidered friction had upset something, put some minute concordance out of order. Now instead

155

of seeing one spectral Prosope, I saw two of them, which over-lapped. My electroscopes had acquired a squint!

"That incident cooled my excitement, and I became conscious of the relative good fortune of which I was the constrained and forced beneficiary. The idea of losing that sort of second sight, that replaced faculty, was painful to me. But the consciousness of my dignity kept me from telling Prosope what had just happened and asking for his help. I hoped that the strabismus would pass—which, fortunately, it did. A few hours later, the conjugation of the two electroscopes re-established itself of its own accord.

"The war-weary Prosope having abandoned me to my foul mood, I had the leisure to contemplate the new face that the old world offered me. At that moment, by comparison with what is displayed to me today, I really could see very little, and poorly. You need to understand that, since their insertion into my orbits and their incorporation into my organism, my scientific eyes have not ceased acquiring more penetration. Thus that evening, the background of the scene was still obscure. It bore a slight resemblance to the nocturnal illumination of a festival, when the houses spread streaks of fire through the darkness and one sees their mass merely as a glimmer. Then again, I had not yet acquired a sense of perspective, a notion of depth. All the lines seemed to me to be equally distant, situated in a single vertical plane, as if traced on a blackboard; and as the new appearances of things made them new things for me, sometimes unrecognizable, I was initially only able to discern their apparent greatness or smallness, without being able to reach any conclusion as to their authentic inequality or their respective remoteness.

"However, minimal as the electrical world still was, from my viewpoint, it nevertheless constituted an *obligatory* luminous spectacle. I did not have the means of separating myself from it by lowering my eyelids upon it; the electromagnetic radiation went through them! I was condemned to see those inexorable fires incessantly before me, shaded by darkenings and brightenings that rendered their perception even more tiring. To put it another way, I was condemned never to sleep again! And that provided the means by which that devil Prosope came to a reckoning with my obstinacy. He vanquished me by means of sleep.

"After three days of insomnia, the phantasmagoria of lights having, perhaps, tripled. Prosope sold me, in exchange for a promise to talk, a pair of compact goggles. They were made by superimposing various insulators which, each one fulfilling its particular task, ultimately intercepted all the radiations. First, I slept; then, true to my word, I talked.

" 'No more blackness now. A general illumination. A degraded illumination, with zones that are alternately bright or twilit. A universal luminosity, eternally undulating and vibrating, whose color passes from the sharpest blue to the most acidic red, through the intermediary of all the violets imaginable.'

"In truth, the violet was almost uniquely sovereign, but red was dominant in the sky and blue on the ground. There was a perpetual exchange between them, a coming-and-going of effluvia, and in the air there was a continual propagation of immense wrinkles, which flowed and intersected indefatigably, while gigantic haloes formed limitless patches there, quivering with centrifugal vibrations. The nucleus of one of them appeared to me *below* the horizon, through the translucent thickness of the terrestrial sphere, like a sapphire hearth in which a fire was lit, and my electroscopes had an extraordinary tendency to turn toward it.

" 'It's the magnetic pole,' Prosope told me, 'and the other haloes are electromagnetic fields. But what is there beneath your feet, Lebris?'

" 'The floors of the house; planes scarcely tinted, sheets of violet light. Someone's lying in the room below...'

" 'What about further down—the Earth, the planet...'

" 'An abyss in which mists quiver, in which denser points emit brighter light...the surface, especially, concentrates the fluid.'

" 'Undoubtedly. And around us—the forest?'

" 'A pale moss, the color of peach-flower, almost un-graspable...ah! The moss is lighting up, sparkling, moving, becoming clearer...it's the wind rising, isn't it? Everything's glowing softly. Phosphorescent plumes are following one another along the walls. The very air is filled with streaks. I can see the wind!'

" 'And when I move my own body?'

" 'Everything that moves surrounds itself with an ephemera flame, and leaves a brief broken wake, a gleaming fringe...'

" 'In front of us...?'

" 'I see a building. Lilac transparency. The angles and corners are much more accentuated than the rest. Admirable azure sprays are escaping from the pointed gables, and the lightning-conductor is giving off an inexhaustible fountain of bluish sparks. All that blue and all that red are perpetually melting into violet, and the violet is constantly busy in dissociating itself into red and blue. That's what produces those eternal fluctuations. Eh? What are you doing? Your hair is catching fire!'

" 'I merely passed my hand through it.'

"On another occasion, Bare, I'll describe to you everything that I described to Prosope and all the observations he made by means of my intermediation. I'll tell you about the various transparencies of bodies, proportional to their conductivity; how certain metals are crystalline to me, although the thinnest glass is often opaque, to the extent that I can sometimes see the hands of my watch more clearly through the entire mechanism than through the glass! I'll tell you about the electromagnetic aureoles with which we are surrounded, as if each of us were, in his tangible being, merely the nucleus of a field of radiations—with the result that, at any moment, our being may be confused with another or influence it. I'll tell you...but we're getting close to Belvoux, and I want to tell you the story of my escape. It was a month ago, to the day...

"I was overwhelmed by depression. My seclusion seemed like a kind of death, and I had lost all hope of every resuming my place among the living. The house in which I was detained was in the middle of a vast deserted region. I had known for a long time that the majority of its occupants never went out. Imagine being in a crystal castle—crystal colored in various shades of amethyst—and that's almost what it was like. The slightest electrical phenomenon made an impression on my sight through the walls.

"Now, every object contains its dose of electricity, every action gives rise to a current; that permitted me to glimpse, at intervals, an automobile arriving and departing, securing a link between the solitary château and an agglomeration of luminous points that I estimated to be very distant—for I had acquired a sense of distance. The automobile penetrated in the heart of the buildings by way of a corridor bordered with high walls—which, continuing all around the grounds, provided it with an insurmountable barrier, supplemented externally by a moat full of water. That is, at least, what I was able to infer, after much contemplation and research, from the height of my cell or during the hygienic walks that Prosope made me take in the courtyard of his fortress.

"It was impossible to escape the surveillance of my guardians. It was impossible to force the bolts on my door. To leap out of the window would have been suicide. I knew everything about my prison that my senses could teach me, and nothing gave me any hope of salvation. My servant remained mute. The others were strangers to me.

"One night, when universal immobility facilitated the work, I counted the inhabitants of the place. There were 30 of us—a number that I believed to be broken down thus: 12 invalids or patients; eight physicians or engineers; and ten domestics, nurses and electricians. The silence was only disturbed by the muffled hum of dynamos. Lodged in the basement, they produced fiery sparks that dazzled me like artificial sunbursts. They sent forth the fluid compressed in heir resplendent accumulators; they launched it into the distance in a spidery web of circuits; and every evening, when the lights were switched on, the conductive wires built the paradoxical edifice of their slender incandescence around me…"

"Forgive me for interrupting, Jean, but tell me: does an illuminated electric lamp appear more or less luminous to you than an electric wire through which a current invisible to our eyes is passing?"

"Remember what I told you about day and night. They're merely shades. I'll continue…

"One morning last month, the customary silence was disturbed by the unusual rumor of an altercation, and I distinguished two human forms standing face to face in the room next to mine. The taller one was Prosope. The smaller, with the unequally developed cerebellum, was my appointed servant. The two men were hurling abuse at one another. The wall must have been an excellent muffler because, in spite of the short distance separating us, I could only perceive confused snatches. By their attitudes and their gestures, and the flamboyances running through their nerves, however, I understood that the quarrel was violent—and the little man's heart was beating with a characteristic precipitation.

"Prosope, although much calmer, struck him in the face with his fist and knocked him down. I saw the slim specter get us and leave the room, with his head bowed, but so iridescent that he seemed to be bristling with light.

"It was lunch-time. Soon, the servant slid back the bolts on my door and spread the elements of my meal on the table with his habitual meticulousness. I had often spoken to him, but in vain. This time, he replied, and I'm damned if I ever heard anyone jabbering French in a more Chinese fashion. I won't try to imitate him. He was furious. Knowing that he would find me a sympathetic and discreet listener, he poured out his rancor, heaping the worst insults imaginable upon Prosope. The reason for their argument was trivial, but I judged the opportunity to be propitious. Without procrastinating, I proposed that he run away with me. He opposed me solely because he, too, was Prosope's prisoner.

" 'Don't you have keys to the house?'

" 'The keys? No problem—but to get out of here'—I'm translating his unbelievable gobbledygook—'there's no practicable route other than the broad corridor between the walls. The locked gate? No problem—but the paving-stones in the corridor aren't all paving-stones! Some of them are electric contacts hidden among the floor-tiles. Anyone who touches them with his foot falls down dead, electrocuted!'

"That explained a peculiarity that puzzled me greatly. I looked down, with a smile, at the floor-tiles of the corridor, the cunning marquetry in which the contacts, hidden from all other eyes, encased sparse luminescences so far as mine were concerned, as easily avoidable as gold plates.

" 'There's only one gate at the end of the corridor,' I remarked.

" 'Yes, at the entrance to the bridge. A child could climb over it—but the corridor! They cut off the current when the automobile comes in or goes out, but the doctor is on his guard these days.'

" 'We'll leave tonight,' I decided.

" 'What about the electric contacts?'

" 'I'll deal with them. Come to find me when everyone else is asleep. I'll take you as far as the gate. After that…'

The supposed Chinaman, overwhelmed by amazement and veneration, kissed my hands. 'Where is this place?' I asked him, releasing myself.

" 'Don't ask me, Lord,' he replied, 'As to where we are, I've sworn never to say. As for escaping, that's something else. I'm at your disposal. I'll take you to the nearest town. I've got money. If you wish, I'll accompany you to the border of your own country. Get me through the corridor and I'll swear an oath to you to deliver you into the hands of your compatriots. Then I'll leave you. Don't ask anything more. I've sworn an oath.'

"Nothing got in the way of our nocturnal flight. The little Asian had an incomparable dexterity in manipulating locks soundlessly. The château, padded like a dentist's office, had a strange muffling power. Prosope, sure of his domestics, was fast asleep—I could see him in his room! There were no guard-dogs or sentries. Finally, it was raining gently, about which I was by no means complaining, as things appear much clearer to me when it's humid. The corridor was negotiated without difficulty, the gate scaled, and we walked for five hours toward the agglomeration of luminous points that I had already located. It was the town.

"My companion said to me: 'If we can catch a train at daybreak, all will be well.' And he added, with an exotic laugh: 'The doctors back there will be asleep for a long time— at least until tomorrow evening. I also have the keys to the pharmacy...'

"*It's Heaven that has sent me this little demon!* I thought. He didn't want to tell me his name or his nationality; I learned nothing from him about the mysterious doctors...that, too, remained a secret to be disentangled. We hurried. The night wore on. Through the diaphanous mass of our globe I followed the Sun's progress with my eyes. To me, it was like a reddish-violet disk among the stars behind the blue fog, the source of a formidable radiance. When it passed the horizon, we were huddled in a narrow railway compartment, crammed with travelers whose unintelligible language did not enlighten me as to their nationality.

"What point is there in describing the fatigues and vicissitudes of that trans-European journey? Toward evening, at the hour when the man I call Prosope was presumably waking up in his château-clinic, we reached the German-speaking countries. To ask questions knowing, as I did, only a few Teutonic words, would have been to call attention to myself and annoy my savior, who had not asked anything of me except to say nothing and *not to try to discover anything.* I therefore limited myself, as I had done until then, to remembering names and noting the configuration of mountains or monumental structures, in order to research them at a later date. Bah! For what purpose? In the morning, the word *Regensburg* struck my ears. We were then traveling on an express along a river as wide as a strait. I then heard *Nuremburg* and *Karlsruhe.* At the Kehl

Bridge, in spite of all my efforts, the Asian slipped away. I crossed the Rhine thanks to a convoy of trucks laden with armaments surrendered to the Allies.

"Then there were all sorts of medical examinations and military interrogations, which I got through by mixing a great many lies with a few truths. You know the rest. Officially, my adventure is closed. I'd like to believe that it's *really* over, but it seems prudent to me always to carry a revolver—and I confess to you, my dear Bare, that your surreptitious presence behind that bush a little while ago gave me a fright."

Jean fell silent and came to a halt. We had arrived. At the other end of the garden, its open windows illuminated, the Lebris house loomed up in the darkness.

"It's very late!" I said.

"Yes," Jean replied, pointing to one place and then another in the grass with the end of his cane. "Look, there's the Sun! And there's the Southern Cross! I'm the first person to have seen it without leaving the northern hemisphere!"

Then having taken them out of his pocket, he put on Doctor Prosope's famous goggles, which, fitted to the surrounds of his eyes like those of an automobilist, completely eclipsed all phosphorescence. One might have taken those opaque lenses for smoked-glass spectacles, and nothing discouraged the assumption that Jean had to wear them from time to time, following the prescription of an oculist.

"Now it's necessary for me to be led," he said. "I'm blind!"

I guided his steps. We went up the stairs—but once he was home, I stayed there for a while, with my hand on the banister, searching with childish fervor for some invented pretext that would permit me to go up to the second floor and see Mademoiselle Grive again, if only for a moment. My heart was beating so strongly that I could hear it. The sound of voices from above rendered me as happy as a schoolboy...

Suddenly, it occurred to me that the extraordinary blind man might perhaps be watching me through the wall, and I went away, meditating on the prodigy that he had revealed to me.

## VII. The Gymkhana

This is the first time that I have set out to write a story. I've just re-read the preceding pages, and I'm amazed that I've carried out my task so badly. I wanted to compose a simple and brief photographic narrative. In spite of that, I've extended myself complacently, sometimes with regard to my amorous desires, sometimes in relation to the prodigy of the sixth sense. However, I should only open my heart to the extent required by the clarity of the story, and it would not be appropriate to talk here about Foucault currents, self-induction and hysteresis, for my technical report contains everything that Jean Lebris was able to make known to me about those subjects with the aid of his electroscopic eyes. From now on, I shall attempt to stick more closely to my brief.

The weeks that followed Jean Lebris' confession left me with the memory of a singularly busy and full period. Love, friendship, devotion to the sick man, scientific curiosity—I had more than one reason to associate myself with the lives of my neighbors. So, within a few days, we had become inseparable—but I recall how difficult it was for me to divide my assiduities equally and to hide the homage of an incessantly-growing passion under the appearance of banal gallantry.

Madame Fontan and Mademoiselle Lebris, gripped by a mutual affection, were hardly ever apart. Fanny, who was free of all constraint, as avid for activity as for charity, and always ready for generosity and pleasure, divided her time between the blind man, sport and the excursions that we organized. All door opened to her gracefulness, her good humor and her misfortune, however; numerous invitations were not long delayed in assailing her. She yielded to them.

Now, it's necessary to know that Belvoux becomes a very fashionable location in summer, because of the country houses and châteaux in its vicinity. On Sundays, the exit from mass assembles all sorts of elegance, and the row of parked cars stretches as far as the main square. Personally, being something of a sportsman and by no means scornful of the joys of the era, I've always frequented that fine society—in which I retain some small status as a scrupulous physician, capable of doing my bit at a bridge table or in front of a tennis net—without any hesitation.

Mademoiselle Grive was a sensation. She was invited everywhere.

I made no complaint about that. Most of the time, Madame Fontan remained at home in her niece's absence, with the effect that Fanny and I often found ourselves alone at gatherings, resulting in a sort of intimacy whose sensation was most welcome to me.

As for Jean Lebris, needless to say, he avoided every occasion that might belie his unsociability like the plague. To break down his shyness to the profit of the charming refugee, it required nothing less than Fanny's irresistible seduction, her obliging generosity, her communicative vivacity, and the 'fellow feeling' that is so exquisite in a young woman endowed with such brilliance. He loved the voice of his reader, the gentility emanating from his guide. Disabled and depressed, however, he always rejected our offers when we talked about taking him to some small party or other.

In spite of the violence of the love that overwhelmed me, Jean Lebris retained an important place in my life. I looked after him with all my heart and all my knowledge, and his gratitude was manifest in the willingness with which he lent himself to my experimental studies.

As will be seen in my report, I employed Jean Lebris for several ends, as follows.

I made use of his intermediation to observe electromagnetic phenomena visually, one after another. My previous studies had not made a specialist in electricity of me, but I obtained the most recent books and purchased a good deal of apparatus. On the pretext of self-education, I obtained authorization to visit, in company with Jean Lebris, the dynamos and transformers of the hydroelectric plant at Saône. Eventually, with the aid of his memory, we were able to replicate, or very nearly, the experiments carried out by Doctor Prosope.

Jean's collaboration was no less precious to me in the exercise of my profession. Placed in the room next to my consulting-room, he distinguished through the wall the nervous systems of certain patients whose nervous systems I thought it worthwhile to submit to electroscopic examination, and more than one was cured, thanks to the indications I obtained by that means.

Finally, I must be careful not to omit the psychophysiological experiments in which I employed that admirable spectator of the functioning of the mind. Here, though, the results were mediocre, the mechanism being entirely unknown, very delicate and complicated. To obtain more success, to overcome the rapidity and the smallness of the phenomena, it would be necessary to possess some instrument that would be, relative to Jean Lebris' electroscopes, what magnifying glasses are in relation to our eyes.

Unfortunately, I was forced to limit my endeavors to the utilization of the scientific observer, without being able to extend them to the captivating study of the eye itself. On that matter, Jean was always unshakable, rebelling against any attempted investigation. "When I'm dead," he repeated. "When I'm dead, you'll have all the latitude…"

That sentence was so painful to me that I eventually abandoned my persistence. Besides, the artificial eyes were difficult to access. There was only one sure means…but I'll talk about that later.

Thus, with my mind content and my heart feverish with hope, I lived intensely for weeks on end, sometimes forgetting, in my egotism, that Jean Lebris' days were numbered, and forgetting just as easily that he was enjoying life, and that his thin face was illuminated by a happiness that nothing seemed to disturb—not the inexorable approach of the end, nor the privation of true sight, nor the menacing existence of the terrible Prosope.

The latter, moreover, offered no reminder of his existence. An attentive surveillance, although suspicious, procured
me no evidence of the slightest danger. The mysterious doctors, rebuffed by the difficulties of the enterprise, or perhaps
confident of Jean's mutism, seemed to have reconciled themselves to his flight. Besides, our precautions never relaxed, in
the sense that Jean was always armed, and never went out
alone, and that my vigilance, by virtue of becoming habitual,
was no less that might be expected of a policeman.

Until Baron d'Arcet's gymkhana, no incident worthy of
note transpired. Even the episode that I am about to describe
was a sentimental occurrence, which remained personal to me
and passed unperceived.

If God exists, God is my witness, Fanny, that I had no
more intention of declaring my love for you on that day than
any other. Oh, I certainly sensed that the moment was approaching. I certainly felt that everything was encouraging me
to love you: your contented glances, your friendly smiles, the
joys and disappointments that I saw passing over your face...a
thousand things, a thousand trivia. Everything! But that was so
good in itself! And then, deep down, yes: I was afraid. At my
age, one already knows so many sad stories...one has already
seen so many lovers go cruelly astray!

That gymkhana was in my destiny.

Do you remember what a fine day it was? It was Sunday
the first of September. The entire population of Belvoux had
set off for the Château d'Arcet. The three kilometer route was
thronged with pedestrians. You had come in the La Helleries'
limousine; I had overtaken you, in my sports car, in Chau-
four...

And the main attraction of the gymkhana, the automobile
race—do you remember that, Fanny?

There were seven competitors, each accompanied by a
young woman. I was sure in advance that you would decline
the offers of the other six in order to come and sit next to me,
behind the windscreen of my roadster. What joy you gave me,
however, in answering my certainty!

There were seven of us, who had to struggle at low speed, jousting skillfully through a labyrinth of skittles, maintain our equilibrium on a swaying bridge like a tightrope-walker, design figures and move in reverse, then race against the clock going back and forth ten times along a hundred-meter track...

I can still see the noble esplanade of the château. I can hear the acclamations that greeted my modest victory. We were covered with flowers. As I went back to the car park, I understood that the public sympathy enveloped both of us, bringing us together. I read one unanimous thought on all the faces. It said: "What a handsome couple!" as we passed by. A sagacious enthusiasm betrothed us...

You were divinely pretty; you had colored cheeks, sparkling eyes. You let all the pleasure you took in that petty triumph show. It was mingled with a slight nervousness, the sporting tourney having had its moments of vertigo, clenched fists, anxiety...it seemed to me that I had won two prizes instead of one!

Our friends, politely complicit, affectionate and merry, made us come back together in my roadster full of roses. A spontaneous conspiracy had been contrived. One could have sworn that our destiny had just become apparent to everyone, and that everyone wanted to contribute to its advent.

We glided smoothly over the shady road. The windscreen, in its garlanded frame, reflected your clouded image for me. On the pretext of avoiding the dust of other vehicles, I took a side road. Someone told me that we were seen from afar, speeding through the fields like a bush escaped from a rose-garden. Soon, we were out of sight.

Then I took your naked hand and, as you let it remain in mine, I raised it to my lips...where I had no need to support it.

You loved me! Oh, there was a God, that day!

You looked at me. I shivered. Our silence was tantamount to a promise. A few minutes later, I said to you: "Would you like to get married next month?"

Awakening abruptly, you exclaimed; "Oh! No—we can't…"

I was astonished. "Why not? We're free. What's the point of waiting? And then, you see, I'd so much like Jean Lebris to be still here!"

"Jean Lebris!" you said. "But it's precisely because of him…"

You looked at me with a surprised expression, and I interrogated you with a fearful gaze.

"I thought…I thought that we shouldn't say anything to him," you murmured, your eyes lowered.

A thunderbolt fell upon me. I must have gone frightfully pale. You seized my hand again, saying: "My love, be patient until the end. I think you've realized…the poor boy would be so unhappy! Oh, don't suppose that he has confessed it to me…no! But I've understood correctly. Can I break his heart? Can I make him suffer, when he will soon be leaving us? Alas, my love, you were fearful yourself just now that Jean Lebris might no longer be here in two months to witness our marriage. So it's necessary to wait, isn't it?"

"Yes," I replied. "We'll wait. That's all right. That's only right. You're the best…I admire you. I love you."

"I love you too," you said to me, slowly.

The blood returned to my face.

We went back, hand in hand. At every instant, I looked at you as one breathes the scent of a flower. The roses, of which you were one, perfumed our privacy. Some left their petals behind us, stripped by the wind of the car's velocity.

## VIII. Radiography

I was bad-tempered and depressed. And I was resentful. So, ever since my debut in the role of lover, I had experienced the traditional blindness! Jean was in love with Fanny, and I, who lived so close to them, had not noticed anything! But was it really possible? What if, after all, Fanny were mistaken? She might have misinterpreted Jean's gentleness. The timid boy was tender, affectionate; his friendship, his most platonic inclinations, were expressed in kind attentions that an adulated young woman might believe to be inspired by other sentiments...

I interrogated my memories, studying the past like an examining magistrate—and then a multitude of facts became apparent...

For several days, I spied on the behavior of the blind man and—shamefully—Fanny.

She was right. We had to wait. We had to remain silent.

"When I'm dead!" Now, Jean Lebris' sinister words had a double meaning. The completion of that funereal term would permit me both to learn Prosope's secret and marry Fanny Grive. A strange chance accumulated consolations in advance around the death of my friend Jean.

There is no doubt that, from the moment of that discovery, I put an unparalleled obstinacy into the prolongation of his life to its utmost limit. I have nothing with which to reproach myself on that score, thank God! And if I am tormented by some remorse today, it's not for having failed in my most sacred duty...

It is only for having not always resisted the need to separate them: *her* and *him*.

Sometimes, in fact, an intolerable anxiety gripped me. In spite of all the proofs of affection that Fanny lavished upon me in secret, I nurtured the dull anguish of jealousy. I was ready to fear Jean's diaphanous beauty, his touching youth, the nuanced delicacy of his sensitive soul, the all-powerful attraction of pity, the contagion of love and even that particular ardor which is the prerogative of consumptives. To know that they were together exasperated me; in addition, though, I was now reluctant to be a third party to their conversations—for the sight of the two young people side by side irritated me like a sarcasm, and, even though I was ordinarily in command of my attitudes, even though my face was accustomed to obey me, I feared that Jean Lebris—who could see emotions setting fire to our nerves as the rest of us see them setting complexions alight—might perceive my anxiety. Finally, I found it difficult to bear the thought of my fiancée being exposed to the indiscretion of those scientific eyes.

In consequence, I multiplied opportunities to be alone with Fanny, and I dragged Jean Lebris into a precipitate series of experiments which obliged him to spend a great deal of time under my roof. By virtue of that, Science gained a number of observations on alternating current, induction and the localization of intellectual centers, but I must admit that Jean Lebris lent himself to the exigencies that so often deprived him of the pleasure of Fanny's company with an ill grace. When he protested, I appealed to his patriotism, representing each of our acquisitions as a national enrichment; he relented in his grumbling, yielding joylessly, and we resumed our work, which was limited only by the requirements of his health.

Toward the end of September, that inspired me with considerable alarm. It was necessary to space out the experiments, which became more exhausting as the finesse of the sixth sense increased incessantly. On the other hand, after a serious auscultation, it seemed to me indispensable to take an X-ray of my friend.

In spite of my objurgations, Jean Lebris had so far refused to do that, denying that it could be useful for any other purpose than allowing me to perceive the structure of his electroscopic eyes. "I can see you coming!" he told me. "Your ruse sticks out a mile. Remember what you promised me? If I start to give in, after this sitting you'll impose another, and I'll turn into a laboratory animal!"

I told him forcefully that there was to be no more beating about the bush, that I no longer had the right to give in to his caprices and that it was necessary to let himself be X-rayed, under penalty of the most serious consequences. I added, on my honor, that scientific curiosity played no part in my motivation and that, niggardly as his suspicions were, I would nevertheless respect them, swearing to him that, if he so desired, I would limit the radioscopy to the examination of his lungs, and not repeat the operation unless it became absolutely necessary.

"It's a matter of life and death," I continued.

"It's a matter of a few weeks more of less," Jeans rectified. "Oh, don't think that life is so burdensome to me that its duration is a matter of indifference! Life is beautiful—and I've never found it more delightful than it is at present…" He continued seriously, as if in a dream: "For some time now, life has been an authentic celebration for me."

"Well, then?" I queried, controlling my voice and my nerves.

He placed his hand on my arm. "It's just that I don't have any right to this happiness, you see. I don't have the right to interrupt the living in their lives, to hold them back in their own journey to Happiness. I'm granting myself, at this moment, an unexpected luxury—I'll be forgiven, I hope—but it's necessary that it doesn't last long. Let me go at my natural hour, Bare. To surpass it would be, on my part, an…indelicacy…an abuse—I might even say: a crime."

"I don't know what you mean," I said, hoarsely. "I don't know anyone who isn't steadfast in wanting you to get better. Personally, I beg you in the name of *all* those who are dear to you to let yourself be X-rayed."

He shook his head. "No," he said. "Let's not mention it again."

I had the intuition that there was only one influence sufficiently powerful to make him alter his decision. That same day, while playing tennis at the Brissots', I told Fanny Grive what had happened.

"He'll certainly expect me to have had recourse to your influence," I told her, "but the important thing is to convince him, for I believe that he's very ill."

Then I told her about the grounds on which Jean Lebris had based his refusal—while keeping quiet, of course, about everything concerning the electroscopic eyes.

It seemed to me that she paled slightly.

I had only come to the Brissots' to meet her and talk to her privately. We were walking along a pathway in the grounds, shielded from all gazes. "Fanny!" I exclaimed, on seeing her go pale. And I stared at her anxiously, bitten by hideous jealousy.

Without raising her head, though, she plunged the gaze of her grey eyes pensively into mine. Then a sad smile, imperceptibly mocking, softened her features, in which I read something akin to reproach and pity.

Confused and desperate, I stammered impassioned excuses. My imploring hands reached out for hers.

I have kept a hazel-leaf that had brushed my temple at the moment of our first kiss. It is here before me on my desk, still green but already withered...

The next day, Jean Lebris capitulated and it was agreed that I would perform the radiography the following morning.

During the war, Belvoux hospital, taken over by the military, had been provided with a quantity of apparatus, some of which had remained at the disposal of the civil staff after the evacuation. The radiographic laboratory, installed in a special outbuilding, was one of the most advanced that could be found. It was rarely used, and I had assumed its direction.

I spent the afternoon at the hospital, checking the machine and assuring myself that it was in working order. Everything was as it should be. I told my assistant that he would not be present the next day's session and that he had, in consequence, to make the preparations with the utmost care. Finally, still hoping that Jean Lebris would permit me to photograph the interior of his electroscopes, and perhaps entertaining the subconscious idea of making them appear and fixing their image without his being aware of it, I prepared several sensitive plates.

Excitement made me very tense, and a great many thoughts crossed my mind at the sight of that milky screen, on which so many various things would be outlined for me, if I wished: where Jean Lebris' skeleton would tell me itself, in an anticipated apparition, the date of his death; or, perhaps—but it was not up to me to strike out that "perhaps"—the formidable invention of the sixth sense would begin to emerge from its impenetrable mystery.

Dusk was falling when I left the hospital.

Back home, I dined rapidly and started looking through the notes that I had made for the composition of my technical report.

I was distracted from my work by a sinister rumor, the noise of hurried footsteps, and a humming noise. The alarm bell began to ring, and a siren began to sound the general alert in the darkness...

The fire was turning the Saint-Fortunat quarter red. The high roofs of the hospital stood out in silhouette against the background of the blaze. So far as I could tell, the focal point of the catastrophe was within the establishment's own grounds. My throat constricted.

"Prosope!" I cried, in the solitude.

A few minutes later, my apprehensions were confirmed. Having run to the location, I could only observe the annihilation of the radiographic laboratory in crackling flames. Fortunately, the isolation of the outbuilding permitted the disaster to be contained, and the wards were preserved from the fire.

## IX. The Last Days of the Phenomenon

The inquiry was unable to discover how the fire had started. It was in vain that I suggested malevolence; more than one person suspected that I did so in order to cover up my own responsibility, to hide some imprudence that I had committed—and I realized that it would have been better to say nothing.

Besides, was it not an "imprudence" to have made preparation for the radiography session without any discretion? For me, the truth was not in any doubt. Prosope was watching; he had hired spies in Belvoux. That being admitted, it was necessary to deduce that Jean Lebris was threatened by direct action.

That was also the opinion of the interested party. Jean and I deliberated. I argued that he should let me warn the police about the dangers surrounding him, but the difficulty of doing so without revealing the secret of his eyes put him off that course and, for that reason, I was obliged to renew my promises of silence. It was agreed, therefore, that we would each take all possible precautions on our own account, and the matter rested there.

Nevertheless, I was momentarily on the point of confiding my fears to Mademoiselle Grive. In fact, Jean could not and would not suddenly stop going out with her, and it appeared to me rather reckless for that imperiled invalid to wander in the woods alone with an unsuspecting and defenseless child. There too I would have like to intervene, but the damned secret still paralyzed my good will. Then again, even if Fanny had accepted vague explanations as to the cause of my anxiety, what measures could she have taken that Jean would not have seen through? How, for example, could the young woman be furnished with a revolver without the false blind man perceiving it and blaming me for it?

Alas, I had not long to be anxious that Jean Lebris might be attacked while out walking. As I made ready to take him to Lyon to carry out the radiography, a violent crisis, accompanied by spitting blood, laid him low.

We put him to bed. He was never to get up again.

I estimated immediately that he would not live for longer than a fortnight. From then on, we no longer had any other concern but to watch over him. Fanny installed herself at his bedside, aided by Césarine, Madame Fontan and—considerable less—poor Madame Lebris. Authorized by the weakness of the sick man, I forbade access to his room to any stranger whatsoever, and I spent as much time with him as I could spare.

To begin with, Jean fell prey to a bout of fever, during which he completely lost touch with reality. The twisting of his face and the oft-repeated gesture of putting his hands over his eyes informed me nevertheless that he was suffering electrical dazzling, and I masked him with opaque spectacles, recommending Fanny to follow my example, even at night, every time Jean seemed discomfited as if by light. Mademoiselle Grive, a docile nurse, had no objection to make, and made none.

On the third day, Jean emerged from his torpor. Fanny and I observed his slow awakening from either side of the bed. The invalid turned his head toward me, then toward her. I had a presentiment that he was about to pronounce our names, thus revealing that he had recognized us—that he could see!—for he had quickly become accustomed to the distinctive electromagnetic appearances of different people. Before he could speak, I prudently said to him: "Mademoiselle Grive and I are here. Can you hear me, Jean?"

He nodded his head affirmatively, remained motionless for a few minutes, then took our hands in his own excessively warm hands, brought them together and joined them, with a slowness that took on an aspect of solemnity.

"Monsieur et Madame…" he murmured.

His face was one of those that would never smile again.

What a glance we exchanged, we two whom he had brought together with such simple generosity! I saw Fanny's eyes suddenly moisten with tears. Unable to master her heart, she let herself fall to her knees beside the bed, and sobbed convulsively.

After a pause, Jean Lebris began to whisper. I leaned over so that I could hear him. It was to me that he was speaking.

"Bare," he said, "in the writing-desk, there…the middle drawer…testament. Take it. Mama…prejudiced…will certainly oppose what you know…but testament…categorical. I leave you my eyes. I authorize…dissection…ah! Prosope is ringing the doorbell! Don't let him in! My revolver…Fanny, do you hear that bell? It's Prosope. He burned the hospital…he shan't have my eyes… How he rings! How he rings!"

The fever had taken hold of him again, and he was becoming delirious. Jean let slip a flood of words, sometime incoherent, but more often revelatory of the secrets of his life. His memories of war and especially of captivity, obsessed him. Fearful of loose talk and curiosity, filled with admiration and gratitude for Fanny's mute zeal, I made sure that from that moment on, Jean Lebris would receive no other care than that of our beloved friend or myself.

His condition worsened, without remedy. Sometimes his mind wandered, sometimes he slept. At intervals, becoming lucid again, he conversed with us weakly about our future nuptials, which seemed to be his sole preoccupation.

On the evening of the sixth day, however, when I had just given him an injection, he pointed to a corner of the room and said: "What have you put there?"

"Up there? There's nothing there, my dear Jean. It's an illusion."

"Why lie to me? Come on, Bare—what is it?"

His eyelids widened over is statuesque eyes, He followed through the air the displacement of a vision that presumably vanished, for he did not persist further.

I did not attribute any importance to what I considered to be a phantom provoked by the fever—but the phenomenon was reproduced so frequently, and the sick man was affected in so remarkable a manner, that I was forced to revise my opinion on the subject.

So far as I could understand, the first apparition had been manifest to Jean Lebris in the form of a disk of violet fog, animated by a rotatory quivering. The disk crossed the room, drawing away by passing through the ceiling, and disappeared. Every day, though, more and more distinctly, other vibrant disks were displayed to the dying man. He described them to himself, without paying any heed to me or to Fanny.

They were no longer merely disks now, but buoyant globes, containing a vertiginous circulation. They wandered unhurriedly, going this way and that, through solids, passing through the atmosphere as easily as through items of furniture, houses and the ground. And they sometimes attached them-selves to objects or individuals, with which their union formed bunches that Jean compared to aggregates of soap-bubbles full of mysterious eddies. He tried to chase the bubbles away when they drew close to him—but could he chase them away? One had to doubt it, on seeing the efforts that he made to snatch them away from his breast, claiming that they were choking him.

Once, he warned me that one of these globes had at-tached itself to my brain, and I realized that I was suffering from a painful headache just then. Was that a coincidence?

The problem presented itself: was Jean Lebris still ob-serving directly? Was the delirium showing him non-existent creatures, or was it necessary to believe that his sixth sense, still in progressive development, still becoming more power-ful, had succeeded in enabling him to perceive hitherto unsus-pected forms?

Until now, the electroscopic eyes had only grasped the electromagnetic aspects of entities perceptible to our ordinary senses. Now, that aspect had never ceased to become more precise, more complete. What proof was there that becoming accustomed to the apparatus fabricated by Prosope might not have permitted Jean Lebris to make further progress, and to discover a clandestine world: a population exclusively formed of electricity, constituted by a fluid so rarefied that our most sensitive detectors were not influenced by them? In sum, had a human being finally been able to glimpse one of those invisi-ble races with which philosophy tells us that we are sur-rounded?[30] And does that race use humankind at its whim, without humankind suspecting it? Do we sometimes owe dis-ease, dementia or death to it?

---

[30] Renard inserts a footnote here recommending the reader to consult, in this regard, J.-H. Rosny's "admirable" short story "Un Autre monde" (1895; tr. as "Another World" in Black Coat Press' collection *The Navigators of Space*).

I could not resolve that question, having been unable to tell exactly when Jean Lebris was delirious and when he was not.

He died on October 22, at daybreak, after a 24 hour coma. Fanny wept on my shoulder.

When Jean Lebris had lost consciousness, certain that death was approaching rapidly, I had taken advantage of a moment of tranquility to open the writing-desk. Contrary to my expectation, the middle drawer was quite empty. I rummaged through the others, but discovered nothing the resembling my friend's will. I searched the whole desk, taking the drawers out to look behind and underneath them. A sudden sweat chilled my temples. There was nothing behind or underneath the desk, nothing in the chest of drawers, nothing anywhere!

There were two alternatives. Either the testament had been stolen, or Jean Lebris, in telling me of its existence, had spoken in the heat of his fever and mistaken his intention for an accomplished fact. The theft seemed more probable to me. How long ago, in fact, had Jean decided to write his will? Doubtless before the crisis that was to carry him off, and which had followed so closely after the fire at the hospital. Before that fire, therefore, at a time when our suspicions had not been alerted, the theft had presumably been committed.

At any rate, there was a considerable risk that, thanks to that larceny, I might be frustrated in my quest for valuable knowledge. At the mere idea of approaching Madame Lebris and admitting to her the necessity of an autopsy, all hope abandoned me. One can imagine my feelings as I closed the blackened pupils over the artificial eyes of my dear friend Jean Lebris.

I had no right to hesitate, though. My duty was to try, by any means possible, to obtain the free disposition of his remains. Would the authorities not laugh at me, though, if I appealed to them? Who, then, could give me such a right if not Madame Lebris?

I asked her for it. She refused. Her religion, her principles and what she called her "common sense" rebelled against it. Her grief gave way to indignation. In spite of all my efforts, she told Madame Fontan, Césarine and Fanny about the "profanation" that I had had the "audacity" to claim. In vain I protested that it was for Science and the Fatherland, that Jean's blindness offered a particularity whose explanation—a prodigious argument!—would make a contribution to the salvation of France, that Jean himself, in an undiscoverable testament...

Madame Lebris shrugged her shoulders. A testament written by a blind man! That was taking "the desire to satisfy the most unhealthy kind of curiosity" too far.

Madame Fontan and Césarine endorsed her opinion. Fanny remained mute, but her charming face, fatigued by sleeplessness and grief, advised me not to persist.

"Let your will be done!" I said to Madame Lebris. And peace was restored among us—but I sensed the formidable empery of Prosope over the funereal house. Occult, it had reigned over us; it reigned still. By two crimes—an arson and a theft—his will had interposed itself victoriously between my desire and his secret. I was defeated. So be it! But I still had to protect Jean's body from any assault. I still had to thwart any forceful move or ruse whose objective was the theft of the electroscopic eyes.

I was sitting in Madame Lebris' drawing-room, with my chin in my hands, plunged in somber and bitter mediation. I felt a caress on my forehead...

Fanny was studying me sadly.

I had no reason to hide the truth from her. The "when I'm dead" had, alas, arrived.

She had suspected something for a long time. From the day when I had warned her that it would be imprudent to speak to me in sign language in the blind man's presence, under the pretext that light sometimes affected him, she had sensed the mystery. Occasions on which we sat together, but never talked, had also intrigued her. Finally, during his delirium, Jean Lebris, surrendered to nature, had no longer concealed the fact that he saw certain appearances.

Fanny had no difficulty forgiving me for having maintained in her respect a silence imposed by a sworn oath.

"Ah!" I said to her. "Your rectitude soothes my pain! But I shall not be tranquil until the moment when our friend is resting in an inviolable sepulcher. Help me, Fanny!"

"What can I do? Tell me?"

Her lovely arms entwined around my neck, and she raised her loving eyes, delicately ringed with mauve, in ardent interrogation. "Tell me!" she repeated.

"You're tired, my poor love," I murmured, tenderly. "And yet, I'm about to impose a surfeit of fatigue upon you. It's necessary that you and I should take turns, until the end, to stand guard. It's necessary that one of us is here, beside him, constantly. Until the end, Fanny! Until the coffin and the cemetery."

"But what about afterwards? Aren't you afraid that some dark night, someone…?"

I explained the plan that I had formulated—after which I left her there, as my substitute, pious and vigilant.

## X. The Exploit

I spent all day giving orders to the mason and the locksmith, with Madame Lebris' consent. She raised no objection to her son's tomb being, in its subterranean part, a kind of unassailable blockhouse. The workmen promised me to do that diligently; in fact, the work had already begun before nightfall.

It was the hour when I had to relieve Fanny of her funereal sentry-duty. I found her worn out, asleep standing up. I led her out of the dead man's room on to the landing, where were able to speak freely. She told me that nothing out of the ordinary had occurred; a few friends had filed in front of the mortal remains, but no suspicious individual had betrayed his presence in the vicinity.

Then, as I looked at her in the twilight, she lamented: "I haven't seen you all day!"

The dear soul crushed herself against me in a dolorous and coaxing collapse—and she would have gone to sleep on my breast if I hadn't said: "Go and get some sleep, my love, for my sake!"

Her lips were burning. One would have thought that she was no longer capable of pulling away. "Fanny!" I said, moved by such fervor. "How happy we shall be!"

Her resistance exhausted, she dissolved in tears, gripped me in a passionate embrace, and then fled, stifling her sobs.

"I love you!" I called, in a restrained voice.

She gestured to me from the top of the stairs. I could scarcely see her. The shadows took possession of her.

Dazedly blessing her, I headed for the silent and sealed room where the pale inanimate figure lay amid autumnal flowers. The servant was keeping vigil. She renewed the candles, gathered up the fallen petals, and asked me if I would be staying up late "beside Monsieur Jean."

"All night," I replied. "You can go to bed, my dear Césarine."

She did so. I installed myself in an armchair and opened a Bible that had been placed there. Soon, though, similarly worn out by fatigue, drained by insomnia, crushed by the weight of an anxiety that Fanny's love could not weaken without causing her to disappear, I was obliged to get up and walk around to vanquish drowsiness.

My thoughts formed a tumultuous confusion within my skull. I do not know how, but suddenly, with the brutality of a blinding light, the implacable idea was established in my head that *it was necessary, at all costs, to steal the electroscopes.*

I was alone with the corpse, free to act...

The church clock chimed 11 p.m.

I had time before dawn to commit several crimes and carry out a number of exploits....but *that* was a praiseworthy act, was it not? Could I hesitate? Could I let the secret of the sixth sense be buried forever? "Never!"—if only for my compatriots! What! Should we Frenchmen remain in ignorance of such a discovery, when the enemy would possess it and perfect it? What! Tomorrow, if war broke out again, should we be subject to the fearful inferiority of having to fight against supermen? To have against us, among our innumerable assailants, extraordinary specialists who could decipher wireless telegraph messages in the sky itself? Who could pinpoint the most deeply buried networks, the most cleverly-concealed artillery batteries? People for whom mountains would be transparent?

I recalled Jean Lebris' astonishing perspicacity, with a thrill of fear. I remembered him indicating unhesitatingly the defective point of a magneto, or the diseased part of a spinal cord. I perceived a hundred practical applications of the sixth sense...

Finally, the evidence shone before me like the Sun! It was not up to my will to satisfy the outdated demands of an old provincial lady. I was the advance sentinel of the national defense. Away with prejudices and superstitions! Fatherland first!

In any case, no one would perceive the violation. It was a matter of 30 or 40 minutes, and I would have several hours to erase all trace of the operation. I even hoped to be able, with a little skill, to take account of the incomprehensible weld between the optic nerves and the electroscopes...

Standing up, with my arms folded, in front of the cadaver that concealed such a vast mystery, I had the feeling of being possessed by impulsive forces that swept away all propriety and convention.

Mechanically, I felt my instrument-case through the cloth of my jacket—and, shivering like a flag, I listened like a thief.

The night was passing with reassuring calmness. The house was padded with silence. For several minutes I heard nothing except for the distant call of a night-bird, the rumble of an automobile out late, and irregular breathing coming from the next room, where Madame Lebris was asleep. Even so, I hesitated, and I don't know why. The desire to delay suddenly overwhelmed me. I feared that I might be dreaming, having one of those nightmares from which one emerges exhausted. My faculties vacillated. It was only a fainting fit.

I stepped forward firmly and, becoming professional again, I raised an as-yet-supple eyelid with a gentle finger…

A muffled exclamation escaped me. Precipitately, I seized a candle, raised the other eyelid…

Instead of the electroscopes, and placed there to simulate their convexity, two small balls of cloth occupied the orbits.

And the goggles! The goggles had also disappeared!

I was suffocating. I was on the point of calling out. My secret wanted to advertise itself now. I needed to pour it out, recount it, argue with some friend full of commiseration about the incredible event that had struck me, and my entire race along with me…

With an effort, however, I succeeded in checking that dangerous excitement. No one must know of my disappointment in its full amplitude. No one, except Fanny. Poor thing, though! Was I egotist enough to disturb her sleep? Besides, how could I wake her up, at this late hour, without provoking the astonishment of her aunt?

Oh, how negligent I had proved to be in abusing her strength! How wrong I had been to impose on her the duty of guarding the dead man in my absence! To leave such a responsibility to a young girl who, for two days, her nerves taut, had not granted herself the slightest relief! Our adversary had taken advantage of that, of course! "No one suspicious has come," she had told me. Well, for a young woman of 20, the undertaker's employee is not suspicious. The carpenter who comes to make measurements is not suspicious. The parish priest, the medical examiner and the bonneted nun are not suspicious!

I waited for morning with an unhealthy impatience. I wanted to know whether Fanny really had followed the instructions I had given point by point; and I was in great haste, too, to seek the appeasement of my distress in her compassion.

At daybreak, incapable of restraining myself any longer, I went up the stairs stealthily, not even knowing how I was going to explain such an early visit to Madame Fontan.

The door of the apartment was ajar. I knocked. A yellow gleam tinted the top of the door-frame.

I knocked for a second time, and pushed the door a little further open—which permitted me to perceive, beyond the reception-room, the young woman's bedroom, in which a lamp was still burning.

"Fanny!" I called, furtively. "Fanny!"

I went in without any further ceremony, suddenly unconscious of what I was doing.

A moment later, I knew how one goes mad.

Three times in the space of two days the same disillusionment had struck me! But this time, it was straight in the heart. The testament had escaped me, the inestimable eyes had been snatched from me, and now…oh, now…!

The beds were not unmade. The dress that Fanny had been wearing the day before lay on the floor, next to the indoor slippers carelessly cast aside. In a wide-open cupboard, the traveling clothes that I knew so well were not with the others. A frightful solitude chilled the dwelling.

Unable to believe what I saw, talking to myself incoherently, I went from room to room, stupid and miserable. I told myself that I was the victim of an atrocious misunderstanding; that everything would be explained in due course; that it was all some abominable coincidence. She would come back, of course! She had not gone away! She was not the one who had taken the eyes! Nor was it her who had taken the testament! Fanny, a thief…and an arsonist? Get away! One could not suppose such a monstrosity!

Logic raised its clear voice, though. Connections formed in my memory. The horror gradually became possible; soon, only my heart refused to admit it.

While letting my stupefied gaze wander over everything, however, I discovered a screwed-up ball of paper in the depths of an empty hearth. It was a note, written by an unknown hand, in an incomprehensible language...

And all of a sudden, despair acquired dominion over my entire being—for I recalled very clearly the rumble of the automobile that had died away into the night, after 11 p.m. had chimed; and on the note—in the *orders* that the traitress had received—I was able to read the number 11 closely following these words, untranslatable from French: *Botasse* and *Saint-Fortunat*—the names of two streets that intersected in the vicinity.

Then I sat down, like a sick man in great pain. I lifted up Fanny's dress in my trembling hands and, immersing my hand in the perfumed muslin, I wept for all the time I had spent on Earth without weeping.

Afterwards...afterwards, it was necessary to go back down, to feign surprise, to calculate a dose of indifference, and to stay silent. To stay silent forever!

Autumn was advancing; it was, therefore, quite natural that Madame Fontan and her niece should leave our rural town to return to the city. People were only surprised that they had left so quickly—"in the English manner"—without even staying for Jean's funeral. Madame Lebris, shamed by the insult, put it about that a letter had summoned them urgently back to Artois.

What do I think? What do I think, today?

Sometimes, I tell myself that she did not love me. I break my heart in convincing myself that she was playing the most ferocious comedy, going so far as to suggest to me the crime of cutting Jean Lebris' days short!

But when I recall, hour by hour, our life; when I evoke the memory—irremediably cherished!—of her gaze, her smiles, her kisses and her tears, I can no longer see as many lies and villainies.

No, no, it isn't so, is it? Fanny, you who are doubtless not named Fanny, you who were only here—oh, God!—as a spy, under a false name, isn't it the case that it's unnecessary to believe in the felony of your eyes? Isn't it the case that *you didn't deceive me in the domain of the heart?* Your odious mission...oh, I want it to have been imposed on you by force! Did you not fulfill it without spilling a single drop of blood? Must not the gentle weakness of Jean Lebris have excited your pity, since you let him fade away slowly?

It might be objected that nothing sharpened your hatred—that, being sure of his imminent death, it was sufficient for you, until then, to keep watch on Prosope's diabolical work...

But it might also be argued that you had less cold reasons for prolonging your sojourn among us—reasons that cause me to hope, in a cowardly fashion, for some unknown future of rediscovery, unworthy forgiveness and happiness in spite of everything! For I, Fanny, I who possess a part of the secret that you serve, I who retain in the incomplete manuscripts in my safe, a little of your master's treasure...would you have spared me, Fanny, if you did not love me?

# THE MAN WHO WANTED TO BE INVISIBLE

*A Story in the British Vein*

*To Octave Uzanne*[31]

"These things didn't happen at Iping, of course," said Mr. Patpington.

Hopkins looked at him in alarm.

"Well, obviously!" his uncle went on. "I mean, in all the time that I've spent here, I assume that someone would have mentioned it to me, if it had happened here!"

Hopkins just sat there, open-mouthed and wide-eyed.

Mr. Patpington was swaying back and forth in a rocking-chair. He was a short, stout man, dressed in black. He had plump rosy cheeks and an exceedingly high forehead, and his unkempt white hair came down over the collar of his frock-coat. A fat little old woman dressed as a man, that was what Mr. Patpington resembled—and to tell the truth, when Dr. Hopkins contemplated his uncle, he sometimes experienced the disturbing sensation of being confronted by his late mother, who had been born in Iping, strangely resurrected and in drag.

---

[31] Octave Uzanne (1851-1931) was a bibliophile and journalist, with a particular expertise in ladies' fashions, well-known on the Parisian literary scene; he seconded Jean Lorrain in the latter's duel with Marcel Proust. He has a peripheral connection with scientific romance by virtue of a small number of satirical futuristic articles, most notably "La Locomotion Future" [Future Locomotion] (1895), which was illustrated by Albert Robida.

"I think, therefore," Mr. Patpington went on, "that Wells wanted to put his reader on the wrong track, by setting the principal exploits of his invisible man in and around Iping."

"But you aren't claiming that those adventures ever actually took place somewhere?" said Hopkins, eventually.

Mr. Patpington darted a disquieting sideways glance at him, and continued swinging back and forth, which he could only do by sliding his arms back and forth along the rocking-chair's arms, given that his short legs were quite unable to touch the ground. An open book lay on Mr. Patpington's rounded thighs. "Personally, Arthur," he said, emphatically, "I maintain that the story is true. It's only too plausible, you know—too plausible not to be true. And don't forget that it's a chemist who's speaking to you!"

At these words, Hopkins—like the narrator of *The Invisible Man* himself—began to see clearly…and he repented of having left a work so liable to excite the imagination in Mr. Patpington's hands. It was, moreover, the only book of that sort to be found in his bookcase. Hopkins, like all scientists in general, and physicians in particular, professed a remarkable disdain for the fantasies of Wells; if he had bought *The Invisible Man* at one time, it was solely because it was set in Iping, because it is always amusing to read things about the place where one lives.

Uncle Patpington had long fulfilled the functions of Professor of Chemistry at the Technical Society in the Strand. Until now, his nephew had only had the pleasure of receiving him at Iping during vacations. Mr. Patpington had, however, arrived two days before, without any warning, even though the school's studies were in full swing, simply saying that he was a little tired and had been advised to take a fortnight' rest. Mr. and Mrs. Hopkins had not asked for any fuller details on that score, happy to observe that the dear old bachelor—who was, in truth, very well-to-do—nourished a faithful affection in their regard, full of future promise.

The strange statements he had just heard regarding *The Invisible Man*, had given birth in Hopkins' mind to the idea that Mr. Patpington had quit the Technical Society in response to solicitations more pressing than he had admitted. He determined, therefore, to maintain a close but covert surveillance of the professor's actions and gestures.

"Just imagine, my love," he said to Mrs. Hopkins. "I was ready to believe that Uncle Pat had gone off his trolley!"

"Is it possible?" asked Mrs. Hopkins, anxiously.

"Judge for yourself. Mary. Do you recall Wells's *The Invisible Man*? Well, Uncle Pat maintains that it's not a fable invented to amuse."

"Heavens!" cried Mrs. Hopkins, putting her hands together and widening her eyes in her turn.

"So, I entreat you to keep an eye on him whenever I'm forced to absent myself. Try to make him talk, too…hmm…I'm wondering whether I ought to go up to London to have a chat with the director of the Technical Society. We'll see about that in a few days."

Thus commenced the methodical observation of Mr. Patpington. Two days passed during which nothing noteworthy occurred. It was merely remarked that Mr. Patpington talked about himself much more than he ever had before. He waxed lyrical about his past endeavors, the papers on chemistry that he had published, and the rewards and distinctions he had obtained. By way of compensation, when he fell silent, one could have said that he fell *more silent*, so obviously did his silences testify to intimate labor. He had finished reading *The Invisible Man*; Mrs. Hopkins had immediately hastened to hide the book, and the old man made no attempt, overt or covert, to find it again. That did not prove anything, though, for his memory was legendary, and it was well-known that a work read by Mr. Patpington was a work integrated, as it were, into Mr. Patpington's soul.

During that couple of days, therefore, no eccentricity on the part of the excellent Mr. Patpington was manifest. Perhaps, at one time, he might have asked why Mrs. Hopkins no longer let Bob and Lily play the game of pulling their grand-uncle's watch-chain or the tails of his frock-coat. Perhaps Mr. Patpington might have made some extravagant statements, if the question of *The Invisible Man* had come up again; let us say to their credit, however, that neither Hopkins nor his wife found the courage to make allusion to it and thus provoke their uncle to divagation.

On the morning of the third day, the postman brought a letter addressed to Mr. Patpington. It was from London, and the envelope bore the words "Technical Society" printed in olive-green in the top left-hand corner. Mr. Patpington received it from Mrs. Hopkins' hands, and then plunged into an intense meditation, pacing back and forth in his room with large and measured steps. Mr. Patpington read the letter, and then, after crumpling it up and hurling it into the fireplace like a cricket ball, with casual expertise, he resumed his meditation as if it nothing had happened.

It was hard for Mrs. Hopkins to go away without saying a word. She made a private note that a certain fireplace concealed a certain ball of manuscript—but at lunch, Mr. Patpington informed them of his own accord that the aforesaid ball signified a conclusive dismissal, based on infinitely honorable pretexts and accompanied by a profusion of eulogies and thanks. Ostensibly, Mr. Patpington had purely and simply disembarked from the Technical Society.

Hopkins asked himself more than once whether Mr. Patpington might not have taken this blow harder than he appeared to—perhaps more grievously than he realized himself—and whether the disgrace might have awkward repercussions on the sequence of events. At any rate, Mr. Patpington ate his ham and eggs with a very hearty appetite. All of that, he said, was of no importance whatsoever. He was, on the contrary, delighted to recover his liberty, in order that he might devote himself to certain fascinating endeavors—and he undoubtedly ought to thank Providence, which had been so abundant in support of his desires.

At that moment, Mr. and Mrs. Hopkins exchanged one of those rapid glances whose spark resembles that of a distant window reflecting sunlight as it is opened or closed.

"I hope, Arthur," added Mr. Patpington, "that you—and you too, Mary—will consent to give me hospitality. I have nothing more to do in London now. Your cottage is vast…"

Such were the circumstances in which Uncle Pat was led to become a citizen of Iping. At his request, Mr. and Mrs. Hopkins installed him on the top floor of their house, and a laboratory was fitted out for him in the attic. Mr. Patpington soon accumulated an impressive quantity of flasks and retorts there. Hopkins, meanwhile, had re-read *The Invisible Man*, as a sort of precaution. When he saw his home invaded by these battalions of receptacles and machines, he no longer had any doubt that Mr. Patpington had got it into his head to rediscover the chimerical secret—and he resolved to set him straight, if he possibly could.

Until then, Hopkins had never dealt with any mental illness, but he was a provincial doctor, ready for anything. Mr. Patpington showed himself, in sum, to be so reasonable in his daily habits, that it seemed quite possible to discuss matters with him and to convince him by force of argument. Psychiatrists will smile at that, but I repeat that Hopkins was not familiar with mental aberrations. He hoped that his uncle, apprised of his error, would begin to think like everyone else again. A few weeks of rest would complete the job, and Mr. Patpington's derangement would thus pass unnoticed—which was singularly preferable for the future of Bob and Lily, because it is always awkward when people can say of you: "Yes, yes, but his great-uncle you know…" and tap their foreheads with their fingers to make the matter understood without saying a word.

While Mr. Patpington aligned algebraic symbols and moved his labeled bottles around up in the attic, Hopkins set to work on the case, treating the problem very seriously, sensing that the chemist would only yield to scientific reasoning. He spent long hours on it and was finally satisfied that he could bring the discussion to a victorious conclusion.

Fortunately, Mr. Patpington agreed to the discussion and did not try—as Hopkins had feared—to deny the goal of his research. Voluptuously surrounded by clouds of cigarette-smoke, sipping with a child-like smile on the little glass of sherry that Mrs. Hopkins had just poured for him, Uncle Pat opened up in response to Hopkins' deferential questions. Of course! He certainly was in pursuit of the discovery of invisibility! He was convinced that an appropriate treatment might render a man as invisible as air. The thing boiled down to a matter of lending the human body the same refractive index as the atmosphere. Wells had explained it admirably...

Hopkins seized the opportunity to strike an initial blow against Wells, which he knew to be a light one, but which would permit him to test the resistance of his interlocutor. "It can, therefore, only be a question of invisibility relative to a certain medium," he said. "In water, for instance, Griffin—Wells's hero, the man invisible in air—would become slightly visible again, like a huge human gas-bubble, since water doesn't have the same refractive index as air. Wells passed over that in silence, but it's a flaw nonetheless."

"What does it matter?" said Mr. Patpington, simply. "Water isn't man's element. For the moment, I'm concerned with the atmosphere."

"Agreed!" Hopkins conceded, pretending to adopt Mr. Patpington's viewpoint. "But Wells didn't give any indication of the means of transforming animal tissues in an optical sense, and I confess that I perceive difficulties, in relation to this point, that seem to me to be insurmountable."

It was this issue on which he had worked assiduously, and he set about enumerating all the histological and physiological reasons opposed to the realization of that brilliant paradox.

He was wasting his time. Mr. Patpington had but one reply. "Don't worry about that, Arthur. Patpington is someone, I think, and am I not Patpington? Just remember that every invention has been in the domain of mirages before passing into that of reality. Suppose, Arthur, that someone had told you twenty years ago that a means existed of seeing inside people—what would you have thought? It's the same with invisibility. Give me credit, and you'll see. You'll see…that you'll no longer be able to see me!"

"Damnation! You intend to operate on yourself?"

Mr. Patpington confirmed it with a joyful laugh.

"But Uncle, you're not an albino, as Griffin was…"

"Oh, pigments!" said Mr. Patpington, scornfully. "I've made them my business, pigments. I give you my word that it's no more complicated to discolor them than it is to discolor blood. Whoever can do one can do the other, and I don't understand why Mr. Wells drew a distinction between the two problems.

*Of course!* thought Hopkins. *Two of a kind! One audacity more or less…*

He remained silent, though, with the result that Mr. Patpington, leaving him bewildered by his check, returned gaily to his calculations and his tinkering.

Hopkins, temporarily unhorsed, got back in the saddle. He had logic on his side. Since old Pat did not recoil before an impossibility of execution, it was necessary to pass on to the next stage and demonstrate to him that if the *tour de force* were accomplished and a man were to become invisible, that man's existence—his rational existence—would encounter insurmountable obstacles.

Demonstrate—easy to say!

*Very difficult*, he thought, *but perhaps Wells's novel is only based on a single sophistry. Perhaps Wells was only dishonest about the invention of the procedure designed to render something or someone invisible. Once that idea is accepted, that postulate admitted, perhaps everything in the book unfolds with irreproachable logic…*

He put it to the proof, and that proof discouraged him. The misadventures of Griffin, the invisible man imagined by Wells, had the ring of truth, down to the smallest detail. On this occasion, Hopkins could not help admiring the artistry with which the author had presented the weak point of his creation, the malicious and admirable fraud he had perpetrated by burying in the middle of the work the weak point that was, however, fundamental, and the clever dexterity with which his illusionist's fingers had concealed the inadmissible postulate. The transition from truth to falsehood was produced by a flick of the wrist; it was dissimulated beneath and elegant gesture, which seemed secondary. A slight shadow fell upon that spot, while clarity reigned over the rest of the story, and one can follow, in the light of the most meticulous common sense, the actions and gestures of the man who had become—by whatever means—invisible.

Hopkins meditated upon this while deploring it, for he knew that Mr. Patpington's derangement was born of the redoubtable and methodical plausibility of the fantastic story and that the story—yes, truly—contained things so finely observed that one had difficulty believing that they had been deduced from a nonsensical premise by rigorous logic.

With a critical eye, Hopkins followed the unfortunate Griffin through the tribulations that his invisibility inflicted upon him. *Nothing!* he complained. *Nothing to find fault with! Griffin's invisible, that's all. He's invisible because light is no longer reflected by his surfaces. He's invisible because light traverses his body without even being refracted. Now, present-day science doesn't tell me whether light, on penetrating our organs, is liable to affect any of their functions. One can't see, in that fashion, why the stomach, integrally illuminated, should cease to digest, or why the heart, impregnated with daylight, should refuse to beat, the ear to hear, the eye…*

"May I be damned!" cried Hopkins. "Old Pat hasn't thought of that. Neither did Wells!"

He went up the stairs four at a time and went into the laboratory like Aeolus, the god of winds.

Mr. Patpington, seated before his figures with his nose in an equation, waved his plump hand to demand silence. Whether he liked it or not, Hopkins had to paw the ground for a few minutes.

"Well?" said Mr. Patpington, finally. "What's the matter?"

"Well," said Hopkins, "it's this: the story's false! Yes, yes, it's understood, you're a chemist of the first order; I have no doubt that you'll find a means to render yourself invisible—but you won't be able to employ that means!"

"And why not?"

"Because," Hopkins cried, triumphantly, "*one can't become invisible without becoming blind*—and Wells is pulling a fast one when he shows us *an invisible man who can see!*"

"It's true that he can't see himself," retorted Mr. Patpington, "since he's invisible. Wells points that out…"

"An invisible man can't see anything at all. First of all, the eye is a *camera obscura*; the eye needs a dark space to produce vision. That's quite sufficient to prove my point. But wait—there's more! With what is it filled, this *camera obscura*, this dark space which light must only penetrate through the round hole of the pupil? Tell me, with what? With *refractive* substances, isn't that so? Substances which, in order to play their optical role, have to refract the luminous rays. Thus, if you take away that property from them, how do you expect them to fulfill their function? And that's not all! Not content with functioning in their entirety like a single lens, some of these substances function individually as mirrors. Now, is a mirror *that no longer reflects anything* still a mirror? And finally, on what screen can these images be projected, in an invisible man, since, hypothetically, his retina will be incapable of interrupting the slightest ray?"

"Ooooh!" groaned Mr. Patpington, exhaling his discomfiture.

"In the order of luminous facts," continued Hopkins, somewhat excitedly, "whoever says *invisible* says *nonexistent*! An invisible eye is inoperative. An invisible man is inevitably a blind man. Griffin is a myth. Conclusion: Uncle Patpington must give up the attempt to imitate him—isn't that so?"

The stout fellow had reckoned without the heroism brooding in the old scientist's heart. He was amazed to see Mr. Patpington, crushed as he was, straighten up tremulously, a pink and resolute little man who seemed to be reinflating with the effect of a noble inhalation. Intrepidity furnished his black pupils with the glint of well-carved jet. "The game's worth the candle!" he declared. "I'll be blind, but I'll be invisible!"

*There's nothing to be done with him!* Hopkins raged.

"Anyway," Mr. Patpington went on, "I shan't embark upon invisibility without being assured, first, of a means of becoming visible again—and, in consequence, I'll only expose myself to a temporary blindness."

His attitude was determined, his tone peremptory; he was animated by a slight resentment. Hopkins judged it perilous to persist. As the maniac sat down again before his algebraic formulas, with the obvious intention of losing himself therein, Hopkins withdrew, his head bowed, conclusively vanquished.

Eighteen days went by between the scene that has just been described and the explosion in the laboratory. During this lapse of time, Mr. and Mrs. Hopkins could only render justice to the gaiety, the friendliness and the joyful charm of Mr. Patpington. Had it not been for his mania, what an adorable companion that dear old uncle would have been! And how could they pluck up the courage to prevent Bob and Lily from leaping on to his knees after the meal and maltreating him like a huge doll brought in a box by the man from the toyshop?

Mr. Patpington, however, worked all day, only mingling with the living at meal-times. On the day when Hopkins visited the laboratory, he employed a lie by way of excuse. He pretended to have a toothache, which, he said, entirely robbed him of his appetite—but when the noise of cutlery filled the dining-room, Hopkins climbed up to the chemist's laboratory, curious to know exactly what the fellow had been doing all day.

In the wake of this investigation, Hopkins seemed singularly preoccupied. Mrs. Hopkins, alarmed, interrogated him. All day, he pretended not to understand her insistence, but he could not sleep all night. The following day, his nervousness betrayed a fit of anxiety and indecision. At 5 p.m., when the laboratory exploded, Hopkins called himself a complete idiot as he climbed the stairs.

"It's necessary to take immediate action!" he mumbled. "Send him and all his reagents packing! It was bound to happen. Give house-room to a madman—oh yes, that's stupid! We're in a fine mess now!"

Good luck had limited the material damage to the destruction of alembics, heaters, test-tubes, retorts and other utensils employed in practical chemistry. The windows, it is true, no longer framed a single pane and the doors had come off their hinges, but the blast had been so powerfully felt throughout the house and the detonation so thunderous, that it was a miracle still to find four walls and a roof there.

Followed by his wife, who was whiter than a sheet, Hopkins went in circumspectly and sniffed the sharp odor that was dissipating rapidly, along with a green smoke. Mr. Patpington was lying on his back, in a tranquil attitude, seemingly fast asleep. The explosive mixture, blowing up under his nose, had nevertheless singed his eyelashes, his eyebrows and his trimmed moustache and covered his face with a green layer, which terrified Mrs. Hopkins at first sight.

Hopkins carried him to his bedroom, laid him down and washed his face. While Mrs. Hopkins went downstairs to reassure the neighbors that the explosion had brought running, the physician ascertained with agreeable certainty that Mr. Patpington had no external cuts or bruises of any sort. The faint ended, thanks to Hopkins' attentions; immediately, Mr. Patpington recovered his color and the use of speech—to the astonishment of his nephew.

"Victory!" he cried. "Victory!"

Transported by delight, Mr. Patpington, propping himself up on his elbow, passed his trembling hands back and forth across his face.

"What? What?" interrogated Hopkins.

"Oh, you're there, Arthur! Well, do you still doubt my genius? Invisible! I'm invisible! Patpington, the great Patpington, has found the secret of invisibility! I'm invisible!"

Hopkins understood that Mr. Patpington was blind.

It only required a few seconds for the doctor to take account of what had occurred in his uncle's brain. The accident had taken Mr. Patpington by surprise in the course of one of the perfectly incoherent experiments that his hobby-horse had suggested to him. He had woken up deprived of sight, for reasons that a subsequent medical examination would ascertain, but, still pursued by his obsession and with his memory disturbed by virtue of the sudden commotion, the eccentric had imagined an entire glorious sequence of events. According to him, his efforts had been crowned by success; he had lost consciousness at the conclusion of the operation during which his body had abandoned all appearance, and, knowing that invisibility was inseparable from blindness, Mr. Patpington believed himself to be invisible to everyone, while only being so, in truth, to himself.

No one wanted to disillusion him. Mr. Patpington was such a nice chap! And he manifested such joy at being invisible! Who could have been so cruel as to transform that innocent happiness into despair? Who would take the responsibility of saying: "Not invisibility, my dear chap, but blindness, pure and simple!" A double heartbreak! No, no, the only thing to do was to praise the Lord for having sustained the illusion that gratuitously completed an infantile desire and draped an infirmity in the very purple of glory.

Thus it was done; and then commenced the most touching comedy. Mr. and Mrs. Hopkins played it admirably, and there is no shame in saying that they kept it up for three months. Yes, for exactly ninety-five days they succeeded in maintaining Mr. Patpington in his salutary aberration. It is true that the deceived individual wanted to be deceived, and that the task was reduced, in sum, to supporting an autosuggestion; all the same, if one considers the normally mistrusting nature of the mentally disturbed and the exceedingly sharp perspicacity with which Mr. Patpington was still endowed, it must be admitted that Mr. and Mrs. Hopkins were worthy of all praise. As for Hopkins, one could not congratulate him too much for the veritably dazzling manner in which he brought the adventure to a close, for the benefit of everyone—especially dear old Mr. Patpington.

We shall draw a rapid sketch of the life that the Hopkinses led during those 95 days. One might say that that life was dominated by the work of benevolent deception and regulated by the obligation to nourish Mr. Patpington's error.

Fortunately, Hopkins was able, from the outset, to isolate Mr. Patpington, and, in consequence, to avoid the blunders that strangers would have been unable to avoid making in his regard. In fact, Mr. Patpington had put his once-famous memory to a stern proof, but was unable—for good reason—to recall the formulas that, according to him, conferred invisibility. Hopkins, affirming that the formulas had been burned, persuaded him without difficulty that his mental genius would enable him to recover them, but that it was necessary in the meantime to keep the whole affair secret.

"Otherwise," he argued, "people would be able to believe that the phenomenon was accidental; some of them would even reckon your invisibility diabolical—and it would all give rise to misapprehensions. It's therefore appropriate that you only go out in my company, dressed from top to toe in effects that conceal your absence, as Wells's hero did. Like Griffin, you'll wear gloves and a large hat pulled down a long way. I'll buy you a wig and dark glasses. For the face, there's the solution of a mask or thick make-up, but I prefer bandages, again like Griffin—it's safer and more natural. We'll say that the explosion in the laboratory has disfigured you and rendered you blind. Furthermore, as I fear some indiscretion on the part of the children, I'll ask you only to appear in front of them in the same get-up."

Mr. Patpington was docile and delighted, and it is only fair to say that he submitted immediately to Hopkins' ascendancy. That very affectionate nephew lent him his eyes, so to speak, and Mr. Patpington surrendered himself to his fate. For him, henceforth, nothing existed but the voice of his guide.

That is why the inhabitants of Iping saw Hopkins taking a stroll every day with a bizarrely-muffled stout little man. It was winter, though, and, thanks to the precaution of only going out after dark—under the pretext that sunlight was harmful to the wounded man's eyes—the matter did not give rise to any comment.

In other respects, Hopkins and his wife became ingenious in treating Mr. Patpington as an invisible man; they did so scrupulously. When one of them went into the blind man's room and they perceived Uncle Pat there, with his clothes on. Mr. and Mrs. Hopkins did not neglect to exclaim: "My God! I'll never get used to it! What a strange sight it is to see a man without a head and hands!" And immediately, Mr. or Mrs. Hopkins would be repaid for their painful lie by the smile of gratitude that spread across the round and rosy face of the beloved Mr. Patpington.

Once, however, in an analogous circumstance, Mrs. Hopkins almost demolished the entire edifice of their pious plot. This is how it happened. Mr. Patpington had a slight cold, which explains why Mrs. Hopkins was bringing him a hot toddy. She knocked on the uncle's door. He was expecting her; a jovial voice replied: "Come in!"—and Mrs. Hopkins went in, without paying any heed to the joyful laughter contained in the voice.

All the charity, excellence and energy of Mrs. Hopkins is measurable in the fact that the toddy was not spilled on the floor, that her scream was strangled into something sufficiently imitative of a cough, that the saintly woman succeeded in going in, in spite of her irreproachable upbringing, and that she exclaimed, in a surprised tone: "Why, there's no one here! Where are you, then, Uncle Patpington?"—even though Mr. Patpington was, in truth, standing in front of her, wearing nothing but a jester's smile, covered in nothing but ridicule.

Oh, that wheeze was no sinecure! It demanded constant vigilance, perpetual self-control, the anticipation of all eventualities and a penetrating surveillance over oneself and everyone else. To recruit Bob and Lily into the familial comedy was unthinkable; it was therefore necessary to forbid them access to the room where Mr. Patpington slept, took his meals and lived for most of the time. The little ones obeyed without prevarication, but when the cat was sold, Bob and Lily were in floods of tears.

Hopkins sold the cat because he had a confused suspicion of the beast and its instinct. He had enough things to worry about on his own account and that of his nearest and dearest, without exposing the success of such a complicated and praiseworthy deception to the gaffes of an animal.

One example will give an idea of all the precautions that it was necessary to take with Mr. Patpington to nourish his delusion. As one may imagine, it was Hopkins who undertook the daily care of the aged infant. Well, what would have happened if, in order to cut Mr. Patpington's fingernails, Hopkins had not thought of first coating them with some kind of paste? Mr. Patpington would have said: "Oh, Arthur, how can you cut my fingernails without being able to see them?" And all would have been lost, exactly as if Madame Hopkins had screamed and fled on the day of the toddy.

But we have talked for too long about Mr. Patpington's blindness without mentioning that Hopkins did what was necessary to figure out its nature and its cause. Here again the inevitable problem arose: to avoid disillusioning Mr. Patpington, and, in this instance, to conceal from him that he was being subjected to an eye examination—since he was convinced that his eyes were invisible.

As chance would have it, Mr. Patpington, never stopped asking his nephew for continual clarifications regarding the optical prodigy of which he believed himself to be the object. The phenomenon of digestion, among others, excited his interest keenly. In *The Invisible Man*, as we know, Wells supposes that the aliments ingurgitated by Griffin only become invisible themselves gradually, as they are assimilated. It was, for Mr. Patpington, a veritable feast to have Hopkins describe the phases of his digestion and the progressive disappearance of the alimentary substances. Hopkins improvised some very nice balanced accounts on that subject; he maintained that such observations were of considerable medical importance, but instead of looking at Mr. Patpington's stomach, or rather his pancreas—which would only have informed him as to the pink plump surface of his uncle's paunch—he took the opportunity to examine, with all the discipline of his art, the eyes that were no longer seeing clearly.

Hopkins could not distinguish anything particular therein. Then he discussed Mr. Patpington's case with a former colleague who was now a celebrated oculist in London, and they concluded together that it one of those commonplace amauroses in which the eye does not present any apparent lesion, and which often have a purely nervous origin. No local treatment could remedy it.

Why should we hide the fact that this result caused Hopkins to rejoice. He had done his duty in obtaining all that science could teach him about Mr. Patpington's blindness, but, having accomplished that duty, he was content with an impotence that permitted him to leave Mr. Patpington to the delights of his illusion. For, in the end, if a treatment had been possible, would Hopkins have had the right to neglect its application? Could he have done otherwise than nag Mr. Patpington to give him back the sight whose deprivation made him so strangely happy? The case of conscience did not arise, and we can easily understand that Hopkins was glad of it.

At any rate, Mr. and Mrs. Hopkins rapidly became accustomed to the new requirements that Mr. Patpington's condition imposed upon them. Now, disemburdened of their initial anxieties, fully adapted to the strange role that they had to play, they drank deeper of the pleasure of being benevolent—to which another pleasure, rarer and more mysterious, would soon be added.

What was that?

It consisted, simply, of enjoying the miracle. It consisted of *behaving as if* a phenomenal being was living under their roof. It consisted of bringing their actions into accord with a marvel, even though that marvel did not exist.

Destiny, taking them by the heart, had obliged Mr. and Mrs. Hopkins to enter into Mr. Patpington's game as into some childish round, and because of that, they felt the mysterious vibration of an obscure, ambiguous and precious sensuality within them. It seemed to rise up from the utmost depths of their being; it returned from the remotest origins of their infancy. As before, the phantoms of their imagination took on substance, to the influence of which they were subject. The enchantment that they interpreted constantly ended up by taking on a sort of artificial form, in the same way that false gods end up being constituted by the smoke of sacrifices. The invisibility that they affirmed incessantly acquired in their affirmation a sort of psychological existence—and such is the prestige of a marvel that its shadow sufficed to generate pleasure.

There is nothing, however, that does not come to an end.

After a time, Mr. Patpington began to show signs of weariness and impatience. He had had enough of being invisible and being blind. He wanted to recover his original properties—not in order to get back to work, for he recognized that he would henceforth be incapable of that, but solely to escape from darkness and cease to be someone who was no longer similar to his peers. His gaiety declined. He became very unhappy and, not being able to find the means of becoming visible again and recovering his sight, he gave way to bitter despair.

Hopkins then became very perplexed. Several times, he was on the point of confessing to Mr. Patpington that he had fooled him. Perhaps, after all, the knowledge that he was not invisible, that he was not abnormal, would bring the old man some relief. But how miserable would it make him to know that he was incurably blind, and devoid of glory?

He suddenly hit upon the solution. One might suppose that Hopkins had had it already, without knowing it, when Mr. Patpington gave him the ingredients of the potion—because, for several days, Hopkins had been obsessed with different memories. His visit to the illustrious colleague in London and

204

a journey that he had once made to the French Pyrenees returned incessantly to his mind, along with other thoughts that, unfortunately, created confusion. Take note also that he continually repeated to himself: "That man obeys me, blindly. The man is completely under my thumb," without seeing where that might lead. Finally, though, it was the discovery of the potion that triggered the denouement.

"Arthur!" called Mr. Patpington, one morning. "Come quickly! Bring a pencil and paper!"

Hopkins did as he was asked, hurriedly. Three lines of alphabetical characters and figures, large and small, were dictated to him in a feverish voice.

"What's that?" he asked.

"The formula! The formula of visibility! To make me visible, Arthur! It's to be drunk. Prepare it for me immediately!"

"To be drunk?"

Hopkins ran his eyes over the "prescription." The preparation was enough to poison all the citizens of Iping. Out of habit, however, he raised no objection, awaiting an opportunity to find a way to get out of it, and he went downstairs, thoughtful and full of annoyance. By degrees, though, Hopkins turned his frown into a hopeful expression, and, having opened the liquor cupboard, he set about mixing a cocktail whose fantasy would have alarmed the least traditional of barmen.

The mixture contained at least a dozen spirits, chosen at hazard, in doses selected in the same way. It made, when complete, a brownish liquid that filled a sherry glass. Hopkins added a few drops of various medicines to it, in order to give the concoction an appropriate aroma. Then he went back up to Mr. Patpington.

"Drink!" he told him. "That's the ticket."

Mrs. Hopkins, who had assisted in the confection of the cocktail, was hot on her husband's heels.

"God grant that it will succeed!" said Mr. Patpington— and he swallowed the mixture in a single draught.

"Lie down on the bed," Hopkins instructed. "It will take effect more rapidly."

Mr. Patpington lay down, meekly.

A minute went by. The congenial old man smiled beatifically and licked his lips.

"Oh, look! *Look!*" cried Hopkins, abruptly. "Your hands, your nose...LOOK! Your ears. *You're reappearing!* Uncle, Uncle, what a pleasure it is to see you again! There! See— your chin is reforming!"

But he could not prevent himself, while he uttered these frightful whoppers, from examining Uncle Pat's expression anxiously. There was a mirror there; he held it out to him. The other, sitting up again, pivoted on his backside hurriedly, sat on the edge of the bed, and paraded his astonished eyes over everything.

"Most agreeable!" he sighed, in ecstasy.

Hopkins felt his breast swelling with pride. "O powerful, redoubtable and mysterious suggestion!" he murmured.

Mr. Patpington contemplated the external world affectionately. "Arthur! Mary! Myself! I can see you and I also can see myself now! But what...what's causing all that dizziness? My word, I'm drunk!"

"No," said Hopkins, sympathetically. "It's just that you haven't yet readapted, you see. Stay seated on the bed."

"Dear, oh, dear little Uncle Pat" said Mrs. Hopkins, kissing Mr. Patpington on both cheeks.

A broad mute laugh enlivened the fresh face of the man who had wanted to realize the most astonishing fable in contemporary literature. He nodded his head and swayed from side to side, struggling against a happy vertigo that was making him lose his balance.

"How do you feel, Uncle Pat?" asked Mrs. Hopkins, maternally.

"Very well! Very well!" proclaimed Mr. Patpington, laughing. His plump little heels pounded the mattress-base. He suddenly launched an oratorical finger toward Hopkins. "When I was invisible..." he began, self-importantly.

Hopkins realized immediately that that was a phrase he would hear repeatedly, until his uncle was deprived of speech—but he loved Mr. Patpington so much that he wanted to go on hearing it until he himself was deprived of hearing.

# SINCE SINBAD

You have asked me, my dear Jean Ray, to write a few lines about "Fantastic literature" for the readers of *L'Ami des livres*.

Like everyone, in fact—including the undersigned—you call "fantastic," for want of a better term, all recreational literary production that does not deal with known realities: the entire oeuvre that extends from *Aladdin; or, The Marvelous Lamp* to *La Mort de la Terre*.[32]

Well, I think that the first thing to do is to limit the domain of the word "fantastic," an adjective evocative of devilry, the supernatural, crazy dreams, even nightmares; an epithet too exclusive of thought, method and knowledge, which is not at all adaptable to the work of a Wells, a Rosny Aîné, or some other writer I am not used to citing.

The application of the word "fantastic" to stories like *The Time Machine* or "Un Autre monde"[33]—or, more accurately, the confusion of genres revealed and consecrated by that application—makes a considerable contribution to the laborious slowness with which the public moves toward distractions that are, however, quite new and delightfully educational. It is because the public sees them only as simple fantasies. It classifies them in the same family as the tales of *The Thousand-and-One Nights*. It takes them for "Ali Babas" arbitrarily accommodated to present-day tastes—which is to say, seasoned with

---

[32] Renard inserts a reference here: "*La Mort de la Terre* (1912) by J.-H. Rosny Aîné." (1895; tr. as "The Death of the Earth" in Black Coat Press' collection *The Navigators of Space*).

[33] Renard inserts further references here to "*The Time Machine* (1895) by H. G. Wells" and "Un Autre monde" (1898) by Rosny Aîné." The latter (q.v.) was actually first published in 1895.

science. It tells itself that Scheherazade's imagination is not of a kind to support the parasitic invasion of electrical or chemical modernities. In its view, science and imagination, thus combined, are reciprocally harmful. The former, in departing from the truth, loses all is value; the latter, touched by reason, creases to sparkle.

All that comes, you see, from the way the public reasons, and from the fact that it reasons badly.

The truth is that in the 19th century, the state of science and the progress of knowledge have put writers in the position of manipulating hypotheses in the speculative field. By virtue of that fact, the physical world has become the object of conjectural, "parascientific" studies, which are not less captivating for arising essentially from philosophy—with the condition, nevertheless, of being considered as what they are, and not being taxed as "fantastic."

It seems to me that the fantastic, properly speaking, attained its highest realization in Hoffmann, and most especially in Poe, and then in Erckmann-Chatrian. I see no one in our era, except Ewers,[34] who can be compared with them, although his oeuvre is tiny compared with Edgar Poe's and appears to us to be tainted by a pervasive sadism, compared with which Poe's cerebral and transient perversity seems almost negligible.

The fantastic is, therefore, not French. We consume it avidly, but we do not know how to prepare it. Excuse me, but

---

[34] Renard inserts a note to identify Hanns Heinz Ewers as the author of two items, "*Mandragore* et *L'Araignée*;" the former has been translated into English under its German title, *Alraune* (1911) and the second—"Die Spinne" in German—as "The Spider." Ewers enjoyed a brief period of fashionability in France when stories from two German collections issued in 1908 and 1909 were translated for such periodicals as the *Mercure de France*, but he lost that fashionability with the outbreak of the Great War, when he became German propagandist in the USA.

it is not the French qualities that I value most highly in the works of the Lorrainean writers Erckmann and Chatrian; and I must say that there is a predominance of idealist anguish and metaphysical torment that is so scarcely American in the work of Edgar Poe that I often wonder about his ancestry. For, even while they are removing genies, enchanters, ogres and fairies from their tales, and their art reveals a singular and troubling poetry in their work, they are serving other causes than that of childhood morality.

Until now, the fantastic tale has been a sort of artificial mythology; now, it is something else entirely. It agitates, in an obscure fashion, the passions, dolor and mental disquiet; it has a human and psychological basis. It continues to be a fable, but one that pushes its allusions into the extreme depths of emotional life, and which, given the amplitude of the means at its disposal and being carelessness of any limitation of implausibility, succeeds in making us perceive strange subtleties in this regard. Because of that, it retains more poetry than the novel. And I do not intend, here, to place these more-or-less ingenious short stories—which are no more than arabesque imaginative play for the reader, and inconsequential amusement for the reader—in the ranks of works worthy of classification and criticism.

The majority of "parascientific" novels and stories (I resolutely proscribe the term "scientific marvelous"[35]) also

---

[35] In 1909, Renard had published an article in *Le Spectateur* on "Du Roman Merveilleux-Scientifique et de son action sur l'intelligence du progrès" [On Scientific Marvel Fiction and its Effect on the Consciousness of Progress], a translation of which is included in volume one of this series, in which he drew a distinction between the traditional genre of "the marvelous" and a nascent genre of fiction extrapolating "the scientific marvelous," along exactly the same lines as the distinction he draws here between "the fantastic" and "the parascientific." He had evidently become dissatisfied with his earlier terminology, perhaps because of negative responses from the

present the merit of being instruments of human observation which in the unusual light of suppositions, cause certain normally-imperceptible interior reliefs to stand out. But what clearly distinguishes the parascientific from the fantastic is that the fabulation of the former must, in itself, possess a "value"—a rational value—in being the development of a logical and fecund hypothesis, while we demand nothing similar of the latter; it is sufficient for us that its subject should be charming, burlesque or terrible, and that there should be something subhuman in it.

Now, the postulate of a parascientific novel can itself embody such a treasure of novelty, possess such a power of evocation, that its exposure, taken for what it is, constitutes an infinitely seductive and fruitful work. That which, in the fantastic, is merely a form, merely an expression, can here become the very foundation, the substance. And if the conceptions that emerge from it are not always related to humankind, or if the psychological element is absent therefrom, I say that no great harm is done.

Since people have been writing novels, every novel is psychological; to the extent that people have been persuaded that no novel exists in which no psychology is manifest, and that the quality of a novel is in direct proportion to the dose of psychology that it contains. I do not approve of that, because it makes me see readers—Aristarchos[36] included—as monkeys crouched in front of mirrors.

I recall what was said, 30 years ago, about the first performances of the works of Claude Debussy. People said, disdainfully, "That's not music"—and the moment that it "wasn't music" it became worthless! Well, let people cease to call stories stripped of psychology "novels," if they insist—but please

---

readers of the earlier article, or simply because it now seemed too cumbersome.

[36] Aristarchos was a renowned critic who became an archetype of rigor by daring to argue—cogently—that even Homer was not perfect.

allow people, from time to time, to interrupt their self-contemplation in order to raise their eyes above their navels, to accept that there are a few other objects in the universe that are not without interest (are there not others, even in humans, than psychology?) and to approach the parascientific novel without arguing about its psychological nature or lack of it, or its ambiguity or lack of it. Let them abandon that "accurate, subtle, powerful" and benevolent fictive opium in order to discover new points of view. Let them play, blissfully, in this artificial paradise…

Artificial? Tell me, is science any less artificial? What are its falsified theories worth today? What will the principles vigorously upheld as I write be worth tomorrow? As much as an outmoded novel—nothing more! Who can affirm, for example, that Wells's *Invisible Man* might not emerge from the unreal tomorrow? That the seemingly-chimerical possibility in question will not become a matter of everyday fact—apart from the error that I subsequently revealed, and which represents a stupidity so unexpected on the part of the English author!

Let us amuse ourselves by comparing the invisibility of a living body (a hypothetical discovery) with radiology (an actual discovery). We might be surprised to observe that these discoveries would have appeared *equally* impossible to one of our forefathers who had had taken it into his head to reflect upon them. How, in fact, would each of them have presented itself to his logical mind? In the form of two fallacies similarly belied by reality.

This is the fallacy of *The Invisible Man*:

Bodies that light passes completely through are invisible.

Now, there is a man through whom light passes completely.

Therefore, there is an invisible man.

And this is the fallacy of radiology:

We can see through bodies through which a certain quantity of light passes.

Now, a quantity of light passes through opaque bodies.

Therefore, we can see through opaque bodies.

I know of no example, moreover, which demonstrates better than this comparison how the parascientific differs from the fantastic, the former primarily provoking the joy of intelligence, the other initial soliciting the pleasure of the emotions.

There is no point in searching any further for the reason for the discouragement that led Wells to stop working in the vein of *The War of the Worlds* and why Rosny Aîné so rarely publishes works like "Les Xipéhuz" or *La Force mystérieuse*.[37] To earn a living by addressing oneself to intelligence—that, indeed, would be truly fantastic!

---

[37] "Les Xipéhuz," tr. as "The Xipehuz," is available in Black Coat Press' collection *The Navigators of Space*; *La Force Mystérieuse*, tr. as "The Mysterious Force," is available in Black Coat Press' collection *The Mysterious Force*.

# THE FROG

I was 13 years old. I had scarcely emerged from the fearful era in which the terror of darkness and solitude reigns over childhood. I was a thin boy devoid of brilliance, whose dreamy eyes dominated a spare face. Timid, impressionable and affectionate, I was perpetually agitated by emotion. The redoubtable and seductive world of the unknown already attracted me with an irresistible force—and when Science offered my youthful avidity some strange marvel or some veiled glimpse of a troubling mist, I felt myself transported by intoxication.

I loved mystery, especially the kind that borders on knowledge as night borders on day: the mystery at which the instruments of knowledge are already aimed. I loved, as I still do, the inexplicable, the future, the possible—and, first and foremost, the divine, exquisite and prestigious Hypothesis, which projects many a fantastic ray of light into every darkness, maintaining legend and fable among us, in new costumes.

I was an assiduous dreamer. Nothing seduced me like venturing to the extreme limits of certainty, leaning over the edge of the pit of obscurity that opens there, challenging the powers suspecting of luring there to a duel and—so to speak—tormenting the hydra crouching in its lair. Then, with a tremulous, keen and perverse kind of joy, I felt the old fears of my early life reborn within me, having become voluptuous.

It was a happy period in which I knew almost nothing, with the result that study reserved a thousand marvels of contrary nature for me, and every day brought me its discovery and its enigma.

Forgive me for extending myself thus in the depiction of my temperament. It is just that I deem it indispensable, in order to judge a fact reported by a witness, to know exactly what tendencies that witness has. It is necessary to know through what sorts of lenses a phenomenon has been observed. Otherwise, all sorts of errors can be produced, from errors of judgment to scientific ones. If I talk about myself, therefore, it is because I was the principal witness to the following adventure, and it is vital that nothing should neglected in the order of psychological precautions when it is a matter of exposing a bizarre incident as delicately ambiguous as the death of Madame Chablas.

I shall insist, therefore—but not out of egotism—on the infinite sadness with which my childish soul was overwhelmed in the era when the vicissitudes of that macabre day unfolded.


My parents, convinced that they were acting in my best interests, had sent me to the Ecole Jean-Jacques Rousseau. It was an expensive boarding school not far from a large town on the coast of Normandy. It could only accommodate some 60 pupils. It provided facilities for sport and for manual labor, but studies did not suffer for that, and I must admit that boarding in those conditions bore as little resemblance to imprisonment as is possible.

Until then, however, I had never left my paternal home, to which tutors had come in relay to educate me, and, pleasant as the Ecole Jean-Jacques Rousseau was, I had difficulty getting used to the abrupt change of environment. Exiled far from my family, deprived of my mother's continual pampering, sensitive to all the frictions of discipline and camaraderie, I sought opportunities to isolate myself, and, in spite of the fact that the rules forbade it, I often found means of returning to my room and indulging myself passionately in the sour and precocious delights of nostalgia.

Every such occasion was like a rendezvous with solitude. I chose in advance some happy memory of the familial past, and savored it delectably, until the illusion dissipated in the wake of mental contention or the bell summoned me back to class.

My room, moreover, possessed another, quite different, attraction—an attraction whose strength I did not suspect but which, however, gradually took hold of me, so powerfully that nowadays, it is in that memory that I delight in penetrating the freshest and purest recess of my youth. That room—it was number 2—was situated on the second floor. The window overlooked the Atlantic Ocean. Beyond the trees in the courtyard—which was almost a garden—one could see the immense rectilinear horizon into which the sun sank every evening. The ridge of the cliffs loomed above the roofs of the school. It was a grandiose and profound spectacle; the future would reveal its cost to me, but a secret need drove me to contemplate it from the very first.

Then again, I would not have been a human child if I had not savored the forbidden pleasure of withdrawing from all surveillance and being able, without being seen behind my half-closed Venetian blinds, to spy on the movements of others—which is what I was doing on that sunlit day, the sinister *day of the frog*, whose date is inscribed on the tomb of Monsieur and Madame Chablas.

I shall explain shortly who Monsieur and Madame Chablas were, but first I must explain who Mourgue was.

Mourgue, the headmaster of the school, had the external appearance of an academic about 37 years old. He had a mottled complexion, a brown beard and long hair. His keen eyes looked through a pince-nez. His manner of dress was negligent. He was reputed—I learned this detail, among others, later—to be a rather distinguished physiologist, impeded in his research by an incessant lack of funds, for which he strove to make up, ingeniously, with stubborn ardor. The man was, in fact, burdened by a terrible vice: gambling—and the casino in the neighboring town swallowed up the profits that his establishment produced as they came in. Such was Mourgue. We did not detest him, by any means, for he treated us benevolently, taking into consideration all the failings of this world. His mother, who had been Madame Mourgue, was now named Madame Chablas, by reason of her remarriage.

Monsieur and Madame Chablas lived at the school. Madame Chablas, who doted on her son and feared the effects that his incurable passion might have on him, had sworn not to leave him until the supreme moment when she would be obliged to quite the world altogether. We had nicknamed Monsieur and Madame Chablas "Philemon and Baucis."[38] They were both 59 years old and even though they were almost sexagenarians they continued to be unashamedly fond of one another. That love, although quite touching, had something slightly ridiculous about it, which its amorous aspect did not diminish at all.

Edgar Chablas—Philemon—was an aged dandy, very well-groomed, with dyed and pomaded hair. He trimmed his jet black moustache carefully and wore his beard in the style of Jules Simon.[39] A glossy comb-over debited from his occipital hair was plastered over his bald spot. A very placid fellow, he never relaxed his smile, as if his dentition merited universal admiration. We took pleasure in seeing him pass through the courtyard, spick and span, with a felt hat pulled down over his ears, his cravat knotted Collin-style,[40] clean

---

[38] The story of Philemon and Baucis is related in Ovid's *Metamorphoses*. While Zeus and Hermes are visiting Phrygia disguised as mortals they are refused hospitality in a thousand homes before being taken in by the eponymous old couple; when offered a reward for their generosity the two aged lovers ask that neither of them should outlive the other, and their wish is granted.

[39] Jules Simon (1814-1896) was a famous statesman and philosopher who shaved his face in a distinctive but rather ridiculous fashion, so as to leave a frame of hair around his face, connecting his side-whiskers under his chin.

[40] References to cravats tied "à la Collin" crop up occasionally in 19th century French literature; one suspects that Renard is borrowing the phrase from literary sources rather than expecting his readers to recognize its rather obscure reference to the comic poet Jean-François Collin d'Harleville (1755-1808).

gaiters on his feet, his hands behind his back, swinging a cane as if it were a pendulum.

Edgar Chablas made every effort not to be an imbecile, and always had, but the poor chap could not flatter himself one having performed very brilliantly in the enterprises of his life. He admitted to anyone and everyone that a strange fatality that condemned him to perennial half-measures and inevitable divisions. Philemon had not even contrived to be born individually; a twin brother, deceased thereafter, had doubled the importance of that initial event. Monsieur Chablas complained frankly of never having done anything worthwhile except with the assistance of a collaborator. He was perpetually astonished to find himself living at addresses that, as if by chance, bore a number supplemented by an A or a B. "To cap it all," he said, "I married a widow. And you'll no doubt find that I shan't even be buried on my own."—a baroque but rational assertion, to which Destiny did not wish to give the lie.

It is necessary to know, furthermore, that Monsieur Chablas played the part of only really being a sort of "supplementary human being" very well, for an alliance with a certain financier had increased his fortune copiously, and Madame Chablas, widow though she was of Monsieur Mourgue senior, augmented it with a love as fine as it was antiquated.

Madame Chablas—Baucis—was in no way outdone by her second husband in the matter of dress. She was one of those old ladies in frills who, by tightening their corsets, obtain in compensation a fearfully slim and rigid figure. She walked stiffly, holding herself erect, but her back was rounded in spite of her stoical efforts. Her hands, which long usage had stigmatized, were covered in rings all day. Her enormous coiffure, stuffed with hair-pieces, as yellow and dull as the hair of corpses, gave her an immeasurable head upon which, in order to go out, she perched imposing combinations of feathers ribbons, tulle and baubles. If you were downwind of her, a strong odor of chypre wafted over you, terrorizing our nostrils, even if the lady was still so far away that her face was only imperfectly revealed by the incredible cosmetic mask with which it was plastered. Those violent colors were more reminiscent of a painted puppet than a creature of flesh and blood. Should the mouth open, it pierced a curiously dark hole within the vermilion systems that represented the lips—and what further emphasized the effect of that remarkable physiognomy was that Madame Chablas continually widened her eyes in fright, by means of which the dear lady seemed to be perpetually in peril.

Monsieur and Madame Chablas! In talking about them, I rediscover the clownish image that they have left in my childhood memory. That age is pitiless. Today, when I remember that they had loved one another madly, that they loved one another still, and so strongly that one of them could not have survived without the other—when I tell myself that all that paltry artifice, and the employment of all those inoffensive coquetries were only intended desperately to prolong, for one another, a vestige of the charms that had once seduced them...

I can no longer reconcile the memory of those two marionettes with the sentiment of so rare an affection.

It was said that Monsieur Chablas was a millionaire and that the Ecole Jean-Jacques Rousseau owed its foundation to him. Nothing was more exact, according to what I subsequently ascertained. It was on the insistence of his beloved wife that Monsieur Chablas had gone into partnership with his stepson, the humble patrimony of the Mourgues having melted through the gambler's fingers. I am certain, furthermore, that Madame Chablas only won that victory after a great deal of effort, for—as events have proved—Monsieur Chablas had no affection for Mourgue save for that channeled through the excellent person who bestirred herself between them. Was it not necessary to be a mother, in fact, to absolve a lunatic who squandered his exceptional gifts to the profit of the deadliest of penchants?

Is it the case, then, that Mourgue was disdainful of Science? I do not believe so. I saw him teach physics, chemistry and the natural sciences. He brought a passion and an extraordinary verve to his lessons. And besides, do we know the exact truth of this matter? Do we know that, in the privacy of his study, Mourgue only studied martingales?[41] He has not left any scientific heritage, but what does that prove? Personally, I doubt it—because of the frog.

And I will explain now what the frog was.

The students of philosophy and the students of elementary mathematics came together in the same room for the course in natural sciences, and every year Mourgue repeated Galvani's experiment—which consists of exciting the muscles of a dead frog with an electric current—for their benefit. Our headmaster presented the demonstration in a manner so novel and impressive, however, that the frog experiment became famous among the pupils of the Ecole Jean-Jacques Rousseau. Those who had seen it longed to see it again. They talked about it in advance, as a sort of periodic festival, and when the great day came, there was always an external audience at the windows of the privileged class, looking avidly in. One was taking advantage of a break, a second was skipping an oral examinations, a third had defected from the infirmary. The junior masters never punished anyone severely in that situation; Mourgue, indulgently, pretended not to see anything as he leaned over the table and produced the classical miracle.

To be perfectly accurate, there were three dead frogs there, already prepared. One of them was reduced to its inferior part, affixed by the legs to a cork mat. The second, pinned like the hindquarters of the first, and partially dissected, was connected, as usual, to the transmissions of a myograph.[42] The third wore a little belt from which extended, at the level of the hips, a double conductive wire, twisted about itself, about a meter long.

As an excitatory source, Mourgue employed a bichromate jar-battery. Fixing two copper wires to the electrodes of

---

[41] A martingale is a primitive betting system, which consists of doubling up on losing bets in order to recover the losses.

[42] A myograph is an instrument for recording and measuring the intensity muscular contractions.

the jar and gripping their free ends, he began by making the miserable hind legs dance the traditional jig, contracting and extending as the current passed through them.

Then came the myograph demonstration.

Finally, Mourgue took the third frog, and connected the flexible conductor—which, one deduced, penetrated the mysterious core of the batrachian's flesh—to the battery. That was the moment we all awaited with anxious impatience.

As soon as the circuit was closed, one saw the frog's four galvanized feet contract beneath it, and lift it up in a lifelike leap—and, convulsively but rhythmically, make the little cadaver move forward in a series of odiously natural hops.

Mourgue, battery in hand, followed the horrible creature, which he seemed to hold on a leash. It made its way to the end of the table, its eyes bleak and withered, an abominable laboratory automaton—and when Mourgue interrupted the current, the miserable thing suddenly collapsed, as if it were dying for a second time and Mourgue really were able to reanimate it, to kill it over and over again, endlessly…

Yes, I was thirteen years old when I saw that for the first time through the classroom windows. Next to me, a new junior master, Monsieur Bernardi, was ecstatic…but I couldn't bear to look at such a scene any longer. I didn't have the heart. I felt that I was about to fall ill, and I turned away, profoundly upset.

Monsieur Bernardi, perceiving my distress, made me sit down on a cement border. A few pupils gathered around me and Mourgue, who came out when the lesson finished, was informed of my fainting fit. "Come with me," he said, paternally. "A little glass of Muscat wine, and that'll be an end to it. Come to my room, my lad."

I followed him.

With his mother and stepfather, Mourgue lived at the back of the courtyard, on the first floor of the central building, whose ground floor comprised the visiting-room and the refectory, while the second and third floors were occupied by our study-bedrooms. The most beautiful rooms in his apartment gave out through French windows on to a vast balcony, simple and truly academic, which ran along the entirely length of the façade. It was there that we often had occasion to see Madame Chablas. Busy with her domestic duties, she would use the balcony to go from one room to another when visitors were waiting in the reception-room for Mourgue to receive them. These appearances gave us pleasure, and we would watch Baucis emerge and vanish in her childish finery, as intriguing as one of those colored statuettes which emerge from the case of an old clock when a church clock chimes, gravely show themselves off, and then return to their place through another opening.

It was 10 a.m. The basement resounded with the noise of the kitchens. We went upstairs. Mourgue took me into the reception-room, and then turned right into the dining-room.

"Sit down," he said—and he headed for a half-open door, with the manifest intention of closing it.

I knew very well that it was the door to Monsieur and Madame Chablas's bedroom, adjacent to the dining-room. Mourgue seemed surprised to find the door ajar. He glanced into the room, and I saw him suddenly precipitate himself into it, pulling the door shut behind him.

I sat still for a few minutes, amazed and discomfited, trying to perceive, above the din of the break and the kitchens, some auditory clue as to what was happening behind the door. Soon, though, it reopened, just enough to allow Mourgue's head through—a pale and nervous Mourgue who said to me, hoarsely: "Go away, my lad. An accident…you shouldn't be here…"

I don't know what he added with regard to medicine and the infirmary. I have wondered, since, whether he sent me to the infirmary in order to drink the medicine or simply to say that I had been sent there. I was no longer listening. I was utterly distraught and I fled precipitately.

In the courtyard boys were capering about and playing games. Monsieur Bernardi and another master, Monsieur La-font, were strolling in the shade of the plane-trees, the former presumably conversing with the latter on the subject of the legal studies he was undertaking.

"Monsieur," I stammered, "there's been an accident in Monsieur Mourgue's apartment, in Monsieur and Madame Chablas's bedroom. I don't know what…an accident!"

They looked by turns at my face and the headmaster's windows. They consulted one another and, after a slight hesitation, ended up setting forth. I can't explain why curiosity overcame my apprehension and how I came to accompany them, but I've explained the attraction that mystery exerted on my mind.

When we arrived at the entrance to the reception-room, Mourgue came through it, from the left. "My stepfather is dead!" he announced, with a tragic gesture. He continued on his way. We followed him, respectfully.

Monsieur Chablas was sitting, fully-dressed—as formally as ever—in a wing-chair. He was no longer smiling. The shadow of death was eating into his lividity.

"And my poor mother!" said Mourgue. "My poor mother! She's mad with distress! I found her next to him, haggard and stupefied, not wanting to understand, refusing to believe…and when she did understand, she suddenly took refuge at the other end of the apartment. She's locked herself in—oh, but I need to comfort her! She has to let me in!"

Then, giving every evidence of feverish anxiety, Mourgue left the room and went back the way he had come. We heard him, through the sequence of rooms, knocking on the door of his study and speaking in an urgent tone, replete with tenderness.

"Let me in, Mother! Don't stay there all alone! Come on, be reasonable. Open the door!"

Madame Chablas seemed to make no reply. Mourgue came back, war-weary but less preoccupied. "She's weeping," he told us. "I heard her. I prefer that. I think it will calm her down, for the time being."

The housekeeper came back from the market. She was bewildered. Mourgue dissuaded her from going to interrupt Madame Chablas's despair.

Suddenly he noticed my presence. "Oh, Messieurs—that child, here!"

I didn't wait for whatever would come next, but made myself scarce, full of confusion, with that weary reproach buzzing in my ears.

The bell rang.

The day continued according to the usual timetable, but in a silence maintained by the masters.

For my part, incapable of paying the slightest attention to the teachers, I couldn't tear my thoughts away from that drama that had disturbed them so violently. The horror of death obsessed me. What a terrible fright, at 13! And in what a frightful light the Galvani experiment had been displayed to me! Must I admit it, in spite of myself? I was less shocked by the death of Monsieur Chablas than the galvanizations exhibited by Mourgue, and among the cadavers that I had observed since the morning, it was not that of the man the haunted me most obstinately.

I did not, however, abandon my relentless enquiries into what had happened in our headmaster's apartment. I learned, in consequence, that the mortuary chamber had been prepared and that Madame Chablas still refused to come out of the study, where her son had rejoined her, by way of the balcony door.

Throughout that afternoon my gaze strayed repeatedly to the mute array of those French windows, veiled by their white curtains. The feeble light of two candles showed through the one furthest to the left. The furthest one to the right—that of the study— evoked for me the well-known disorder of that picturesque location, full of heaped-up papers and apparatus, where I now imagined the unfortunate Baucis sobbing on Mourgue's shoulder and stubbornly insisting on remaining there, far from her Philemon, who was no longer a person.

As evening approached, I felt very tired. The timetable gave us a break of three-quarters of an hour before dinner. I took advantage of it to escape from communal life and went back to my room surreptitiously. Everything there rested in a peaceful inertia, bathed in warmth and shadow. I opened the Venetian blinds slightly, and the serene vision of the sun setting over the sea appeared to me through the slit. That was probably what had brought me to my high-set cell, avid as I was for the mysterious consolation that human beings extract from the reassuring splendors of Nature.

The sun was low enough to be seen declining with a promptitude that seemed to be accelerating. Its descent testified to a sort of voluptuous haste, as if the sea had beckoned it; and toward it, over the waves, sharing their moving extent, ran a fiery road, a glorious carpet—as if to invite it not to disappear, but rather to roll from the shore of the sky to the strand of the ocean.

I was drawn out of my ecstasy by confused noises, which reminded me that Mourgue's study was situated directly beneath my room. That brought me back to the funereal day. With my ear stuck to the wall, I listened fruitlessly for a few minutes—then I heard someone open the French window, and I leaned out.

Down below, the upper school pupils were arranged in two rows, facing me, ready to go into the refectory. They saw, as I did, Madame Chablas come out of the study. The poor woman seemed to be exhausted. Absorbed in her grief, she moved absent-mindedly, with a hesitant step. A powerful scent of chypre rose up, enveloping me.

So she had finally decided to fulfill her duties as a widow! Poor, poor Madame Chablas! I followed her with my eyes from behind my blinds. She stiffened herself as best she could, but nothing could have modified the somnambulistic gait pushing her toward the most redoubtable obligation of all! Nothing could ameliorate the emotion that the sight of that good woman, going where she was going, inspired in me. Nothing: not the burlesque make-up that still begrimed her, nor the jewels on her sagging hands, nor the accessories of her complicated dress, so blue and so green—all the things that had given rise to so many gibes!

I thought I could hear a sort of rustling sound beneath my window. My gaze left the walking woman, and I perceived what my comrades could not see from below—which is to say, *a long flexible wire, which Madame Chablas was dragging behind her, the other end of which disappeared through the French windows of the study…*

Before my stupefaction had even become manifest, however, I had witnessed the drama's denouement. Madame Chablas, all of a sudden and without a moan, had collapsed.

Cries rang out.

Mourgue ran forward. I threw myself backwards. It was vital, above all, that he did not catch a glimpse of me. He must not! For me, at that moment, it was a matter of life and death. For at that moment, there was, for me, no doubt as to the truth!

My teeth chattered. Suppressed panic made me shiver.

I crept downstairs. I mingled with my comrades. Everyone was repeating that Madame Chablas, too, had just died. Mourgue had only picked up a corpse. Vanquished by fatigue, he had, it was said, fallen asleep by his mother's side. She had gone out by herself without waking him, and he was now in despair at only having been brought to his feet by the clamor of the pupils.

As these items of information reached me randomly, their plausibility imposed itself on my reason; doubt entered into me, and the terror that had gripped me gave way to a disordered conflict of antagonistic ideas. I was too nervous to get a grip on myself, too young to discipline my thoughts, and I would not have entrusted anyone with the task of clarifying their tumult.

Sometimes I perceived, confusedly, the extent to which the Galvani experiment, as improved by Mourgue, had influenced me, and what tenacious obsession had amalgamated that memory with all my other thoughts—and then I lost all confidence in my lucidity.

Sometimes, on the other hand, the scene on the balcony reproduced itself on the screen of my memory with an extraordinary precision, with the enigmatic wire unrolling behind Madame Chablas. I saw her collapse again; I wondered what fluid had suddenly run out (was it electricity, or was it life?) and who had cut off that current (was it Mourgue or was it God?).

After that, a rush of arguments was precipitated within my head, toward the idea of a galvanization of Madame Chablas, and my intelligence, overwhelmed by their number, ceased functioning momentarily…just as the bubbles of gas in a battery precipitate themselves upon the negative electrode, and the battery becomes polarized.

The years now permit me to disengage the irrefutable facts that imposed themselves upon me more-or-less dully that evening: the presence of the wire; its invisibility relative to the witnesses in the courtyard; Mourgue's conviction that no other witness was positioned on the upper floors; the coincidence of the emergence of Madame Chablas with the assembly of the pupils formed up facing the balcony; the irreducible distance—not rapidly reducible, at least—between the spectators in the courtyard and the spectacle on the balcony; the extraordinarily automatic gait of Madame Chablas; her perfume, more vehement than ever; her dead gaze, which my position had prevented me from seeing very well; the layer of make-up that could have dissimulated a sepulchral pallor; and finally, the school's electric lighting, implying the existence of many power-points capable of feeding any kind of apparatus at a moment's notice.

Now, had not Mourgue stayed shut up in his study for a long time, able to construct at his leisure, within human limitations, the galvanizer he had invented? Had not Mourgue, in an excitement that might have been feigned, jealously reserved to himself the duty of taking away and undressing his mother's body?

All that formed an impressive array of charges against him, which could not be contradicted. But nothing, either, opposed the more natural version of the event. To be fair, ought it not to be remembered that Mourgue's study was the indescribable receptacle of a host of machines? Electric wires were strewn over the floor, some of them interminable and equipped with plugs or sockets perfectly capable of catching on the hem of a skirt. And, I ask you, does a woman in distress think about anything other than her distress? Besides, as was well-known, Madame Chablas usually walked in a mechanical fashion; despair and mental torment explain perfectly adequately why that particularity should be exaggerated. Her make-up was no novelty either. Finally, what interest could Mourgue have had in hiding and delaying the official recognition of his mother's death? That was what I could not explain, to begin with—without giving the question the importance that it merited, because I was hallucinated by the horror of my hypothesis.

The problem, in sum, remained unsolved for the child I was, as it remains unsolved for the man I am.

*Was it a living person that was seen to die?*

Where did Madame Chablas die? Was it on the balcony, as everyone believed? Was it in the study? Did she really take refuge there in a fit of grief? Did she emerge therefrom not as a living person, but a corpse galvanized and piloted by Professor Mourgue? Was it not rather, that same morning, in the conjugal bedroom? Had her son found her dead by Monsieur Chablas's side, and had he carried her into the study while I went to fetch Monsieur Bernardi? In that case, which had died first: Philemon, or Baucis?

In my soul and my conscience, I have no idea. And if my mission is to pass judgment on the affair, I can only rely on the testimony of an impressionable child—that child being myself.

"Pass judgment?" you say. Does the Law, then, anticipate a punishment for such actions? They are sacrilegious, to be sure, and grotesque, but might find an excuse in scientific curiosity. And, in the final analysis, they injured no one, in a legal sense.

No one? Do you think so? Listen, then, to this fragment of dialogue, which I overheard a few days after the death of the Chablases, between Monsieur Bernardi—the law student—and Monsieur Lafont.

"There's been mention of 120,000 francs!" said Monsieur Bernardi.

"And Mourgue gets it all?" asked Monsieur Lafont.

"Everything! An only son…he can think himself lucky to have the chance! When one thinks that, on the morning of her death, Madame Chablas hadn't a *sou*!"

"How's that?"

"Follow me carefully, Lafont. Monsieur Chablas had no other heir than his wife. Remember that Mourgue was no relation to him and that the dead man left no will. For Mourgue to profit from his stepfather's will, it was necessary that his mother should first inherit from Monsieur Chablas, and that Mourgue should then inherit from his mother…"

"So," said Lafont, "if Madame Chablas had died before Monsieur Chablas, the latter's inheritance would have gone to the State? And Mourgue wouldn't have got anything?"

"Exactly. But it would have been sufficient, in law, for Madame Chablas to have died at the same time as her husband, or for the circumstances of their decease not to have permitted it to be determined with certainty which of the two had preceded the other to the tomb."

"Really?"

"It's called the *presumption of co-decease*. Article 722 of the Civil Code states: *'If those who die together are over 50 years old and less than 60, the male is always presumed to have survived, where there is an equality of age, or if the difference does not exceed one year.'* That's the case."

"Indeed," concluded Monsieur Lafont, with a laugh. "In those conditions, Mourgue, I dare say, has had a lucky escape. A few hours earlier…"

"And the Queen of Spades would have lost a pretty penny!" Monsieur Bernardi concluded.[43]

That was the last echo that reached me of the doubtful and dramatic adventure, Mourgue lived to a ripe old age in easy circumstances. He was wise enough, although rich, to continue as headmaster of the Ecole Jean-Jacques Rousseau and to live there thriftily in the capacity of a professor of natural sciences—to the extent that he repeated Galvani's experiment every year for the benefit of his pupils.

I witnessed it punctually from behind the windows until my turn came to sit on the philosophy benches. By then, though, I was rather blasé about a prodigy that I had seen so many times. The moderation of grown-ups increased its hold on me every day; Mourgue's frog no longer intrigued me.

---

[43] The reference to the Queen of Spades is intended to remind the reader of Alexander Pushkin's famous novella, first published in 1834, in which that card—reflected in the person of a sinister temptress—is fatal to the gambler who is the story's protagonist.

# HYPOTHETICAL FICTION

Sometimes, when a writer assembles his words and sentences, he does not require them so much to express his thoughts as to suggest certain sentiments and sensations to the reader. In consequence, the person who reads such books in the same way that he reads the Civil Code or some informative newspaper—which is to say, remaining deaf to the mysterious appeals of the text, striving only to understand them instead of allowing himself to feel them—is like a blacksmith or a locksmith placed before the gate of a park, who only thinks of examining the grille, without perceiving the park through the bars.

Now what is true for certain kinds of style is no less true for certain kinds of composition. Thus, the person who sets out to read a hypothetical novel without reading between the lines, without glimpsing, beyond the story, certain conceptions that it is impossible to translate, or the exposure of which would necessitate the employment of a forbidding language contrary to the principles of the novel, is also only seeing the grille, neglecting the park, and will answer with reference to the lock when you talk to him about the flowers.

I have taken the trouble to clarify this point before saying what I think about the genre of fiction that is often identified as "scientific marvel fiction," to which I now prefer the appellation "hypothetical fiction." There would, in fact, be no point in writing it—or, at least, in publishing it—if everyone read as everyone calculates, coldly and flatly. The imagination of the writer of hypothetical fiction requires that readers are willing to "dance with him." J.-H. Rosny Aîné's *La Force mystérieuse* and *La Mort de la Terre*, or H. G. Wells's *The Invisible Man* and *The Island of Doctor Moreau* are as many invitations to the waltz of worlds. If the reader remains passive and inert, if he does not perceive the profound rhythm of the universal jazz that is the music of the spheres, he is done for; he will not enter into the mentality of the hypothetical novel—which mentality consists, by means of a story that is ingenious and attractive in itself, of supposing that which is not, in order to acquire an idea of that which might be, of that which might perhaps happen in future or that which might exist beyond the range of our senses; and also in order to gain a better understanding of that which we know, whether by studying that which our world is not, or by adopting unusual viewpoints in order to look at it.

Between the thick shadows of the unknown and the luminous body of our knowledge, there is an extremely captivating zone, which is the zone of hypotheses: an extremely narrow region into which all the efforts of scientists and philosophers are hurled. It forms a sort of phantasmal halo. It is like the fringe of science, the feathery down of certainty. That is where the characters of hypothetical fiction operate; that is where lights are ignited which, although entirely artificial, radiate knowledge into ignorance—so to speak—and give us, if not the power itself, at least the delightful illusion of obtaining some slight understanding of the inexplicable.

That is an amusement of the intelligence, a fecund game of the mind, which is sometimes justified in an impressive manner by the reality of discoveries, and which then acquires the name of *anticipation*. It is reckless to call a novel that attempts to divine the future an "anticipation." At the very most, one may say "attempted anticipation," insofar as the prophecy is unrealized.

It is not in any case, works of that sort that seem to me to be the most interesting among hypothetical novels. Others give me more pleasure, appearing to me to satisfy more appropriately, by means of a mirage, our impatience to know, and to calm the nervous tension from which we suffer because we feel irremediably ill-equipped with physical organs to pierce the mystery that surrounds us, the encirclement of which only retreats very slowly. They are the stories which, taking a judiciously-chosen supposition as a point of departure, examine the consequences that flow therefrom, according to logic. When Rosny, in *La Force mystérieuse*, studies the influence of a celestial body endowed with certain properties passing close to the Earth, while, in "Les Xipéhuz," he depicts the struggle of ancient humans against a race of creatures that dispute their supremacy, and when Wells, in *The War of the Worlds*, describes the invasion of our globe by the inhabitants of Mars, or, in "The New Accelerator," reviews the consequences of all our functions being accomplished more rapidly, it can be claimed that we obtain more therefrom than a transient pleasure or an illusory satisfaction. It is, at any rate, a little better than a cigarette given to us to smoke in order to appease our hunger.

Why? Because it is always efficacious to put things in a new light, even if the light in question is artificial. Our knowledge gains substantially thereby.

We do not give sufficient thought to the fact that, in order to observe an object or a creature—a human being, for example—more clearly, it is an excellent idea to observe what that object or creature—the human being—is not. That is a negative study, which we are not accustomed to making, but which is nevertheless precious, and nonetheless striking. When, on a sheet of paper, you have shaded the whole area external to the face whose features you have set out to draw, what remains in white upon that background? The silhouette of the face, the contours obtained by a negative procedure.

Except that author should only make one single slip. From the moment when we have accepted his initial supposition—the only one that he has the right to impose upon us—he has a duty to avoid the slightest error of judgment; otherwise, the works falls to the level of fairy-tales. An inflexible logic must govern the action—a logic equal to the disciplined imagination that presides over the choice of the initial supposition. One of the grand masters of hypothetical fiction, Wells, has presented us with an invisible man *who can see*, which is much more inadmissible scientifically than the invisibility of a living body. I add that one sometimes has great surprises in store regarding the originality of a theme for development; in my own case, I believed one day that I had discovered an entirely new idea—that of *Le Péril bleu*—but perceived, to my amazement, that an eminent colleague had formulated it before me...well before! That colleague was none other than Plato. What a lesson in humility![44]

In the 19th and 20th centuries hypothetical fiction has replaced the 18th century *conte philosophique*. "Today," Wells has said, "utopia needs a world." That world is the zone of which I spoke just now, and which is situated between the known and the unknown. And it is entirely natural that, in an era when science is absolutely predominant, one makes use of science to erect the framework of those novels that are conceived less for providing distraction during reading than for giving rise to dreams after they have been read. "They give the imagination a shake," as Jacques Copeau[45] has said of them. Without a doubt, if Voltaire and Swift were to reappear among us, the former would not have failed to import into *Micromégas* and the latter into *Gulliver* a series of issues descendant from the scientific knowledge that we have acquired in the century of Edison and the Curies—and, scant as our belief might be in the possibilities of metempsychosis, it is easy enough to imagine that the soul of Voltaire nowadays animates our great Rosny, and that Swift's has passed into the body of Wells.

---

[44] This observation is a trifle disingenuous. The reference is presumably to the story of Gyges in the *Republic*, to which reference is made more than once in *Le Péril bleu*, but Renard's purpose in quoting it here is presumably to defend himself against the charge that he had been imitating Wells in compiling his own romance of invisibility, by emphasizing the antiquity of the idea.

[45] Jacques Copeau (1879-1949) was most famous as a theater director and dramatist—he founded the Théâtre du Vieux-Colombier—but he was also an active promoter of literary work and helped to found the *Nouvelle Revue Française*.

We know, however, that in the 18th century, the *conte philosophique* was exclusively a pretext for satires. *Micromégas* and *Gulliver*, which only retain a delightful inventiveness for us, both had the object of railing at certain contemporary individuals and institutions. In our time, however, if the hypothetical novel permits a Wells to express sociological opinions in the form of an apologue, many writers, by way of compensation, are able to work in the genre with no other preoccupation that causing it to exhale all the aromas of its own nature.

Does this mean that a hypothetical novel ought to be confined within the limits of the physico-chemical world? Far be it from me to think so. On the contrary, the finest works of the genre are those in which old anxieties that have always obsessed human daydreams, haunted our minds and clutched at our hearts drift like eternal effluvia. The wind of destiny blows through the laboratory door. Isn't that so, Edgar Poe? Isn't that so, Villiers de l'Isle-Adam? But that is not what is essential; what is essential resides in the metaphysical fog that inevitably rises within the romantic narrative.

It follows from this, necessarily, that the most enthusiastic lovers of the hypothetical novel are to be found on the far side of the Rhine. We (forgive me for that "we," which is almost as detestable as "I") do not understand it any better than the people of central Europe. The Latin peoples already show us much more indifference. The English consider works like *The Food of the Gods* or *The First Men In the Moon* to be secondary within the oeuvre of their Wells. As for the Americans, they are still a trifle young, and it was surely by virtue of an error that Edgar Poe as born in Baltimore more than 100 years ago.[46]

---

[46] This judgment might seem a trifle odd to modern science fiction readers, but if Renard knew, in 1928, of the existence of Hugo Gernsback's *Amazing Stories* and other examples of "scientifiction," he might well have considered them to be products of German rather than American enterprise. He was

I apologize for not having presented this brief survey more simply. The subject is complex, and I consider that it can only be treated appropriately by employing, as I have tried to do, indirect procedures that do not attack it directly but delimit it, like the aforementioned design, from without.

One image, in order to finish with a *cul-de-lampe*:[47] hypothetical fiction seems to me to be perfectly symbolized, in its fantasy and its rationality, by the sculptor Jean de Bologne's *Mercury*: that young and handsome god whose wings, although fantastic, do not make a monster; who flies with a powerful grace, but who still maintains—and always will maintain—a single toe in contact with the Earth of human beings.[48]

---

probably better acquainted with the success in the 1920s of the German *Zukunftsroman* [futuristic fiction], whose technophilic practitioners included the best-selling Hans Dominik, but his plaintive comment about hypothetical fiction being better appreciated on the far side of the Rhine may well have more to do with his familiarity with Fritz Lang's movie *Metropolis* (1926) and the fact that his own modestly hypothetical novel *Les Mains d'Orlac* had been filmed in Germany (in 1925) rather than France—the American version was not made until 1935.

[47] Literally, the bottom of a lamp—but the term is used in architecture to refer to any rounded suspended ornament, and is thus suggestive here of "rounding out" the argument. Although *culs-de-lampes* play a highly significant role in the art of the imaginary world featured in *Un Homme chez les microbes* (tr. in volume 2 of this series as "A Man Among the Microbes"), the term is not used in the version that had recently been published (very belatedly) shortly before this article appeared in the December 15, 1928 issue of *A.B.C.*

[48] The bronze statue by Jean de Bologne (1529-1608) to which Renard refers is to be found in the Louvre; it became an oft-copied stereotype.

# THE DISCOVERY

"Well, Ralph," said the dazzling Mrs. Parker, "Tell me what this new instrument is. It looks like a photograph frame…"

It was evening in New York, after dinner, in the marvelous hall of the marble palace in which Randolph Parker, the second Edison, resides at the expense of the United States.

A surprising hall, in truth. Almost everywhere, ebonite, steel and nickel added a cold and industrial note to that sumptuous environment. Electricity triumphed amid the draperies, the complex items of furniture, the supremely comfortable chairs and all the abundance of plutocratic architecture.

This evening, a diffuse light, like that of day, illuminated the phonographs, automatic organs and the piano that played itself with the touch of a Paderewski. Various telephones were strewn about the heavy tables, overloaded with luminous glassware, There were electric lighters and parabolic heaters scattered here and there. A silvered wall awaited the projection of an invisible cinematograph. The mysterious and absurd maws of loudspeakers protruded from the corners.

Old Randolph Parker, still svelte in his smoking-jacket, was moving from one apparatus to another, incapable of remaining still for a single moment. He had taken a little pair of forceps and a screwdriver from his pocket, and he was contentedly regulating his machines, which sometimes crackled as they emitted minuscule blue sparks. Rolling his Havana cigar from one corner of his mouth to the other, he approached the "instrument" that had intrigued his young wife: a sort of milky screen framed in wood, in the form that photographers call a "card-album."

"Tell me, Ralph—what is it?"

The master of the lightning turned to Mrs. Parker with the smiling eyes that characterize phlegmatic Yankee good humor. "A surprise!" he said, his cigar still moving.

There were four of us in the hall: Parker, his wife, his nephew Teddy and me.

"Oh, Ralph! Why make me wait?"

The illustrious old man started laughing silently, and his turquoise eyes, in his clear face, gazed with infinite tenderness at the delightful creature who was brightening his declining years. He took her child-like hand and kissed it.

Teddy examined the screen in his turn in a disinterested manner. To tell the truth, all of his uncle's science left him indifferent. He was a colossal young man, an athletic sportsman, who always seemed to be fresh from the bathroom after a game of polo or rugby. I knew him through the tennis club, and he was the person who had introduced me to Parker a year before. "Radiography?" he suggested, however.

Randolph Parker, more cheerful than I had ever seen him, exclaimed: "You too, Teddy! Well, in a little while, I'll reveal the surprise! But first, if our friend would like to follow me, I'll show him something that wouldn't interest a little girl or a young heavyweight boxer. It's upstairs, in my laboratory. Have a little patience, Mary. We'll be down again in five minutes."

I followed him. The elevator took us up, and we went into the laboratory.

Parker was radiant. He took me by the arm and said: "The finest hour of my life!"

I studied him curiously, transported myself by a contagious cheerfulness, because I liked him very much and because I knew that only some immense good fortune could have given him that radiant face.

"A discovery?" I asked him.

He put his hand on my shoulder. "Yes, naturally. Randolph Parker's great discovery! Look. Here, next to the telephone: this little screen, exactly similar to the one in the hall—which, you might have noticed, is also next to a telephone.

The two telephones enable us to communicate directly—my wife and I—when she's in the hall and I'm here in my laboratory.

"The surprise is the same one that I'll reveal later to Mary and Teddy. My friend, you're about to witness a veritable scientific event: an invention that everyone has been seeking avidly; a marvel that humankind has been awaiting feverishly since the progress of science made the promise to its appetite, ever since it has become possible to transmit engravings and drawings electrically..."

"Vision at a distance!" I exclaimed.

"You've said it. I only have to unhook the speaker. Immediately, at the moment when the customary bell rings in the hall, my image will appear on the screen downstairs, as if that screen were a mirror, and as if I were standing in front of that mirror! And at the same instant, this screen here will reflect the hall for our eyes, and you'll see the image of my wife there! Watch!"

Parker had placed his white hand, marbled with glorious burns, on the nickel-plated receiver.

I could not retain an impulsive gesture that I will regret forever. With an instinctive promptness that surpassed the speed of my thought, I seized the scientist's wrist in order to immobilize it.

"What are you doing?" he asked, astonished.

"Nothing..." I replied. "The emotion..."

I released him—for, after all, my gesture was stupid. It betrayed Mrs. Parker more surely and more definitively than the consequences that might not even have followed! Who could tell whether the lovers had taken advantage of Parker's brief absence? Who could tell whether the screen in the laboratory might not reflect the most innocent scene in the world?

Alas, the stupidity had been committed! Parker, who was staring at me, suddenly went pale. Then he lowered his head silently—and I found nothing to say to him, for I thought him greater than he was.

Greater, certainly. I had not suspected that love could be so forceful in that old wounded heart, and that Parker was about to do what he did.

"My friend," he said to me, dryly, "would you care to go downstairs. Tell them that the surprise is not ready, that my invention is not complete, contrary to what I had hoped. You may add, to console Mary, that I have made a discovery even more important…"

So saying, Parker set about dismantling the screen with a trembling screwdriver.

I was in despair.

"Go on!" he said. "I beg you—and have no regrets. All things considered, you see, our discoveries have done more harm than good. Then again, such discoveries are always 'in the air' at a certain moment. Vision at a distance…someone else will invent it tomorrow."

"But what about the glory?" I stammered.

"Go!" he repeated.

But I had detected a brief indecision in his movements of demolition—and ever since, having returned to France, I have been waiting for the newspaper fanfare telling the world about Parker's discovery to let me know that I have been forgiven.

# THE TRUTH ABOUT FAUST

Doctor Faust, a graying quinquenagarian, looked at his visitor thoughtfully.

Mephistopheles was sitting very comfortably in a large winged armchair, the leather of which was burning slowly, with a nauseating odor, in response to contact with his person. The Devil was tapping the arm-rests with a clawed hand, which left marks like a hot iron. He affected to be waiting, not without impatience, for the alchemist's decision, and scanned the surroundings with an indifferent gaze.

Shadows were massing in the laboratory. Rain pattered on the panes of the arched window. The embers of the furnace, which projected a red light, could be heard crackling amid the retorts. Occasional drops of water fell from the humid vault, and whenever one of them touched the Demon, steam and a hissing sound advertised the fact.

"Decide, Doctor," said Mephistopheles. "Once again, what do you need? It's not that I'm in a hurry—eternity awaits me—but I'm as fearful of catching a chill as anyone else. Then again, I've warned you—if you meditate for as much as another quarter-hour, the armchair will be burned through, and you'll have to get it repaired, or sit on the trunk…"

The indecisive Faust, his arm extended upon a thick table-top, mechanically rotated the cup that was filed with the poisoned beverage.

"You have a famous flaw," Mephistopheles went on. "And that, meaning no insult, is thinking too much. My word, you've cut a hair from a woman's head into four—which is quite remarkable, in is day and age."

Perplexed, Faust ran through the notions of his philosophy in his head. What should he ask for, by virtue of the pact? The fulfillment of what wish would restore his desire to live?"

"I'm off!" said the Devil, getting up. "*Au revoir*, Doctor—I'll come back another time. Between now and then, you'll have come to a decision."

"No!" cried the thinker. "Stay! Just a moment! One more moment!"

"All right!" accepted the Devil, sitting down again.

Faust offered him a chocolate box. "Would you like a bonbon?" he asked.

"Gladly." Neglecting the candy, however, the Devil delicately selected a still-ardent ember and crunched it between his teeth.

Shrugging his shoulders, Faust murmured: "Show-off!"

And nothing more was heard, save for the downpour and the furnace.

To distract himself, Mephitopheles drew smoking arabesques on the arm of the chair with the tip of his claw. "Pyrogravure," he said, improvising the word.

"Pardon?" said Faust.

"Nothing, Doctor. Anticipation."

"No more whimsy—I've found it!"

"Archimedes said that in Greek."

"I know what I want!"

"Go on."

"Youth."

"Damnation, Monsieur! Anything but that!"

"More than that," said Faust, with a penetrating gaze.

"More than that?" said the Evil One, bewildered. "Me!"

"What do you mean by that 'Me!' Master of Obscurity?"

"I said 'Me!' as you might say 'The Devil!' And you must recognize that one might swear for less. What! Youth and more than youth!"

"Listen," Faust retorted. "If I were an old man, and old man abandoned by desire, you know as well as I do that the recovery of youth would have no attraction in my eyes. But I'm 58 years old, if I'm not mistaken, and my soul is often troubled by desires that the state of my body prevents me from satisfying…"

"Yes," the Devil interrupted, with a smile that might have been described as licentious, "but youth alone…"

Faust stamped his foot. "Incorrigible goat!" he protested. "Understand me, then! The best part of youth is neither its strength nor its seduction, but the future that extends before it!"

"In truth," Mephistopheles remarked, "it's you that's being obscure. I know a witch who can give you back your twenties. Do you consent? With that done, what will your happiness lack?"

"The consciousness of being young. The sentiment of the future. I remember, you know. I was handsome. My limbs were powerful, my brain contained a world. Life and happiness were the same thing. But listen: *I didn't appreciate it.* Young men don't know…the joy of their spring-time is unknown to them, O my guest, until the first snows of their winter fall. And it's only today that all the grace of my past is resplendent in my old memory. For one does not know that one is young; and does that which one does not know really exist?"

"In brief," Mephistopheles concluded, "you want to be young and not to be young at the same time. You're a wise man and a madman. Wise, when you imagine the dream of which you speak, mad when you want to realize it. Oh, Monsieur! To enclose your soul, full of experience, in the dazzling flesh of a juvenile body! To make, in combination, knowledgeable youth and powerful old age! What an admirable monster you would be within Creation! But don't you think that such a prodigy is impossible, even for…the Other, up there, who did not wish that the color black could become white and yet remain black?" And as Faust remained somber, he added: "Come on, Doctor, it's not that I'm reluctant to perform. A pact is a pact—but no one can do the impossible. And if I were to give you some advice—listen to me, in your turn—then you must choose: either one is young, without, as you put it, knowing it, or one is no longer young, and able to savor one's youth. Which will you plump for, in the end? To recover your twenties without taking pleasure therein, or to remember gladly having lived them?"

Discouraged by a sullen silence, he made a dismissive gesture, and took a few steps away.

"*Prosit!*" said Faust.

The Spirit of Evil turned his head, and saw the philosopher drink a draught from the poisoned cup.

"As you please!" groaned the Devil. "Much good may it do you!" And he retired, presumably, whence he had come. No one knows how.

# THEM

They had a very nice house in Passy. Florine walked very carefully through the garden, with its neat lawn and hortensias, which separated the little house from the laboratory building. Midday had just sounded. Philippe's two assistants came out of the outbuilding. They bowed to Madame Chambrun with respectful briskness, visibly surprised by the familiar but unexpected sight of so much grace and elegance. She replied with a pretty and benevolent smile and headed for the staircase in the shade of the corridor.

At the very top, a door opened on to a hall of vast dimensions. It had once been a painter's studio, but rows of chemical vats and sets of electrical apparatus now made it a place of science—redoubtable, to be sure.

"You've changed the door!" said Florine. "Is it because of air currents? Indeed, it must be…"

She closed the rubber-lined door behind her; it made a muffled sound as it sealed itself with a rigorous exactitude.

Philippe Chambrun laughed. He was just as the newspapers depicted him from time to time: tall and bony, with lively and kindly eyes and a broad forehead surmounted by rebellious hair that stuck out oddly. All sorts of multicolored stains spattered his white smock. He was pouring a bluish liquid into a glass flask, which he was holding up in order to see it better.

Without ceasing to laugh he put down the glassware, took off his glorious stains and came to meet his wife, whom he took by the shoulders in order to contemplate her before embracing her.

She was exactly 23 years old. He was 40. They had been married for 18 months.

Florine looked up at him sulkily and muttered: "I know perfectly well that it isn't because of air currents."

"What is the cause, then?" he set, leaning his head maliciously to one side.

Suddenly—which almost never happened—femininity got the upper hand. Caprice possessed Florine. She pulled away and said, peevishly: "You're mocking me. Let me go! Why don't you want to tell me what you're doing? Do you think I'm incapable of understanding?"

"Oh, Florine!" he said, reproachfully.

"Or of keeping a secret?"

Disconcerted, he looked at her, searching for an explanation. "Come on, Florine, my love, you're not serious? What's got into you?"

There are days when the most reasonable of women are only temperamental little girls. This one, habitually so affectionate, and in reality so wise, abruptly burst into tears. Someone other than Philippe—less of a scientist, perhaps—would have understood what kind of annoyance had caused those tears to flow He only saw someone shedding them upon herself because she thought herself stupid, odious and pitiful. He believed her words, since she had not retracted them—and he was distressed to see his little Florine so strangely unhappy.

He reflected. His face became extraordinary grave and pensive. "All right, I'll tell you. Are you satisfied?"

"Yes," she said, with an exquisite smile, wiping her eyes. "And I swear that I'll keep your secret. For there is one, isn't there?"

"A secret—yes, a truly strange secret," he murmured. And he began to march hither and yon, without saying anything further, seemingly perplexed.

"So," she said, pointing at the apparatus, "all of this…"

As he was about to speak, though, he seemed to be seized by a sudden dread. "Not here! Not here! It would doubtless be more prudent…"

In her turn, Florine looked at him curiously. "Come on, Philippe—we're alone! Your assistants have gone. We are alone, aren't we, Philippe?"

"Does one ever know?" he said, in a bizarre tone.

Anxiety took hold of Florine. She no longer felt safe in the laboratory—and she was painfully amazed by that.

"Let's go," Philippe went on, more calmly. "I presume you came to fetch me for lunch."

"Yes..."

She dared not interrogate him during the meal. He continued in his silence. He pondered and reflected, sometimes screwing up his eyes, as if to follow the imaginary curve of his thoughts through space. Then his gaze returned to Florine and, relaxing, he smiled at her—but he was still absorbed.

Once, while the domestic who was serving them was out of the room, he said: "My assistants...they don't know anything. I haven't confided anything, thus far, to anyone. And it's noticeable that I've worked in peace, which seems to prove...seems to prove..."

"What?" she asked.

"Nothing," he relied, frowning.

She had the impression that he was still afraid that someone was listening to them, and, while a disagreeable frisson made her shudder, she made a proposal: "Speak English!"

He shrugged his shoulders, and fell silent again. After a pause, he resumed, fixing her with an anxious gaze. "To modify the atmosphere of the laboratory. There it is. By operating the transformation from the viewpoint of..." He stopped, his finger on his lips, his eyes furtive.

"I don't understand at all," she admitted.

"Evidently. You can't understand like that. Listen, we're going out. Spare me any comments. We'll get the car and go for a drive...a long drive. We'll come back this evening, late."

"Good," she said.

Many times over, she had already told herself that it would definitely be better to give up on knowing the secret of Philippe's research. She could not go back now, though. Not because she wanted to take things far enough to find out whether she ought to suspect some derangement of that splendid intelligence—no such thought ever entered her head—but because she was prey to a passionate curiosity, which it was necessary to satisfy.

The car was easily capable of an average speed of 70. At 5 p.m., Monsieur and Madame Chambrun were installed beneath an arbor on the bank of the Loire, taking tea.

"230 kilometers," said Philippe. "That's quite something. Perhaps, however, the precaution was entirely unnecessary. Enough! After all, it's doubtless preferable that I should no longer be the only one with the secret. If it's a matter of my approval, the thing is, in any case, certain."

But he seemed as anxious as he had been in Paris, regarding the consequences of an explanation.

"I'll try to make you understand as rapidly as possible, with the fewest words. Don't speak. Listen to me in silence. Act exactly as if it were certain that someone were spying on us."

He paused then for several minutes, preoccupied with his deliberations, and finally took from his pocket one of those little portable slates from which one can erase in the blink of an eye, by the flicker of a shutter, the words that one has traced. It was thus that he wrote, piece by piece, what Florine read by degrees behind the screen of his hand.

*Our senses feeble. Not very numerous. Can only allow us to perceive an infinitesimal part of nature. Would be absurd to think that only the things we can see and touch exist. Odds strongly favor that we are living amid a multitude of invisible and impalpable beings. If they exist, what are they? Mystery. Perhaps they, too, are unsuspecting of our existence. Perhaps, on the contrary, they exercise all sorts of influence upon us. One might even suppose—at the worst—that they control us without our knowing it. What if it's to* them *that we some-times—or always—owe what happens to us, even our maladies? That when we die, it's* they *who kill us.*

Florine, very pale, opened her mouth.

"Ssh!" he said, cutting the air with a curt gesture. And he continued writing:

*I believe that they can't read our thoughts be-
cause...because then, I have reason to believe that they would
have interfered with my work. But...but if they exist and if
they're intelligent, do they overhear, and do they understand,
our speech? Can they read our writing?*

He erased the last sentence very quickly, under the influence of a reflex, looked Florine deeply in the eyes and continued.

*In a few days, I expect to finish. Goal: fill the laboratory
with certain emanations, modifying the air in such a way that
the invisible ceases to be invisible. So that the hidden world
appears. So that it can be studied, or at least observed, photo-
graphed. If it exists. As I believe it does.*

"It doesn't exist!" protested Florine, outraged. "No! It's
not possible!"

"Silence, now," Philippe instructed. "Not a word. I
promise to call you as soon as I obtain a result."

"But how do you imagine them? In what form?"

"All hypotheses are permissible..."

She was in the grip of an intolerable malaise. "No, no!"
she repeated, agitated by anguish. "Such a thing!"

"We shall see—we shall *see!*" he concluded, with a
smile. "Now, we can go home."

They walked a little way back into the countryside to
where the car was parked. The landscape was charming in the
beautiful summer evening. A gentle, caressing breeze was
blowing along the river.

"The wind's frightening me, now," said Florine. "One
might think that someone you can't see is brushing past you."

Philippe cheered up. "Put like that," he said, "it's a
joke."

"I don't think so." And she widened her eyes, staring
tragically into space, like someone advancing into the darkness, gropingly.

They reached the car. They filled it up with gasoline, and
Philippe resumed his place at the steering-wheel. There was
silence at first, but after 50 kilometers or so she thought aloud:

"So far. Was that really necessary?"

"I don't know, I tell you. I don't know anything. How quickly the darkness falls! What time is it, then?" He switched on the headlights.

"What are you doing?" she asked.

He stopped immediately, surprised by the tone of the question. "What?" he asked, anxiously.

"It's still very bright, and you just switched the headlights on…"

"Ah! Ah!" he said, strangely severe. "I thought that they were illuminating…that they were illuminating poorly…" He switched off the headlights and passed his hand over his eyes. "I don't understand what happened…a shadow…it seems to me that it's getting dark. It will pass…probably…"

"You work too hard. You're overtiring your nerves, your sight…."

"Hmm! Yes, perhaps."

"What do you think it is?" she asked him, suddenly frightened by his attitude. An idea—a disturbing idea—was making her heart beat faster.

"Drive," he said, curtly. "Take the controls. I…I don't have any confidence in myself this evening. I'm afraid that my eyesight might fail."

It was thus that they returned to Paris, very late that night. When they were back inside, she put her arms around him. "How do you feel? Are you ill?"

"Not at all—except that there's still a shadow over things."

She hesitated, then said: "Is it any worse?"

"No…"

She had no doubt that he was lying. With affected placidity, Philippe declared: "I'll go to see the optician tomorrow."

"Understood," she said. "As early as possible."

Neither of them slept. At dawn, Florine inquired: "Well?"

He admitted that a thicker fog was extended before him. Then he delivered himself, at length, to considerations regarding atavism. His mother had had weak eyesight. One of his great-grandfathers had gone blind. Anyway, as Florine had said the previous evening, the fatigues…

Thoughtfully, she listened to him searching for ordinary causes for his trouble, in order to reassure her, to put one over on her.

*Taking everything into account*, she said to herself, *there are incredible coincidences…*

He wanted to go to the optician, whom Florine had telephoned, by himself. She did not insist on accompanying him. He came back an hour later, joyful and exultant.

"Cured! Cured, my love! It was nothing at all. A few drops of lotion, an application of electricity, and here I am, as before."

"But what was wrong with you, Philippe? What was the diagnosis?"

"Vague. Very vague. I have a suspicion that I was being treated at hazard. What does it matter? I'm better now, that's the main thing."

"The doctor didn't advise you to avoid overwork?"

"Yes," Philippe confessed, "but that won't prevent me from continuing with you know what. Weren't we silly, last night? Admit it—we both thought that…"

"I still think it, you know."

"Get away!" he mocked. "The best proof of our error is that human medicine put a stop to the darkening effect, quite abruptly."

Slowly, she said: "Are you sure of that? Are you quite sure that it was human medicine?"

This disorientated him. "But…" he said, half-indecisive and half-mocking, "it seems so to me!"

"We never know," Florine continued, in the same slow and deliberate voice.

"What, for example? Let's see! Have I renounced my enterprise? Have I made an oath to abandon my work? Thus, the invisibles have no reason to reward me!"

"You've done none of that. But I…you must forgive me, Philippe, because I love you dearly…because, you see, for me, all the discoveries and all the glory in the world count for nothing, by comparison with your health, your sanity…"

"My life's not in danger," he said, precipitately. "But explain…"

"Your life's not in danger? That's the question. Suppose…do me the kindness of supposing, for a moment, that what happened is imputable to *their* will, that *they* determined it…*Them*…"

"But Florine…."

"Let me finish. Mightn't it be a *warning?* A *first* warning?"

"Let's be illogical. In the case that you're supposing, it would be necessary to admit—I insist—that they consider my offensive concluded."

"It is, Philippe."

"Why is that?"

"During your absence, I smashed everything in the laboratory."

Silence fell. Philippe bit his lip. "Ah!" he said, eventually. "Oh! Ah!"

"Do you forgive me?"

"Great gods, my love!" he said, distraughtly. "What wouldn't I forgive you?"

He embraced her wholeheartedly—but she found his face pained and pale, the skin seemingly taught.

"I…I'll go take a look," he said.

"Shall I come?" He was still embracing her.

"Not worth the trouble, Besides, it's nearly lunch-time. Time to take stock, and I'll come back down."

He turned round in the doorway and blew her a kiss, a sign of perfect harmony, accompanied by the most affectionate of smiles.

"Thank you," said Florine.

At the top of the stairs he opened the new door with the hermetic seals.

The two distressed assistants were gathering up the debris, in the midst of a chaos that recalled visions of war. He helped them, without saying a word—and when mid-day chimed and they had gone he continued sweeping mechanically, alone.

As he worked, he dreamed. The air became populated, in his imagination, by prodigious creatures that slithered and glided like creatures at the bottom of the sea. Their forms were translucent. There were of all possible sizes: minuscule ones; immense ones; ones much too enormous for the laboratory to contain them in their entirety. They passed through it, however, cloudy and buoyant, for neither the walls nor any material object of any kind was an obstacle to them. They passed through everything, as electrical waves do, as if their substance were composed of waves. They were only visible, though, in the cube of air contained in the laboratory, scientifically prepared for that effect.

It was a magical dream—and the scientist's eyes shone.

"Bah!" he said. "Who takes no risks…"

He looked at what he was holding: a commutator, which Florine's hammer had torn away from a dynamo. Philippe found the dynamo in the heap, but the damaged piece could no longer be reconnected to it. "Six months and 100,000 francs," he calculated, in a low voice. "This time, of course, not a word! Florine mustn't know anything."

Florine climbed up the stairs, anxious to know what could have delayed him much longer than he had said.

She found him lying on the floor, not moving.

The doctor could not revive him. He attributed the death to a stroke, brought on by overwork, and said that the previous day's visual disturbances had been a symptom, the seriousness of which the optician had, unfortunately, failed to understand.

Which proved absolutely nothing.

# THE SHARK

"Eight months in the China Seas…"

"That's a fine voyage," I said to him. "You were lucky, Fabrice."

"Doctor Brandt has always been an excellent friend to me. I hope that he'll take me again. I'll retain a nostalgic memory of the *Orion* and life aboard…"

"The *Orion*'s a three-masted schooner, isn't she?"

"Exactly. You're much more knowledgeable that I was when I embarked!"

"Oh," I said, blushing, "It's just that I've seen photographs in the magazines…tell me, Fabrice, what made the deepest impression on you in the course of your oceanographic cruise?"

"On the return journey," he said, after a moment's reflection, "we crossed…"

Then he hesitated, and darted a slightly anxious glance at me, as if he regretted having stupidly started a story that I might be unworthy to hear. He continued, however.

"One night, after dinner, Brandt and I were strolling on the deck. It was somewhere the other side of Malacca. A warm and magnificently starry night…the boat was moving slowly. Some crewmen, with Captain Fall, were busy with some work or other at the side. I asked Brandt what they were doing, assuming that it was some kind of fishing enterprise. I'd seen them employ so many different kinds of apparatus while we were exploring the depths…

"Brandt said: 'We're not fishing. I'm taking depth-soundings. It will take all night and much of tomorrow, until the afternoon…'

"Naturally, I had nothing to say in reply. It was all quite banal. But Brandt went on: 'Do you know where we are? Do you know what this sea is?' And with a grand gesture of the hand that was holding his pipe he indicated the circular moving expanse of which the *Orion* was at the center. The waves were rising placidly, stirring the innumerable reflections of the firmament. The marine desert had no particular attributes.

" 'Of all the mysteries that the ocean conceals,' the doctor said, 'perhaps the strangest is what it hides down there. Beneath these waters there must be unsuspected rocks, and it's those rocks that I'd like to reveal. That's why we're taking soundings, patiently. The marine charts indicate great depths everywhere. They're mistaken. They're badly mistaken.'

" 'Why?' I asked, quite interested.

" 'Look at these surroundings,' Brandt said, repeating his gesture. 'In the last 30 years, 22 ships have sunk hereabouts. 22 ships have been swallowed up in a relatively restricted area.'

" 'Is that so extraordinary, then?' I objected. '30 years is quite a long time—and typhoons, as you've told me, are frequent in these latitudes.'

"I saw Brandt's eyes gleaming in the shadow of his peaked cap; he was staring at me fixedly. 'It's not a matter of shipwrecks caused by bad weather,' he told me. 'The 22 vessels I'm talking about disappeared with no apparent reason, in calm seas, beneath a cloudless sky. The men who survived these disasters and lived to tell the tale couldn't explain what had happened. All the ships had sunk abruptly, with frightful rapidity. I tell you, Fabrice, that this can only be explained by the presence of reefs treacherously concealed beneath the surface. The 22 vessels must have been spiked by a rocky point, the summit of some submarine mountain.'

" 'Couldn't your divers go down to the wrecks to investigate?' I asked, timidly.

"Brandt smiled. 'The wrecks haven't been located,' he replied benevolently. 'Besides, it's a safe bet that they've slid down the rocks all the way to the sea bed—which is to say, to the bottom of an abyss so deep that no man can dream of reaching them, given the present state of science. No diving-bell exists capable of descending several kilometers below sea level.'

" 'Damnation!' I said. 'Really? Several kilometers!'

" 'In any case,' Doctor Brandt continued, 'even if we find the presumed rocks, that won't explain everything.'

" 'Evidently,' I agreed.

" 'They were frightful disasters,' the doctor continued, after a pause, 'and so prompt that there was never time to get the lifeboats into the water. Even worse, perhaps, was…'

" 'What?' I asked, alarmed by my companion's tone.

"Brant took me by the arm and let me toward the *Orion*'s stern, to the very edge.

" 'Can you see them?' he said to me, in a low voice.

" 'What do you mean?'

"He made no reply, but his gaze never quit the waves. I looked harder. Then I saw, amid the undulations of the sea, other curves appearing and disappearing, glistening momentarily, leaving an impression of long, swift tapering bodies.

" 'Oh!' I said. 'The sharks!'

" 'Yes—the sharks. This region is infested with them. They surround ships in distress…'

" 'As they're surrounding us at this moment,' I remarked.

" 'Don't worry. We're making headway too slowly for any harm to come to us, and the sounding-line will reveal any danger to us before it's too late.'

" 'May God hear you, Doctor! That must be a frightful death…'

"I had become accustomed to the darkness. I could see the sharks more clearly. They were very numerous. Sometimes, a fin or a forked tail emerged from the water, only to plunge back into it immediately. I thought, fearfully, of the windfall that those voracious carnivores must have enjoyed as large ships, loaded with human beings, poured out their crews and passengers into these very waters. The emotion that I experienced was so strong that I covered my eyes with both hands.

" 'I share your sentiments,' Brandt told me. 'How happy I would be if I were able to discover those rocks and, in consequence, avoid the recurrence of similar abominations!'

"We chatted in that fashion for another hour. I delayed going to bed stubbornly. For the first time since our departure, my sojourn on the *Orion* didn't appear to me to be absolutely safe, and I was conscious of all the redoubtable mystery that threatens a ship in the immense solitudes of the sea. Eventually, it was necessary to go back to my cabin—but I slept very badly, unable to deflect my thoughts away from the twenty-two wrecks lying at the bottom of the gulf, or the multitude of sharks that were encircling us.

"I woke up anxious the next morning, and I had to make an effort to conceal my malaise. The *Orion*, still escorted by sharks in large numbers, was continuing to take soundings. The day went by without any result. The apparatus indicated no shallows...

"That went on for a week, a pure waste of time—a week of which I retain one strange memory. I've told you why Brandt did me the favor of taking me with him that year. It was a matter, you'll recall, of giving me a change of air, of helping me to forget a bitter sentimental deception. The excellent fellow noticed that I had become nervous again, and besides, he too seemed as annoyed as he was surprised by the futility of the soundings—to the extent that, while having them continue, he wanted to break the monotony of the scorching days during which the population of sharks never ceased to surround us, as if they were waiting for the sudden sinking of the *Orion*.

"Brandt decided to catch one or two of them. He thought, rightly, that a fishing party would distract me. No other motive led him to do it. I must admit that, if any spectacle is designed for excitement, it was that of the dogged struggle offered to us by the two monsters that our crew caught. In the meantime, the vain sounding operations were uninterrupted.

"Brought on to the deck one after the other, the two enormous and truly hideous creatures were of quite different species. One of them, a brownish grey in color, intrigued the doctor by virtue of the dimensions of its head. He decided to dissect the animal.

"Doctor Brandt had not been at that task for more than half an hour when we saw him come out of his laboratory, with his face set hard, not finding it easy to conceal his amazement.

" 'Stop the soundings,' he said to the captain, 'and let's get moving. Let's get moving right away!'

"At table, that evening, he never opened his mouth. The *Orion* sailed on at top speed. The sharks around us became rarer. The next day, Brandt called me into his cabin. I found him very excited. He was contemplating a bowl in which an anatomical preparation, which appeared to me to be a section of brain, was submerged in alcohol.

" 'Can you tell that this is a mutation?' he asked me. 'No? Well, it is. Understand me, Fabrice: there aren't any rocks down below. There are no rocks, but a species of shark—which, due to the effect of a mutation, has undergone an abrupt and formidable transformation, and has suddenly become a superior species, certainly capable of reasoning, understanding, carrying out plans...'

" 'Are you sure?' I asked him, fearfully.

"He put both hands to his forehead. 'No,' he said, 'no, I can't be sure. It's necessary to perform experiments; it's necessary to turn back...'

"We didn't turn back," Fabrice concluded. "And inasmuch as Brandt could not elucidate that enigma, the most frightful mystery must be added to all those that already reign over the submarine darkness."

# WHEN HENS HAD TEETH

I was woken up in the middle of the night by a distant mournful clamor.

I had passed some difficult examinations at the end of October, and as soon as I obtained the happy results, I had made haste to leave Paris for a fortnight. An old friend of my father's, Doctor Templier, had invited me to stay with him, as I had the previous year, on a large island in the South-West, where he was accustomed to prolong his pleasant sojourns for as long as the temperature permitted.

The wind was blowing up a storm when I arrived at my destination, after having been rudely shaken in the sea's arms. The doctor was waiting for me at the quay with his two daughters, Pauline and Simone. He was apologetic for greeting me in such brutal and inhospitable weather. "While this lasts," he said, regretfully, "we can't shoot birds."

That was his favorite occupation: hunting along the shore—not so much to provision his larder as to enrich his ornithological museum.

It is necessary to say that no region of the vast Earth is visited by as many birds as the island on which I had just landed. You would not believe the flights of multicolored birds that the stroller on its beaches and in its pine-woods perpetually causes to rise up with every step. It would take an entire year to count the multitudes of winged voyagers, large and small, which take a rest there in the course of their migration, for a few days or only a few hours.

My host's little motor car, lurching in the gusts of winds, brought us by some miracle to the low-set house with the tiled roof charged with flat stones, where I paid my respects to the worthy Madame Templier. The glass cases of the ornithological collection garnished the periphery of the large hall; they contained a profusion of stuffed specimens, whose ranks were ever-increasing.

"As soon as the storm lets up, young man, we'll take our rifles. It's the seasons of great migrations and this terrible wind can't have failed to drive certain birds to the island that don't ordinarily use it as a port of call. A windfall!"

Dinner was very pleasant, but we didn't stay up long thereafter. Nothing is more tiring than the wind. My cheeks were glowing, my eyes stinging. I went to my bed gladly. Nevertheless, I didn't fall asleep right away. The squalls were whistling furiously. One would have thought that the house was about to blow away at any moment.

It was the clamor that woke me up. I found myself suddenly sitting up in the darkness, my ears pricked.

I lit the oil-lamp, whose flame flickered in the draughts, and again I heard—very distantly, it seemed—in spite of the howling of the storm wind, a desperate bellowing. That was the last. After a few minutes of expectancy, familiar noises animated the dwelling. I had certainly not been the only one to hear those sinister appeals. I got up. Doctor Templier had done likewise; we ran into one another in the large hall. He wasn't anxious.

"I thought I heard the bellowing of an animal in distress," he said. "There are pastures two kilometers away, between the woods—perhaps you remember them. The animals haven't been brought in yet; in bad weather, they shelter in a half-enclosed barn. The herd belongs to a smallholder whose farm is too far away for him to be able to hear anything at all. Something tragic is happening over there, but I confess that the prospect going out in complete darkness to face the wrath of the unleashed elements isn't at all tempting. If it were a matter of a human being...so much the worst for the beast. Let's go back to bed. Tomorrow morning, we'll go take a look..."

I couldn't go back to sleep, and I read until dawn—which found me impatient to find out what I could about the cause of that frightful bellowing.

The tempest hadn't died down. We set off—the doctor, Pauline and I—braced against the assaults of the imperious wind, which pelted us with vaporous rain. The clouds sped by, raveling out; the grey sky was nothing but a world in flight.

We followed a route through the woods, in order to take advantage of the shelter they offered. The sand of the pathway was whipped up, and the wind through it in our faces.

The edge of the wood ran along the meadow; the livestock barn was nearby. A dozen horned beasts were huddled therein, pressed against one another, silent and miserable. Some distance away, on the grass, something white, black and red attracted our attention. It was the cadaver, three-quarters devoured, of a piebald heifer. The hard ground in the vicinity had not preserved any footprints.

"What can have done that?" asked the doctor, greatly intrigued. "We have no carnivores on the island, thank God! And yet, and yet…look at these tooth-marks…little pointed teeth…narrow little jaws. No, those aren't the jaws of a fox; their extremity forms too sharp and angle. Besides, in the absence of more ample information, the fox is unknown here."

I caught sight of a muddy spot not far away where the aggression had undoubtedly taken place. "Note, if you please, doctor, that there are no prints visible in the mud, except for those of that poor beast—which did not stop prancing, I imagine, while launching those poignant cries for help."

"That's true," the doctor admitted. "Damnation! But in that case, its assailants can't have touched the ground? Imagine that!"

Pauline picked something up a short distance away. "A feather!" she said. "Here's another…and another…"

The doctor examined these feathers with an indescribable stupefaction. Then he came back to the massacred and partly-devoured ruminant.

"If they were birds," he murmured, "the skin of their victim ought to bear…but yes! Look! These holes, these talons. They're the claws of raptors, which dug into the heifer's hide!"

"Birds armed with teeth?" I said, incredulously. "Only *Archaeopteryx* was provided with them—and if I'm not mistaken, that antediluvian monster has only ever been seen in a fossilized state…"

"Yes!" he said, shivering, his eyes illuminated by a strange gleam. "*Archaeopteryx*—a species extinct for millennia! The creature intermediate between the reptiles and the birds."

We looked at one another in bewilderment.

At that moment, as the tempest eased slightly, we saw a flight of huge, heavy and very awkward birds rise up from a distant wood, which the wind bore away in a jostling mass.

Since then, one can admire three long grey feathers in one of Dr. Templier's glass cases, boldly labeled: *Archaeopteryx pinion-feathers*.

Does the ancestor of birds still survive in some unknown place? That feverish adventure leads me to believe so, and sometimes to tremble.

# ON THE PLANET MARS

"Monsieur le Directeur," said the inhabitant of the planet Mars, manifesting a great agitation, "the Earth is inhabited! I'm now certain of it!"

"Really?" said the other Martian, with the utmost calm.

We are able to transcribe in these terms, for the usage of human brains, this commencement of an extraterrestrial dialogue—but will the reader please accept that the reality did not correspond in the slightest to the images that the preceding sentences will have suggested to him?

First of all, did this exchange of ideas produce any vibration of sound in the planet's atmosphere? No words had emerged from the mouths of the two Martians; they were conversing by means of silent waves of which we can give no better definition. Did they, in fact, possess mouths? One could not see any trace of them. To our human eyes, they presented themselves in the form of two lenses[49] about two meters in diameter, standing upright on the ground thanks to the temporary flattening of their bases. These lenses, of which one was reddish and the other bluish, were very thick and perfectly opaque in the middle, but that thickness decreased toward a periphery which, so to speak, did not exist, for the lentil was not delimited by a sharp and precise border; they faded gradually into space like a nebula.

Imagine two lenticular nuclei, variously colored, each fading away into a peripheral fog, and you will have an approximate idea of the two superior Martians in question. No

---

[49] The original referent of the French term for a glass lens, *lentille,* is a lentil. Although it makes little difference merely as a specification of shape, the choice of translation is bound to have a considerable effect on the reader's conceptualization of the Martians, and the other possibility needs to be noted.

faces, meaning no physiognomy; and if we have permitted ourselves to say that one of them manifested a great agitation, it is because that is what its color indicated, by way of an unaccustomed glare.

"Yes," it continued. "Inhabited! I haven't left my observation apparatus for several days, and I've clearly perceived intermittent lights that can only be signals produced by intelligent beings with an awareness of mathematics."

"You're young, my friend!" said the blue Martian, whose body took on a lovely moiré effect of green-tinted concentric ripples.

"I assure you, Monsieur le Directeur, that I'm not the victim of an optical illusion. This is a matter of *signals*, which are being sent from there *to us*, and to which we can reply without difficulty, given the advanced state of our Martian science."

"Ta ta ta!" said the director. "Chimeras and foolishness!"

His interlocutor's red tint suddenly paled, only to become, a moment later, deeper than before. "In spite of the respect I owe you," he said, "in spite of your age and your scientific knowledge, Maître, I cannot admit your skepticism and I stand my ground. I don't have the right. The question is more important than us—you as well as me. Just think! The plurality of inhabited worlds! The problem of communication between the people of the universe! Maître, we have brothers on the Earth—I can prove it to you. Are we to remain indifferent to their efforts, deaf to their appeals?"

As it expressed itself thus, the young Martian—who was undoubtedly some astronomer attached to an observatory—became increasingly animated, moving back and forth by rotating itself as if it were a wheel, which is the fashion in which such individuals progress.

"Do you think you're the first to discover that the Earth is inhabited?" the old Martian replied, softly.

"Pardon?" said the young one, nonplussed, suddenly ceasing to rotate.

"These lights have already been noticed by others. Others have drawn the necessary conclusions from those manifestations. Let me tell you, furthermore, that we did not have to wait for them to be produced to discover what you have just discovered. For many years, we have known that the Earth is inhabited by a great quantity of diverse creatures, one species of which has dominated the others for thousands of years by virtue of the power of the mind. That is humankind. It is, down there, what we are here. Certain instruments of observation, of a range that you cannot imagine, allow us to know with great precision what is happening on Earth."

"What do you mean? What instruments? Are they kept secret, then?"

"Oh yes. Only our elders, of which I am one, know the whole truth concerning the Earth. There is nothing we don't know about the mores of humankind and its history."

"Is it possible?" exclaimed the neophyte, utterly flabbergasted.

"You need, my young friend, to forget these signals that you've glimpsed. Swear to me that you will never mention them to anyone—for the Grand Council had decided that it will not reply, under any pretext, to Earth's solicitations."

"But why?" asked the other, desperately.

After a pause, the old Martian continued, in his mute language. "If you were a human on Earth, you would have some difficulty in believing that the inhabitants of our Mars are peaceful, and that they live wisely and quietly—for the Terrans have given our globe the name of their god of war, and they are convinced that we are bellicose. You will agree with me, however, that life is pleasant here and that nothing ever happens to trouble the harmony that reigns among us. Alas, my son, I cannot say as much for the Earth. Everything is certainly not perfect on Mars—but down there! If you only knew!"

"All the more reason, Maître, to communicate the benefits of our civilization to the Terrans!"

"Hmmm! It's just that, you see, the Grand Council decided otherwise—and it would be only prudent, my young friend, for you to conform to their decisions! Believe me, we have nothing to gain from commerce with humans, but everything to lose! Come on, let's repeat it together: the Earth is uninhabited!" Perceiving the hesitation that he had provoked, the blue Martian went on, paternally: "Give in. It's a matter of orders that one does not debate. We are no longer in the domain of science, but that of public safety. Humans equal danger! Danger! It's necessary that they don't exist, so far as we're concerned."

For a moment, the young Martian contemplated the Earth-star shining in the sky with a lovely blue light. And as he revered the wisdom of the elders, he said: "Very well. The Earth is uninhabited."

# *Afterword*

As with *Un Homme chez les microbes*, it is impossible to resist the temptation to begin a discussion of "L'Homme truqué" with some speculations as to what the fuller length version might have looked like, had Renard not decided to cut the intended novel short at some 27,000 words and wrap it up rather abruptly, referring his readers to J.-H. Rosny Aîné's "Un Autre monde" for further speculations regarding the exotic life-forms that the character equipped with a new kind of sight had begun to notice.

Presumably, the author's original intention had been to offer a much fuller explanation of the secret world revealed by Jean Lebris' marvelous "electroscopic sight." He would have given a fuller description of the known world as seen from this hypothetical viewpoint, and a much more elaborate account of the hidden world that it revealed, previously inaccessible to our senses. As to why he changed his mind, we can only speculate. Perhaps he realized, belatedly, that he had made a fundamental mistake in his characterization of the world of electricity in confusing electrons with photons. Perhaps he realized, when *Un Homme chez les microbes* failed to find a publisher for the third time, that the kind of extensive and languid exposition required by such imaginary exploration was something that put editors and readers off, and that there was no place for such exercises in the contemporary literary marketplace, which was besotted with murder mysteries and love stories to an extent that the tokenistic nature of his attempt to dress his story up with both would be obvious. The fact that he was consciously re-treading imaginative ground previously broken by Rosny might have been another factor weakening his resolve. At any rate, he took the decision, and left us with a novella that is very obviously unbalanced and truncated, probably less than half of the work it had originally set out to be. The fact that it remains fascinating anyway, and by no means ineffective, in both speculative and literary terms, is some compensation, but the published version can only leave the minority of readers who are sympathetic to his original cause a trifle disappointed.

As with many of Renard's hypothetical marvels, the parasitic "electrical" entities glimpsed in the story were to receive further consideration in subsequent works, but only in a very scat fashion. As the reader of this collection has observed, Renard provided another tantalizing glimpse of something similar in "Eux." As with some of the other marvels in question, however, other writers took up the task that he abandoned. The possibility of such parasitism between individual human beings had been previously mooted in numerous literary works of "psychic vampirism" predating "L'Homme truqué," including Jean Lorrain's "L'Egrégore" (1887)—which Renard might well have read—J. Maclaren Cobban's *Master of His Fate* (1890) and Arthur Conan Doyle's *The Parasite* (1895), and it was inevitable that the notion would be generalized again in the way that Rosny's "Un Autre monde" and Renard's "L'Homme truqué" had set out to do.

The science fiction story that makes the most spectacular use of the motif in question—if only because it was the first to do so in an extended melodramatic mode—is Eric Frank Russell's *Sinister Barrier*, first published in 1939. Russell took his own inspiration from the writings of the assiduous collector of curious reportage Charles Fort, who had made the laconic suggestion, after aggregating one collection of such reports that humans might be the "property" of some alien race which maintained them like livestock, in order to feed surreptitiously on some kind of "life force." Russell's pulp fiction fantasy could not, however, develop the idea in the careful and methodical way that Renard had originally intended, any more than Renard had been able to do, and other science fiction stories following Russell's example also elected to exaggerate the horrific element, and to plan potential rebellions of humankind against their invisible oppressors. "L'Homme truqué" thus took its place in the same restricted group of philosophical fantasies as *Un Homme chez les microbes* and the relatively obscure titles cited in the afterword to *A Man Among the Microbes and Other Stories*.

The philosophical foundations of the notion briefly introduced into "L'Homme truqué" and placed at the core of "Eux" lie in the same source as those of many earlier stories: the apparent corollaries of Cartesian dualism. *Le Docteur Lerne* had already introduced a kind of psychic vampirism in the startling scene in which Klotz/Lerne's "soul" suppresses and largely displaces Nicolas's "soul" while he is engaged in sexual intercourse with Emma. Although the subsequent development of that story posits that souls cannot exist in a "free-floating" state independent of some physical anchorage, it only requires one more small step of the imagination to envisage alien entities composed of an alternative kind of matter closely akin to the stuff of human souls—so closely akin, in fact, that they can aliment themselves upon it in mysteriously horrific ways. In "L'Homme truqué," however, that notion remains stubbornly unextrapolated, and it seemed more appropriate to concentrate discussion on the aspect of the story that is much more fully developed: Renard's second attempt to compile a narrative account of a new sense.

Although there are problems with the hypothetical scientific foundations cited in "L'Homme truqué," resulting from the mistaken allegation that electricity is a form of electromagnetic radiation, it might only require a slight adjustment to the jargon employed to rescue the possibility that is envisaged there. Renard had, after all, based the fundamental assumption of his story, and the fundamental analogy of his scientific marvel, on the functioning of "electroscopes"—presumably referring to gold-leaf electroscopes—which were manifestly capable of reacting to electrical charges at a distance. He probably did not fully appreciate the difference between static electricity and electric currents, although Jean Lebris' altered vision does seem sensitive to that difference; however confused his knowledge might have been, though, he was not incorrect in recognizing that electromagnetic phenomena are associated with detectable "fields of force," and his confidence in the possibility of their sensory perception cannot be ruled out *a priori*.

Nowadays, of course, it is a matter of general knowledge—rather than the esoteric theoretical opinion of a group of physicists whose views were not uncontroversial—that an electric current consists of a flow of electrons. Any modern science fiction writer ought to be aware—although the routine and unrepentant idiocy of much television and movie "sci-fi" makes the issue debatable—that vision depends on the interception by the retina of photons emitted directly by light-sources or reflected from surfaces, and that no parallel method of information-transfer exists with respect to distant flows of electrons. This only means, however, that a sense of "electroscopic sight" would have to be shored up by another sort of hypothetical reasoning.

It is arguable that, in searching to imagine, characterize and describe a sixth sense different from the one imagined in *Un Homme chez les microbes*, Renard was being a little too conscientious in giving his character the ability to "see" something as specific and already well-defined as electrical activity. Most of his predecessors and successors took freer advantage of the inherent psychological plausibility of Cartesian dualism by making the nature of their hypothetical "energy beings," and the objects of their imaginary predation, something much more closely akin to the alternative "substance of the soul."

Given Renard's willingness, in the *Le Péril bleu*, to imagine vast macrocosmic entities compounded out of alternative matter, he could easily have extended that same line of thought to the potential complexities of the human microcosm and its possible relationships with external entities invisible to the five senses with which humans are routinely under-equipped. Indeed, although the brief story is inevitably vague, that is what he seems to do in "Eux." In "L'Homme truqué, however, he seems to have been trying to avoid such an imaginative leap of faith, for conscientious reasons, and deliberately attempting to stick more closely to scientifically-recognized phenomena. Alas, his attempt to characterize electroscopic sight, further confused by Prosope's allegation that electricity is *the* fundamental component of matter—which may be a misunderstanding of the Einsteinian equivalence of matter and energy—revealed his limitations in that regard.

As suggested above, it is possible that a belated realization of the fact that he was ill-equipped to work so closely with actual scientific theory was one of the reasons why Renard decided to abort the novel that "L'Homme truqué" was originally intended to be. What is not in doubt, however, is the fact that the novel clearly reflects the general disenchantment with the social role of science that had occurred as a result of the Great War. Even the maniacal villain of *Le Docteur Lerne* is a less sinister figure, in some ways, than Doctor Prosope, who speaks to his colleagues in an unintelligible language and operates in a strangely hostile moral environment, in which Science is a demanding and arbitrary god addicted to mysterious ways. It is not obvious why Prosope behaves as he does—there seems to be no real reason for his utter disregard for the principle of informed consent—but in so doing, he is merely representing the manner in which people had come to see science in the wake of the horrible contributions that scientists had made to technologies of human destruction in the Great War.

Whether or not the novel was originally planned to end on the neat but direly downbeat note with which the novella reaches its *conte cruel* conclusion we cannot know, but it is tempting to assume that the extant ending reflects something of Renard's own disillusionment at the time, with respect to his intimate personal life as well as his recent military service and continuing writing career. It was not the first time he had treated the subject of love in a despairingly cynical manner, but it was to be the last, as he bowed to conventional demand, and he might have added an extra kick to it in consequence. On the other hand, since the general paranoia of the story so obviously reflects the fact that it was written in the immediate aftermath of the Great War, the specific treatment of the romantic subplot might simply reflect the same state of post-traumatic distress.

"L'Homme truqué" remains the weakest of Renard's five major scientific marvel stories, as his effective abandonment mid-way through clearly recognizes, but it is certainly not without interest as a further step in the particular exploration that *Un Homme chez les microbes* had begun. Given that Renard could not have known at the time he set out to plan and write "L'Homme truqué" that the earlier work would ever be published, he might have thought of it merely as a more reader-friendly way to introduce the fundamental notion of senses other than the familiar five, in order to prepare the way for the much more elaborate description of the operation and corollaries of the Mandarin tuft, but it really might have been a significant expedition into unknown territory in its own right. In spite of its faults, it still qualifies as a significant experiment in the amalgamation of scientific marvel fiction and detective fiction, even though it eventually turned out to be less successful in that respect than *Les Mains d'Orlac*, or even—in an admittedly perverse fashion—*Le Péril bleu*.

It is hardly surprising that "L'Homme truqué" ran into difficulties of rational plausibility; indeed, it is arguable that very few such stories contrive to avoid that fate when subjected to keen scrutiny—as Renard was enthusiastic to point out when he found a flaw in the logic of *The Invisible Man*. It might appear at first glance that the story in the present collection worst afflicted by such difficulties is "L'Homme au corps subtil," in that it is not at all obvious how Bouvancourt's stratagem of shielding his feet from saturation by Y-light could save him from the same fate as Morand. Why does his superirradiated upper body not simply fall through his untransformed feet as well as the ground beneath? This apparent error might, however, be more easily salvageable than the one afflicting "L'Homme truqué."

The answer to the enigma, if it is treated as such, is presumably not unconnected with a corollary problem, which is brought into its clearest focus in the story in Bouvancourt's description of what must have happened to Morand as a result of his fall. Why is Morand's oscillation as he moves continually back and forth through the Earth's center of gravity subject to a progressive diminution of velocity? Obviously, in spite of the ability that bodies transformed by Y-light have to pass through untransformed material object, they are still subject to some form of friction—a fact confirmed by Bouvancourt's observations of his own experience of having things pass through him. How does this mysterious friction arise? Presumably, the phenomenon must be linked to the mysterious integrity of Bouvancourt's partly-transformed body, which prevents him from falling through his own feet.

This can be tentatively explained by further recourse to the fundamental thesis of Cartesian dualism: the notion that the soul, or mind, consists of an alternative kind of matter, which interacts with the ordinary matter of the body via some kind of interface. Presumably, it is an interaction of this admittedly-mysterious nature that is responsible for the fact that ordinary matter still exerts a "frictional" drag on matter transformed by Y-light, and for the fact that the integrity of Bouvancourt's person—maintained if not actually constituted by his soul—takes precedence over the tendency of his superirradiated legs to part company with his untransformed feet.

Another objection that might be raised to the logic of "L'Homme au corps subtil" is the question of how permeable individuals can breathe, even in the open air. Why do the untransformed oxygen molecules in the air not pass through their lung-tissue rather than being absorbed into the blood-stream? (If a similar thought occurred subsequently to Renard, it might conceivably have prompted his objection to *The Invisible Man*.) The story's central hypothesis is, however, strictly concerned with the permeability of *solids*, and the question of the relationship of a Y-light-saturated object with respect to gases—or, for that matter, liquids—remains tantalizingly unexplored. A gas is, in effect, already an "alternative state of matter," whose potential interactions with other such states remain speculatively unexplored in the story, but evidently do not prevent a permeable individual from breathing.

If Renard did begin to develop a greater sensitivity to such logical flaws after the war, and if that realization did play a part in his decision to cut "L'Homme truqué" short, it might help to explain not merely the form and nostalgically sentimental tone of "L'Homme qui voulait être invisible," but also the two parables of disillusionment that follow it in this collection: the article "Depuis Sinbad" and the story "La Grenouille." The conclusion of the article may be the clearest and most explicit indication Renard gave of why, in spite of his own tastes and inclinations, he had given up writing "parascientific" fiction by 1923 (save for two subsequent "salvage missions" undertaken in respect of previously-completed but as-yet-unpublished works), devoting himself instead to popular crime fiction and conventional fantastic fiction that never attempted to offer any serious competition to Edgar Poe.

As the article indicates, although Rosny had not quite given up on scientific marvel fiction—he contrived to publish "Les Navigateurs de l'infini"[50] in 1925—his work in that vein had always been rare, and it became rarer. It is significant that the sequel to "Les Navigateurs de l'infini," "Les Astronautes" [The Astronauts], remained unpublished until long after his death, finally appearing in 1960. Although he published a further handful of the largely marvel-free prehistoric fantasies for which he was already well-known, he only published one further story with any significant scientific marvel content, "Dans le monde des Variants,"[51] which might well have been written long before its first appearance in 1939. It is also worth noting that the prolific Jean Ray, who was at the beginning of his career when he interviewed Renard and asked him to write the

---

[50] Translated in the Black Coat Press collection *The Navigators of Space*, which also includes "The Astronauts."
[51] Translated in the Black Coat Press collection as *The World of the Variants*.

article in 1923, very rarely strayed into the "parascientific," always preferring the comfort zone of the *fantastique*.

However explicit the article might be, however, its impact pales into insignificance by comparison with the careful description of the narrator's disillusionment contained in "La Grenouille." It is tempting to believe that Renard is talking about his own childhood fascinations when the narrator describes his early state of mind, especially when one considers the possible resonance of the reference to "tempting the hydra:":a monster whose traditional location—Lerne, in French—gave a name to the villainous scientist of Renard's first novel. Not unlike "L'Homme qui voulait être invisible," although in a very different way, "La Grenouille" is only a "parascientific" story in a marginal sense; it is eager to make much of its own ambiguity and flatly refuses to consider any further possibility attached to what the significantly-named Mourgue might have accomplished except for the single purpose imagined.

None of the subsequent items in the collection make any determined attempt to go beyond that sort of marginality, even if some of them do include token suggestions of broader implication. Like the narrator of "La Grenouille," their author is a man who no longer cared to dabble in that sort of speculation—except by way of salvaging work he had already done, when he was younger and in a more adventurous frame of mind. The brief article on "Hypothetical Fiction," the brief story "The Discovery" and—most of all—the exceedingly brief account of "The Truth About Faust," all continue in the same gradually-weakening vein of disillusionment, tinged with nostalgic regret. There is a certain wry propriety in the fact that the last item of all—the last item of "parascientific" or "hypothetical" fiction that Renard was ever to write—is a valedictory vignette in which a young entity receiving advice from an older and wiser one decides that it might be better, after all, to deny the existence of anything that might trouble the harmony of the blissfully ignorant imagination. We, of course, are not obliged—or even intended—to agree with the nebulous individual in question.

# SF & FANTASY

Guy d'Armen. *Doc Ardan: The City of Gold and Lepers*
G.-J. Arnaud. *The Ice Company*
Aloysius Bertrand. *Gaspard de la Nuit*
Félix Bodin. *The Novel of the Future*
André Caroff. *The Terror of Madame Atomos*
Didier de Chousy. *Ignis*
C. I. Defontenay. *Star (Psi Cassiopeia)*
Charles Derennes. *The People of the Pole*
Harry Dickson. *The Heir of Dracula*
Sâr Dubnotal *vs. Jack the Ripper*
Alexandre Dumas. *The Return of Lord Ruthven*
J.-C. Dunyach. *The Night Orchid. The Thieves of Silence*
Paul Féval. *Anne of the Isles. Knightshade. Revenants. Vampire City. The Vampire Countess. The Wandering Jew's Daughter*
Paul Féval, *fils. Felifax, the Tiger-Man*
Arnould Galopin. *Doctor Omega*
V. Hugo, Foucher & Meurice. *The Hunchback of Notre-Dame*
O. Joncquel & Theo Varlet. *The Martian Epic*
Jean de La Hire. *Enter the Nyctalope. The Nyctalope on Mars. The Nyctalope vs. Lucifer*
G. Le Faure & H. de Graffigny. *The Extraordinary Adventures of a Russian Scientist Across the Solar System* (2 vols.)
Gustave Le Rouge. *The Vampires of Mars*
Jules Lermina. *Mysteryville. Panic in Paris. To-Ho and the Gold Destroyers*
Jean-Marc & Randy Lofficier. *Edgar Allan Poe on Mars. The Katrina Protocol. Pacifica. Robonocchio.* (anthologies) *Tales of the Shadowmen* (6 vols.) (non-fiction) *Shadowmen* (2 vols.)
Xavier Mauméjean. *The League of Heroes*
Marie Nizet. *Captain Vampire*
C. Nodier, Beraud & Toussaint-Merle. *Frankenstein*
Henri de Parville. *An Inhabitant of the Planet Mars*
Polidori, C. Nodier, E. Scribe. *Lord Ruthven the Vampire*
P.-A. Ponson du Terrail. *The Vampire and the Devil's Son*

Maurice Renard. *Doctor Lerne. A Man Among the Microbes. The Blue Peril. The Doctored Man*
Albert Robida. *The Adventures of Saturnin Farandoul. The Clock of the Centuries*
J.-H. Rosny Aîné. *The Navigators of Space. The World of the Variants. The Mysterious Force*
Brian Stableford. *The Shadow of Frankenstein. Frankenstein and the Vampire Countess. The New Faust at the Tragicomique. Sherlock Holmes & The Vampires of Eternity. The Stones of Camelot. The Wayward Muse.* (anthologies) *The Germans on Venus. News from the Moon*
Kurt Steiner. *Ortog*
Villiers de l'Isle-Adam. *The Scaffold. The Vampire Soul*
Philippe Ward. *Artahe*

## MYSTERIES & THRILLERS

M. Allain & P. Souvestre. *The Daughter of Fantômas*
Anicet-Bourgeois, Lucien Dabril. *Rocambole*
A. Bisson & G. Livet. *Nick Carter vs. Fantômas*
V. Darlay & H. de Gorsse. *Lupin vs. Holmes: The Stage Play*
Paul Féval. *The Black Coats: The Companions of the Treasure. Heart of Steel. The Invisible Weapon. The Parisian Jungle. 'Salem Street. Gentlemen of the Night. John Devil*
Emile Gaboriau. *Monsieur Lecoq*
Steve Leadley. *Sherlock Holmes: The Circle of Blood*
Maurice Leblanc. *Arsène Lupin: The Hollow Needle. The Blonde Phantom*
Gaston Leroux. *Chéri-Bibi. The Phantom of the Opera. Rouletabille & the Mystery of the Yellow Room*
William Patrick Maynard. *The Terror of Fu Manchu*
Frank J. Morlock. *Sherlock Holmes: The Grand Horizontals*
P. de Wattyne & Y. Walter. *Sherlock Holmes vs. Fantômas*
David White. *Fantômas in America*